ABOVE THE SNOWLINE

Also by Steph Swainston from Gollancz:

The Year of Our War
No Present Like Time
The Modern World

The Castle Omnibus

ABOVE THE SNOWLINE

Steph Swainston

GOLLANCZ
LONDON

First published in Great Britain in 2010 by
Gollancz
An imprint of the Orion Publishing Group
Orion House, 5 Upper St Martin's Lane,
London WC2H 9EA
An Hachette UK Company

A CIP catalogue record for this book
is available from the British Library.

ISBN 978 0 575 08158 1 (Cased)
ISBN 978 0 575 08159 8 (Trade Paperback)

1 3 5 7 9 10 8 6 4 2

Typeset by Deltatype Ltd, Birkenhead, Merseyside

Printed and bound in the UK by
CPI Mackays, Chatham ME5 8TD

www.stephswainston.co.uk
www.orionbooks.co.uk

'There can be no hearts above the snowline'
–Herman Melville

TWO HUNTERS

A stone rattled down the scree slope, bouncing and clacking, speeding up as it descended and dislodging further stones. It hit the side of a great boulder, ricocheted off and came to rest. Another followed it, tumbling past and sending up tiny puffs of the grey ground-rock dust that underlay the scree. Then a section of frost-shattered granite gave way under the boot sole of a Rhydanne girl. She was running down the steep slope with bounding strides and sliding crunches. She crossed the narrow stone chute diagonally, reached the larger slabs on its outside edge and turned to descend across it again. Behind and far above her, her husband was making his way down. She smiled, thinking: he never keeps up with me.

She rejoiced in her speed. She loved the exhilaration of being nearly, but not quite, out of control, revelling in the feeling of leaving her feet behind her; in the co-ordination of her long legs; in her ankles and knees jarring when she planted a foot into the scree and jumped again. She knew how to find footholds so precarious, thinking ahead with such fast instinct, her grace would put a chamois to shame.

She reached the bottom of the slope, a relatively flat terrace covered in gigantic, angular shards from cliff-falls and old avalanches. As the scree petered out onto grass she slowed to a halt and glanced back to see her husband still descending between the massive, uneven pillars of rock. In the distance his footfalls sounded tiny and high-pitched, as if the scree was broken glass.

She crouched and tightened the laces of her moccasin boots, then pulled a strip of wind-dried meat from her pack and began to chew it. She popped the bung from her waterskin and washed the sharp pieces down with neat whisky.

Her husband stopped beside her. 'All right, Dellin?'

She nodded. 'Hungry, though.'

'I'm starving.'

She passed him one of the strips like stringy leather and as he munched it they pressed on, running in step between the boulders, picking their way with extraordinary rapidity. Dellin breathed deeply; the clean, cold air caught in her sinuses. Above the screes, the pure snowfields had taken on the dazzling blue of the early morning sky.

They ran along a natural balcony, a plateau below the soaring needles of rock, covered in rubble vivid green with lichen, which sheltered mosses and tiny mountain flowers. They were searching for ibex but there had been few sightings of any game above the tree line for weeks and they were becoming desperate.

'Do you think there'll be anything over in Caigeann?' Dellin asked eventually.

Laochan bowed his head, meaning, the herders have left for the high pasture so there won't be any goats.

'Well, let's follow them.'

'If we get any hungrier we'll have to. But it's a long way and unless we eat first we might not be able.'

Dellin showed all her teeth in a smile that was more a grimace. She loved preying on the goats of those Rhydanne who lived as herders. She liked to swoop in, take what she wanted and run away pursued by the stupid, exasperated goatherds hurling stones.

Since the start of the melt season, the deer had become scarce and now the smaller prey also seemed frightened and elusive. Dellin and Laochan were not sure why, they hadn't met any other hunters and the weather had been fair. But they knew that if they did not make a kill soon, they would starve.

Their pace matched exactly as they ran, sparse and concentrated. They even breathed together, leaving identical puffs of misted breath on the air. The rocks underfoot were no longer sealed together with ice and the footholds were treacherous, but Dellin jumped from one to the next, picking them out with perfect judgement, scarcely needing to think.

Rhydanne are to humans as cheetahs are to alley cats, as greyhounds are to lapdogs, as hares are to rabbits and as falcons, the swift-winged cutters of the air, are to blackbirds whose predatory instinct extends only to worms and insects. They are lithe-limbed, cat-eyed and pale. They were human once, unlike the winged Awians, but millennia of evolution in the extreme mountains had adapted them to altitude and to the cold: it had keened their senses, honed their bodies and charged their speed. They are solitary, independent and, although they hunt in pairs, cannot even conceive of acting as a society. They are the ultimate hunters. They are also drunk nine tenths of the time.

A cliff top jutting out from the terrace formed a promontory and good lookout point. Dellin jogged onto it and gazed out over the contours of the slope. The mountainside curved away, pastel green and grey, but she could see no movement, no sign of deer. She leant on her spear for support, turned and looked back up-slope to where Carnich Glacier knuckled its way down from the high summits. Its spiny projections and rugged surface smoothed towards the snowfields. And far beyond them, a wall of jagged black pinnacles too sheer to hold snow cut against the sky.

The meltwater torrent leaving the glacier plunged into a deep ravine; even at this distance its roar made Dellin's ears ring. It emerged much lower down in a series of waterfalls that seemed solid, like white veils, and poured into the top of a pine forest where it disappeared from view. Condors were sailing, broad-winged, over the topmost spires of the pines.

On the other side of the ravine, the balcony jutted out onto a great crag. Dellin cried, 'Laochan! Look!' The top of the crag was bare. It was below the tree line and should have been forest, but its flat summit had been stripped. Rocks were showing in the grey-yellow scar. She could just distinguish the trunks of the pines at the edge of the felled area. She squinted and discerned piles of lumber, looking no bigger than tinder spills. There were square mounds of stone there too, all larger than any trading post she knew, and penned in with fences and walls as if they were goats. 'Someone's cut all those trees down. And they're building huge huts!'

Laochan tapped his spear butt on the rock apprehensively. 'Could it be Karbhainn?'

'Karbhainn couldn't do that. It must be Awians.'

'Aliens?'

'Awians. Featherbacks. They build, don't they ...?'

He tried to tell the huts from the rock. 'It's bigger than Scree pueblo ... It's like three pueblos joined together ...'

'On our hunting ground.'

They stood for some time, watching the bald promontory and the forest lapping up around it. Its cloak of pines descended unbroken into a thick cloudbank. Some gaps far out in the cumulus showed flatter ground and vague bistre and green shapes, framed by the cloud as if floating. There was nothing of interest down there.

She nudged Laochan and pointed. Some white boxes were emerging from the margin of the trees, on the Turbary Track. One by one they turned off the track and slowly crawled like ticks onto the top of the promontory, where they stopped in a line. 'Wheeled sledges. They *are* flatlanders. Can you see any?'

He slitted his eyes against the breeze. 'Amazing. Sledges never come up this far.'

'Laochan! Trust your own eyes!'

'Yes, I trust my eyes, but I trust my nose more. Can you smell burning?'

She stood breathing in the scents carried on the cool breeze: woodsmoke, pine resin, and something stronger, too, something she couldn't identify. Faint noises came to her – stone being hammered and a man's shout – cut short when the gust died down. 'So much noise. No wonder the ibex are scarce.'

'Ibex! They could wake a hibernating bear.' He stared intently at the promontory, moving his head slightly from side to side, the way a hawk does when it focuses on prey. Dellin glanced at him, so he pointed out some brown blots on its summit, on a patch of sparse grass. 'What are they? Deer?'

She shaded her eyes. 'Horses. They'll be horses. A larger type of mule.'

'Why aren't they running away?'

'I don't know.' She gave him a fleeting look. 'Are you thinking what I'm thinking?'

He licked his lips. 'Think so!'

They turned and dashed back to the slope. They sped past outcrops of bulging rock onto a cliff and jumped down its ledges, using their spears to balance. Dellin's nails rasped when she dug them, like pitons, into cracks. They descended through almost-sheer swathes of tough grass and bilberries. The ragged scatters of stunted pines at the tree line brushed their trousers. They raced between them and into the forest, among taller and taller pines until the great conifers blocked out the sky.

The air was rich with the smell of damp humus and deep-textured bark. Meshed branches softened the ice-bright sunlight to an aquamarine glow that dappled the ground. Dellin and Laochan's light tread made no sound on the compacted needles as they ran past ferns, ant mounds, and the trees' roots covered in inedible red-capped fungi. She was alert to every sound, yearning to hear the scuffling of a deer fleeing, but nothing came to her except the fluttering of small birds in the branches.

She swung her arms, loving her spear's perfect balance. Its steel tip arced to and fro at the edge of her vision. Laochan's spear bounced against his back in a tubular bone holder.

Notches had been freshly hacked in the larger trunks. Laochan slowed and sent Dellin a worried glance, but she simply ran on and he had to follow. They peered down between the trunks to the trading post road. A new track left its nearest hairpin bend, leading up towards the top of the promontory. It was freshly scuffed and very wide, with two ruts where wheels had churned the pine needles muddy brown.

Laochan whispered, 'It looks too *used*.'

'Don't worry. We can spot the horses without leaving cover.'

They ran alongside the track until the forest stopped abruptly. Laochan threw his arm out to warn her and crouched behind a rowan bush. She sank down beside him. The track curved out in front of them and where the forest had been was nothing but stumps, the boles of recently felled pines, pale chips and branches all over the ground as if strewn by the most terrific storm of all time. The wheeled sledges, like boxes with arched canvas roofs, were lined up at the end of the track. Behind them, a high wall with a gap in it surrounded the buildings.

Laochan darted horrified glances around. 'Have they built all this since last time?'

'They must have. No! Don't dash off! I'm hungry.'

'What are they doing?'

'I don't know. Look.' The horses were grazing on the other side of the track inside a sort of large pen, an enclosure like the ones goats are kept in, but *huge*, so huge Dellin couldn't see across it. Eight, nine, ten brown mares were tugging mouthfuls of dry grass from a manger in the centre. One magnificent black stallion stood apart, swishing his tail and raising his head to sniff the air. Laochan watched them with a fascinated light in his eyes. 'They look strong.'

'Yes, but they're easy pickings. No claws or horns to gore us, and they won't dive underground.'

'Where are the featherbacks?'

'I've no idea. They must be in their pueblo.'

He nodded. 'They'll probably be drinking if they've trapped this much food.'

'Then let's take some.'

They glanced at each other. They had hunted together for so long he easily read her expression. He nodded seriously, took his spear's detachable bone point and eased it in its socket to make its string run free, then ran his beautiful hands over the bolas cord wound around his waist. He met her eyes and said, 'Wait for my call,' then slipped round the bush and was gone. He ran, stooped, across the track and circled around the pen to approach from upwind. He reached the wheeled sledges, gave a frightened glance at the height of their roofs, then dropped to hands and knees and crept between them.

Dellin snaked out and down to the near side of the strange pen. It seemed to be circular, more than a hundred strides across, and its far side almost touched the cliff edge. She squirmed closer on her belly, holding her spear off the ground. The damp grass brushed the front of her parka and grit pressed into her palms.

The male horse whinnied. Shit, she thought, he's scented us already. The mares bunched together, holding their heads high, rolling their eyes and flaring their nostrils. The cold breeze lifted hairs from their manes and tails, turned their every puff of breath to wreaths of steam that hung around them in the pale air. Lumps of dry mud clung to their hooves. Dellin wondered at the mud – it wasn't the thin soil of Carnich, it had come from somewhere else entirely. She picked out one of the mares but they were clustered near the manger with the enormous stallion pacing round and round.

He'll be better eating than squirrels and toadstools, she thought, but the pain in her belly was so intense and she felt so weak, she knew she was better choosing one of the mares. She crouched and waited, ignoring the strain in her knees, thinking, come on, Laochan.

She heard his low whistle on the other side of the enclosure and sprang up – grabbed the rail and vaulted it, shouting, 'Hey! Hey!'

He leapt the fence, spear in hand, landed and dashed at the horses. Dellin's mare bolted with the rest towards the barrier and she thought they'd all jump it, but frightened by the precipice they swerved and ran alongside, Dellin's mare in the middle.

She raised her spear beside her cheek, its point steady in front. She balanced it in her hand, steering the shaft with her thumb. She ran faster, halted and hurled the spear with all her strength, all her momentum, the whole long fulcrum of her body. She tipped forward, started running, watching its flight.

The spear arced up, descended point first and plunged into the horse's hindquarters, sinking in two thirds of its length. The horse stumbled, incredibly regained its footing, but the others raced past and left it behind.

It ran after them, its back leg jolting the shaft back and forth, sawing the spear point and cutting its flesh. A second later the point emerged under its belly, shining with blood. The wound widened and a pad of intestine protruded and slipped out until two loops hung down.

A kill, Dellin thought. A kill in one throw! The mare was tiring – it still tried to keep up with the herd, but hampered by pain and the dragging shaft couldn't lift its hooves as high. Dellin smelt its terror and howled with excitement. *I'm going to catch it*! She bounded forward and pounced. She buffeted into the hard wall of its shoulder, threw her arm over its neck, jolted and dug her nails in. The horse lifted her off her feet and dragged her along.

Her toes bumped on the stones. The mare's tough hair rubbed her cheek, but before it could turn its head to bite, Dellin grabbed its mane, flexed her arms and pulled herself up to sit astride. She was riding!

'Hey!' she cried. 'Hey, Laochan!'

His face turned up in astonishment from beside a brown mound – his prey was lying quivering, and he was trying to work his spear free.

Under Dellin's thighs the mare's shoulders surged and thumped. Its mane swished her trousers and its hooves threw up clods of turf. She wasn't satisfied with a messy kill; she wanted to make it clean. She drew her knife, grasped it in both hands and stabbed it down through the tough neck.

Blood whipped back, splattered her and pattered on the ground. The foam around its mouth streaked with red. Bits flew back and stuck to her. She pushed and the knife disappeared up to its hilt. The mare's legs buckled, it pitched forward and Dellin jumped clear. She landed on hands and feet, was up again in an instant and saw the mare lying on its side. It rolled onto its belly and tried to pull itself up by its straight front legs, then collapsed completely, breathing heavily.

Dellin ran to its back, out of the way of its frantically kicking hooves, grabbed the waving shaft and pulled it free. Then she raised the spear above its eye and for a second saw the point reflect on the shining brown orb. She thrust the spear, jumped onto the shaft, and felt it sink home.

She released her weight from the shaft and stepped back. She loved taking an animal's movement and stilling it. She loved being able to see closely all the details of its body, and the rich smell of its sweat was making her giddy. She stroked its flank. The coarse hairs felt silky when smoothed along their grain. Underneath, its muscles flickered in their last spasms.

Dellin's hands were sticky with the tremendous amount of blood pouring freely from its neck. She retrieved her knife, slipped it into the suede sheath on her thigh, settled back on her haunches and meticulously licked her fingers clean. Then she leant over the horse's bulk and poked her tongue into the wound, where the hair-bearing skin had pulled back from the slick red flesh, so wet and warm. She bit the flat expanse of its neck, feeling her teeth slide over the hard hairs. She pressed her lips against them, relishing the overpowering scent, and breathed it in through nose and open mouth – filling her lungs with it, filling her mind as if she had become part of it. She felt the horse relax and its smell changed from enticing prey to fresh meat – it was dead.

Food at last! Dellin bowed her head and sucked, sucked at the wound. She drank her fill, then looked to Laochan. He had not made his kill as cleanly as hers, since he stubbornly still used a bone spear, and its uppermost back leg was twitching. Behind him, the other prey stampeded round and round, crazed with fear and streaming ragged scarves of breath.

The handsome black stallion caught Dellin's eye. It was indeed a prestigious beast. If she killed it, she could thread one of its teeth on her necklace. Her strength was flowing back now; the mare's blood was so wholesome she lusted for more. She fancied she could smell the blood of the stallion coursing in its very veins. She wrenched her spear from the mare's skull with a pull and a twist, then gave a double whistle.

Laochan looked up, his mouth and chin shining red. Dellin pointed at the stallion. He wiped his sleeve across his face and grinned.

He stood, digging his thumb under the bolas cord coiled around his waist, loosened the knot and unwound the three cords, releasing the stone balls that had been bound at his hip. He gracefully lifted the handle so they hung loose at the end of each cord, and whistled he was ready.

Dellin whistled, 'I'll chase it to you,' and leapt forward over the tussocks. Her soft boots were silent but her bangles jangled and inside the neck of her parka her strings of beads rattled. The stallion sensed it had been singled out. For a second she thought it might turn and attack her. But it continued racing its fastest, neck stretched and head thrust forward, as if it would burst through the barrier and go tumbling, mane, tail and hooves, down the cliff.

She manoeuvred between it and the fence, matched speed with it and turned it towards Laochan. Few animals had ever outrun her, even when they were fleeing for their lives. She put on a spurt and made it charge quicker, ecstatic that her reflexes were so much faster, she could turn it whenever she wanted.

The stallion saw Laochan and tried to cut in front of Dellin to escape, but a jab of her spear forced it closer. He slipped the three round weights off his shoulder, let them drop free and swung them to and fro. Then he raised the handle and twirled the bolas above his head.

She halted and let the stallion race on. As Laochan's hand swung towards the horse he released the bolas. The three balls on their ropes spun through the air, looped into the stallion's legs and tangled them together.

It went over hard onto its withers and head, thumped back onto its side – Dellin heard a leg break – and lay struggling, lifting its head, arcing its body, thrashing its hopelessly wrapped-up hooves. She pounced, her knife drawn like a single talon, and shredded its throat so thoroughly its eyes were already beginning to glaze by the time Laochan sprinted over.

His shadow cast across her and striped the stallion's broad body. She looked up, seeing the wind ruffle his long hair. His eyes reflected the sunlight and shone with joy. He smiled with blood in the corners of his mouth and Dellin beamed back. 'We've enough meat for weeks!'

'We can't carry it all,' he said. 'We'll have to make a cache ... At least one.'

Dellin nodded. 'The tall spruce is best. Remember the one above the ravine? If we tie our packs in its branches the wolves won't get them. Oh, this is just like last summer!' She went down on hands and knees and examined the horse's incisors; great yellow plaques, with chewed grass and mashed blue flowers between them. Small bubbles of saliva clung around its pulled-back lips. 'Good,' she said. 'I'm going to take a front tooth.' She found a rock and began to bash its gums.

Laochan bent a leg and examined its hoof. 'Look! Look! It grows metal underneath. Wow. Metal hooves!'

She wiggled an incisor free and drew out its very long root.

Laochan poked his finger into an old spur-scar over its ribs. 'What's this?'

'Some kind of thorn scratch.'

'Wait till they hear how I brought it down ...'

'They'll think you've grown ten dicks. Hurry up! We have to butcher it before the wolves appear.'

'After we've eaten, I'll pounce on you and you'll be my prey!'

Dellin bit his shoulder lovingly and he grinned at her. He felt along the rounded edge of the horse's back leg, and scored with his flint knife an arc along the line of the joint, again and again until the tough hide gradually split and he cut through to the muscle beneath. He dug his fingernails under the hide and slowly tore it back, using his knife to slice it away from the clinging meat.

Tiny flakes broke off his knife edge and remained in the flesh as glittering dust, the sharp new stone shining cleanly where they had detached. Dellin yelped in disapproval and pushed his hand away. 'Let me do that. I don't want to eat steak full of flint spalls again. You know my favourite – get the stomach.'

'All right.' He pushed back his sleeves, then drew his knife down the middle of the stallion's belly from breastbone to between its back legs. The skin began to part. He was careful not to pierce the intestines, the pungent reek would attract wolves, but he neatly cut the tubes at top and bottom, took the stomach out and presented it to her.

She cut the hard ball of muscle in half and greedily bit out a mouthful of the mashed grass inside. It was so piquant! She chewed the acidic fibres slowly and passed the other half to Laochan, who looked like he needed some nourishment.

He cut out the liver; purple, smooth and gleaming, and slopped it into his rucksack, then pulled the slippery mess of intestines forward and reached his arm over it into the body cavity to pluck out the kidneys. He stripped them of valuable white fat and tossed them in his pack.

'Ay!' he said. 'Try some of this fat. There's four times as much as on a deer!'

His tempting musk tingled Dellin's nose. But first things first: with fast, economical movements she peeled the skin down no further than the hock because the lower leg bore no meat, and began filling her bag with thick steaks from its haunch.

A shout made them look up. Featherback men were running out of the opening in the wall, waving their arms and shouting madly. More men behind them turned to beckon to yet more dashing from their shacks. Dellin gasped. She had never seen so many! Their clothes were – colourful! – too bright – and they actually had wings folded at their backs. They really grew *feathers*. The stiff tips of one man's wings protruded from his coat. Their hair was short and many shades of brown, even yellow, like dry grass. They were stocky and bulky and moved too slowly – comically slowly. Some held wood staffs and they yelled with fury. A hail of stones was bound to follow. She grabbed her spear.

Laochan was elbow-deep in the horse's ribcage, feeling about for its heart. The featherback men stopped at the barrier, aghast expressions contorting their faces. They raised their staffs in front of their eyes.

'Run! Run!'

Laochan sprang up – and cried out. A stick had appeared projecting from his hip. He clutched both hands around it, turned in wonder to the featherbacks – and another stick with feathers on the end appeared exactly in the middle of his chest.

He dropped to his knees, staring at Dellin. His eyes were full of terror and confusion. Then they set and he fell.

She tentatively touched him. He's dead. Laochan's *dead*. Feathered sticks were appearing all around her, embedding in the ground, in the horse's carcass and in her husband's body.

She wrenched herself away from him and instinct told her to crawl. The forest edge seemed impossibly far. Something whooshed by – a stick hit the stones in front of her, jamming between them at an angle. It had a sharp metal tip. Then she was up and sprinting her fastest. The thin pines with a few bushes between them, the unnatural cut stumps much too white, the strip of dark boughs over trunks and undergrowth jumped and bounded, never getting any nearer.

Sticks were cracking against the rocks all around. She sped past them and kept going straight, aiming for the darkness between the trunks. She vaulted the barrier, landed atop a boulder, sprang off and across the track.

At last, the forest! She caught her breath in a bound over the brambles at its edge and landed, both feet, both hands, on the pine litter.

She heard no pursuit. She dashed deeper in, skidded to her knees behind the rowan bush, pulled herself into the smallest possible area and peered out between its leaves. Four featherback men were climbing into the enclosure. The horses were mad with panic, stampeding round and round inside the fence as far as they could get from the kills. The strangers seemed cautious of them and walked instead to Laochan, who lay on his side with his legs crooked. One bent down, obscured by the tussocks, straightened up with Laochan's knife in his hand and inspected it.

Tears were pouring down Dellin's face but she kept watching. She started sobbing, catching each breath short and sharp.

The tallest Awian crouched beside the stallion and pressed his hand to its neck. The second turned Laochan's body over with his foot. Dellin saw in a flash his white skin and trailing black hair. She cried out and all four men looked in her direction.

She shrank back and clamped her hand over her mouth. The man stroking the dead stallion said something and the others began to walk towards her. They left her husband lying face down and drew new feather-ended sticks, fitted them to the strings on their wooden staves.

Dellin glanced uphill, towards the familiar screes. She fled.

LIGHTNING

November, 1890

I ran up the spiral staircase as fast as I could, beside myself with excitement. I couldn't wait to tell him. Three hundred and thirty steps later I came to a little bare landing and the arched door of his apartment. I reached out a hand and rapped on it. There was no answer. Of course there was no answer; the Messenger was rarely seen before ten o'clock in the morning, when he leaves his tower with his girl of the previous night and goes in search of breakfast.

On the other hand, he is keen to be accessible and usually leaves his door unlocked. That was well known. I pushed down the catch and swung it wide. 'Jant?'

He wasn't in this half of the circular room, but bedclothes were rustling on the other side of the velvet curtain drawn across it. I stepped through the doorway and waited for a reply. 'Jant? *Jant*?'

'Just a minute!' came from behind the curtain.

This is the fastest person in the world and it is always 'just a minute' with him. The room was half in impenetrable gloom but a little light leaked in from the shutters, and with the odour of stale coffee, the air was quite a fug. I picked my way across the semicircular study to the window, between a trio of smeared wine glasses on the floor, plates sticky with the remains of what seemed to be cherry gateau, big curled feathers from the tops of someone's wings, and a pair of women's shoes with pointed toes, kicked off in a hurry. I opened the shutters. One of them was broken, and as I propped it wide I thought, it's extraordinary. Jant does look very much like her. Broader, of course; but she could be his sister. Watch me shock him out of bed.

'Jant!' I called. 'There's a Rhydanne in the Castle!'

The bedclothes crinkled with increased asperity, then with a jingle of brass rings on the rail the curtain twitched apart in the middle and Jant's face appeared, looking somewhat hungover. 'What?'

'A Rhydanne!'

'Where?'

'Down by Carillon.'

He blinked in surprise. I continued, satisfied, 'Called Shira. Standing by Serein's fishpond. So I thought I should—'

Jant interrupted me, 'He's called Shira?'

I smiled and something in my smile informed him he should alter the question.

'*She's* called Shira?'

'Yes. That much I understood.'

He poked his upper body through and drew the drapes about his waist, so I was no longer speaking to a disembodied head but also to a hairless torso. 'Is she speaking Scree?'

'I assume so. You can speak it, surely?'

'Well, it's been a long time but ... yes, yes, of course ...'

'Well, come on then! If she harpoons any of Serein's prize koi, he'll run her through.'

'Ha! Serein and his bloody fish.'

'You and your bloody women.'

Jant shrugged, withdrew behind the curtains and tweaked them into place. A few seconds later he slipped through and descended the three steps to the lower half of the room, buttoning his shirt cuffs.

'She's standing on the wall of the pond,' I said, 'with a *spear* – some kind of harpoon – watching the carp.' I raised my arm and struck the pose. 'I was going to the hall when I saw her. A groundsman tried to talk to her as well, but he couldn't. I mean, she talks but we couldn't fathom a word she said. It's all V's and K's.'

'Bh's and Ich's.'

'Exactly!'

He picked a corset from the back of the chair, gathered its dangling laces, scooped up the shoes and disappeared behind the curtain.

Typical, I thought. Apart from the clutter on the floor, his room was cluttered on every wall, the top of his desk and dresser, and it wouldn't have surprised me if the clutter had extended across the ceiling as well. The desk was covered in coach route maps, folded in zigzag fashion, and other necessities of his job: pens, paper, a walnut box of seals and stubs of sealing wax – crimson for the Castle's correspondence, black for his own.

On his travels he had collected such a vast miscellany of articles that his room resembled the den of an undiscerning buccaneer. There was a little cup and saucer with gold rims compulsively lifted from the Rachiswater Royal Café. There were books of matches pinched from various hotels; a scallop shell ('A Souvenir From Cobalt'); horse racing spurs from Eske; a glazed green roof ornament of a sea serpent from Ghallain; a bunch of silk sky-blue roses of Awia given him in secret by a Lady Governor, stuffed into a Litanee knotwork vase; a series of small gouache paintings of local scenes popular in my own manor; a pack of cards I know to be false, with extra aces; and several half-dried bottles of eyeliner, which I believe was all the rage in Hacilith and the sort of thing that Jant latched onto rapidly.

Clay animal figurines from past Shatterings crowded the mantelpiece and in the grate were a very blackened kettle and toasting fork. Rather than descend the three hundred steps to the hall, he sat up here of a night and made his own toast and black coffee, from a great coffee tin embossed with baroque scrollwork and a dense little cylinder of dark chocolate, which he grated into it.

On a stand, pride of place, stood a black and scarlet chessboard, with ebony and red maple pieces inlaid with jet and carnelian. It had cost Jant so much he never stopped flaunting it, but it was no more than a pose because he doesn't have the slightest idea how to play. The bric-a-brac and interesting junk picked up in flea markets around the world gave off a mothy smell of dust, but the more subtle smell of wood polish underlay everything, with old newspaper and the peppery scent of ink.

Beside the door, the wall was taken up by pigeonholes, each compartment labelled with the name of one of the Eszai or the Castle's staff. Bundles of letters and slips of paper projected from most of them.

The curtain was pushed aside and a half-dressed woman emerged, apologetically bowed over a bundle of her clothes. She backed to the door and disappeared down the spiral stairs as fast as she could go. Jant came out on the other side and began preening in the mirror.

I said, 'A Rhydanne, right here in the Castle! What do you think she wants?'

'I have a landslide of a hangover ...'

More rustling, and another pale and interesting girl crept out of the bedroom – all dishevelled hair and white shift – and departed as quickly as her flip-flops would let her. Jant didn't spare her a glance.

'Who was that?'

'I'm not really sure ...' He pulled on his boots and searched around. 'Where's my sword? I can't go down there looking like a Zascai. Oh, here we are.' He unhooked his jacket from the back of the door and a Wrought sword was hanging underneath, on a belt with the Castle's sun as its buckle. He put it on then sailed out of the room, leaving the door open. He took the stairs two at a time, leaning around the tight curve. 'What a time to come knocking. There I was, lying in the sunlight with a sleeping beauty on either side. The blonde's leg *there,* hidden in the duvet; the brunette's plump tits *there*. I was enjoying wondering how to wake them and you rush in, shouting.'

'I'm sure you'll manage to find some more.'

'It's the eyes.' He smirked. 'They can't resist the eyes.'

We reached the bottom of the staircase, emerged onto the grass and turned onto the path that runs between the kitchens and the end of Carillon which houses the Treasury. All the windows of the Treasury were caged and the flagstones of the path were dipped in the centre by the progress and egress of so many thousands of feet over the centuries. We passed the Treasurer's apartments, then the Cook's, and on either side the verdant lawns exhaled the moisture of last night's rain. Although it was late November, the warmth of autumn still lingered and the baroque, red-tiled roof of Carillon looked more beautiful than ever against the cloudless sky.

'Maybe we should be careful,' I said. 'She seems wary. If she's come all the way from Darkling, imagine how strange the Castle must be to her.' Jant strode beside me without saying anything. 'Remember how you felt when you first arrived.'

'I didn't come all the way from Darkling.'

'Sh!'

'We don't have to creep up on her,' he said loudly. He rounded the corner and stopped dead.

The Rhydanne woman stood on the wall of the fishpond, poised motionless like a heron. Her spear pointed, unwavering, at the water.

Jant murmured, 'I haven't ... It's ...' He took two steps forward and halted again.

Her long black hair hung straight down and we could not see her face apart from the tip of her white nose. She was petite in stature but she held herself very erect. Her limbs in a peculiar black vest were unnatural – too long for her build, too sinewy. A leather thong looped up from the butt of her spear and was wrapped around the hand holding the shaft.

Her vest was meagre compared with her white suede trousers – they were sewn with thongs, giving a moccasin effect to every seam with wisps of the fur lining protruding. She wore boots of the sort worn by trappers pulled up to her knees. Some crude metal bracelets decorated her bare arms and, looped around her neck, were several strands of beads, mostly ivory-white but some dyed black and red. They were bones and teeth! A white suede jacket hung on a backpack with a frame of stark polished bone, resting against the wall.

I waited uncertainly, like a traveller privileged to catch a glimpse of a snow leopard, but half hopeful it will cross his path quickly and slink back into the forest without showing its fangs.

Jant thrust his chest out, flexed his wings and sauntered closer. The girl snapped round, levelling her spear at his throat. He flinched, then, disgusted with himself, brushed the point aside. 'Dein,' he said softly.

The girl blinked. Now I could see her eyes, striking sea-glass-green with vertical pupils like those of a cat. Her face was quite angular, cheekbones stretching skin as fine as kid leather, surrounded by the mane of her hair. She appraised Jant and drew a breath. She studied his eyes just like hers, the same moth's-wing pale skin and wiry build, then she swayed side to side to examine his wings. She stirred her spear and its razor point circled his face like a steel mosquito.

He placed a hand on his chest and introduced himself. A frown creased her forehead. She snatched out her arm, grabbed a handful of his feathers and yanked them.

'Ow!'

She laughed, said something, and at Jant's perturbed expression laughed some more. The ice was broken. She lowered her spear and crouched on the wall top. She tapped a pointed talon on her breastbone and said, 'Shira Dellin.'

He answered, and they started talking in a guttural torrent so fast I couldn't distinguish words. I let it wash over me and watched her curiously: her obvious but alien intelligence, her distilled strength which shone through every movement. She was scarcely human, more like a wild animal masquerading as a girl.

'What is she saying?' I asked eventually.

Jant turned as if he'd forgotten I was there. 'Oh, Lightning. Yes, Shira Dellin here says she's come to find the silver man.'

'Who is the silver man?'

'It's ... it's a character from a story.' He wouldn't meet my eye. 'It's hardly important.'

'Tell me.'

Memories long-buried by silt stirred under the dredge, weighty years he had hidden and didn't want to examine. 'Oh, for god's sake. I think she's been out in the sun too long. When I was a kid my grandmother told me that, long ago, the "silver man" came to Darkling. He stayed with us for a while – with the Rhydanne people, I mean – and during that time everyone had enough to eat. But sadly, he left, and now he lives in the flatlands.'

'That's a story?'

'As Rhydanne stories go, it's about the most substantial I ever heard. That's why it stuck in my mind. Eilean impressed on me that if anything terrible happened, anything really disastrous, we should find the silver man and he would help us. To that lot "silver" means "important", you see. Dellin first thought *I* could be him. But she's changed her mind. It must be my lack of bangles. In fact, she thought I was a Rhydanne in disguise. Fake wings, do you see? I explained I'm half-and-half, but she scarcely believes me.'

'By "silver man" could she mean the Emperor?'

'Don't be ridiculous. San has never lived in the mountains.'

'As far as you know.'

'He's been sitting in the Throne Room for fifteen hundred years!'

'But before then?'

Jant shrugged and kicked the grass. 'What would a Rhydanne want with the Emperor?'

Dellin sat down cross-legged on the wall top with the spear across her knees, and her gaze flickered over us. She clearly hated the fact she couldn't understand. She was formulating something to say but kept being distracted by the calico carp gathering in our shadows cast over the pond. They were used to being fed and were rising like blotched orange, black and white balloons to mouth at the surface tension. I dabbled my fingers in the water and the fish nibbled at them, to her complete astonishment.

'Rule one,' I said. 'If anyone wishes an audience with the Emperor, he or she may. Rule two: if she asks us to lead her to the Throne Room, we are obliged to do so. You know that.'

'But ... me, in the Throne Room, with ...' He jutted his thumb at the huntress. 'I mean, she won't understand anything, and San will completely terrify her. And, look, Lightning, I'm just out of bed, I haven't even—'

'She may be trying to apply to him in a time of need.'

'And besides, she smells. Why don't you take her? I—'

'Jant! She needs you to translate.'

'All right, all right. If the Emperor will appreciate the services of the world's best translator, I'll do it. And besides, it could be a laugh.' He beckoned and she sprang up, donned her rucksack and twirled her spear. I was actually glad that she couldn't understand Awian, given that the world's best translator seemed determined to belittle her as much as possible.

She loped ahead of us like a lithe wolf, over the striped lawn past the Breckan Wing. Her footprints set far apart on the dewy grass drew great circles around us; her pace was longer than a human woman's. I could tell she was used to travelling immense distances on foot – she was more at ease moving than sitting still.

We turned the corner of Breckan Wing to the front of the palace. 'How did she get in, anyway?'

Jant smirked. 'She climbed the Skein Gate Barbican.'

'Really? And no one saw her?'

'Judging by the number of trophies she's wearing, she must be a fantastic hunter. Even though she's so small – I've never seen such a miniature Rhydanne. If she didn't want to be observed, those bloody lazy Imperial guards wouldn't have noticed her. She probably only took a couple of minutes to climb the tower.' He shrugged. 'They couldn't have caught her by hand.'

'By god. Do you have the urge to climb like that?'

'Certainly not!' He rounded on me. 'I'm the Emperor's Messenger, not some bloody savage!'

'Sorry.'

'Don't compare me with ... that thing. I'm civilised. She doesn't have the most basic manners!'

'I know.'

'I was fifteen when I left Darkling. They *hunted* me out. I haven't been back since. Yes, my mother was like her; yes, my grandmother too. But it's just an accident of birth. I can't help it.'

'Jant, I said I'm sorry.'

But of course he had to have the last word. 'You might as well ask if Awians have the urge to eat bird seed.'

We passed the broad, open arches of the gallery that runs along the ground floor of the Breckan Wing, and turned the corner into the Starglass Quadrangle. The Throne Room's grand entrance reared ahead of us, four steps up into an arched portal covered with carvings. Dellin looked about her with an air of satisfaction, then knelt and rubbed a fingertip on one of the cobbles of black flint chipped square. I approached so close I caught a whiff of her smell, a not unpleasant tang of old leather and the musty spiciness of dried blood. She smelt like a poacher's game bag, of meat so old it was no longer foul, but patinated like the soles of birds' feet and smelling as warm as the fur of hares. Her fingernails were filthy and her jacket glazed with dirt. Red flakes of old gore embedded the grain of her spear shaft. 'What could she possibly want to consult the Emperor about?'

'She won't tell me,' Jant admitted.

We ascended the four steps into the portal, Dellin gazing all the time at the statues in its recessed walls, and passed under the deep-relief carving into the corridor before the Throne Room. It seemed very dim after the sunlight and Dellin walked straight in, almost blind, and startled the guards standing either side of the Throne Room door. They jumped, levelled their spears, and she found herself facing two points. She twisted her body and brought her spear to bear.

Jant jumped forward and grabbed it. He yelled something but she didn't move.

'Stand at ease!' I shouted.

'Her first,' said the older guard.

'With all due respect, Lightning,' the other guard said. 'She's got to drop it.'

I said, 'Jant, tell her the silver man is behind that door. If she wants to meet him she must give up her weapons.'

'That'll insult her.'

'Tell her it is only temporary.'

He did so, then said to me, 'She doesn't want San to mistake her for a herder. The hunters look down on the herders. God, nothing ever changes in Darkling. I told her not to worry – San will know she's a hunter from her trophies – but she won't co-operate. She thinks bloody highly of herself, despite that she's a Shira.'

The guards craned forward. 'What is it?'

'Fascinating,' said his comrade.

'But what is it?'

I said, 'If flattery doesn't work, tell her that if she carries her spear inside, the archers will shoot her on sight.'

'Archers? They don't have a word for "archers". Um ... This is bloody ridiculous.' He paused, then smiled, clicked his fingers and mimed drawing a bow.

Dellin snarled and shrank into a crouch, her fingers white on the shaft. The guards tensed, which frightened her even more.

'At ease! At ease!' I said, shocked. 'She isn't threatening; she's scared. Jant, tell her we'll keep her safe.'

He told her and she offered the spear submissively. He took it and passed it to one of the guards. She shrugged off her pack, then hesitantly unwound the thong from her thigh and removed her knife. Its scabbard was decorated with hammered silver beads and tatty tassels. She reeled the thong around it and handed it over.

'Cheers.' The guard nudged his friend. 'Comet's brought in the cat. Eh?'

'She's beautiful ...'

'Striking, rather,' I said.

Jant was preoccupied with psyching himself up to speak with the Emperor, and made no comment.

'Comet, may we ask ... what is it?'

'It – *she* – is a Rhydanne, a predator fresh from the biting wastes and freezing summits of Darkling. Uncivilised she may be, ninety per cent carnivore she definitely is, but she has travelled here alone, facing untold dangers and overcoming who knows how many tribulations in her haste to bring a secret message to the Castle for the ears of none but the Emperor San himself!'

'Wow.'

'So shut up and let us in.'

They turned to each other and pushed the doors wide. Dellin looked at the ornate lock, at the curlicued hinges. The deep architrave of solid amber had been carved into voluminous honey-coloured drapes, as if frozen in time, mid-flow. Jant grasped her shoulder firmly, since if she ran in unaccompanied the Imperial Fyrd guards might take fright and shoot her. He led her through the doors with a few quiet words. 'I told her not to fear the Emperor.'

'She is bound to,' I said. 'We all do.'

*

Dellin paused and a delighted expression broke over her face. She looked around but no one can take in the whole Throne Room at once; only the Emperor, at the centre of the perspective, can see the main aisle and the side aisles together, all the way to the great rose window at the end. She examined the glittering, mosaic-covered arches and looked up to the archers on the gallery. Twelve Imperial Fyrd archers stand there, six on each side. Seeing them, she crouched again and fingered a large horse's incisor on her necklace.

'She thinks it's a trap,' I said.

'I know, I know,' said Jant. He spoke to her rapidly. He stood over her, blocking her view of the bowmen, shielding her – as she would see it – and her bony fingers curled around his with a powerful grip. She rose to her feet and stood with a hunter's readiness.

'She doesn't like archers for some reason,' he said.

'I can see that,' I said. 'I will go first and she will see they won't move.' I walked down the aisle and through the highly carved screen to where the Emperor was sitting on the sunburst throne. I bowed low before him and went to sit on the end of the front bench nearest the throne, so in relating these events to you I am easy in my mind that I heard every word spoken that day.

Tornado and a few other immortals were assembled on the benches at the far side. Since the last few years had been relatively peaceful many of us were residing in our apartments here rather than at the Insect front. Tornado smiled and raised his hand to me in a familiar salute, then when Dellin and Jant came in, he hefted to his feet and boggled at her.

The sunlight shone through the walls pierced with so many pointed arched windows they were nothing but stone frames for stained glass, casting heraldic light on the benches, arches and dais. Jant and Dellin seemed unreal, moving effortlessly through the slanting rays. Citrine, azure and malachite green slipped over them until they reached the end of the scarlet carpet, where Jant tried to manoeuvre Dellin in front of the throne. She shook herself free. She ran to the dais, pushed her bangles loose, leaving embossed red lines around her arms, and looked up at the Emperor. Jant swept an elegant bow but she just stood there, knees slightly bent, very tense as if to pounce. Jant was puzzled and annoyed that she didn't kneel. He placed his hands on her shoulders and tried to push her down but she just snatched herself away, her hand on her thigh where her dagger should be.

'Comet,' said the Emperor. 'That is no way to welcome a guest.'

'My lord,' Jant announced. 'Shira Dellin has come from Darkling and wishes an audience with the "silver man". I found her waiting in Carillon – she can only speak Scree, so I will translate.'

The Emperor made a strident sound, directly to Dellin. Jant's mouth dropped open, and so did his wings. Dellin smiled, showing fine white teeth, and started chattering eagerly. The Emperor said something to Jant, who was still too astonished to do more than make a clipped, automatic bow and sit down next to me.

'What's going on?'

He leant to whisper, 'The Emperor speaks Scree! My first language ...'

'What did he say?'

'He told me to sit down.'

I chuckled. 'Serves you right. You underestimate everyone, even San. Now do something useful and tell me what she is saying.'

'Um ... She just called him a flatlander.'

'What an excellent diplomat!'

He leant back on the hard ebony seat – there are no cushions, to remind us that we must be vigilant and dutiful at all times – stretched his arms along the top of the backrest, crossed his legs and spoke quietly. 'She just said, "My name is Dellin Shira, but I call myself Shira Dellin, putting my caste name first because I am not afraid of being a Shira, born out of wedlock. Why should I be blamed if my mother ran too slowly?" Hear, hear! I couldn't agree more.'

Other immortals were arriving all the time, and filing into the benches. From the footsteps behind the screen I could tell the mortals' benches were filling up too; the news of a Rhydanne in the Throne Room was making its rounds and everyone was coming to see for themselves.

The Emperor pointed at Jant and crooked a finger in beckoning. Jant shuddered and rose to his feet. San said, 'I wish everyone to hear her words. Translate for the benefit of all.'

Dellin stepped from side to side, warily watching the Emperor. The silence intensified as everyone listened and Jant prepared to echo her. She began. 'People are like flint. It is hard and resists much harsh treatment, but when it does break its edge is sharper than steel. The Rhydanne are starving. The hunters are famished, and I was too, before I left. The Awians have taken the promontory; they are killing the game and driving us away, either with their feathered darts or on horseback. They ...' She mimed an archer in the same way Jant had.

'Shoot,' he said.

'Shoot,' she copied, feeling the word. 'Shoot Laochan. My husband.' She rubbed the back of her hand across her eyes, which suddenly wet with tears, but whether from grief or frustration I couldn't tell. 'Now I have no husband, nobody to defend me if other men chase me, or to tend me if I am injured or pregnant. I have to hunt alone, but what is the point in hunting now? Any animals the Awians haven't trapped and slaughtered they have frightened away with their noise and bad tracking.' She paused. 'Laochan Dara was from the summit of Klannich. It took me many years to find a hunting partner since I am a Shira. I may never find another. The Awians murdered him and they shoot at others, too. They don't let us onto the promontory. I don't understand why.

'I have been travelling since the melt season, till I saw the pinnacle of this house on the horizon. The silver man must live in the biggest house in the flatlands, I thought. I was right. Here you have silver in abundance, more colours than all the mountain flowers, and you must be great hunters.'

I realised that she could not have spoken to anyone for six months and, savage as she was, I began to feel warmth for her. Half a year alone may not be much for a Rhydanne, but she must find the Plainslands strange and the Castle daunting. I admired her determination. Even immortals, Challengers and kings freeze in fear when they face the Emperor, but Dellin's fortitude shone like a standard. She kept glancing up into the spire lined with gold mosaics, as if its point had pierced the sun and siphoned out liquid flame to run down inside and coat the galleries.

Without turning her back on the Emperor, she swept a glance over the massed immortals, taking in our unfamiliar clothes. She saw Tornado and gaped at his bulk, shook herself and returned to gaze at the Emperor through fine fronds of her black hair. The other Eszai entering were amazed at her lack of respect, and there was so much whispering going on I could hardly follow Jant's translation.

The Emperor said, 'Why did the Awians shoot Laochan?'

Dellin ducked her head. 'We were hunting ...'

'What were you hunting?'

'Some horses. We were starving so we ventured close and took one.'

'You killed one of their horses?'

'We took three!'

'I see.'

'They enclosed their animals on land where anyone may walk. All animals are fair game.'

'Only in the hunters' minds. Do you often prey on herders' animals?'

'Yes, goats and llamas.'

'Would you expect them to defend their livestock?'

'They try.'

'Would they kill you if they could?'

'Yes.'

'So you do know you are stealing their property. Why is stealing from Awians any different? That the Awians used bows and arrows when you were expecting slings and stones is not something for which we can blame them.'

She hissed in frustration. 'Do you mean we must starve? I do blame the Awians because they force us from the land where we have always run and they take the food and shelter that should be free for all. All things on the mountainside are for the taking and we gather them if we can. But the Awians are building fences over it as if they are goats penning themselves. The whole mountainside is not the Awians' shieling, my-friend-the-silver-man.'

'Indeed not.'

'Nor is it their pen. But they would corral the mountain itself. I know they want to take the rocks themselves away – the shiny stones – and the very trees. If they could pick Carnich up and carry it down to the flatlands, they would.'

'Carnich!' Jant said. He spread his wings excitedly. 'Carniss, my lord – where the king sent his brother!'

The Emperor nodded, as if this fitted something he had already concluded. A rustle of interest flurried over the benches. Anyone who read the papers knew the story. Last year it had been the main subject of conversation from Summerday to Ghallain, but as my manor borders Rachiswater and I am a friend of the king, I had been in the thick of it.

The Rachiswaters are a recent dynasty. King Tarmigan Rachiswater's grandfather had taken the throne from the bankrupt

Tanager dynasty only sixty-two years before, and they were an even more ambitious and vigorous warrior family than the Tanagers had been. It was natural for dynasties of my country to begin in such a fashion. King Tarmigan, who was rather profligate, had been interested in Darkling for years, as the mountain rock yields silver and the terrain other precious goods. He was the first king to formally extend Awia in fifteen hundred years. He founded a new manor adjoining his on the slopes of the Awian highlands and sent his twin brother to administer it as the first governor of Carniss. This neatly served as a way of distancing his brother from him, as there was bad blood between the two.

Dellin thought for a while and the Emperor, giving her time, did not say anything. She extended one leg, turned her toes up and looked thoughtfully down the length of her leg at her foot. She rubbed at the palest beige patch on her thigh, rendering it as grimy as the rest of her trousers. Then she took a couple of steps almost too fast to follow and raised her face to San again.

'The featherbacks themselves are more like antler than flint – they are spreading and branching out. More wheeled sledges arrive every day. Since the melt season before last they have been building a house of stone. It grows every day, boulders climbing around a timber frame as if it is a grey adder sheathing on its skin.'

'How large is it?' said the Emperor.

She glanced up into the heights of the spire above his head. 'Not quite as big as this, but very big. Nearly as big as Coomb Mhor. Diédre Pinnacle ... As tall as the round bulges in the wall outside ...' She gestured expansively, her bangles jangling, and indicated the rear of the Throne Room beyond which was the north curtain wall.

'She came in over the Skein Gate,' Jant said.

San smiled. Wrinkles spread from the corners of his eyes, around his cheeks to the corners of his mouth. They intensified, vanished as fast as breath on a glass. 'Did she really? This sounds like Raven Rachiswater's settlement.'

'Yes, my lord. Most likely his manor house.'

'Dellin, I thank you for coming to the Castle,' the Emperor said, then he addressed the court in Awian. 'The king did not seek my advice before colonising Carnich. His new manor is in Darkling, on Dellin's hunting ground. Kings may act as they please, but it is the Castle's duty to protect the Fourlands and maintain peace between its peoples. Beside the blue column of Awia there is a silver column for Darkling.' He raised a hand to indicate the four columns in the niche behind the throne; one each to symbolise a country of the Fourlands.

'Darkling is one of the Fourlands in its own right,' he continued, 'and the Rhydanne are the people of Darkling. However, the mountain range is mostly unpopulated and there has never been a formal boundary between it and the other lands as there is, say, between Awia and the Plainslands.'

He turned to Dellin. 'Tarmigan and Raven Rachiswater consider Carnich to be part of Awia. This incident must be resolved to the satisfaction of all: either Rhydanne and Awians must find a way to live comfortably side by side, or Raven must offer you acceptable compensation. Comet?'

Jant translated and then said, 'Yes, my lord?'

'You will accompany Dellin back to Carniss and speak with Governor Raven. Speak also to the Rhydanne and discover their opinions. If no simple solution presents itself, return and report to me.'

'Yes, my lord.' Jant swelled with pride. He had not had such an important assignment before; he was only a young Eszai, the most recent to join us, only seventy years ago. In Awian he said, 'Rhydanne are nomads. If she's famished, I don't understand why she just doesn't walk away from Carnich.'

'Her husband was killed, Comet.'

Jant stepped back a little to address us all. Now he was an authority on the subject, it seemed. 'She isn't like any other Rhydanne I've ever met. The others would just roam off and find food somewhere else.'

He was holding his wings half-spread, an impressive effect, but I think he was consciously trying to distance himself from Dellin, and standing in an attentive but supplicant attitude as Awian as he could make it.

The Emperor appraised him. 'Consider Dellin an ambassador and see her safely to Carnich.'

'My lord ... she can't speak for other Rhydanne. She's only concerned with herself – as all Rhydanne are. Her complaint was very personal.'

'She says they are starving to death. Such a grievance cannot be disregarded.'

Jant brought his wings forward and hugged his body with them; stood completely enclosed in black plumes with the strong limbs crossed over his chest. The sharp tips of his flight feathers brushed the floor. As you and I know well, he never overlooked an opportunity to pose.

San said, 'Find her rooms in the Herst Building and offer her the hospitality of the Castle.'

'I would prefer to entertain her in my rooms.'

'Would you? That is very irregular.'

'My lord, every visitor finds the Castle overwhelming. How much more so will a Rhydanne who has just run in from the Darkling wastes?'

'Very well,' the Emperor conceded.

Dellin was listening intently but could not keep still. She stalked up and down, exploring the area before the throne and between the front benches on either side. She never turned her back on the Emperor – silver-haired San in his white robes with a collar of colourless jewels seemed to eminently satisfy her expectations of the 'silver man'. Her wary stance drew many whispered comments from the audience, but I thought it to be a show of respect in Rhydanne terms. She knew San was a man of prowess and therefore a possible danger to herself. She knew he was beneficent; she knew he would help and, as far as she could tell, he had existed for ever. No wonder she was anxious.

She inspected the wax-encrusted torchères, their braided stems, cabriole legs, and claw-and-ball feet, amused to see eagle talons rendered in gold. She poked her fingers into the deep carvings on the poppyheads of the bench ends, ebony inlaid with mother-of-pearl. She moved with the delicacy of a cat, more gracefully than a cat, more like a puma, over as far as the door to the Emperor's private room and back to the dais.

She wrinkled her nose at the frankincense smoke rising from the censer on the lowest dais step, and waved her hand through its stream. She tentatively touched the ring on the conical lid, flicked it open and peered at the coals inside. Then she actually sat down on the step beside it and unfastened the bone toggle of her jacket's deep pocket. I heard twelve bows bend as the archers drew on her, but instead of a weapon she took out a strip of what seemed to be dried meat and chewed it, clacking it on her back teeth.

Jant regarded her antics smugly, though his little, cat-with-the-cream smile wasn't as relaxed as usual. He said a word to her. She darted to him and cheerfully offered him the strip that glistened with her saliva, but he pushed her hand away. He showed her how to bow and she copied it with natural grace – standing side by side, they looked like identical puppets. Then she raced ahead of him as they walked out.

I took my leave of the Emperor and followed them past immortals and mortals, all turning their heads as Dellin passed. The whole hall trailed out behind me, leaving the Emperor alone on his throne. Well, a pure Rhydanne had never been seen in the Castle before and few people had seen a Rhydanne at all. Very occasionally individuals do travel down from the mountains and may be found anywhere in the Fourlands, but the occurrence is so rare that I have only seen a pure Rhydanne once before and I am nearly fourteen hundred years old. She was telling fortunes in a fair and, compared to petite Dellin, had been tall and rather mannish.

I caught up with Jant and Dellin at the door, where the guard was returning her spear. She snatched it back, and took her rucksack and knife with righteous annoyance.

'What do you think of that?' said Jant. 'The Emperor speaking Scree?'

I said, 'There are more dangerous pitfalls here than for you to worry about the Emperor's linguistic skills.'

'He spoke it accurately and well, but some words weren't quite right, as if the pronunciation had drifted. Some of his phrases were unusual too, things Rhydanne wouldn't quite say these days.' He jammed a thumb in his belt and we walked out of the dim narthex and down the steps. 'How long ago did he visit Darkling? Two thousand years? Maybe when god was still in the world!'

I shrugged. Unlike Jant, I see no point in febrile questioning. 'I am not surprised. If San intended to be adviser to the world, he would want to live for a while in each of its four corners.'

'Imagine him sitting in a tent, eating goat stew ... regaling Rhydanne with words they think are wise.'

'I find that wisdom is universal, Jant. It transcends era and language.'

The path through the Starglass Quadrangle, the only entrance to the Throne Room, is paved with the marble gravestones of former immortals who have died in their role – serving the Castle – rather than those who have lost a Challenge and been displaced to become mortal again. Those who died in battle are buried here, as a place of honour for all eternity. Each tombstone is a different colour of marble, and each has the name and heraldic device of the immortal engraved and gilt in the same style. They form a wide path running down the prime meridian of the Fourlands, with the flint cobbles on either side. I had known every one of them, I had been present when each was initiated into the Circle, and I remember every one of them hoping that his immortality would be for ever.

Behind us, Tornado shouted, 'Wait!' The crowd parted at the sight of him hurrying towards us. Dellin was crouching and stroking with admiration the deep etching on Lir Serein's grave. When Tornado loomed over her she cried out in shock. She snarled at the Castle's Strongman, over two metres tall and proven to be the strongest warrior in the world – at least for eight hundred years, but probably for all time. He dwarfed me and I am not small. He had more muscle in one arm than Jant had in his entire body. He beamed down upon Dellin, radiating amusement and approval so strongly that she recovered, and smiled back.

'Well done, girl,' he said. 'I've never seen a performance like that in front of the Emperor.'

'If she knew we're immortal, she'd be more impressed,' said Jant.

'Rubbish. She's a fighter, anyone can see. So the Emperor's sending you to Darkling, is he?'

'To Carniss, yes.'

'Well, I'd give my axe hand to come with you. How about it?'

'Certainly not,' said Jant.

'Why not? I'd like to see her in her real surroundings, maybe come across more like her. I've never seen Darkling.'

'Because,' said Jant, nettled, 'this is my first real assignment. Seventy years doing Messenger's errands, flying letters round the Fourlands till I'm bored sick, and you older Eszai always take the plum jobs. This is my chance to show I can do more than struggle with the Black Coach. San will give me better missions after this, the sort that you hog. So you're not taking over!'

'Didn't want to. I want to come with you, climb some mountains, that sort of thing.'

'You'd slow me down. Don't you know it's freezing up there? And you'll hardly be able to breathe at the altitude where she feels at home.'

'Excellent,' said Tornado, scratching his shaved head. 'A real challenge!'

'Good for fitness,' I said.

'Just what I was thinking, Saker.'

'No!' said Jant. 'I hardly want to return to Darkling myself, let alone take every Plainslander and Awian inside these eight walls. Anyway, you two can't possibly get any fitter.'

Tornado laughed. We continued through the quadrangle, which is full of instruments astronomical, horological and meteorological, the world's most modern and ingenious, which the Castle collects here. They surround the great gold Starglass like courtiers around a king. The servants uncovering their awnings and taking readings from the Starglass paused to watch Dellin. She gave them not a glance, but ran to inspect the gleaming brass of an orrery taller than a man. Dew had beaded on its rings and a servant was wiping the ivory model of the Castle itself, at its very centre. Around it, two agate orbs representing the planets, an opal moon and a topaz sun, were fixed on embellished rings and pivots. The servant threw the lever for her, and they began to spin in an accurate simulation. Dellin stepped back, gripped her spear and watched them defiantly.

Jant sniggered. 'Look at her. More metal than she's seen in her whole life before.'

'Don't they have metal in the mountains?' asked Tornado.

'Yes, if they only knew how to mine it.'

'Tell me what Darkling's like,' he said eagerly.

'Unbelievable. The mountains soar fifteen hundred metres high. You can see all the way to the western ocean. There are creatures there like nothing else in the world, denizens that make even me jittery: white wolves with dripping fangs and eyes like the Summerday lighthouses ...'

'What, three of them?'

'At least. Ah, Darkling, the land of elk and bunnies. There's a race of wild men with antlers growing from their foreheads, which spread wider than arms and weigh so much that old men have to walk around with their heads bowed and their antlers dragging on the ground. There are sucker deer – the bottoms of their hooves are concave and soft and act like sucker cups, so they can climb vertical, smooth rock faces and stand upside down on the underside of overhangs.'

'Wow,' said Tornado. 'I'm going! Take your crossbow and bring one back to show us.'

'Certainly,' said Jant, seriously. 'But you haven't heard anything yet. There are hundreds of creatures that Dellin takes for granted which you're unfortunately going to miss. There are mountain seals.'

'*Mountain* seals?'

'Of course. Left over from before the mountains started growing, when they were on a level with the sea. As you know,' he proclaimed, finding his pace, 'mountain seals live on diametrically opposed peaks. As they have flippers they can't climb, obviously, so when they need food they drag themselves to the lip of the ledge and teeter for a few seconds before sledging down, faster and faster; god, they reach tremendous speeds ... They snatch what food they can on the way, and have enough momentum to toboggan up the mountain on the other side. They reach a ledge and stop there in readiness for sliding back.'

I glanced at Tornado, who was lapping this up, and then looked away quickly because I could not refrain from smiling.

'You're pulling my leg,' Tornado said abruptly. Maybe he had seen my expression.

'Not at all. I've seen one go past. I was climbing Stravaig when – whoosh – I looked in its direction – "What the fuck was that?" '

'You're taking the piss. He's taking the piss, Lightning, isn't he?'

I said, 'Safer to ignore him when he spouts nonsense.'

'Damn you, Jant. I believed you then! I bloody believed you – up until the seals.'

'Mountain seals,' he averred, in hurt tones, and then burst out laughing. 'Should have seen your face. It would never work, anyway. They'd end up in the valley. Then they'd have to wait for winter, for enough snow to build up and leave them at the top of the mountain again.'

'Damn you, I'll pay you back one day.'

'You'd have to get up so early in the morning it would be the middle of the night.'

Tornado smiled. 'Should have realised when you said the mountains grew.'

'The mountains *do* grow,' Jant insisted. 'That one's true. It causes the earthquakes, and I've lived through one myself. It causes volcanoes too, like Mhadaidh, which means 'The Fox', you see, because its slopes are red with sulphur and all kinds of noxious chemicals. Some mountains, like Bhachnadich, have holes that actually smoke.'

'Smoking mountains,' said Tornado. 'Nice.'

'More nonsense,' I agreed.

'Saker,' Jant said to me. 'Don't you want to come and see?'

'Not particularly.'

'Have you ever seen Darkling?'

I sighed. 'I have occasionally hunted in Eyrie.'

'That's the foothills!'

'I plan to spend the New Year in Foin; I have no wish to travel to Carniss.'

Comet and Tornado glanced at each other. Neither was inclined to broach the topic, but I know they were thinking that ... well, it has been seventy years since Savory, and perhaps I should leave her in the past and seek more society than the quiet backwaters of Foin, but where I spend New Year is my choice. It is the best place to salve the spells of wistfulness I still suffer from time to time.

'You are incurious,' Jant said. 'How long have you been alive without visiting Darkling?'

'Don't criticise me.'

'You've no sense of adventure. I thought that was the advantage of being immortal. You can go everywhere, see everything! The Emperor seems to have done so, before he ended up in the Throne Room. Take a leaf from his book! What have you been *doing* all these years?'

Shooting Insects and lasting longer than you will, I thought, but he plunged on, 'You should jump at the chance to see something new. What's your problem?'

I shrugged, piqued. Doesn't every man fall short of his own self-image? 'It seems that when you were learning Awian and I let you run riot in my manor, you failed to absorb a point of etiquette. One should—'

'Never been to Darkling. Never been to Ressond. Never been to Addald Island or Cape Brattice.'

'I sailed around Cape Brattice in the year twelve hundred, *before* it became easy.'

'Never even been to Cathee before Savory dragged you there.'

'Savory didn't drag me anywhere,' I snapped. His wits are quicker than mine, but I know my manor is superior to any of those places.

It is layered as thickly with memories as a canvas reworked with many successive paintings. I wanted to sequester myself in Foin, in the midst of them, as if in a gallery, and peruse them to my heart's content.

'Savory was more adventurous than he is,' Jant said to Tornado, who good-humouredly let the matter drop. He knows me well and recognises, far better than Jant does, when to stop aggravating me.

We passed between the Breckan and Simurgh Wings, following the processional route from the quadrangle. Only a few leaves remained on the poplars bordering the avenue down to the Yett Gate. We walked past the shaded arcade on the ground floor of Breckan. Dellin sprinted to the wall, seized the smooth stone in both hands and pulled herself up. She climbed with such gusto her rucksack with her spear attached bounced on her back. I couldn't see any handholds; she just *spidered* up. She reached the roof, flexed her arms and pulled her body over the balustrade. A second later she stood tall on its parapet, backgrounded by the old white buttresses of the Throne Room that soar high behind Breckan. She ran easily along the balustrade until she came to Breckan's neoclassical pediment, then ran up the side of it and stood on its peak.

Tornado, staring at her, rubbed his neck. 'What skill! Wish I was that agile.'

'Nothing I couldn't do,' said Jant.

'I'd like to put her against Insects in the amphitheatre.'

'Her spear is crude. No balance.'

'I wonder what heft it has,' I said.

Tornado glanced at me. 'Rhydanne in the amphitheatre, eh, Saker? We'd have the biggest paying crowd of all time. Not least cause she has a body like a lynx!'

Jant shrugged. 'If they had more human minds they wouldn't need such lynx-like bodies.'

'It's a good thing they don't,' Tornado said. 'If they had human minds *and* lynx-like bodies, then most of the places in the Circle would be filled by Rhydanne, mark my words.'

I said, 'It is a pity they can't join the fight against Insects. She'd make an excellent scout.'

'Oh, yeah,' said Jant sarcastically. 'She'd throw rocks at the Insects for – oh, twenty minutes – before getting bored and wandering off.'

I disagreed. Dellin's determination was obvious to me, if not to him. I said, 'I bet I could teach her to use a bow.'

'She'd just slope away, and you'd achieve no more than to damage the fyrd's morale. You might as well herd pumas.'

'But you're not like that,' said Tornado. 'After all, Jant Shira *is* a Rhydanne name. If you don't wander off, why should she?'

'Because I'm half Awian!'

Dellin reached the end of Breckan's roof and crouched on the balustrade. Although she was above a drop of fifteen metres she looked as steady as on the ground. She drew back and disappeared from sight.

'Fuck it,' said Jant. 'I've lost her already.'

She reappeared, sprinting, and jumped into the sky. She seemed to hang there, between the two buildings, falling with one leg and arm stretched out. She landed on the lower roof of Carillon, dropped to her knees, and was up and running again along the tiles. That image is still fixed in my mind: Dellin sailing in the air without wings, her hair flying behind her, in the gap between the two magnificent buildings, against the dazzling sun.

Tornado gave a low whistle. 'Wow. You can almost believe they turn into lynxes on their birthdays.'

'Don't tempt her.'

Dellin reached the end of the roof, knocking off a few tiles, and shimmied easily down a drainpipe. Without glancing at us she hurtled off joyfully, following her nose towards the kitchens. She was full of excitement from having spoken to San. The release of tension drove her to climb every building as far as the Dining Hall, where Jant reined her in.

Jant ordered food to be delivered to his room. The hall was buzzing with gossip, so I did not follow Tornado inside. I said farewell to Jant and made him promise to tell me all when he came back in the New Year. I kissed Shira Dellin's bony hand, which she found most peculiar, and returned to my own apartments.

JANT

Dellin ran ahead up the spiral staircase, taking absolutely no notice of me. She crammed herself into the recesses funnelling down to each slit window and tried to peer out of the cracks in their narrow shutters. She pulled herself up by the thick rope handrail. At length I opened my door and released her into my room.

She darted about investigating everything rapidly but thoroughly – the curtains, the furniture, the hearth and the desk. She started pulling all the letters from the pigeonholes.

'Hey!' I said, 'Stop that!' I stood in front and guarded them – and off she dashed again.

She looked into the beaten-bronze bowl on its wrought-iron wash stand, then caught sight of herself in the mirror above it and a startled expression crossed her face. She tried a sly smile, then ripped the mirror from the wall and gazed down into it, studying her reflection. That didn't last long; she tossed the mirror on the divan and pulled dictionaries of various languages out of the bookcase, flicking through them while sniffing the paper then letting them drop.

Butterfly, my Insect trophy, dominated the room on one side of the window; a dated but carefully maintained suit of scale armour stood to attention on the other. She approached the huge dead Insect cautiously – I doubt she had seen one before – seemed to realise it was just animal remains and reached out to knock on its hollow thorax. She leant from side to side observing it, her angular face a centimetre away from its globular eyes, the tip of her nose almost touching the shell, its reedy antennae and razor jaws. Beneath the mandibles are jaws like paired trapdoors, then under them many layers of maxillae. I have a recurring nightmare of being caught by an Insect and held down while the maxillae like circular saws rasp away at my flesh, scraping it down to the bone while I'm still alive.

Dellin knew nothing of the horror of Insects. She left Butterfly and disappeared behind the blue curtain. I sighed and walked it back along its rail, just in time to see her looking under my four-poster bed. She pushed head and shoulders underneath then pulled back into a crouch and emerged, sleeves and hood white with dust and smelling of camphor.

'Nothing under the bed, is there?' I said. 'No one in it, either, thanks to you.'

She examined its posts entwined with variegated ivy and topped with bunches of peacock plumes, the drapes and canopy of bottle-green damask. A series of pennants hung along the top frame, embroidered with cockerels and daisies, with red tassels on each point, actually the bunting from a jousting tent. Dellin was still trying to figure out what the bed was for – she pulled off the bolsters and green sheets edged with gold silk.

I fended her off and replaced them, but a chinking sound made me look round. She had taken one of my wine bottles from the mantelpiece and, holding it between her feet on the floor, was stabbing at the cork with her spear.

'Stop it! For god's sake! Sit down. Here ...' I moved my chair away from the desk but she ignored it. She made camp under the desk itself. She took off her snow-leopard-skin parka, spread it on the floor with the soft fur lining turned uppermost, and sat down cross-legged on it, her long legs folded like a grasshopper's.

'Where is your wife?' she asked.

'I don't have a wife.'

'So old and not married?'

'Dellin, I wish you had the slightest idea how tiring it is trying to speak in your terms. I'm a Shira. My mother died while giving birth to me; my father was Awian, so how could they arrange a match for me?'

'And you haven't found your own partner? Are you slow or something?'

'No, I'm not bloody slow! I'm the fastest man in the world!'

She opened her pack and brought out a waterskin, unplugged it and drank it dry, then squeezed it flat and shook it mournfully.

I caught a whiff. 'Gin, Dellin? That's not Rhydanne poteen. Have you been through Eske?'

'It's good.'

'Have you been stealing drink all the way across the flatlands?'

'All the flatlands! They have a lot of alcohol. They can spare some.'

I envisaged a trail of broken-into vintners and pubs from Carniss to the demesne. And – oh, god – how had she been eating? Catching livestock? Chasing down sheep and cattle and slaughtering them in the fields? 'I bet you found animals on the plains easy to spear?'

'Very easy. They are fat and slow.'

'That's because they're farm animals! I'm surprised the owners didn't set their dogs on you.'

'Some did. The dogs were not as tasty.'

I sighed, thinking of newspaper headlines proclaiming packs of wild women ransacking the plains. Dellin turned to look speculatively at the bottles on the mantelpiece. I had been trying to cultivate a knowledge of wine, as the connoisseurship of certain older Eszai impressed me, but Dellin had limbered up on gin and was dying to attack the vintages I had carefully purloined from the Castle's cellars.

'I can't believe you drank a whole waterskin of gin.'

'Two waterskins, Jant. This is the second.'

'The second? When did you drink the first?'

'Before talking to the silver man.'

'Mmm. I don't blame you.'

'I am not drunk,' she said suspiciously, just as there was a knock on the door.

She started and grabbed her spear, but I called 'Enter!' and the door creaked wide. Three servants nudged their way in, carrying platters piled high with bread and meat, fruit and salad, and another boy behind them staggering under the weight of a majolica jug of wine.

'Ah, excellent. Put them down there ...' I indicated the middle of the floor. 'Just there. And you can take the old plates back. Don't mind the Rhydanne. That was an excellent cake, by the way. And those glasses. Wonderful. Thank you. Much obliged. Bye!'

I passed her the jug. She lifted it with both hands and started guzzling wine. She stuck her talon into an apple, inspected it impaled on her fingernail and threw it away. Then she turned to the meat – with Tornado's appetite and the manners of a wolf. She snatched a slice of fillet steak and it vanished. Two more, one in each hand, and both disappeared. She chewed with her mouth full to bursting and all the time pulled the platters closer to her knees.

She snatched a roast chicken, done the Awian way with garlic and capers, and deftly twisted it apart. She dug out the buttery-juicy meat with her fingernails and fed her maw with both hands. It turned my stomach and, worse, it brought back memories I would rather not explore.

'Steady, steady!'

'I'm hungry!'

'Take your time. No one will steal it. We have food and drink enough.'

The meat went into her mouth as a child would eat sweets. She chomped on a leg, gristle, skin and sinew, all together, then placed the clean bones down neatly as if she had a use for them too. For all her gobbling she didn't waste a single crumb or drop of wine; she thought it much too valuable.

She finished the chicken, then batted the tray aside and pulled another, of ham arranged in a spiral, towards her. I tried to slow her but she glared, her eyes sparking and her hair wild. I could almost see her putting on weight.

'You must be ravenous?' I asked, amused.

'I haven't eaten since last night. When I saw the spire I started running.'

'Tell you what, I'll eat the salad.'

She paused in the act of screwing ham rind into a little ball so she could fit it into her already full mouth. 'Who were those men in pale blue?'

'Only servants.'

'They must be excellent hunters,' she said, in a tone indicating that perhaps she should be talking to them rather than me.

'No, we Eszai do the hunting. *I* am a hunter; they just cook the food.'

'How do you stop them stealing it, then?'

'I know it's hard to believe, but there's enough to spare.'

'Then you must have a lot of time on your hands.' She nodded towards my silk shirt. 'No wonder you have such good clothes.'

'I don't make my own clothes either.'

'Ha! I knew there was something wrong with you.'

'Dellin! For god's sake! Try to understand. I'm not ill, or disabled, or childish, or slow. I'm *rich*! Well, I'm far from being rich, but the Castle is. Extremely wealthy, and I live here because I'm the Emperor's Messenger, called Comet, the fastest man in the world.'

I explained my position, which took a very long time because Scree doesn't have the words. I told her that the Emperor makes the Circle's warriors immortal, and maintains our immortality through the Circle, for each who is the best in the world at his speciality. I said there were fifty of us, but each could be replaced if someone beats them in a fair and open competition. Tornado was the strongest man in the world and Lightning the best archer, and they prove it every time they are Challenged.

It was even more difficult to relate my childhood in Darkling, because she thought being a goatherd was lowly, and I kept shrinking from the images that came to mind of that terrible time. To admit my past was to recognise memories that were more like unfocused patches of pain than clear recollections. I skirted round them with care.

'So you see,' I finished. 'The Castle buys more meat every day than in all the cliff-fall hunts you've ever seen put together.'

'The silver man is powerful.' She smiled.

'He stops time from ageing us. What greater power can there be? For example, I am ninety-five – or thereabouts – because I don't know the exact year I was born.'

She just gave me an incredulous look: the number was too large. It was several Rhydanne lifetimes and completely at odds with my appearance.

'Ninety-five melt seasons, ninety-five freeze seasons.'

Her gaze wandered over me steadily, noting the lack of bangles and beads and, worse still, the clothes of a soft flatlander and the scent of aftershave redolent of male Awians. She turned her attention pointedly back to a tray of succulent pink venison. 'So many flavours,' she murmured, scooped the meat up and tipped it into her rucksack.

'You don't have to do that!'

In went the rest of the venison and a whole bowl of granary rolls. She was dropping them into a sort of leather pouch in the main sack.

'Stop! It's disgusting!'

She picked up a tray of songbirds wrapped in vine leaves and stowed a handful carefully behind the cushion on my divan. I tried to take the platter, but she wouldn't let me.

'You don't have to cache it! We can order more any time!'

'You can't have my food! Go find your own food!' She escaped with the platter and jumped the double step to my bedroom. She piled stuffed quails on the sill behind the shutter, checked they were hidden from view, and cached all the chicken bones under the bed. Then, satisfied her food was safe, she wiped her hands on the curtain, seated herself under my desk and washed down her meal with mouthful after mouthful of wine. She may have been calm but I was infuriated, more because she was paying no attention to me than because of the foul mess. I have learnt, from attending governors and the king, how much appearances matter. Now to impress Dellin, did I have to act like a savage as well as reverting to her lingo?

I unclipped my sword and sat down on the divan with the scabbard between my knees. 'Look, I may not be wearing any trinkets but I am a good hunter. See how much metal?' I pulled the hilt up and bared a little of the blade.

Dellin immediately held her hand out for it. I shook my head and offered her my gold ring, but she pointed to one of a pair of brass candlesticks on the side table. 'I like that better. It's bigger.'

'But it's just brass. It's cheap.'

'Great. You could own a lot of them and then you'd be really important.'

I passed her a candlestick. 'Here.'

'Yes,' she said, and just pointed to the other of the pair.

'Here.'

'Yes.' She tucked them under her rucksack straps and pointed at my ring. So she would just take whatever I gave her and think me a damn fool for parting with it. I put my ring back on. As no more riches were forthcoming, Dellin simply lay down on the fur. She curled into a remarkably small space, with her hands together in front of her face, and immediately went to sleep.

'Thank you very much,' I said, and regarded her frankly. 'You smell. I'll have to ask Ata to give you a shower. If this morning has been a culture shock wait till you discover the delights of a flushing toilet.'

I left her, locked the door for the first time in months, pocketed the key and descended again. I visited all the women I could find, female Eszai and male Eszai's wives. Many immortals were away, training or pursuing business, interests, pleasures and rivalries from their other residences, but I found several servants whom I knew well, doctors in Rayne's hospital, librarians in Lisade and accountants in Carillon. I borrowed jewellery from them all. They thought it was hilarious and I faced a blizzard of questions about Dellin. I joked with them as they laughed at me trying on their beads, but after an hour I had an arm full of plain bangles fit for the best hunter in Darkling.

I ran to the stables and ordered a coach, then back to my room, rather enjoying the dissonance of silver, opened my door – and Dellin had gone. Her parka was rucked up and the shutters swung wide.

Damn her. I ran to the window and leant out. Far below, the grassy slope of the glacis led down to the moat, which rippled black and white like damask steel in the afternoon sunlight. Nobody was down there; she could be kilometres away by now.

'Hey!' A shout from directly above. I twisted round and looked straight up the wall. Giddyingly, Dellin's worn moccasin soles dangled from a notch between two of the crenellations. They bounced against the stone and arced out as she swung her feet.

'What are you doing up there, *sguniach*?'

Her face appeared, looking over, 'Come up!'

Swearing, I stomped back to the landing and up a ladder to a trapdoor in the ceiling. I slipped back the bolt and shoved up the trapdoor. It swung over and crashed flat against the roof above, showering grit into my eyes.

Swearing even more loudly, I climbed out into the bright air, the trapdoor frame smearing tar down my trousers. Dellin was perched between the merlons, her legs hanging over the edge. She craned round to see me and blinked, surprised at my bangles.

'I have more but I cached them,' I said. I walked around the low cone of the lead roof and sat down next to her. She was still eating but obviously forcing it down. Close to, the suede rounded over her skinny thighs was scratched and pockmarked with the bites and scars the leopard had received when it was alive. The thick seams shone with bone grease rubbed in to waterproof them. Her long ponytail down her back was surprisingly clean.

In addition to her small size, she was probably younger than she looked, because Rhydanne grow and mature faster than humans or Awians. I guessed her to be twenty, which would be the equivalent of early thirties for us. Crow's-feet clasped the corners of her eyes, and over hard muscles, her skin had a wind-burnt shine. There is no such thing as an elderly Rhydanne. Their bodies take the brunt of their harsh existence and they live and run at full speed until they drop dead at around age forty.

Above us my flag, the Waterwheel emblem black on white, fissled and rustled. This tower was my haunt, my eyrie, my silent kingdom, and the serrated peaks of Darkling lurked out of sight below the horizon. I did not want to go back there; I had been away too long. Like climbers who have attained the summit and gained a sudden peace, we looked out across the meadows to the frothy tops of oak trees at the start of the Eske woods. Beyond the wide strip of the moat, the river glittered into a series of locks. Two channels ran from it, into the second moat and the fishponds. The banks of the ponds were dotted with people fishing, and a nodding carthorse was towing a barge on a return journey from the kitchen's postern gate to the river.

Dellin looked left to the edge of the earthworks, right to the bridge of the Skein Gate. 'This is better! Inside, I feel trapped. The walls are too close. It's too small and dark.'

'Even the Throne Room?'

'Even the Throne Room. So many people! It must be a sight.'

'What must?'

'When you move for winter.' She pointed to the pale Skein Road, which ran out of the barbican, across both moats and straight as a die through the water meadows in the direction of Binnard. 'I bet people and herds fill that whole track.'

'You think we move to winter quarters? You think everyone in the Castle moves?' I laughed, then stopped abruptly, because a joke gets bitter quickly when there's no one to share it with. 'Wait till I tell Tornado ... No, no, Dellin. We stay here all year round. Flatlanders tend to live in one place.'

She was silent for a while. Below us, ninety metres of masonry slitted with windows plunged to the moat. The guard was changing on the Skein Gate and snatches of jocular conversation drifted up.

'So, then, the featherbacks won't move from Carnich?'

'No, Dellin, not in the winter.'

She laughed derisively, which angered me.

'You don't appreciate the might of Awia! This has repercussions; if you drop a pebble you could cause an avalanche. It goes all the way to the king himself! You might as well try to push down that bloody spire!'

She glanced over her shoulder, looking across the tower top

and through the gap between two battlements, past the tip of the theatre's cupola, beyond which, just visible, rose the Throne Room's octagonal spire. 'The weather itself may push it down one day, Jant Shira. And the Awians? Trying to stay at Carnich through the winter? Do they really know what the mountains can do?'

When our coach was ready I took Dellin down to the gate. A crowd had gathered around the coach, including Lightning and Tornado. Really, you would think they had something better to do. I explained all to the driver, opened the door and Dellin jumped inside. I climbed in behind her, sat down on the bench and slammed the door. The Sailor's wife had helped her to take a shower, which had left her much cleaner, but somewhat bedraggled and subdued, and her hair still smelt of lanolin.

The second the door closed she looked frightened. She half-stood and shoved the door, turned round and barged past my knees, then shoved the door on the other side. I couldn't make her sit down. Bowed beneath the padded ceiling, she grabbed the handle and tugged it. The door sprang wide and she jumped out.

The coach rocked on its flat springs and a nervous titter went through the crowd. I stepped out. Dellin, terrified, was backing away into the crowd, which was separating to watch as she passed.

The driver called, 'What's the problem?'

'She! She is the problem!'

I put Dellin inside again and the same thing happened. She threw her weight from side to side and the chassis bounced. She kicked open the door and leapt to the ground.

'It's a tiny space,' she gasped. 'I'm trapped!'

'Look out the window.'

'No! It's too small!'

Now the horses scented her. They raised their heads, trying to see around their blinkers. The mare nearest her stamped its front hoof, edged away from her, and in two steps was up against the harness beam. So began a *pas de quatre* which should have been carried out to a slow waltz tune. The horses on the other side stepped away from Dellin too and the coach began to tilt. The wheels on my side rose off the ground. The driver grabbed his seat to stop himself slipping and the coach bit further and further into its suspension, its step and running board cutting into the grass.

The crowd seemed content to watch rather than help so I pulled

Dellin away from the horses. The driver walked them forward to realign them, the coach rocked back and its step flicked off a lip of soil and grass.

'It's perfectly safe,' I said. Dellin showed her teeth.

I took her arm and tried to drag her inside but she braced herself in the doorway with both feet and one hand. I couldn't tug her in, her limbs were so rigid, and the crowd fell about laughing.

The driver, flustered with embarrassment, said, 'What's the matter with her?'

'She doesn't like the confined space.'

Dellin had darted round and was regarding the horses inquisitively. They were veering away from her on that side now, shying and tossing their heads, chewing their bits, twisting the harness bar and lifting the left wheels off the ground. I don't know how the driver managed to stop them from bolting. He waved her away, so I moved her to a safe distance and shouted, 'If she can't sit inside she'll have to go on the luggage rack!'

'Won't she be chilly?'

'Not at all!'

I explained to Dellin, who swung up on the brass brackets and settled happily next to the trunk. I stepped onto the running board and called, 'Let's get this show on the road!'

'Hah!' The driver cracked his whip. The horses bowed their heads and took the strain, the reins slipped through his fingers, and the glossy black coach rolled forward. The sound of the hooves echoed back hollowly from the Castle walls. I was about to duck inside when Dellin jumped down, ran around us and ahead, up the road. The lad pulled the horses to a halt and looked round at me.

'What now?' I called to Dellin.

'Why go in a box when you can run? Much faster than the horses!' she exclaimed and cheerfully bounced from one foot to the other.

'Because it's a long way. I have a lot of luggage, and ...'

She sneered.

'All right, all right!' Well, if I am trying to be conspicuous, then surely Raven and the Rhydanne will be far more impressed to see me flying in, than if I arrive by coach.

I turned to the driver. 'Dellin can't bear the coach. She wants to run, so I'll run with her.'

Someone in the crowd cheered – do you know, I think it was

Tornado – and the rest followed suit. I acknowledged them with a wave. Then I climbed up onto the luggage rack, flipped open the trunk and stuffed as much into my haversack as I could carry, ending with my grey velvet army hat, which has had more than its fair share of fame.

I settled the sack between my wings, then jumped down and set off after Dellin without another word. But never let it be said that Comet ran all the way to Carniss. As I crossed the drawbridge I was running fast enough to fly. I spread my wings and flapped up, labouring higher, passed over Dellin, and fanned her with the down-draft of my wings. It was a shame I missed her expression, but I felt her staring after me.

That surprised you! I thought. Now you know why I'm the fastest man in the world! I turned on the breeze and circled. Dellin was a little black and white figure far below, running steadily along the road. She tried to beckon me down, but I ignored her and she stopped trying. After that she only rarely looked up, but when she did I dropped height to show I had seen her.

Behind us, the tiny coach and the crowd surrounding it shrank into distance across the water meadows. Shallow pools flooded the waterlogged common here and there, like mirrors framed with grass. Lines of debris on the road marked the highest extent of the flooding, and the breeze bore the tangled, hairy smell of wet nettles and mud. The last we heard of the Castle was the faint peal of the Starglass, striking two p.m.

Tornado could never run in such a sustained fashion and, unlike Dellin and myself, he isn't immune to all but the most intense cold. He might be the anvil-splitting Strongman who once dragged a canal boat up Dace Weir, and the nemesis of a hundred thousand Insects, but this job is best left to the expert.

I was also disappointed by Lightning. He used to be a good deal more outgoing, but he has spent too long moping over Savory – and, of course, being continually upstaged by my good self. His so-called love for Savory was ridiculous in the first place, but to spend seventy years in mourning, growing his hair in a ponytail and avoiding the limelight, goes from the ridiculous to the sublimely absurd. He is putting it on, you know. Instead of hiding in Foin he should cut his hair and make this New Year a night to remember.

In fact, just as Savory gave *me* a night to remember, and more than once – whenever I carried one of Lightning's love letters to her at the Front. I would walk past the lines of Cathee soldiers' tents, and their boar skull standard on a pole, to the captain's pavilion.

'Captain Savory?' I would call, and a young, ginger-haired woman would answer at the tent flap. The first time I saw her, she was clad in pieces of Lightning's sun-golden armour, greaves, vambraces and shoulder plates, which he had given her to wear. She also had a lentil skin stuck between her teeth. I would deliver his blue rose – by now somewhat wilted – and his letter, which was as embarrassingly dramatic as it was simple in style, because Lightning's knowledge of Morenzian was basic at best and Savory could scarcely read at all. Then we would lie down on her sheepskin bed ... She wasn't a virgin; she was wild.

So you see, all he thinks of is l-o-v-e, and it's a fool's delusion, always a fraud. We don't win wars through *lurve*. We exist to fight for the Castle, that's all, and lovers only succeed in destroying themselves. No wonder Lightning got hurt: he heaped all his affections on one mortal woman when there are so many women to pleasure us. When Savory was killed in a blood feud in her own part of the back of beyond I could have said, 'I told you so!' But Lightning wants to live in the gilded cage he has constructed for himself and forgets the fact that the world outside is freezing, dark and cruel. Many people think that the world is too harsh to inhabit without a cage, but the bars they build can only ever be scant protection and the real world will break in upon them. Better to live in the raw, the way I do. We live too much in fantasy in the first place, for Lightning to delude himself further with feisty Savory, flirtatious Savory, the woodsman's daughter and the dreamer's fodder.

They are whores, all those women: they are hay to our baser nature. Back in eighteen eighteen, when I joined the Circle, he had already been courting Savory for three years. I could in no way believe he was really in love. I thought he must be bored and seeking trysts to enliven and complicate his life. Why otherwise would a lord of Awia intrigue with a backwoods boar-netter and show no trace of shame? Being new to the Castle I was always wanting to run, fly, put my life on the line, for anything and at any time, and the fact I was shagging Lightning's betrothed was highly amusing. Perhaps it would have continued even if they'd married.

As for marriage, well, he was talking like a mortal. What need does an Eszai have of a wife? It was distasteful to see him following

Savory around – immortals should remain independent. Mortal women are trouble: they are branded with death like everyone else, and like we once were. My girlfriend in Hacilith died. Savory died too and so soon, kneeling in her cottage rank with the smell of pork fat and potato peelings. Lightning told me as he picked a blue rose in the gardens of Micawater that he would give up his manor to follow her beauty. And I say? I say such a sentiment makes me feel sick. I say that, as for love, I have all the whores in Hacilith and that is all you need.

Which reminds me, Dellin is down there. The evening is drawing in and the lights on the horizon are those of Melick village, in Fescue manor, where I know a good brothel called the Tired Concubine. I think we will reach it a little after nightfall.

So, Lightning, the Castle's Archer, was damned impulsive when he fell in love with Savory, and I must be right because I proved her to be as loose as every woman secretly is. But he'd find it very easy to shoot a flying target, so he must never know I shagged her, all right? He must never, ever know.

ZOYSIA

There was me, Wagtail, 'Textbook' Ana and Cisticola 'Slow' who were the best. My name is Zoysia, Fescue born and bred. I haven't never been out of the muster, nor out of the village hardly, since I turned sixteen and first came to the Tired Concubine.

I was in my boudoir, sitting on my bed, painting my toenails by candlelight because business was quite slack, there being few travellers this late in the year. There was a mighty thump on the roof and all the girls in the attic shrieked. Ana's voice in the corridor thrilled, 'Did you hear that?'

'Yes!' I called, and so did Cisti from her room.

Ana knew I wasn't with a client so she barges in. 'It shook the gable!'

'It might be Comet,' I said. 'Like last time.'

'Yes. Sh!'

We listened and sure enough we heard footsteps tap-tapping, directly above, along the ridge. We stared up at the angle between the rickety ceilings. Ana shuddered and pulled her white fur stole closer round her shoulders. The attic fell quiet – we were all holding our breath and listening.

On occasion Comet did use our house for overnight stops, and our madame, 'Lady' Spelt (a jaded old harlot if there ever was one) said he found the Concubine of use because us girls asked no questions and pestered him only in the way he wanted to be pestered. No more, no less. Spelt had let him have a free ride when she was young – so she could say the Concubine had been patronised by an Eszai – and he came back again and again, so it turned out to be a sound investment.

The footsteps halted and a powerful sound of wings swooshed down past the window. I rushed to the shutters but saw nothing but darkness. A second later, loud knocking sounded from the porch and the dog started barking madly.

'Lady' Spelt hurried to unbar the door, and every single one of us rushed to the stairs. Ana and I looked down the stairwell. Girls on the two floors below were peering over the banisters and peeking between the rails, all in their lace, diamantés and stockings. The more adventurous arranged themselves sitting on the steps or leaning on the post, showing a lot of leg and trailing their feathers.

In came Comet, folding his wings behind him. He was *gorgeous*. Tall and thin, with a taut body and wonderful cheekbones, jet-black hair cropped very short and ragged, and lots of bracelets which, y' see, was probably the new fashion. He was wearing army clothes, not the fine suits you expect immortals to wear in the Castle, but a dark jacket and trousers, and a leather knapsack embossed with his Wheel. We were all taking note, but he spoke, very assured, to Spelt in a low voice and we couldn't hear. Oh, I burned for him, and how! I wanted him more than anything in the world and thought I'd die if I couldn't have him.

I loved the mystery, y' see – that we'd never know what secret Imperial business he was about. He would stay a night and then leave, bound for exotic places to parley with the king in a marble palace, or with bigwigs, nabobs and hoitytoits in the city, which I told myself I'd visit one day. But I never will, you know, because I never have enough money.

Spelt nodded and was making a tick in the ledger when in bounded something – so quick it was hard to see – but it skidded to a halt on the floor behind Comet's boots. It was a girl, but in shape like nothing I'd ever seen. I thought it must be one of the orphans who sometimes came begging for a crust or who throw themselves on our mercy wanting to join the house. The doorman tried to drag her out but Comet placed his hand on her head. 'No! She's with me!'

Spelt, who was clutching the ledger to her chest in astonishment, pulled herself together and motioned the doorman away. He went out, casting a glance behind him. Through the fanlight we could see his big shape in the porch, which worried us 'cause he normally stood out of view.

Spelt put her pen down and called, 'Wagtail!'

Well, I was so envious of Wagtail I could have killed her. She was the girl Comet, having seen us all on display once, had picked out and often asked for when he didn't want the rigmarole of choosing again. The others gossiped it was because her name was the only one he remembered, but I believed it was because she'd shown the biggest rack of tits on the line-up. She was filthy and had no shame whatsoever – she'd do anything. She read magazines the subject of which would make *my* hair curl, but hers was quite straight.

Wagtail descended the stairs in a most slinky walk, legs scissoring, bum swaying, head tilted with a slow smile. So much make-up plastered her face she seemed to be wearing a mask. Net tights led down to little patent-leather pumps; her blue silk bodice was wired into an hourglass shape and striped with coral lace. Long strings of fake pearls bounced off her breasts. She blinked underlined eyes and smiled with baby-pink lips.

Comet looked her up and down and cast a speculative eye over the rest of us. We fell into poses as his gaze passed over. Then he indicated the waif-woman by his feet. Spelt nodded and called my name. *My* name! I couldn't believe it! Was the Messenger to be my client? I was so heated and flustered, Spelt had to call again, a note of anger in her voice. Ana pushed me, for I was rooted to the spot. The others pulled away with jealous hisses and I followed Wagtail downstairs, primping my hair and tweaking my bra as I passed through the shadows in each storey. Then I reached solid ground in the hall and walked towards ... the never-dying Emperor's Messenger, looking carelessly up.

Wagtail was stroking his wing and murmuring in Awian. She led him to the ground-floor suite. The urchin would have followed but Wagtail shut the door firmly in her face.

Spelt said, 'You take Dellin,' and gestured at the poor thing. I saw it was a woman older than I'd thought, who looked skinny, in thick white clothes.

'What? Do you want me to sleep with her?'

'Zoysia, you daft mare! Look after it. Give it dinner or something, but get it out of the hall, instant!'

I bobbed down on my high heels – to put myself on her level – saw her cat eyes and recoiled in surprise. A Rhydanne! Really a Rhydanne! And, judging by her get-up, she was a wild one. But of course Comet would be with another Rhydanne, I thought. Maybe she was his girlfriend.

I spoke to her, but she gave a deep sigh and muttered in her language. I guessed she'd never even been in the country before. So Comet was happy to leave a foreigner who didn't speak Plainslands, and who was dragging the most frightening spear, alone in a knocking shop?

Spelt cried out behind me, 'Go on, lazy! Take it down to the kitchen! I don't want the pub party tripping over it! Comet said to watch it well till tomorrow, and tell him immediate if it gives you the slip.'

I beckoned her and she sprang to her feet. As I led her down the hall she flapped her arms, pointed at the door where Comet had gone and conveyed amazement with an expansive shrug.

'Yes, he can fly. Were you shocked? I'm not surprised.'

She pointed at the winged girls, out at the night sky and flapped again, questioningly.

'No. Only Comet can fly,' I said, fluttering my hands in appropriate gestures. 'Is your name Dellin?'

'Dellin,' she agreed quietly. Then, by god, she took some horrible, old crawling piece of meat from her pocket and started chewing on it. I led her down to the kitchen, my heels clacking on the greasy stone, and she began to scurry – no, I mean, *zoom* – about, investigating everything. I wrapped myself in a spare dressing gown hanging on the door for the purpose, sat down at the table, slopped some gin into a tin mug, lit a cigarette and watched.

She moved like a man, directly, always purposefully with an object in mind. She pulled open all the drawers, cupboard doors and the oven hatch. I wished she could carve up her energy and give us all a slice.

I drew on my cigarette and she stared in horror. 'Want one?' I asked, and threw the box on the table, but she ignored me and laid her spear and kit on the floor in front of the range. She dragged the table and chairs around them to build a sort of lair. I blew out smoke and thought she would actually be quite pretty if she was made up and if she had some less disgusting clothes. It was true, y' see: in a good light or with pressed powder her face would be elegant. Her skin was very clear. I bet she hadn't had so much as a grain of sugar in her life. Her colour was somewhat pallid, but with a little foundation she'd look like a normal woman. Her chest was flat, but if she put on some weight and wore the right neckline that wouldn't matter too much. And if I taught her not to move in such a masculine way but how to loiter a little, I could make her extremely sexy.

She seated herself triumphantly inside the den, opened her mouth and pointed into it.

'Food? Yes, there's some left over. There has to be,' I said conversationally. 'Cook leaves at six but we work all hours.' I used a towel to grab the handle of the oven compartment, pulled open the heavy door, and brought out a risotto all burnt onto the baking dish. I ladled some of the raisiny, mushroomy rice onto a plate, dolloped a generous helping of cauliflower cheese next to it and spooned on beans from a pan on the cooker top. Dellin crawled out from behind her barricade, knelt on the floor with her elbows on the table, sniffed at it and shuddered.

'This is good Fescue fare,' I told her and fetched her a fork, but when I turned back she was already wolfing it with her fingers. She ate two platters full in front of my very eyes, then opened her rucksack and produced horrible, gross bits of meat, ate most of them and dumped the rest in the corner. She slurped wine from some sort of smelly bag. Wine from the Castle itself, I guessed, more excellent than I would ever taste! Then she retired under the table and watched me with intense curiosity.

Woodcock the gigolo sauntered in and seated his big self at the table. 'What's your game?' I asked.

'Just wanted a look at her.'

'Oh yes. I should charge admission. Roll up! Roll up! Come see the savage!'

'She's not just a savage; she's a woman,' he pointed out.

'A woman who doesn't want your services.'

'As I thought, she's a rare one. Have you spoken to her?'

'She only speaks Rhydanne.'

'As far as you know,' he said, and tried her with Awian, but nothing doing.

'Did she build that den with the chairs?' he said.

'Yes. I suppose they do that in the mountains to lie in wait for victims.'

'Or it's to make her feel safe in our kitchen.'

Dellin opened her mouth and repeated, 'Feel safe.'

'My god!'

'Is she just imitating? Or does she want to talk to us?' He tapped the bench top. 'Table.'

'Taible,' said Dellin, dutifully.

'Table.'

'Tay-bull.'

'Good enough. Chairs.'

'Chairz.'

'She does have an accent. Chairs.'

'Chairs!' Dellin mimicked.

'She's from Darkling,' I said, rather struck by how romantic it was.

'Spear,' said Woodcock.

'Spear. One spear point. Steel. Yes!'

'She knows more than she's letting on,' I said.

'The Awians would have sold her that. And the knife.'

'Nife!'

'Fair enough ... Plate.'

'Plate.'

After ten minutes of this I became bored and left Dellin with the gigolo. I climbed the dark cellar steps and at the top, enough light filtered in from the hall to cast my shadow all the way down to the kitchen. It dimly illuminated the decrepit wood panelling.

I put my palm on a panel directly in front of my face and pushed it left. It clicked onto a greased runner and slid aside easily. I slipped the panel below it aside in the same way and the one below and the one below that, until I had an opening one panel wide and as tall as I was. Behind was a passage. I peered in to see the tiny pinpricks and shafts of light shining through from the ground-floor suite. I kicked off my shoes because they made too much noise, turned sideways, sucked in my stomach and slipped in.

Once inside there was enough room to turn straight and walk naturally, y' see. I edged along, feeling the crunchy ancient lumps of plaster and flakes of whitewash under my stockinged feet. The yellow light slid over my bare skin, shining in dots and lines from wormholes, splits and the edges of panels that didn't quite meet. The dust tickled my nose so I pressed the collar of my dressing gown to my face and, horripilating at the thought of spiders, I pulled my other hand back into the dressing gown sleeve and waved the drooping cuff ahead of me to ward them off. At eye level a chalk arrow indicated a crack larger than the others. I peered through and there was Comet. Comet and Wagtail ... and Cisticola!

I watched them avidly until a 'Hist!' from the mouth of the passage made me glance round. 'Hey, sister. Get your fat butt out of there!'

I shuffled carefully away and crept back down the passage to the hall. All eight whores were queuing outside the passage and along the hall, waiting their turn to spy on him. The first two giggled and slipped inside, and the rest stared at me cattily.

I retreated to the kitchen. Woodcock was still there, chatting merrily to Dellin. 'She's very fast,' he said to me approvingly.

'Huh?' I wondered what he had been doing to her. 'Aren't they famed for it?'

'Not "fast" running; I mean "fast" intelligent. Listen ...' He spoke to Dellin in Awian: 'Say what you learnt.'

Dellin took a deep breath and glanced around the room. 'Table. Chairz. Plate. Spear. Knife. Oven. Bucket. Glass. Rice. Herbs. Eyes – nose – mouth. Hair. Feet. Wings. High. Low. Asleep! No asleep ... awake. Beans! Dog! Chimney! Coal! Porn mag! Woodcock! Zoysia Einkorn!'

'My god.'

He nodded. 'Does Comet know she can do this?'

'I don't know.'

In the silence we could hear the boing, boing, boing of Comet's bed in the ground-floor suite. I sighed. I'd never even have the chance to serve his dinner, let alone whisper, 'Would you like to sleep with me?'

'Let's teach her some more words,' said Woodcock eagerly. Having seen so many women's bodies, he was prone to be impressed when a girl preferred to use her mind. Dellin had broken the tedium and he was keen to talk to someone who wasn't either a tart or desperate for his service. And, y' see, Dellin was physically different too, so of course that piqued his interest. Nobody wants to be a gigolo – or a whore, come to that. It's just that there's very little work in Fescue for those of us who are too poor to escape.

'One, two, three, four, five,' Dellin recited. *'Amre, demre, shanre, larore, keem.'*

'Is that counting in Rhydanne?'

'Keem-am, keem-dem, keem-shan—'

'Let me guess: *keem-laro*?'

'Keem-laro, yes!'

'You see!' He beamed at me. 'I'm learning Rhydanne too. I'd love to see her in her natural habitat, climbing, catching edelweiss, or whatever it is she does. Spear, Dellin?'

'Sleagh.'

We named the objects in the room until long past midnight, and our eyelids grew heavy. Dellin was very keen to learn more and forced herself to continue, bringing us stuff to name, but we ground to a halt and Woodcock went to bed. Dellin cleaned her teeth carefully with water and a pine twig, which surprised me, then curled like a squirrel on her jacket on the floor. Mindful of Spelt's instructions to keep her in sight I kipped on the kitchen bench beside her for a couple of hours, no more, because y' see, she woke me at the crack of dawn, pulling my hair and demanding, 'Food!'

'You never stop.' I gave her some bread and tried to introduce her to make-up. She ate all the bread after a summary sniff and would have eaten all the butter too, but no amount of cajoling would make her submit to lipstick and foundation cream. I was still trying when Spelt called down, 'Zoysia? Bring that thing upstairs!'

Comet was standing at the reception desk, counting coins from his wallet to pay the enormous bill. 'Here she is ...' I faltered, melting.

Comet smiled and looked at me properly for the first time. He opened a wing to block Spelt's view, leant and whispered, 'Thanks. Here ...'

I felt his warm lips brush my ear, and by the time I had recovered he had his back to me and I realised he'd pushed a roll of banknotes into my hand. I whipped it behind my back, gripped the notes tightly – it was a solid roll! – and tucked it up under my bodice.

He said something to Spelt and left with Dellin. Outside she ran off and he followed at a most unnatural pace, as if they'd become two-legged racehorses. Everyone crowded into the porch and blocked my view, but did I care? Not me! I turned and dashed up the stairs, piled all my outdoor clothes on my bed, threw myself among them and began to count the money Comet had given me. At last! At last! I'm going to catch the southbound mail coach – from the stop by the green! I'm going to the city!

REEVE MARRAM

It was late, at the end of a warm autumn, after a summer finer than we had any right to expect, the weather on the fells being what it is, and I was at the high table eating my supper, a thrifty pease pottage such as is my habit. All of a sudden the watchman was standing at my elbow. At the shock I put my spoon down harder than I intended and splashed soup on my jumper. 'What do you mean by creeping up on me?' I snapped. 'And what are you standing there for, anyway? Ey?'

'Someone's at the gate ...'

'Well, didn't I tell you to ring the bell? Ring the bell if we have a visitor, I said, and announce them. No need to stand there jarring me as if we're at the quarry face!'

The lad protested that he had been sounding the bell for ten minutes and nothing had happened. Typical of young men these days: they first disregard your orders and then lie with barefaced cheek. I was halfway through telling him so when he glanced at the ceiling and pointed to the porch. 'Comet is waiting in the gatehouse,' he complained.

'Comet? The Emperor's Messenger?'

'Yes.'

'You kept Comet *himself* outside? You idiot! Go and welcome him in! And stop staring at the ceiling – don't think I haven't noticed – there are no tiles loose. I know, I had 'em all fixed in that dry spell. Wait! Wait! As you're going, take these plates ...' I pushed the soup bowl and bread board towards him. 'No need to wake the cook, is there?'

The lad took the dishes, all the while rolling his eyes to check the tiles, and I sat back in my chair and felt in my coat pocket for my short pipe and baccy pouch. An after-dinner smoke is one of my few pleasures and I like to take time to fill my pipe. While tamping it with the Marram muster seal I reflected: I hope the Messenger doesn't stay long. It's a drain on the resources of the household. Though thankfully he never expected the ceremony he was entitled to.

He hasn't been here for years. About ten years, and although I'm the first to admit those years haven't been kind, Comet will look just the same. I surveyed the surroundings that he would soon see, and felt proud. Though I run Marram as tightly and scrupulously as I used to manage the mines, the house is growing increasingly eccentric with age and needs constant work to keep it even halfway habitable. It used to be a manor in its own right, Marram did, before it became a muster of Fescue, and that's why this hall is so spacious compared to those of other reeves.

The lad had typically left the door open, so the night air was blowing in and wavering the flames on the candleholder hanging from the rafters. The lamp in the courtyard shone through the leaded panes and cast a net of shadows across the switchback floorboards and the somewhat threadbare rug. I would like to replace it but the accounts won't allow.

The lad's clogs clattered on every single cobble across the courtyard. I saw him go by the array of little bay windows with Comet and another boy following, their outlines distorted and rippled as they passed the bull's-eye glass. My lad entered at the far end of the hall and announced ... something. He muttered too softly to hear over the sound of the crackling fire.

Comet's head appeared in the doorway, he raised his arm in greeting and strode in. What always strikes me is his incredible exuberance. He came down the hall, creaking the floorboards with his swinging walk and a big grin on his face. The other young man, similarly vigorous, followed in his wake.

I felt for the handle of my walking stick – it was hanging from the table – and, pressing heavily on it, gained my feet. 'Comet!' I called. 'Welcome!'

'Reeve Marram! Call me Jant. How many times do I have to tell you?'

I considered. 'You've only told me twice. Who is this young man?'

'This young man is a Rhydanne woman.'

'Indeed?' I picked my spectacles from a side dish, wiped butter off them, fitted them on my nose and leant forward, the better to see her. 'So she is, by San's flat bottom! Well, well, well. Sit down, both of you.' I gestured at the bench, and relaxed back onto my own chair because I was obliged to take the weight off my bad leg.

I picked up my briar pipe and pressed its warm bowl in the palm of my hand. The Rhydanne girl seemed to have a folded chair on her back and a home-made spear in the crook of her arm. 'Any news?' I asked politely.

'She is the news.' Jant pointed at her. 'Nothing happening at the Front. Lightning's still prone to morose spells. Mist is away sailing the tempest until his throat fills with salt. But the biggest news of the moment has walked right into your hall! May I introduce you? Reeve Marram; Shira Dellin.'

'Pleased to meet you.'

'Hello,' she enunciated in Awian.

'She's changed a lot since I first met her,' Jant said triumphantly. 'You wouldn't believe how wild she was. Completely untamed.'

He spoke to her quickly in her tongue, and I noticed she didn't sit wholly facing the table but astride the bench so she could see both me and down the length of the hall to the porch. 'Is she wanted by the law?'

He laughed. 'No, that's just a Rhydanne thing. They're chary.' He explained who the odd lady was and the bare bones of his assignment.

'My, my,' I said. 'Is this to do with Raven's exile?'

'Yes.'

'Goodness. I do remember it. We get so little news these days that I followed the whole story. Year before last, it was. Ah yes, I do recall it ... Thinking back, it was October ...'

'I have to negotiate on her behalf,' said Jant. 'Though if compensation is her aim, I'm a cat's aunty.'

The Rhydanne girl did indeed look vengeful and seemed to be following much of our conversation. Her thick hair draped over her shoulder and down her front, like a scarf, and her chin came almost to a point. The folded chair on her back was actually a rucksack frame of bone struts handsomely joined, just as the timbers of this house are pegged together at every corner. She freed herself from its weight and rested it against the bench, though it nearly came up to the level of the tabletop.

I lit a match, cupped my hand around the bowl and sucked the flame into it. I puffed out a mouthful of the sweet-leather smoke, which makes me think more clearly, and looked about for the lad. 'Rustle up a meal for Comet. Bring cheese pie and the roast ... What about her?' I asked Jant. 'Does she eat ... um ... civilised food?'

'She'll be happy with the roast.'

'Well, then. The end of the beef, laddie; as lavish as possible.'

The lad glanced at the ceiling again, knowing that lavish in Marram terms would be nothing to the Messenger, then slouched away. 'We need to stay the night,' Jant said. 'We have to start early tomorrow to get as much distance covered as possible before the weather breaks. Can we have a room?'

'Of course. Messenger's prerogative. Take the best room, such as it is. The doors of Marram are always open to you and your couriers.' I tilted my pipe stem at the lady. 'What about her ... does she sleep outside? Or in the stable?'

'She will sleep in my room.'

I nodded thoughtfully, careful not to let the surprise show on my face. I knew he was decadent but I hadn't been aware how far his tastes extended.

'You can't expect me to know very much about her kind,' I said, and addressed her directly: 'I'm very sorry for my ignorance, young lady.' She found it funny that I puffed out pipe smoke with my words. 'Mountainlanders don't come down as far as Fescue. Pardon my curiosity, and if I make mistakes don't take offence because there's none meant. And I would be obliged if the Messenger would translate for me.'

Jant did so and I was pleased to see her smile – a little ferret smile, with very white teeth.

'So you're going up into Darkling?' I prompted.

'Yes. Hence all the gear. Where we're going, even Rhydanne will feel the cold.'

'I see. Can I help you with anything else? A packhorse, perhaps? We have tough ponies.'

'I think she'd prefer a tender pony.'

'Tender pony? I don't know that breed. Oh, I see.' I chuckled, finished my pipe and tapped the dottle onto my plate. I opened my clasp knife and reamed out the bowl. Then I opened my old baccy pouch and set about rubbing the moist flakes into shreds. 'Sorry the cook is taking so long. It's not good to keep hungry guests waiting.' Jant pushed the apology away but I continued, 'I just can't get the staff these days. The lad's family is from Garron Mill and the lead fumes go to their brains ... And it's easier to raise the dead than it is to wake that damn cook—'

But as I spoke they came in, bringing a platter of roast beef, oat bread and some beer. The bleary-eyed cook set the beef down in front of me with a bowl of horseradish – though it was the last of the market heifer and supposed to last a week – blinked innocently and departed before I could give him any more orders.

I carved it as thinly as I could, aware of Dellin's stare, like being watched by a half-starved lion. I passed the first plate to Jant, naturally, but he gave it to her. She carefully picked up a knife and fork, watching our reactions all the time, and began to eat with them in a contrived fashion. She was copying us; she used both quite dextrously but they were certainly new to her.

Jant poured her some beer and she drained the tankard! She slammed it down, helped herself to more and gulped that too. What a feisty lass! She snatched a quick glance into the furthest corner, which was quite dark. Another glance, like a falcon, and she put her mug down. Her shoulders rounded and her head lowered; she stared into the corner. She swung her leg over the bench and, graceful but hunched, crept away from the table, so lightly she didn't even creak the boards.

'I don't see anything,' I said, but Jant put his finger on his lips. She was halfway across when – a mouse! In a flash a tiny mouse streaked towards the wall, its tail and hind legs flying.

Dellin burst into a sprint and pounced. Her arm shot out, she landed in a crouch, lunged forward and grabbed it. She settled on her haunches, brought her fist in, and sure enough the mouse was clenched there. She pinched its tail with thumb and forefinger, dangled it in front of her face and examined it from all angles. I thought she was going to drop it into her mouth and swallow it whole.

She knelt more comfortably and let it go – caught it with her other hand and giggled. She released it, deflected its path with an open palm, and snatched it up again. She played with it for a long while, laughing quietly until I began to feel quite sorry for the poor thing. Then, holding it in her fierce little fist with its struggling head poking out, she broke its neck with a flick of her thumb, just as I would flick a match. She crossed to the door and threw its broken body into the courtyard, then jogged back to the table as if nothing had happened. Jant sighed heavily. 'Excuse her. Please.'

I tapped the pleasantly worn stem of my pipe against my teeth.

'Excuse her? I think it's great! Translate for me: you're welcome to live here any time, my dear. You're a much better mouser than our old tabby.'

Dellin said, 'Thank you for giving us meat. One mouse would leave me hungry.'

'Ah, there are enough mice in Marram to feed a whole army of Rhydanne. What do you think of the hall, my dear?'

'We passed by the mines. So much metal ... but your hall is poor.'

'Ah. Well, Lord Fescue takes all the profit, doesn't he? He spends it on parties in the city, and with what's left over he renovates his own house. It's a good deal more splendid than this.'

'The Awians steal silver from Carniss too.'

'Well, lady mouser, there's nothing either of us can do.'

She made a noise deep in her throat, just like a growl, which discouraged me from questioning her further. Just because she was with Comet didn't mean she wasn't dangerous. I filled my pipe, scraped a match and pulled the flame into the bowl until the tobacco shreds glowed red.

Her inquisitive face looked around, taking everything in as if she saw the world anew every minute. Maybe all Rhydanne do, and you would too if you were a hunter; there is always something new to look out for.

'It's a blessing and a lesson to hear what an outsider thinks of us,' I reflected profoundly. 'It's salutary to hear an unusual perspective. There hasn't been such an outsider in all of upland Fescue since I was a boy.'

'If she were a hunter instead of a hunt*ress* you wouldn't dote on her half as much,' said Jant.

I chuckled. 'Go on, now. Ask her what she thinks of us.'

'Are you sure?'

'Indeed. In-deed. I want to know what the wildcat thinks of us folk who can't catch mice.'

Jant asked her and Dellin replied, 'Reeve Marram, you think your people are poor, but any Rhydanne can see they are very rich because, every day, every woman manages to put enough on her plate for herself or her family. Since I came to the flatlands I have seen so many riches that no Rhydanne will believe me when I tell them. Flatlanders are sick with greed and racing against each other to possess the most. It's a disease that dims their minds and slows their bodies. Tell me, why are they so eager to own the earth and turn it into fancy goods and fancy clothes? Don't you find it exhausting? Rhydanne live simply but everyone else strives to multiply their possessions, even though they already have more than they can use. They own many clothes, but can only wear one coat at a time. They have so much food it rots before they can eat it. And that is why I fear for Carnich.'

Articulate girl, I thought; I hadn't anticipated a speech. 'This disease, of covetousness you say, well, the Awian nobility have caught it much worse than the miners of Marram.'

She nodded unhappily. 'And I despair, because there are more Awians than stones in a scree slope, than stars on a freezing night. We could live side by side with them, but they are taking so many furs that they are wiping out the animals they depend on. Jant is conducting me to see Raven, their leading hunter. I will convince him and the rest will follow.'

Jant shook his head and added to his translation, 'She's so naive.'

'Not at all, not at all. Tell her this. Lady mouser, speaking bluntly works with me, but it won't affect Raven when you meet him. Awian nobles are crafty. They hint at things and never talk straight. In fact, they speak a language within a language, and if you don't know it, they'll ignore you. An old foreman like me couldn't sway Governor Raven, let alone a huntress like yourself.'

'I will make him listen.'

Jant glanced up at the underside of the roof tiles visible atop the rafters, just as the lad had done, although I swear to you on my mother's grave not a single one was loose. 'We've imposed on you long enough. It's late and I think we'd better retire. Can we have a light?'

'Certainly. Lad, go fetch a lamp.' The boy clattered off to prepare the guest room in the north wing, which I feared Comet and his ward might find rather too damp and draughty. Like the rest of the house it had been built somewhat imprudently without foundations. The weight of its roof was gradually breaking my house's back. Huddled under the gritstone tiles with their lichens as big as dinner plates, every wall had settled its own crooked way into the earth over the centuries.

I stroked my beard smooth and observed Dellin. Her skeletal fingers had picked up my gnarled old pipe and she examined it carefully with eyes the same dark green as the field of the Fescue flag. 'Good luck in your endeavour, brave huntress,' I said, and god knows the sentiment was heartfelt. 'Good luck. Now I can say I've met the cat who dared to look at a king.'

JANT

We crossed the packhorse bridge and jogged up a walled lane out of Bromedale onto Marram Moor. Granite outcrops cresting the hills had sloughed massive blocks of stone down their slopes like dice. Behind every tilted escarpment a fragile netting of black drystone walls draped over the hillside, penning a few lean, bedraggled sheep. As we passed they looked up suspiciously, still chewing, and the ones in the distance bleated to each other. Flies hazed around them. Their thick wool was matted and splodged with red dye. Their arses were caked with dung.

By midday we had left them and the moor far behind and were onto the wild lower slopes of Darkling. The hills became more craggy still, broken with the rock beneath bursting through, but between the outcrops the grass was as smooth as moleskin. Tussocks the colour of rabbit fur grew in marshy patches, in the saddles between each summit. But in front, and always in sight above us, were the naked granite peaks – jagged mountains topped with permanent snowfields, with higher summits behind them and a still more imposing third cordillera just visible, forming the horizon. Dellin stretched and smiled, replenished now she could feel their chill.

She trotted on ahead, murmuring to herself. Mutter, mutter, mutter, in pace with her jogging, like one of the short proverbs Rhydanne sometimes tell. I caught up with her, so the spear tied to the upright of her rucksack was bumping along beside me. She was reciting Awian words. 'Oven ... bucket ... table ... feet ...' she said. 'Feet ... legs ... tits ... bums.'

'Good grief,' I said. 'Did you learn your Awian in a whorehouse? Oh, I see ... You did.'

She skipped round and, walking backwards, looked at me accusingly. 'You left me with a house of slow runners. Zoysia and Woodcock taught me some words.'

'*Woodcock*?'

'Are the words correct?'

'Yes, yes. The words are fine.'

'They taught me more than you did. Why did you leave me there?'

'What do you expect? You appeared from nowhere and dragged me away from a very eventful social life. I've been missing it. I like the Castle's gossip. I like doing the rounds of manors and coaching inns, keeping up with the news. It's what I do best. You stopped me enjoying myself, so I thought I'd talk to people along the way.'

'You could talk to me.'

'Yes, but ...' I stared at her. 'It really isn't the same thing.'

'You've been sulking. You haven't said a word in hours.'

'I thought Rhydanne never said a word in *days*! We could have ridden by coach but you insist on climbing. What is there to say?'

'You could teach me some more Awian,' she suggested brightly.

'Why? Oh, OK. Seeing as there's no one else to talk to ... Um, "sky", that's Awian for *athar*. "Blue sky", *athar guirme*.'

She jogged on, this time allowing me to keep pace beside her. Our steps crunched on the gritty erosion patches, swished over the short grass, splashed through the marshes in the dips. My visual field was full of the thin grass and soil, the worn bedrock, for hours and hours on end until I thought I'd see it in my sleep. We crossed no prints of sheep nor men, heard nothing but our own voices and the shush of the wind.

She said, 'I've learnt the words for sky, clouds, sun and blue. I don't think they will help me talk to Raven.'

'The weather is a major topic in Awia, actually.'

'It isn't what I want to know. Tell me about Raven himself. Reeve Marram used the word "nobility". Tell me what it means.'

She was heading all the time straight towards the backdrop of ice-clad peaks. A small, wooded gorge cut through the last of the foothills and up to a pine forest on their slopes, and towards this she naturally made her way. She was wrong – I wasn't prepared to travel so far at altitude and there weren't any places to stay up there. We had been having this argument since the first turn on the road through Fescue and she was adamant.

The fact that I can fly had really rattled her. She hadn't known about it, and I had given her a shock when I took off. She was impressed, despite herself, because Rhydanne value speed. Flying obviously made me faster than her, and she could imagine the advantages that it would have in hunting game. Having being forced to accept the staggering reality of a flying Rhydanne-Awian man she was now trying to reassert herself by forcing me into her world.

I said, 'Look, I know a hamlet, further on, called Scatterstones. They're all shepherds, but there's a drovers' inn where we can stay. Then we can go on to Cushat Cote, Foin, and take the Pelt Road to Carniss. The sensible way.'

'I know. You tried to put me in a box.'

'A coach.'

'We are going to the peaks,' she said obstinately. 'Away from the mosquitoes. Where the water is pure.'

'Do you expect me to sleep in the open? Fyrd-issue tents weigh a tonne; I'm not carrying one.'

'I can make you a shelter.'

'But there's nothing up there! No paths, no tracks!'

'Only goats need tracks.'

I pointed ahead to the rugged gorge. The wind constantly swished in the boughs of meagre pine and mountain ash trees. The stream hissed and chuckled over its cobbles and cascades. 'Look. You don't know where you are.'

'That doesn't matter if I know where I'm going!'

'I didn't bring a map. You don't even know what that mountain's called.'

'Why should I need to? Why should it have a name? Are you Awian, or something?' She walked faster, striding high above the tussocks.

'That's not the way!' I practically howled with frustration.

'It's *my* way. Darkling is my home. I just want to get out of these horrible hills!'

'Come back! OK, come here and we can talk about it.'

'*Talking*! You *are* an Awian. You're useless!'

'We're guaranteed a bed for the night at Scatterstones.'

'I'm carrying a howff.'

'Well, I'm not!'

'I'll make you one.' Her voice had a sincere tone, but as she headed away it faded and I was forced to follow. 'I've been in the flatlands for weeks, and everything was strange and new. I've had enough of staying in rooms where the walls press in at me from all sides. I've had enough of sleeping where I can't see the sky. I have had *enough* of eating meat which someone else has cooked to their taste. I even built shelters from furniture to pretend I was camping. Oh, I know you were laughing, but I had to follow my habit and not let any of the strangeness in, or all the strangeness would rush in at once and overwhelm me. You flatlanders are very weak. Now I am going home and you can either come with me or flutter off back to your Castle.'

I watched her climb some rubble from an old avalanche and disappear into the gorge, then emerge further up clambering over boulders, using her hands on the steeper parts. I was convinced she'd look back, but she didn't even pause. I had forgotten how decisively Rhydanne behave. Stupid! I told myself. Are you going to tell San you lost her?

I spread my wings and flapped up the incline, flying so low with my legs dangling that my toes bumped off tufts all the way. I entered the gorge and searched for flat ground. There was none so I landed on the slope and ran down to Dellin. She didn't register me but kept trudging, reciting, 'Blue ... sky ... king ... prince ... manor ...' as if it was the doctrine that would win her Carnich.

I followed her up the uneven steps of natural rock beside the stream. 'Would you really have walked all the way to Carnich without me?' She didn't reply and I realised it was a flatlander's question – of course she would. Nevertheless I made one last try: 'If we're going to climb I should have brought more supplies. Scatterstones would give us mutton pie; otherwise we'll have nothing to eat tonight.'

She rounded on me incredulously. 'What are you blathering about? We're surrounded by food!'

I glanced round but there were no sheep in the gorge. In fact, I hadn't seen any since morning. 'If you're talking about those ewes, they belong to ...'

She started giggling. Her face lit up, her eyes danced. She saw my surprise and laughter overcame her. She shook her head, swishing her ponytail; doubled up and beat her fists on her thighs. 'Oh, Jant ... Oh, Jant, we've been surrounded by food ever since we left the Castle ... and you insist on carrying it!' Then she must have had another thought, because her expression grew serious. 'The gorge is full of food. If you grew up in Darkling, how could you possibly not know? Every child knows it. I taught both my daughters. Picking food is children's work, even for goatherds.'

'I'm not a goatherd!' I repeated for the *n*th time. 'I'm used to *feasts*. I *have* been in your position. I've been there, done all that poverty-stricken berry-picking stuff, and it was shit. I've improved my life since then.'

'But you can't remember any of it? You must be as bad at being a messenger as you were at being a goatherd, if you have such a poor memory.'

'Damn it! I remember! There are bilberries, sure, but—'

'So you do know bilberries.' She giggled with contempt. 'Come on, I'll show you!' She ran lightly to the pouring waterfall, climbed the boulders beside it and disappeared onto the higher level. I sighed and followed.

When I reached her side, she pointed to the verge. 'Look, we have ramsons, garlic roots, not at their best this time of year but still good to accompany meat.' She unearthed them with her knife and popped them in her pack. 'Up here are rowan berries, cloudberries ... blackberry brambles, see? Hawthorn and briar hips, sour but very nourishing. Come and collect them!'

'Great. A light snack.'

'That's not all!' She bounded around so quickly that I didn't follow her but watched her crossing and re-crossing my path. 'Onions. Hazelnuts. Pignuts. Look here! These delicate blue mushrooms are wood blewits. The spear-shaped leaves are sorrel. Take the seeds as well. Those tall stalks are orache – better than spinach! You can bake meat wrapped in their leaves. These flaky plates are bracket fungus ... and such a lot! Help me pick the small ones. They tenderise better. And below, boletus and parasol mushroom. That red one's russula. The wrinkled one's sparassis! Put them all together in your pack! Over here, turnips. Yarrow and thyme! Take as much as you can; they're good to flavour meat. Bulk them out with sage and mint; they taste fine together. Oh, by the Huntress, don't you *know*? This is sage, this is mint. Come further up – I've spotted puffballs on the opposite slope!'

She ran beside the stream, crossed it on tiny stepping stones, and dashed up and down the nearly sheer banks, finding footholds on eroded steps of soil. She paused to pick berries from a bush, harvested handfuls of leaves and uprooted whole plants, one here, one there, into her rucksack. But I thought this horrible muck, not fit to eat at all. Why, when I could have a plate of beef and dumplings, had I let myself in for this? My heart sank even further when she began plucking snails off a rock and throwing them into her rucksack too.

We reached the highest cliff of the gorge, worn smooth by the glistening waterfall. Dellin climbed it straight. I zigzagged up the bank beside it, which was so steep it was hell on the thighs, and all I could hear was my heart booming and my breathing *in-in-out-out, in-in-out-out*. Whenever I felt I wasn't going to slip I looked up to the edge of the slope and Dellin's face was there peering down at me.

I emerged and there before me a pine forest rose up to the massive rock faces of Darkling. Their sheer size took my breath away, and as I looked around for a place to sit down I saw a fallen tree lying in the stream. Its roots had torn up a crown of black earth and its topmost twigs were trailing in the water, latticing it into silver ripples. 'There's plenty more food by that tree. Come and look!' Dellin pointed with a dirty hand to some yellow, wrinkled fungi in the damp grass around its trunk.

'I'm not touching those! They look revolting!'

'But they're chanterelles. They're almost as good as field mushrooms.'

'I don't care! This is all inedible, Dellin. Are you trying to kill us both?'

'What else are you going to eat?' she said, crouching to wash the nuts and mushrooms in the stream.

'Roast beef, hopefully!'

'Jant Shira, there will be good prey higher up: ibex, chamois, big game. Winter food in fact. I like it better too. It's less effort for more meat and I have all the gear to hunt it. So let's climb higher and in the meantime take what we can. Pick those, they're oyster fungus and honey fungus.'

'The slimy goo and the squidgy orange stuff.' I sighed and complied, while Dellin gathered some weeds she called marjoram and, from the cliffs wet with spray, pocketed bunches of fleshy hart's tongue fern. We continued through the forest, where she showed me we could eat the soft, pale green shoots at the tips of conifer branches. Yew trees are poisonous, but she peeled off the red flesh of the berries, which was sweet and sticky and tasted of pine. She declared that juniper berries could be made edible by cooking and, as we ascended, we snacked on waxy, yellow pine nuts, levering them out of cones with our knives.

And then we left the forest, through a zone where the pines grew stunted, and emerged onto the bare Darkling mountainside. Here she found more fruit on the shrubs among the rocks – barberries, cranberries, cowberries – but they hardly stopped my stomach from rumbling. When she dug up gentian root 'to go in our kutch', I turned and looked back over the vast landscape through which we had travelled. No way was I drinking kutch.

The forest's uneven pelt covered the hill. The stream sucked the hillside smoothly down into the gorge, and from its foot clear water bled out and bisected the grassy expanse of Marram Moor. Marram town itself was too far to see, tucked into a fold of Bromedale in the grey distance. The moor stretched to the north as well, and at some point, just before the horizon, it must become Micawater. To the south it continued towards Rilldale. I turned; before me the bare granite clutched and combed into vertiginous peaks.

We were in a bizarre landscape of naked, angular rock with only the smallest rowan trees at the foot of the cliffs. Enormous, dark grey boulders surrounded us, almost entirely covered with green lichen. Everything was either grey or pale green, as if seen through coloured glass, and I was trying to get used to the weird effect. We had done eighty kilometres so far and, since we were losing the light, Dellin began looking for a place to camp. Eighty kilometres on foot over bad terrain. I grinned, despite myself, at the incredible rate of Rhydanne travel.

Dellin called out ahead. I ran up and found her fastening a dead mountain hare to her pack. Her spear lay bloodied on the ground. Now I was impressed – if she could hit such a small target at distance with a thrown spear she was better than most trained spearmen. She gutted the hare without skinning it and slung it over the top of her rucksack. 'Its fur has turned white, see?'

'Yes.'

'Soon it will snow. I knew I would be coming back through the snows.'

A few minutes later she speared another, which I hadn't even noticed, and I readied my crossbow, determined not to let a Rhydanne get the better of me. She caught yet another by hand, then, thankfully, I managed to shoot one. We now had enough to eat, so she called a halt to hunting.

'You hit it with a tiny arrow,' she said, tying the carcass to her pack.

'A bolt. Give it back; I can reuse it.'

She held out her hand for the bow and examined it as we walked. I had given her food for thought, but not, it seemed, for long. 'My spear is much better,' she concluded and passed the bow back abruptly.

'This is the best the Castle ever designed!'

'Ha! When snow starts falling, it will be less than useless. We'll have to rely on my spear. Do the Awians use crossbows like this?'

'Some do, but they mostly have longbows.'

'The damp will affect them too.'

'They keep them in cases.'

'Much good that'll do in the driving sleet!' She laughed. 'Snow must have started sticking in Carnich by now and Awians won't murder us any longer! Oh, Jant, the shape of the mountains tells me I'm nearing home!'

The sun dipped into the lilac-grey haze above the toothed peaks, and Dellin beckoned me on, uphill to the base of the cliff. It had weathered to a concavity along its base and had an overhang at head height. She ran along it; she seemed to be looking for something. After a while she halted. 'This is perfect, Jant. Some Rhydanne have been here. It's good to see their signs after so long.' She stretched, shrugged off her rucksack and untied the animals from it.

A sudden dusk breeze sprang up, blowing the chill of the high peaks against my body. I lay down in the shelter of the cliff, and immediately felt the sun's rays again, strong enough to burn. It was strange, as if we had reached the point where autumn and winter joined. The late-summer sun was making one last effort before winter overwhelmed it.

Dellin began skinning the animals. She looked up, annoyed. 'You're doing nothing while we have to secure camp. We have to work together; didn't your grandmother tell you this is the most vulnerable time?'

'Yes, but there aren't any wolves here.'

'That's what you think! You have no idea! Take out the wood we gathered and make a hearth.'

I did as I was told, with very bad grace. I am used to giving orders to mortals, not obeying them. But I know how to build a campfire. I'm not as hopeless in her world as she is in mine. I made a big cooking fire such as the fyrd use and was just about to light it when she glanced over and yelled, 'No! Too many sticks!'

'What?'

'The wood has to last us!' She ran to my hearth and dismantled it in a matter of seconds. 'We're above the tree line, Jant. Do you want to end up using bone as fuel? Because it burns dismally, let me tell you.' She placed three flat stones in a triangle with small gaps between them, so that air could enter at the points of the triangle, and set the hearth in the space between them. She lit it with a flint and dry grass, and stood a small brass pot of water on top.

'I'm making kutch!' she said happily. 'It's been days since I last had any. Do you want some?'

'Oh, no. Not kutch. Certainly not.'

'Kutch is good for you.'

'I have water.'

'Only the dying drink water.'

The brass pot was well scrubbed, but still blackened and patched with iridescence from hundreds of campfires. Dellin laid out one of the hares, shredded its meat and dropped it into the boiling water. Then she poured in a generous amount of Marram beer.

'I'm not drinking that concoction,' I said.

'You can't afford to be choosy.'

'Oh, god ...'

'And *don't* use that water to wash! It has to last till tomorrow.'

'How am I supposed to get clean, then?'

'Rub snow on yourself.'

'But there isn't any snow.'

'Yet. There will be tomorrow! And besides,' she continued, 'you smell better if you don't wash. Less fake, more like a man. Maybe one day you'll explain to me why flatland men go around smelling of flowers.'

I knew this had been a mistake. I got up and wandered around while she made the alcoholic gravy called kutch. The Rhydanne are as obsessed with kutch as Awians are with coffee and habitually brew the disgusting broth from whatever meat and spirit is available. Dellin poured some into a mug and drank it with every sign of enjoyment, but it really reeked. I was determined not to touch any but I was ravenous and craved almost any food. Roast potatoes, golden and translucent-crisp; chocolate cake; I could almost smell it; shortbread fingers and fresh coffee ... why hadn't I brought any? Coffee would be perfect, but Dellin would have to stick to kutch. One cup of espresso and she would probably explode.

'Sure you don't want some?' she said.

'No! It pongs! My reputation will be marred badly enough when I arrive at Carnich as filthy as a wolf, without eating like one too.'

Revitalised, she laid down her empty pack and began rolling out her tent, a wide tube of supple leather which had been packed in the base. She unpegged the rucksack frame and took the three longest struts, each just less than a metre long, threaded them into hems at the tent opening and slotted them together. To keep this triangular opening upright she pushed her spear into the ground as a tent pole and hooked the apex of the triangle to it. Then she propped up the other end of the tent with the last of the rucksack frame's struts – in no more than five minutes she had built a camp out of no more than what she was carrying.

She supported the spear with stones, then sat down beside the fire.

'What about me?' I asked.

'Here.' She tossed a folded tarpaulin and a length of cord at my feet.

'What am I supposed to do with that?'

She laughed, annoying me even further. 'The anchor points are above you.'

I looked up, to the smooth underside of the overhang above my head. She spoke slowly, clearly thinking I was stupid. 'This is a rock shelter, Jant. When you were a goatherd, did you live in a house?'

'In a shieling, actually.'

'You can't have travelled much.'

'I spent my first ten years in Mhor Darkling valley.'

'I'm not surprised you know nothing. There are holes in the rock, look ...' She came over and, standing on tiptoe, passed her fingers through a loop that had been carved out of the cliff face. 'Here's one. And another. All the way along, see?'

Sure enough half a dozen rugged holes were chiselled from solid rock along the edge of the overhang – I would never have noticed if she hadn't pointed them out. I set about unfolding the canvas sheet, threaded the cord through its eyeholes and tied it to the loops in the overhang. It hung down like a curtain and made a chamber of the dry recess at the base of the cliff. I stretched the curtain out into an awning and selected some rocks to weigh down its bottom edge. Then I crawled into the serviceable shelter between it and the cliff, stowed my rucksack and joined Dellin at the hearth.

By this time I was so famished I felt faint, and Dellin's cooking smelt scrumptious. She had threaded slivers of hare meat on bone skewers and laid them across the fire, so the meat was browning already and dripping juices. She had fried the nuts and mushrooms together and left the pan on a warm hearth stone. She had placed all the fruits on the back of her jacket spread on the ground and we snacked from them while she pounded the herbs into paste in a tin bowl.

She was bare-armed in her black vest, her hunched shoulders pointed as she basted the meat with the paste and at length gave me one of the kebabs. It tasted wonderful. The meat, herb-crusted and succulent inside, was every bit as good as one of the Castle's feasts. Even the spring water, pure and cool, was better than the water on the Plains.

She set the pot to brew more kutch, then used her nails to pull the steaming meat from the skewer. She didn't blow it cool but chomped it noisily with her back teeth. Then she pointed along the mountainside with the empty skewer. 'That's the way we're going. Good visibility. You can see for about forty kilometres, the full distance we will cover tomorrow.'

'We should be able to cover fifty.'

'No. Because tomorrow it will snow.'

Nothing seemed less likely. The sky above the cliff was a rose-pink haze and a cloudless blue out to the east. We were already in shade, as the sun set behind the highest peaks, which cast their long shadows over us and down to stripe the mountainside.

'Are you sure?'

'I can smell it. Can't you?'

'No.'

'You've been in the flatlands too long,' she said contentedly. 'I can smell the snowfields. The glaciers, Jant! After a morning's ascent we'll have to use snowshoes. I hope for a little snow at first, to break you in—'

'I can cope with a bit of snow!'

'Oh, really?'

I gazed ahead to the endless terrain of pinnacled cliffs stretching out above boulders and scree slopes. It didn't seem so difficult.

She sipped her beery broth. 'Do you want some?'

It was easier to refuse this time. 'No, I'll never drink kutch!'

'Please yourself. But take some more nuts. You can't live on hare alone. It's too lean so, no matter how much you eat, you will end up starving. You need a mixture of food, plenty of fat – the hazelnuts are best ... How wonderful this is! We have made tomorrow safe. Our equipment is sound and we have enough food. So we have left nothing to chance. We will start tomorrow well.'

She fell silent, and gradually I became aware of the crackling of the undergrowth, the very sound of plants growing, respiring, dead plants decaying and water permeating down through the soil. I could smell the mountains! My senses unblocked, first hearing, then acute smell. I could scent the fragrance of grass and lichen, woodsmoke, the stone itself. The air was full of the clean, crystalline smell of snow. This is what Dellin must feel like all the time. I glanced at her. She watched the mountainside, relaxed. This is what it's like to be Rhydanne, senses alert all the time, confidently aware of your surroundings. With her cat eyes, their reflective membrane protection against snow glare, and her thick hair, each strand of which is hollow for insulation, the higher Dellin climbed, the more at home she was. She knew all the sounds, the capercaillie clucking and the bellowing of deer. The mountains are in constant communication with her, telling her about themselves and what tomorrow will bring. The mountains themselves talk to her like friends. No wonder the solitary Rhydanne are incapable of loneliness.

The sun set and a fine line of roseate haze above the peaks shone on the snowfields and turned them pink. Higher up, it merged into peach, then pale yellow segueing into blue, then darker and darker towards the zenith. To the east, the sky was growing velvety blue-black and several stars appeared. Above the ridges bright platinum streaks of cloud still reflected the light of the sun below the horizon. The air was decidedly chilly. I shuffled closer to the little hearth, which seemed to give out as much heat as one of the fyrd's big bonfires.

Dellin watched me shrewdly. 'Your clothes are inadequate, Jant. Even your overcoat ... and that ridiculous long-tailed hat.'

I was indignant. 'These are the best fyrd-issue kit. The Castle designed them! Every soldier at the front in winter wears them.'

She didn't even bother to snigger, just shook her head, swishing her ponytail from side to side. 'They're silly.'

I took off my grey velvet hat and turned it over. 'I thought it would be perfect for Carnich.'

'Even hunters feel the cold up by the Frozen Hound Hotel.' She stirred the fire. 'Will the Awians be wearing similar sorts of clothes?'

'Yes.'

'Good. Good.'

I could no longer distinguish the features of the cliffs. They were all black, and as I strained to make out the rest of the camp, tiny blue specks prickled in my vision. Dellin's skinny front and sharp chin were lighted orange by the embers; the dying fire hollowed her eyes and blotted her hair into a mane. Her head was bowed; she seemed thoughtful. 'No signals. If there are any Rhydanne nearby they don't suspect our presence. Well, that is good too, I suppose ... Are you hungry?'

'No.'

'Then I'm going to sleep.' She unlaced her boots, stood nimbly and put them inside her tent. She took off her parka and trousers in front of me, without any shame – her skin was vividly white in the darkness against her cotton vest and drawstring shorts. She crouched and spread out her overclothes in the tent.

'Don't leave anything edible outside or the wolves will come,' she said. 'Bury the hare bones, put a few more sticks on the fire and leave it burning.' She climbed into the tent with her head poking out, plumped up her parka hood as a cushion and went to sleep. The haze was clearing in the cool air and constellations spread across the sky. More distant knife-sharp peaks were becoming visible as their ragged shapes blacked-out the familiar stars.

There were no lights at all, and the stars between stars made a nonsense of the constellations you would recognise from the plains or the city. So many stars, so brilliant they outshone the noctilucent clouds. I made out the Strongman, with a square of four for his chest and three for his vaunting axe, and the Archer, near the zenith, but the Messenger hadn't risen yet. There was Lynette, 'the Beauty', standing on her tiptoes as she does in winter, but now I could see a haze of fainter stars around her seven bright points. And, spanning the entire sky, the dusting of tiny stars in a milky river that Awians called the Whitewater. So many awe-inspiring millions that I was glad of Dellin's presence or I might have lost myself among their lonely points of light. Dellin and I had the mountains to ourselves.

*

Next day, when I woke and crawled out of the cosy shelter, everything was covered in snow. Dellin struck camp quickly and practically with no trace of smugness, while I gazed at the monochrome landscape. A thick blanket smoothed the irregularities of the slope and whited-out everything apart from the sheer cliffs above us. I dreaded having to walk in it.

The snow continued for two weeks, until all but the most tremendous boulders were covered. We walked all that time. Dellin no longer bothered to pitch her tent each night but dug a snowhole and we crammed together inside it. Yes, I could have flown to Carniss in a couple of hours. I resented having to walk with her for the best part of a month, but she was an ambassador, in a way. The Emperor had commanded me to travel with her and I didn't want to arrive at Raven's house without her. However, in the snowholes I scarcely slept a wink, because such close proximity to her fur clothes and musty scent reminded me too much of my boyhood. Everything we did seemed to exhume a new memory and I shuddered with each one. I had plenty of time to tell Dellin about my past, but she didn't reciprocate with hers. It's only in the flatlands that gossip makes the world go round; if a Rhydanne has a secret, she keeps it to herself.

But I'm such a household name everyone knows my background. It was odd to recount it to Dellin who, moreover, didn't care. I found myself being sensational in an attempt to interest her. My mother was a Rhydanne hunter, I said, and my Awian father some kind of pervert. I was a rape child, a Shira born out of wedlock, and a murderer before I drew breath: my mother died giving birth to me. The anatomical differences between Rhydanne and Awian made that likely. She had narrow hips, as Rhydanne do, on account of being superb sprinters, but I had wings which could only get trapped.

The Rhydanne of Scree pueblo would certainly have killed me, but my grandmother, Eilean Dara, thirty ferocious years old, stepped in and brought me up as her own. I can only guess why – I think I reminded Eilean of her beloved daughter, and she never lost a chance to blame me for her death. Eilean discovered that looking after me meant relinquishing her hunting life. I developed as slowly as an Awian and was good for nothing but herding. Her rancour deepened. She hid me in empty Mhor Darkling valley, and filled my head with warnings against hunters and herders alike. I led a grim and lonely existence there until an avalanche ripped the mountainside down and utterly buried our shieling, with Eilean inside. I spent that wild night clinging to the crag, yelling into the cacophony as the invisible valley liquefied below me. Next morning, amid the devastation, I started walking. Out of the valley, out of Darkling. One foot in front of the other, for hours and days, and years and decades, you can get a very long way. I still haven't stopped walking and I never will.

I related all this graphically. Dellin pondered it deeply, and said, 'Eilean should have built her shieling higher up the slope.'

I trudged, head down, treading in Dellin's shallow prints, but her tiny frame gave me no protection from the driving blizzard. I lifted my feet and compressed the snow with a crunch, kilometre after kilometre. After three weeks I had become used to it, but I felt unwashed, itchy and uncomfortable inside my clothes. Bits of meat between my teeth irritated me. My sword scabbard and crossbow bag, tied on my rucksack, chafed and dragged me back. My feet sank in the knee-deep drifts and I swore with every step.

'It's your turn to take the lead,' Dellin chimed.

'My boots are soaking,' I said.

'This is good snow, so don't complain.'

'What sort of snow can ever be good?'

'It fell on damp ground,' said Dellin. 'So it will stick. If the ground had frozen solid first, it would be slippery, but this snow is secure so there'll be fewer avalanches later.'

'Avalanches! I never want to see another.'

'This is just the beginning!' She took the lead again, sloshing along on her snowshoes. Her hood was raised and its wide fur trim framed her face. My liripipe hat didn't have a brim and the flakes blew straight into my eyes. They melted on my collar and dripped down my back. We walked uphill all day through an empty landscape of ever greater, ever sharper spires of rock. The cliffs were too sheer to hold snow but in every crack fine flutings of powder snow trailed like veils a thousand metres long. Ice in my water bottle rattled when I drank from it. As we walked we snacked on a sort of burger made from an ibex Dellin had speared, then pounded the meat to a paste and cooked it between two hot stones. It was revolting but it was all we had. I was still determined not to drink kutch, though.

The snowflakes became smaller as the day progressed, until in the evening they were graupel, tiny balls no bigger than hailstones. A few at a time drifted down from the leaden sky, and rested on the compacted snow.

Dellin looked back. 'We don't have far to go now. We're nearly at my cave.'

'You live in a *cave*?'

'No. It's one of the fissures I use as a store and an emergency shelter. The Rhydanne around here call it Dellin's Cave – Uaimh Dellin. We can stay there for the night and reach Carnich tomorrow.'

'I want to press on to Carnich now. It's only a few kilometres past the glacier.'

'No, because in an hour or so it will be too dark to see. The last thing I want is for you to fall and break an ankle.'

'I never fall!'

She shrugged. 'Maybe not on the plains, but up here even the most sure-footed can slip. Besides, Laochan stored his winter clothes in the cave. You can have them. Knowledge of the land saves you from disaster.'

She repeated this last as if it was a casual aphorism. I soon saw its wisdom, because she led me, sliding and cursing, down a precipitous chasm. We picked our way carefully up the other side to the base of a range of cliffs as pleated as a lady's fan. They were topped with pinnacles that I first thought were Rhydanne standing watching us. As my eyes grew used to the distance I realised each narrow flame of stone soared as tall as the Castle's towers.

'You said "We're nearly there" hours ago. *Are* we nearly there?'

Dellin turned to laugh and the wind parted the fur on her hood, showing its soft, grey roots. 'You sound like a baby! Yes, the cave's just up here.'

We rounded an outcrop, and there, high above us, a deep fissure struck down the cliff face like a black bolt of lightning. It opened at the bottom into a steep-sided entrance and I saw dry earth and rocks inside before the floor disappeared into darkness. Great boulders, mostly covered in snow, formed a terrace around it, their black tops slanting out and points projecting. The snow lay in hummocks all around, signs of yet more boulders completely buried. The wind howled around the cliff's buttress with tremendous force and whined through the upper reaches of the crack.

'This is it! Uaimh Dellin!' Her face, lost in its fur frame, again became the bulky back of the hood as she turned away and hastened up the slope. She diminished, black-and-grey against the black-and-whiteout, and, with something of a smile, I floundered after her. She stopped outside the entrance of the towering rift.

'Well, come on,' I said. 'I can't wait to be free of this coat and dry off.'

I stepped forward but she shot out a hand and grabbed me. 'No! There might be wolves. Whole packs and lone wolves sometimes den here ...' She looked all around, as she had done in my room in the Castle. The thought of wolves stirred yet another memory. A pack of five once treed me like a cat halfway up a cliff. They were too hungry to fear my sling. They had jumped and snapped while I crouched on a narrow ledge sucking my skinned fingers, I'd climbed up so fast. Eilean appeared hours later, scattered the wolves and then boxed my ears for letting them get the better of me.

I unpacked my crossbow and loaded it. Dellin said, 'You have to think like a wolf,' and sniffed the air and examined the rocks. 'No urine. I don't see anything and I can't smell them. Can you?'

'No,' I said flatly.

'But they might be further in. Come downwind. You're standing in the wrong place. Stay in the lee of that stone and they won't scent you.' She kicked off her snowshoes and took her spear in both hands, close to her side. Very slowly she walked inside. Her parka merged with the gloom.

'Ha!' a yell echoed out – the exertion of a spear thrust. Then a scuffling and an immense roar. Dellin flew out backwards as if blown by it, skipping over the cave soil with her spear pointing – at a bear!

It appeared from the darkness at an extraordinary speed. It lowered its wide head, mouth open in a snarl. Its gleaming eyes were fixed on her and its glistening nose twitched furiously. It lumbered at a run, its fur rolling over enormous shoulders, huge paws thudding the ground – claws ticking on the rock then crunching the snow. Blood ran freely down its neck from a deep wound behind its ear.

I shot it in the side but it didn't even notice. I scrabbled for another bolt. Dellin kept her spear pointing straight at its eyes. She was holding the shaft nearly at its end, thrusting with the strength of both arms. The bear threw its head side to side, immense teeth bristling, and growled so loud it vibrated the ground.

Dellin retreated, jabbing at the accessible spots between its front legs, its chest, face and muzzle. She didn't lift her spear to its forehead, or it would charge under the shaft. She kept trying to hit its blood-wet throat but had no chance as it thrashed its head.

'Get back!' she yelled. 'I don't need help!'

What, retreat and leave a mortal to die? No way! It slashed a paw at me. I jumped back just in time, felt the air move as it tore past, landed well but dropped the bolt.

The bear was now free of the cave. It stood up on its back legs, drew itself to its full two and a half metres and roared. Dellin was not daunted. She stepped back and stabbed it under the armpit. It lunged towards her and landed on all four paws. It covered metres but Dellin was already up on an ice-clad rock, braced with her legs bent. As it reared she belted her spear with all her strength into its eye socket.

It fell back and – 'Ya!' – she jerked the spear out and stabbed again, into its throat. She couldn't force the whole point through the fur and it swung away, blinded and yowling. Its fangs and great furrowed forehead swiped past. Its nose dripped blood and foam – the snow was melting under its pads into a scarlet slick.

I loosed a bolt which vanished into its hump. Neither the bear nor Dellin cared. She jumped down off the rock, nimble in the snow, keeping distance as the bear lunged at her. I lost sight of her behind its backside. I sent a bolt in above its tail, and Dellin emerged on my left, her face intent. She darted about, thrusting whenever she found space, snatching the spear back with its thong round her palm. She landed puncture after puncture, moving with agility. Ten minutes passed but she wasn't even panting.

The bear began stumbling from blood loss but she couldn't land a mortal blow. It swayed its head, making a chomping noise and scattering drops of blood. It looked like a portly man being attacked by a little black-and-white wasp.

Its jaws snapped a centimetre from my knee. I tried to draw my crossbow again but the string was stretching each time and it was quickly losing its power. I dropped it and drew my sword – how do you fight a bear with a sword? I only know how to kill Insects. I backed away; the bear followed me. It turned side-on to Dellin and she saw her chance. She ran forward and with all her weight drove the spear under its left front leg.

The bear drooped its head and gnashed at the shaft. Holding it with its teeth, it began to moan. A surprisingly human sound. It lowered itself down onto its belly and folded its forelegs under its muzzle like an old man folding his arms. It rested its chin on them and closed its eyes – one still bright, the other a red, slimy hole. Dellin lowered her spear to prevent its weight breaking the shaft. We watched its sides heave, more weakly and weaker still, and its misty puffs of breath grew fainter and fainter, until it died.

Dellin worked her spear out triumphantly. She threw off her parka and pulled the front of her damp vest. The normally concave veins on her forearms stood as proud as branches. 'Bear!' she explained and began to laugh.

'You mauled it.'

This made her laugh even more. She wiped the back of her hand over her face, sinewy neck and collarbones, and flicked the sweat off onto the slush. Clouds of breath wreathed from her mouth. 'No bear hibernates in my cave! Ha ha ha. No, wait! Don't go near it yet! You can never tell.'

Her laughter made me smile. Together, exhilarated, we looked down on the bear. It was a drop-shaped mound, with a wide backside, pantaloon hind legs and pointed snout. Foam dotted the short whiskers on its muzzle. Its two-tone fur was more obvious now: a deep black on its forehead, its rounded ears, its great hump and the hairs protruding from between its toes. The rest was shaggy brown, covered with sleek black guard-hairs. Its once-mobile nose was already dulling with ice.

When you face death your senses are alive. The world is bright! We were elated, switched on to the utmost. No future, no past, just the current moment! Now the danger had passed we were relaxing and feeling the adrenaline ebb away.

She leant on her spear. 'What *is* that thing you're holding?'

'A sword.'

'A sword. Is that to skin it with? Ouzel would pay five bangles for this pelt.' She brushed her hand against the grain of the fur, revealing the depth of its fluffy undercoat.

I was so impressed I could scarcely string a sentence together. 'It's for killing Insects, but ...'

'But not bears. And has your bow become damp? Well, well, you need a bolas, like Laochan.'

'Dellin, I can't believe you just killed a buck bear. I mean, I helped, but ... you were amazing. Tornado said he'd love to see you fight an Insect, and he's right. When Awians bait bears they don't even go *near* them. They use longbows and packs of dogs.'

'I bet they don't eat them, either.' She took hold of its hump and heaved it onto its side. 'This is a stroke of luck. The damn Awians might have killed all the game in Carnich, and I doubt we'll find anything tomorrow, but at least we'll eat well tonight. And I can cache some,' she continued, and gestured at the entrance. 'It's safe now. Take in the packs.'

I did as she said, wondering. Here on the verge of Carniss she was on her home ground, the top predator, at the height of her career. She was making me look ridiculous.

The snow faded to a wet margin at the cave mouth and then onto a hard-packed earth floor. Dellin had built a hearth just inside, with a more prodigal use of fuel than usual, and its flames throve high. I crouched down and began rubbing some life back into my hands. My fingertips hurt excruciatingly as they defrosted, as if they were being crushed.

The firelight enhanced the glow of ivory-yellow lamps along the base of the walls, three on each side. Their flames illuminated the entire chamber. They were a peculiar shape, with dents and protuberances. I picked up the nearest and felt its smooth, warm surface. It was a bear's skull turned upside down. Dellin had secured each one on its lower jaw as a stand, then filled each brain pan with lamp oil and fitted a wick in the holes where their spinal columns had once attached. White fangs spiked from their palates and cast shifting, jumping shadows.

Near the entrance the chamber was nearly oval and as wide as a normal room, then it narrowed towards the rear where the slanting walls met smoothly in a crevice. A sheaf of spear shafts neatly bound with sinew were propped there and, just in front, a round hollow worn in the clayey earth, spotted with blood, showed where the bear had been asleep.

I knelt close to the fire. Its smoke rose straight up into the point of the ceiling and was blowing out the top of the entrance past a crusty overhang of snow and icicles. As I tracked its course I noticed a natural ledge three quarters of the way up the wall – the shadows of some objects on it reared and shrank. I stood, and a fan of seven of my shadows joined them, their heads curving over the ceiling.

A large, rough wooden chest filled the depth of the shelf,

together with six or seven rolled rugs in drawstring bags, bundles of twigs and an earthenware oil jar carefully wedged between them. Dellin's ladder leaned against the shelf, a slender pine trunk with the branches lopped off leaving stumps. I smiled as I examined it. Her little cave was unexpectedly snug.

She poked her face in at the entrance. 'Hurry up! I have to butcher this bear quickly!'

I slipped out of the rift fringed with ice and was surprised how much darker the terrace had become in the last few minutes. The peaks around us were darkening stage by stage, as if candles were being blown out one by one in a boundless hall. The bear's back was a black silhouette. The rocks all around it jutted against a sky bloated purple with unfallen snow. Behind the further of Klannich's two peaks, as jagged as a child's drawing of Darkling, the heavy, dull-red sun sagged like a yew berry.

Dellin nodded and echoed my thoughts: 'There's a lot of snow still to fall tonight. At least it will cover our scent.'

'And deter wolves?'

'Yes. The wolves ...' She crouched abruptly and began cutting through the bear's nearest wrist. I drew my sword to assist but she rocked back on her heels and growled, 'This is my kill.'

'Yes, but ...'

'I don't need your help!' She detached one paw and started to saw through another wrist, evidently taking them as prizes. No bears lived at the extreme altitude where I spent my boyhood, but Eilean sometimes met hunters with wind-dried paws sewn on their rucksacks or whole strings dangling from their tent poles. Eilean had told me that they were adept hunters who must be treated with respect – but what do such codes mean to me now? It was just embarrassing. The other Eszai, sporting immortality as a sign of status, would laugh themselves silly to see Dellin recovering scabby, blood-matted bear feet.

'Leave them,' I said. 'Please.'

'No! Why?'

'I can go baiting any time and send you any number of paws. A whole cartload, if you like.'

She ignored me. She lay them aside carefully and made a cut all the way around the bear's neck and down its front over chest and belly. She gradually peeled the fur back, leaving muscle and guts enclosed in a silvery-grey membrane. Then she pressed the muscle of the bear's shoulders, to find the hollows around its scapulae where the thick layer of muscle kept the forelimbs in place. She cut round them and lifted off the right forelimb, then the left. They looked remarkably like human arms. She laid them in the snow and said, 'Go fetch a pickaxe from the back of the cave.'

'We don't need a cache, Dellin. There'll be plenty of food at Carniss.'

'If you think I'm eating with Raven, you're mad. This is my food, Jant. I bet you've dug caches before.'

'A long time ago. In another life, that wasn't really me ...'

'It'll last all winter, till the melt.'

The melt, I thought. In Mhor Darkling we didn't even have a melt season. The ground was solid with permafrost and our caches kept fresh for years. In fact, they're probably still there now, and still edible.

I found the pickaxe, of cheap Awian manufacture, returned to the terrace, scraped away the snow where Dellin indicated, and began hacking at the frozen soil. She continued to peel the bear's skin down, over its bottom and pulled the tail through, leaving its tuft of fur on the naked buttocks. She skinned the back legs and cut the thighs, calves and hamstrings from them. The thin, pink-white bones still attached to the hips seemed quite pathetic with trimmings and flanges of dark red muscle remaining. She filleted the two long muscles of its back. She was bloodied up to the elbows and the iron smell of clots was overpowering.

The soil was hard as stone and, despite the intense cold, I was sweating. I threw the pick down. 'This will do!'

'But it's just a shallow scrape.'

'Dellin, do the wolves have shovels?'

She shrugged and bundled the bear meat up in its pelt, the fur on the outside, and toggled a bone through to fasten it. She put the package in the pit and I scooped earth, then snow, over it, packed it down and marked it with a broken spear shaft.

Dellin had decanted the bear's guts into its ribcage and she pointed at it, brushing snow from her eyelashes with her other arm. 'Drag that upwind a few hundred strides. Be careful.'

'I'll be fine.'

'Dump it in the direction we'll travel tomorrow. It will draw wolves away and when we pass it we'll see their footprints and assess how many are about. Though I think it will soon be buried.'

I thought so, too, judging by the snow-burdened sky. I grabbed the bear's ear and dragged its remains away, though I wanted more than anything to defrost by the fire. I wasn't used to being cold! In the Plainslands winter I can wander around in a T-shirt; everybody envies my immunity from the cold. I didn't remember feeling dangerously cold when I was a child either, so I had assumed my normal clothes would be adequate. Now I had to admit Dellin was right: the Darkling winter sheared straight through them.

I returned, flurries driving hard into my face, but the welcoming glow emanated from the cave mouth to guide me. The terrace had frozen into a dark slick. I slid inside, to where Dellin knelt, forelit as she leant over the fire. She had spread furs around it and stripped down to her underclothes. Her jacket and trousers hung on an A-frame – a rack for wind-drying fillets of meat out on the terrace in autumn – to which some mummified strands still clung.

I'd drawn my fists back into my sleeves and clamped my jaw to stop my teeth chattering. I stomped straight to the hearth and huddled over it.

Dellin glanced up. 'Are you cold?'

'No, I'm fine.'

'You're freezing!'

'Well, I do ache a bit.'

'Take your ridiculous coat off!'

I couldn't open my hands to unfasten the buttons, so she had to help, standing close, no taller than my shoulder, and clicking her tongue disparagingly. I slowly uncurled my fingers – the army gloves were less than useless – stripped off all my clothes, which went on the drying rack. My hands were so numb I couldn't feel the flames, reached too close and nearly burnt them. I couldn't warm my wings at all without scorching the feathers so I spread them like a cloak and rubbed them vigorously.

'Warm up more slowly,' Dellin said. 'You'll hurt yourself. Sit on the pelts.'

I did so and she folded them around me. 'Now you need a hot drink. I've made some kutch.'

'I said no kutch.'

'You're hypothermic! You have to drink something. Here.' She handed me a mug that smelt of whisky. I held it for a while, letting it defrost my fingers, but without sipping any.

The smell of hot stone and brass from the hearth mingled with bug-repelling pine resin on the reverse of the furs and the shiny smell of melting ice. At the far end of the cave Dellin had erected a tripod and stretched something like a bladder over it, opened out at the top to form a bowl and knotted like a stocking at the end that trailed down between the three stakes.

She looked me over professionally, taking my lithe legs and hairless chest for granted but studying the broad joints of my wings. I made no impact on her whatsoever; she had the detachment of a doctor. 'Wings take a long time to dry,' she stated. 'I'll get you some better clothes.' She squirreled up the pine-bole ladder and balanced on the top two branches. She opened the lid of the trunk and rummaged inside it, her bottom bobbing about. She lifted out a crucible used to melt hare skin mastic, a bag of the glue chips and a pack of skins.

'That's your store?' I asked.

'My *laaba*. Animals can't reach it.'

'What about Rhydanne? Don't they steal your stuff?'

Her head still buried in the box, she chuckled. 'Not with a bear to guard it! No, hunters know they can borrow in desperate straits. If a hunter is far from her usual ground and dying from starvation she can use my stores ... if she finds them. That's why I build the hearth in view of the door: if any hunter sees the fire tonight she can come in.'

'I thought it was to keep wolves away.'

'That too, but don't you know a hungry wolf would brave a fire? Hunters appreciate that if they use stores, they must replace them. Think if I came in, starving, and found my food gone? I'd die! It's true ... Another hunter's hoard saved my life once, when I was chasing ibex way over on Bhachnadich.'

'A stash in a cave?'

'Yes, but I don't know whose. I've never met anyone on Bhachnadich. Never heard any signals. I was caught in a blizzard and I had exposure. I was desperate, at the end of my strength, so I sheltered there by chance. I found some dried salmon, kindling and spirits, so I brewed some kutch and revived myself. Two days I spent there ... I replaced the stocks, of course, and I know where to find that refuge, if I need it again.'

What a life, I thought. What a bloody life. There but for the grace of the avalanche go I.

She took out a suede parka, lined and trimmed with fur, and

another pair of hazel-withy and twisted-gut snowshoes. Trousers and boots followed; they were white, like hers, so it must have been a winter suit. Every Rhydanne hunter has two, a brown buckskin outfit for summer camouflage and a thicker one of chamois and snow leopard fur for winter.

'This is Laochan's,' she said. 'He was wearing his other clothes when he died. I left him there ... I didn't return.'

'I'm sorry,' I said.

'What do you mean? You can have them.'

'No,' I said more tenderly. 'Raven won't think I'm a neutral negotiator if I arrive looking like a Rhydanne.' I had recovered enough from the cold to begin taking off my bangles and bracelets.

Dellin simply pointed at my soaked jacket. 'It's freezing outside. If you wear that you will die. I will trade you Laochan's clothes for those bangles.'

How like a Rhydanne. 'All right,' I said. 'Take them.'

She nodded and gave me her dead husband's clothes. Selling them had no effect on her; in fact she began cooking again. She scooped more snow into her pot on the cracked and reddened hearthstones. It quickly turned translucent, its crest fell in and the water boiled much sooner than it would on the plains. Tiny bubbles coated the sides and bottom of the pan, and rushed to the surface till they turned it grey.

Her camp craft impressed me as much as her hunting prowess. She turned some strips of fat spitting in the fire. It looked like bacon.

'Is that from the bear?'

'Yes. Brown fat. It's the most nutritious sort of meat there is. And it tastes the best too. Hibernating bears have it – that's the only source apart from cubs – so you're lucky.'

Outside, the night blizzard howled and drove snow horizontally past the cave mouth. A drift was building up there, already half-filling the entrance with a soft wall, coloured orange by our firelight. 'We'll have to dig ourselves out.'

'Perhaps. Doesn't matter.'

Sure enough, it didn't matter. Nothing mattered here. It was strange to think of other Eszai sitting down to feast in the Castle's hall, when five hundred kilometres away I was sequestered in a cave with a huntress, the only inhabitants of our secret world. Snow sealed the cave mouth completely and shadows flickered in the eye sockets of each skull lantern, bringing life to the long-dead beasts.

When we had eaten Dellin stirred some of her whisky into the melted bear's grease. 'What's that for?' I asked.

'It's an ointment. I'm going to massage your feet.'

'Really? Um ...' I wondered where this was leading. 'I'm not so sure about that.'

'Jant, you have blisters. The slush has softened your skin. It's dangerous. You might fall prey to frostbite or blood poisoning. Here ...' She held out her hand and I wriggled round to present her with my right foot, while keeping the rest of my body wrapped in the soft furs. I was naked, after all.

She washed my feet with warm water and then began to give me the most soothing and reinvigorating massage I have ever had. Her head bowed thoughtfully as she worked in silence. Her profile was sharp, with a shadow under the angle of her jaw. Her hair was tied back, her pale body fantastically athletic, with bone pointing from the muscle at elbows and shoulders. The notch at her throat was as deeply hollowed as an ice sculpture. Her breasts were just two nipples pushing out the vest, which, lower down, hung loose over her hard, concave stomach. The black vest and pants revealed more of her long limbs, making them lengthier still. I watched the play of indentations in her muscles as she moved. There was so much power locked up in her small frame.

In our snug sanctuary I moved closer to her, although Dellin never looked up to meet my eye. She worked practically, kneading my sole and separating my toes, which so many other women had massaged before. She forced her strong fingers between every muscle, loosened every joint, and it felt magnificent. I had to ruck the furs around my waist to disguise a secret erection. If she had noticed, I think it would have shocked her.

'Now your feet are safe,' she said at last. 'It's your turn to do mine.'

'This ankle is still stiff. There ...'

'Feels all right to me.'

'Can you do it again? Ahh ...'

Then I took her tiny feet, washed and massaged them. They were surprisingly charming; every nail perfect and no calluses at all. Cleanliness was a matter of life and death to her, not a quest for beauty, but the result was the same. I felt her skin warm and soften under my hands and I couldn't prevent my massage strokes becoming erotic touches. I was long-practised at massage and proud of my prowess. She relaxed and lay down close to me, and the deep furs folded between us. Was she attracted to me, or was this just another way of 'making tomorrow safe'? I felt a new interest in her lifestyle. After all, I was returning to normal tomorrow, one night's holiday as a Rhydanne wouldn't do me any harm.

'Laochan's clothes remind me of those I wore as a child,' I said serenely. 'They're much the same, magnified to adult size. That smell of worn suede takes me back to Mhor Darkling. Eilean made my clothes; I didn't know how. I still don't, even though I'm ninety-five. Laochan's stitching is so fine, he must have had a lot of spare time.'

'Oh yes. He was a wonderful hunter. He had time to beat lots of bangles, carve lots of beads. You can see some on the laces.' She sighed and I squeezed her instep to let her know she wasn't alone.

'I may not have learnt how to make clothes, but I taught myself to fly.'

'You are fast,' she murmured – a compliment! I felt a mounting desire to caress the rest of her body, lean forward and run my hands over her legs, very slowly under the furs. I wanted to tell her more.

Instead, she sat up. 'You've drunk all your kutch.'

I blinked. 'Um ... yes. Yes, I have.'

She laughed. 'It was good, wasn't it?'

'It was all right.'

'Do you want some more?'

'Er ... yes. Yes, I do. It's very warming. Show me how to make it.'

'Very well,' she said. 'But first fetch your flowery foam – your soap. You should wash and smell like an Awian again, because Raven will expect it. Come on.' She used her mittens to ease four hot cobbles from the hearth and carried them to the tripod in the rear of the cave. She plunged them into the cone of pink flesh: there was a sudden hiss and a cloud of steam hid her.

I peered into the wobbly sink. 'What's this made out of?'

'It's a section of the bear's gut.'

Surprisingly, the water was clean and wonderfully hot. Dellin lay on the furs and watched with regret as I shaved and brushed my teeth. Then I returned to the hearth and pulled the silky pelts around my legs, comfortable with exhaustion, hot water, massage and kutch. Now I was rid of a fortnight's filth I felt extremely fresh, as if preened for a special occasion, and I basked in a tranquillity I'd hardly imagined could exist in Darkling at all. 'Thank you, Dellin.'

She snorted. 'You don't smell like a man; you smell like a bunch of violets. Tomorrow you must speak for the Carnich Rhydanne.'

'Yes ...' I murmured.

'Look at me! Look me in the eye. Don't take the Awians' side because you grow feathers and so do they.'

'Dellin, I—'

'Don't take Raven's side because you are accustomed to speaking with princes and he puts you at your ease. Don't feel as if you're a boy again, because Darkling brings back memories. I think Raven is the sort of man who has no time for boys.'

'Hah! I grew up in the city backstreets, Dellin. I had a gang behind me then, and now I have the Castle.'

She nodded slowly. 'And most of all, don't take his side because you think it's what the silver man secretly wants. He wants to benefit his people, not the Castle.'

'I know! I *swear* I'll represent you fairly!'

She stirred the embers, and when a single, elongated flame licked up around the pan, she glared at it. 'The lies of Awians are as powerful as their bright colours. They carry you away.'

'Dellin, I can handle Raven Rachiswater; I've known him since he was a boy. In fact, I remember him playing on a rocking horse with his brother ... and they squabbled over it. I remember his father. Damn it, I remember his *grandfather*, who died on the battlefield. Yes, Carnich is your home, and you're wonderfully in your element here, but wait until you see me in the milieu to which *I've* become accustomed.'

Next morning, Dellin's fur sleeping bag was already empty and the skillet of water was simmering noisily on the hearth. A clear blue light shone from the tunnel she had dug through the drift in the cave mouth, and rhythmic tapping told me she was out on the terrace.

I slit Laochan's jacket up the back twice for my wings, put it on and popped the toggles through their holes. I dressed myself in his other clothes, though they were a bit tight, and crawled out into the bright sunlight with my mittens slipping over the crystalline snow.

What a sight it was! The mountainside dropped away nearly

sheer into a steep, wide ravine filled by Carnich Glacier. We were on the bank high above it. I looked down onto its surface, which wasn't flat but corrugated into regular waves taller than a man and banded equally white and dust-grey with ground rock. At its mouth the titan pressure of the weight of ice had thrust out clusters of blue-white shards, which stood sharp and monolithic, or splayed like quartz crystals. They cast long shadows each the length of a ship over the river of ice.

On the far side, the immense bulk of Klannich rose more than halfway up the sky. Its M-shaped double summit was unmistakable. The nearer pinnacle was higher, but the further one was visible beyond it, since Klannich curved slightly to the east as if shrugging. Further on still, a wall of snow-clad ridges continued the immense cordillera with a breathless impression of space. Peaks behind peaks, and yet more crested into the distance, each ridge a paler shade of blue until only the points were visible in a blue-white haze.

Clouds piled around Klannich mountain, not the thin wisps we had seen as we climbed, but great, cumbrous stacks of coppery nimbus, dark at the base where they hid the pointed summits here and there. A peach-pink, heavy dawn light shone from them, which, together with the lupin-blue sky, stippled the snowfield and the glacier's ridged surface blue and orange. As the light shifted from a thundery brown to violet, the snowfields changed too, reflecting every nameable colour. Only Klannich's two pinnacles remained pure white, like canines.

Ice had sealed the snow in a glassy crust over the whole slope and there was no sign of the bear's blood. Half a metre of snow must have fallen last night – the heaviest fall I'd seen in eighty years. Dellin was busy with breakfast. She was sitting on one of the boulders, tenderising a chunk of bear thigh by holding it on the flat top and bashing it with a stone. 'What do you think?' she said.

'I'm missing my coffee and biscuits.'

'What? No. I mean, weren't you looking at Raven's house?'

'Can I see Carniss from here?' I said excitedly. 'Where? Show me.'

She stood up and pointed across the ravine. The far bank was a vertical cliff, but Klannich projected beyond the end of the glacier into a promontory. In silhouette, topping this headland, was a wall and a big square tower.

'Oh god,' I breathed. 'Oh god – oh *no*!'

'Raven's pueblo,' said Dellin.

'You didn't tell me he was building a *fucking castle*! It's … it's *huge*!'

'I told you it was big.'

'Oh, shit, Raven, what the fuck are you trying to *do*?'

Dellin couldn't understand a rhetorical address to Raven. She looked at me as if I was mad.

I said, 'It's a keep. He's built a bloody fortress up there! Easily as big as the ones at the Front! Why didn't you *tell* us?'

'I told the silver man it was as big as the Skein Gate,' she said, taken aback.

'A *house*, you said. Not a fucking *tower*!'

Dellin seemed so frightened that I tried to calm down. 'How long did it take him to build?'

'Last year and this year, from the melt to the melt.'

'Impressive.' I indicated the sloppy meat. 'Were you going to make kutch with that?'

'Yes.'

'Well, bring me the whisky. I need a stiff drink.'

She dashed into the cave and emerged with a bottle. I swigged from it, grimaced, and said, 'Raven doesn't have a licence to fortify. If he did, I'd know about it, because he needs permission from the Emperor. Nobody can fortify without a licence and nobody ever has, not since the Eske Rebellion …' I tailed off because the fortress drew my gaze. Its blocky profile was so much at odds with the mountains I wondered why I hadn't seen it at once. A curtain wall ran along the top of the sheer cliff, and at the end nearest Klannich a square tower surmounted it, with a tiny movement fluttering – a flag flying from its roof. Raven might have disturbed a few Rhydanne, fine, but I couldn't let him cross the Emperor.

'I'm the first immortal to know this. I have to deal with it properly. Have your moonshine back, Dellin. It's got a kick like a mule.'

She slopped some into a steaming mug and offered it to me with some oatcakes. I broke one in half and stirred the kutch with it, breaking up the layer of translucent fat on its surface into amber globules. The chill air was nipping my skin and the sun's rays were tangible too, a sick radiation making me feel light-headed. The air in my clothes was a warm cocoon and I dreaded the moment when excessive movement would expel it.

'I'm right, aren't I?' she said. 'Raven wants to rid Carnich of Rhydanne, every one.'

'But he has the might of Awia behind him. Surely Rhydanne can't be such a threat that he needs to build a *keep*? He can't be protecting himself against Insects, either; there aren't any up here. There are wolves ...'

'A timber barricade is proof against wolves,' said Dellin.

'Exactly. There's no need for a keep.'

'Will you still speak to him?'

'Yes, certainly! I want to know what the fuck he's playing at. San will want to know too.'

She looked relieved and began to prowl about, tidying and packing. Then she swung herself onto the boulder's slanting top and dropped onto one knee. On all fours, she grasped its edge and stretched the other leg out behind. She took a deep breath, threw her head back and howled: 'Ah-ooo!'

What was she doing?

She took another breath and yowled into the air: 'Ah-ooo! Ah-ooo!' More high-pitched than a wolf.

I backed off until a boulder pressed cold against my calves, then sat down heavily on it, crunching the snow. The respect I'd had for her vanished. How could I have felt close to her last night? I couldn't possibly know her! Her actions were so alien, her thoughts must be worse!

She paused, head bowed gracefully, but I felt repulsed. I had no idea what to say. What does one say to a wild animal?

'Ah-ooo! Ah-ooo!' And now the first howl echoed back from the surrounding cliffs. Dellin tilted her head and listened: those weren't echoes, they were *replies*.

Another ululation resounded from further up the far bank. A third, definitely an older female, amplified on the breeze gusting down the glacier.

Dellin breathed deeply then bayed again, leaning forward on hands and toes, putting her whole strength into the call. Echoes redoubled the cries and they reverberated together, nearly-human voices straining lupine howls into the wails of mourners. Abruptly, they stopped. The ravine resounded with echoes, which gradually died away until, at length, I could hear the whistling breeze. The hair on my arms prickled. My mother had been one of these!

Dellin closed her eyes and turned to the source of the glacier, as if listening with her whole face, but the wind brought not the faintest sound. She shrugged and wiped her mouth. 'There's a pair nearly opposite, another pair some way up the Carniss side of the glacier and a lone huntress down in the forest. That's all – I heard nothing from the trading post.' She crossed a foot onto her thigh and began lacing a crampon to her boot. 'I'm sure I heard Karbhainn, though. I'm glad the stinking Awians haven't killed him.'

'Can you really recognise their howls?'

'Their signals, Jant. Only wolves howl. Yes, of course I can; these are people I've come to know.'

The wind was whipping round the cliff edge beside her cave and, judging by the curling clouds, the air currents were treacherous. Hopefully I could gain enough altitude on the more constant flow along the ridge to soar high above the glacier.

Dellin tied her crampon laces and stamped around to test them. She looked innocuous enough now, but I was still shuddering at the sight of her stretched out like a pointing hound. I hadn't known Rhydanne howled ... But then another scene from my shieling resolved in my mind: the wind clamouring down our valley carried a fluid, diaphanous voice. A yearning sound, it rode the gale effortlessly but with no trace of sentience, as bestial as a fox. I had heard nothing like it before; it matched no animal I knew. It had to be Barguest, the great wolf, outside in the sightless abyss. How many times had Eilean told me, 'Barguest will come and get you'? I pulled the rugs over my head and lay as still as if frozen, but the howling drifted into my bunk, calling me to come outside, feel the strong teeth plunge into my flesh and be shaken into thousands of pieces. Eilean heard it too, and gasped. She grabbed her parka and dashed out, leaving the door swinging on its leather hinge.

Dellin poked me with the butt of her spear. 'Wake up, Jant. Will you fly over the glacier?'

'Yes.'

'Then meet me at the other side. If I approach alone they'll shoot me.'

'Oh, then I'll catch the arrow in mid-air.'

She grinned and set off with a swinging gait, using her spear as a staff, towards the ravine sliced by Carnich Glacier through the white skirts of Klannich.

RAVEN

I retired to the window seat to peruse my book while the servants cleared the remains of breakfast from the table in my solar. But I wasn't paying much attention to *Myths and Legends of Ancient Awia* – I have re-read it so many times before, with the few others I managed to bring here. I kept glancing up from its worn pages, through the diamond-shaped panes of leaded glass to the heights of Capercaillie and the thronging peaks. They repelled me. They fascinated me too. Their silence belied their terrible potential: they could take a man's life at any time, in any number of ways.

Clouds were lifting off the summits and out of the hanging valleys between them. Each valley extruded its own glacier, meeting in the bulk of Carniss Glacier. Clouds hung below the double crown of Capercaillie, which, I am told, is about five thousand metres high. Nobody has charted the others; there are far too many. According to the theory of Phalarope, the range, the backbone of the continent from the top of Ghallain Peninsula all the way into the Paperlands, is slowly but constantly increasing in height as the pressure from the seabed under the western ocean pushes it up. Difficult to imagine, but I am told the theory is supported by the sharpness of the peaks too young to be worn down, the straight west coast and the frequent earthquakes.

I looked up to the triangular, vertical rock face of Capercaillie. Blown powder snow had stuck to it, revealing its diagonal strata. Far below my window, the settlers' cabins were dotted about between my tower and the edge of the forest, where the tree boughs hung low with ice. The snow around the long latrine shack was stained brown, and in front of it tracks converged on a manger, from which several russet-cream llamas were imperiously pulling straw.

I appreciated the beauty of the peaks surrounding us, but they were innately deadly too, like a coiled viper which may at any moment rear and strike. They engender an apprehension in me, just the same as when I used to wait in the amphitheatre, sword in hand, alone on the sand-strewn ground, the crowd fell silent, and the gate at the opposite end began slowly, slowly to ratchet open ...

I do not understand the mountains. No human terms can fancifully be applied to them; they are as cold as my brother's heart. I will never be able to tame them but they add to the challenge I have set myself, and I admit I find it exhilarating.

A low howl, very mournful and faint, emanated from the direction of the glacier. More howls joined it, making my people below look around anxiously and glance at each other. The goats and llamas started up and their bells began tonkling all over the settlement and echoing back from the quarry face. The Rhydanne are howling again. It sent a shiver down my spine. I slipped a bookmark between the pages and placed the book down on the seat, stood up and looked out over the treetops, but there was nothing to see bar the plumes of spindrift curling off the nearest ridge. I supported myself with my hands on the columns either side of the window and listened to the howls. The snow out there looked soft as carded wool, but its terrible cold constantly stole into my solar and wrapped around my ankles. The mountains want to suck the life from us. You feel the heat of your body dissipating into the chill air.

Eventually the howls ceased and the silence returned, as deep as the drifts. The servants by the table were looking up at me apprehensively. 'Not wolves; only savages,' I said. 'You can go now.'

I descended from the recess and sat down at the table. A scatter of coins lay next to my ledger – I have just given an advance on next month's pay to my steward, who is inordinately fond of drinking in the Frozen Hound. The gold coins glittered and caught my eye, my brother's profile on each one. I picked one up. It might as well be my face, since no one can tell us apart. I pressed my thumbnail on the cheek as if to scar it. It could be my face, and why shouldn't it be? It's simply a matter of chance. He drew breath a minute before me, so he inherits the kingdom. He always had to be first. He was always the bully.

I permitted myself a sour smile. He becomes king and I end up trapped on this damn rock. Scarcely aware of doing it, I tossed up and caught the coin. I clicked my thumbnail into the ridges on its sides, and it gradually warmed to the heat of my palm. I tossed it again. My brother's head, 'Tarm. Rach. 73RD Rex Awia' inscribed around it. Again. The Rachiswater eagle close on the obverse. My twin brother's head. The florid eagle with his eye keen and his wings folded. My twin's head. The eagle. My twin's head. My twin's head. The eagle. My twin's head. Why does his head turn up more often? I clenched my fist. It is just like him – rearing his head into every affair where he's not wanted! He's ubiquitous! I unfolded my hand, index to little finger, and looked down at his profile, identical to mine. Except that while I wear my hair short, he is jolly and cavalier, or at least feigns it, and grows his dark locks to shoulder length.

I do hate him (tossing up the coin again). He doesn't manage the kingdom as well as I could. He has no interest in the affairs of the people, no appetite for the details of justice and trade, only for feasting, hunting and sycophancy. He does not have a practical attitude ... But, damn him, his laughing mind has so political a bent that whatever I do anywhere in the kingdom he seems to know of it. He gainsays me. He forestalls my every step. And he does it in so humorous a manner that the courtiers laugh themselves sick. Laugh themselves sick and on to another feast at my expense.

So I am here.

I was surprised to find I was clenching my fist again and the hot pound coin was digging into my palm. I calmed myself as a good swordsman should and glanced out at Capercaillie Mountain – its ominous bulk was a fine stimulant.

No, I can't conquer the mountains but I can still conquer my brother. Carniss Keep is impregnable. No one can assail this cliff top. With the storehouses and cisterns for both water and snow we can withstand a siege. Work on the fortifications is proceeding according to plan – the ones I can't afford to build yet I've left space for, to throw up if necessary. The colonists are coping admirably – proof I know how to govern, but he only knows how to reign. My forces are nearly ready. I have enlisted the fortune hunters who flocked here, and Francolin's soldiers will arrive soon. Then my sweet brother had better look to his own.

I know it does no good to pick over the past but in hindsight my mistake was so obvious the memory still smarts. I should have distanced myself from the coup. Then, when the net closed around the plotters, I would not have been caught in its mesh.

*

Two years ago this month, in the Langrel Room of Wrought Manor, candles were lit on black candlesticks so tall their flames were depositing rings of soot on the sloping ceilings. I sit opposite Francolin, Lord Governor of Wrought, across a card table on which burns a lamp. It is night outside and the oddly shaped corners of the large room are in shadow. The lamplight, so dark yellow as to seem almost brown, does not venture into them but plays on the table, skipping over the surfaces of every object and baulking from the shadows beneath. Beside the lamp, a pile of ash on a silver plate is all that remains of the letters that brought us here.

Reeve Estaminet has been quiet all evening, listening without comment, but Snipe, who has just checked the door for the hundredth time, stirs uneasily from foot to foot and looks back over his shoulder at us.

'So, it's settled,' Wrought says. 'We make our move next week. It's a shame we don't have the support of any other reeve.'

'Only Estaminet,' I say. 'I can vouch for several reeves from other manors, but only Estaminet from Rachiswater.'

'What about the steward?'

I shake my head. 'No. My brother's steward is loyal. I've taken pains to keep this from him. If he had the slightest whiff of what we were doing, he'd run straight to Tarmigan.'

Grey-haired, old Wrought carefully examines his fingernails and the backs of his hands. 'Let me recap. Tarmigan ... *King* Tarmigan,' he amends sarcastically, 'is preparing to march to the Front and resume his campaign against the Insects. On his first night in camp a group of soldiers in my pay will enter his pavilion and will ensure he never wakes again. They will make his death appear as if an Insect has attacked him. How it will be done, neither you nor I know and we do not want to know.'

'Sh!' says Snipe from the doorway. 'Not so loud.'

'Will you sit down!' Wrought snaps. 'You're giving me the jitters. This whole wing is deserted!'

I say, 'Nobody's there, Snipe. Do as he says.'

My servant obeys, tentatively dragging a chair to the table and sitting astride it. His skin is so sallow it resembles ivory and deep shadows ring his eyes. The growing stress we had suffered as we watched Wrought's plans take shape had reached fever pitch. I recoiled from them so much that I was no longer even sure whether my surroundings were real, or simply a backdrop to a mad play.

Wrought appraises Snipe shrewdly. 'He's nervous.'

'Of course he's bloody nervous. We all are!'

Wrought licks his dry lips. He has the peculiarly smooth lips of an old man whose looks age has dignified rather than ravaged. 'Raven,' he says, 'you will be ready to ascend the throne as soon as the messenger arrives with the news.'

'Yes, immediately. I don't want the fyrd stepping in.'

'Good.'

There is another long pause. To prevent any more last-minute fears setting in, Wrought clears his throat and says briskly, 'This is our final meeting. We know what we have to do. We all have safeguards ensuring we can rely on each other. We all know what we stand to gain. Now, let us separate and go about our business; not a word nor glance will pass between us till it's over.' He stands up, scraping his chair on the parquet, and unlocks the door. Reeve Estaminet goes through without looking back and his footsteps recede down the corridor. Snipe sweeps the room with a quick scowl and follows him out.

'Francolin,' I ask, 'why are you doing this?'

He chuckles, goes to the window and pulls the curtain aside a little, to look through the rain-streaked panes at the sodden and rotten scrub woodland extending down to the smokestacks of the weapons factories. 'When you are king, as is your right to be, you'll remember the hand I had in your accession. I've had a good life, Raven. I've done almost everything I wanted to do; slept and feasted with whomever I wanted. Still do.' He rubs at the pane. 'My coffers are full and at supper time my lovely daughter comes to the table and gives her old dad a kiss on the cheek. You've seen her, haven't you?'

'Yes, but she's usually pushed forward to speak to my brother.'

'All that will change. I've achieved most of what I wanted in life and, now death is round the corner, I have nothing to lose. It would be good to be father of the Queen of Awia. I'd like to see my line continue in the Rachiswater dynasty.'

I see. 'I would be pleased to wed your daughter,' I said.

'Thought you'd say that. Thought you would. Tern's a beauty, is she not?'

'As beautiful as the legendary Lynette herself.'

'Our families will join and my grandson will accede to the throne instead of your brother's brat Sarcelle. I offer you this manor as

Tern's dowry. You will inherit it as well as Rachiswater and my blood will be part of the royal dynasty for years to come. That means a lot to an old man.' His withered neck flaps, rather like a tortoise's, and I suddenly hate him. The lusty, conniving old goat doesn't deserve his woods and marshes, his foundries, his beautiful and scandalously young wife whom he found as a serving girl – and his even more stunning daughter whom every man in Awia is watching like a hawk. Now I understand why Francolin has been shielding her: he intends her for me.

'A double prize,' I say. 'The throne and your daughter. I agree. We shall be the first of a long dynasty: Rachiswater-Wrought.'

Francolin bows. Then he reaches out a thumb and forefinger, turns down the lamp and with a hiss the room is plunged into darkness.

I dropped the coin. It clattered on the floor and rolled under the table. 'Damn Francolin!' I said, bent down and retrieved it.

A group of mountaineers entered the gate, and I heard their boisterous talk as they clattered through the undercroft below me. I went to the window, looked down and saw the last of them enter with crampons on their boots and ropes across their bodies. I had sent them to explore an ice cave in one of the rifts of Capercaillie.

'Snipe!' I called. 'Tell the climbers I'll dine with them tonight. I want to hear what they've found!'

'Very good, my lord.'

I returned to sit on the tall pine chair. I missed Rachiswater intensely. I yearned for the palace and the capital town so much I ached. The fruits of Awia's glorious culture were denied me: conversations with people who know literature, visits to the theatre, the opera and the ballet. There was nothing in the mountains. None of the coarse and grasping settlers had even heard of the Tambrine poets. Of course, my philistine brother knew this part of the punishment would bite most deeply. He forbade my friends in artistic circles to correspond with me, at pain of losing royal patronage. I wished that I had strangled him in the womb.

In Carniss the winter afternoons were freezing and deadly. I missed the crisp brightness of our hunting woods. I missed the beautiful lemon-yellow chestnut leaves against the pale blue sky, as it was this time two years ago, on my last day in Rachiswater, when Tarmigan dealt our lot with a simple wave of his hand. Everyone involved had known how much was at stake, and now I think of that day with a mixture of fear and defiance. I can still hear the hunting horn that signalled my life in Rachiswater coming to an end.

The sound of the hunting horn far off in the woods at Rachis: Hoo-oo! Hoo-oo! Dogs barking and scrambling bell a counterpoint to its resonant note. Crashes in the undergrowth grow louder as they approach, and now the first dogs burst through, their forepaws raised in dives. They snuffle the ground, their eyes bright but with a detached look: they are concentrating on the scent.

My twin is the first to turn his horse and race after them. His helmet visor is raised and his eyes sparkle. His horse's rear hooves drag nettles and brambles out of the patch. I follow on black Rabicano and six more huntsmen spur on, one after another, behind me.

My reins are slippery in one hand, and in the other my longbow held down tight against Rabicano's flank. Tarmigan races ahead and through gaps in the screen of twigs and hawthorn leaves I see flashes of his iridescent armour – beetle-carapace green, now turquoise, now metallic purple. Out of the corner of my eye the huntsmen are glints of steel and harlequin velvet – diamonds of crimson and primrose, violet and rose-blue, on their bay and dapple mounts.

Autumn light has a golden quality that you never see at other times of the year. The sun is so low its long yellow light casts our shadows far into the woods. I am still young enough to prefer autumn to summer, dusk rather than dawn, late-night conversations, not early-morning graft. I am thoroughly enjoying myself.

We skirt round a copse of saplings growing close together, spiralled with ivy and hung with glossy mistletoe as if festooned for New Year's Eve. Tarmigan jumps his purebred over a wide ditch. He dips his lance tip and disappears into a thicket. I urge Rabicano to follow him, feeling twigs buff off my armour. I am beside myself with gladness that soon I'll have to follow him no more.

We duck low, over our horses' necks as the branches sweep above our heads. My arrow shafts and flights squeak as they rub together in the quiver over my shoulder. Our hooves crunch the fallen leaves, then we emerge into a clearing with hassocks of grass bearing seed stalks. We charge through, splashing the shallow water lying between them.

The hounds know they are closing in and give tongue again. The screen of grass waves ahead of us and a rustling marks where our quarry has come to bay. The dogs are all around us now, slowing down and hanging back, looking up at us expectantly. Among the tussocks we sight the sinuous profile of the mountain lion.

I nock a barbed arrow, draw, and my hooked fingertips press white on the string. Then suddenly my brother's horse plunges forward in front of me, completely blocking my shot.

'Ya!' He levels his lance at the lion. It draws back liquidly on deep-sculpted haunches. Its ears lie flat and its face creases into a snarl. Threads of saliva link its fangs as it opens its mouth and roars.

The lance tip pierces its shoulder and at the same time it leaps. It seizes his thigh, sticks there like a burr, its claws in the saddle and its tawny reflection shining on his leg armour. Its shoulder runs with scarlet. Slowly it releases its hold, slips down and slides off the lance. It falls on its side, showing its white belly – and my horse baulks away. The lion lies still and the fire dulls from its burning eyes. When they glaze over I lower my bow and see with satisfaction that my first arrow is still lodged in its hindquarters – peacock-feather fledgings and gold foil. All the other hunters had missed; my shot was the one that had brought it to bay.

Tarmigan alights, pulls off his gauntlets and touches the lion's wound with his finger, then, according to the boorish custom, smears blood across his cheeks.

'Well done, Your Highness!' calls Oscen.

'A powerful beast!'

'An excellent bag!'

My twin turns to the hunters his laughing, panting face shining with blood. His chest and shoulders are heaving and his feet, clad in pointed sabots, are sinking in the grass.

'Mortals could almost count you Eszai!' says Oscen.

'I shot it first,' I say, but nobody pays me the slightest attention.

Tarmigan wipes his face on his leaf-fringed mantle. 'The deer in our woods will be safe now with no lions to prey on them.'

'Indeed. We knew you'd be its match!' cries Oscen.

'Right!' Tarmigan says. 'Let's go back to the pavilion and release another one!'

I am always amazed how they can ignore me when I look identical to him. I repeat, 'I shot it first.'

'Yes. You damn well put an unnecessary hole in a fine pelt.'

Flushed with success, he stands with his lance clasped in both hands. 'I think, Raven, you should be more careful of your own hide.'

'What do you mean?'

'We bring new quarry to bay! Tanager! Oscen!'

The courtiers draw their bows *on me*! I gasp, looking from razor-sharp arrow head to arrow head – all six of them. The closest courtiers begin backing their horses slightly to take better aim.

'What's going on? How dare you?'

'My own twin, a traitor,' Tarmigan says calmly.

'What? Certainly not! Whoever gave—'

He looks directly at me but speaks to Oscen. 'What shall we do with him? Hang him on the Broad Road? Is that gibbet empty yet?'

Oscen swallows. 'Your Highness ...'

'What is this about?' I shout.

'I know you are planning to depose me. Dismount!'

I do so and he approaches. 'How could you expect to keep it secret? How could you imagine you would succeed?' He throws the question open and the courtiers shake their heads uneasily. Mindful of the fact I am still their target, I raise my hands. He comes closer and places his palm on my forehead. 'Oh, Raven. Are we not the same? Don't I know your thoughts every minute, every day? I even know what you're thinking now.' I flinch away but he continues. 'You're wondering whether to bluster you've no idea what this means. Well, pleading ignorance won't do; I know everything. Oscen, if you please ...'

Reeve Oscen steps from his courser and draws a coil of cord from the saddlebag. He takes my bow, unclips my quiver from the saddle, then holds out his hand for my sword. I unbuckle my belt and hand it to him, with rapier and poniard. It is the ultimate disgrace. I hang my head and my wings droop open and brush the wet grass. I say, 'I demand a fair trial.'

'This *is* your trial,' says Tarmigan.

Oscen gives him my weapons then forces my arms behind my back, crosses my wrists and binds them tightly. Overcome with emotion, I glance down to hide it, then feel a burst of defiance and sneer, 'You're very sure of yourself.'

'Yes, I am.'

'But if you're wrong ...'

Tarmigan smiles and with his lance point goads me back onto my horse, which is difficult to mount with my hands tied, and they all snigger at the comedy. Another courtier has skinned the lion and presents the pelt to Tarmigan, who arranges it on his cantle. He leads back to the encampment constructed in a clearing for the week's hunts and nightly feasts. Oscen takes my horse's reins and follows in procession, then the courtiers at my back, still with arrows at string. As we ride the wind blows the long grass in waves and above us the boughs hiss my shame. I sit straight-backed, looking forward, trying to maintain a semblance of dignity, though I have a dry lump of bile blocking the back of my throat. I had hoped for the silver throne, and now my future is to be a dank jail cell – or, more likely, a fatal hunting 'accident' by the end of the day.

Ladies run out of the beautiful pavilions of organza silk and millefleurs-painted wood to meet us. They see me and their smiles become looks of horror. Their hands fly to their mouths. They turn to each other questioning, chattering. I stay expressionless and all the time the trees shush like surf on shingle.

Tarmigan shoves me ahead, through the doorway surrounded by blue climbing roses, down a passage of ruched velvet and cloque satin artificed to resemble the forest, and into a milk-white hall of dovetailed planks with columns and a fake balustrade above the portal – a copy of the Rachiswater throne room. Tarmigan has had the silver throne of Awia brought to his hunting camp.

A huge, liver-coloured pointer rises from her cushion and schoozles her nose into his hand. He leaves me standing in the middle of the hall and throws himself into the throne. He turns sideways, kicks his legs over the armrest, crosses them and says, 'Francolin Wrought put you up to it.'

I hesitate, then decide not to compound my indignity with bluster. 'Who told you?'

'A king's ears are everywhere.' He takes a glass of wine from a side table which matches the elegant throne. 'Would you believe Reeve Estaminet has very uncharacteristically volunteered to become a gladiator?'

I nod unhappily.

'Francolin has taken a hands-on interest in the Insect war.'

'No, he hasn't. Tell me what you've done to him.'

Tarmigan drains his glass. 'I petitioned the Emperor to make him governor of Lowespass. As the position is currently empty, and as

Francolin was a distinguished warrior in his youth, San agreed to send him to the front.'

'He's seventy.'

'He's a traitor. He is moving to Lowespass Fortress as we speak, where as governor he will answer directly to the Castle. Isn't it useful that the Castle has one manor under its control? Naturally, he was obliged to resign governorship of Wrought, and leave it to his daughter. Now, all traitors to the crown may be hung—'

'By law, only the common people.'

'Fuck the law. You were going to bloody *kill me*!' He unhooks his knees from the armrest, straightens up and leans forward. 'How could you plan to kill me, Raven? Wouldn't it be destroying part of yourself? Wouldn't it be like seeing yourself die? God knows, I couldn't do it ...' His expression of refined mock sorrow makes him look as if he almost believes what he's saying. 'I will send you to the fortress prison on Teron Island, where you will remain in solitary confinement but for one mute guard until the end of your days.'

I look at the painted vines above his head; curling stalks and stylised bunches of grapes. A golden eagle perching on a stand in the corner watched us solemnly, and I returned its gaze.

My brother suddenly beamed. 'You won't plead, will you? Neither would I. You're not afraid; you just want to know your fate. I would, in your place! Well, then, I have a proposal, Raven, and you have a choice ... Hm ... You can't be comfortable with your arms tied?'

'I've lost all sensation.'

'Oscen? Where are you, Oscen? Undo him so he can sit down.'

This being accomplished I sit on a bench rubbing my wrists, and my brother pulls a chest from behind a gauze divider. He drags it to my feet, snaps the catch back and raises the lid. Inside is a luxurious grey fur. He lifts it out, revealing a stack of silver bars beneath, and runs one arm under it, as if he is a merchant.

'For years our outposts in Darkling have been sending us such sought-after pelts. They also send us silver and precious stones, and the mountain lions we enjoy hunting so much.' He produces a purse and shakes cabochons of sapphire, ruby and emerald onto his palm. 'A few prospectors venture into the wilderness but mostly, I am told, the savages can be taught to fetch these. The mountain limit of my manor yields tall pines too, even fit for masts. Some of my subjects make a life for themselves there and exploit them. I would like to further the opportunity. I would like to, pardon the expression, kill two birds with one stone. I propose that you extend Awia by leaving the western reaches of this manor to found your own beside it. And *never return*.'

'This is exile,' I say.

'So it is.'

A folded map is lying on the silver ingots. I begin to feel tentatively relieved that I might survive the day, so I pick up the map and concertina it open. It represents the lower Darkling peaks, where the Pelt Road peters into the alien Turbary Track, and a near-rectangular area has been carefully outlined with red dots. 'Carnich,' I say. My accent scuffs the pronunciation and it comes out 'Carniss.'

My brother nods. 'It would bring glory to our family and to Awia. I know you're ambitious and frustrated; you've been in my shadow too long. I'm giving you a chance to govern your own manor, manage it however you wish, and make it prosper. You will, of course, send us taxes. In time you could expand it. You could even send hardy mountain soldiers to the fyrd. Think how that would impress the Emperor!'

This is just a rock surrounded by snow, I reflect. I might as well be on Teron Island. 'But—'

'Ah! Raven intrigues against his king and then raises a "but"! Oscen, did you hear that? Shut up, brother; you're in no position to bargain. You have choice enough: exile in Darkling as the governor of a new manor, or life imprisonment in Teron. Or you could top the bill with Estaminet the Gladiator and go out in a blaze of glory in a ring full of Insects ...'

I say nothing.

Tarmigan continues, 'I will give you a loan every year in return for the goods –' he clenched his fist to make the jewels clack '– and little by little I will decrease the loan until you are rightfully selling them to Rachiswater. You will be self-sufficient, no longer reliant on the palace. Then you will rule the manor in your own right and it is yours to bequeath.'

I nod reluctantly.

Reeve Oscen pipes up, 'Your lancers are ready, Your Highness.'

Tarmigan becomes more serious. 'You're exiled for life, Raven. When you reach Carniss you may never set foot across the boundary again, or you'll *plead* to be sent to Teron. If you return to lowland

Awia, unscrupulous governors or reeves could use you in their schemes. I can't let it happen.' His hand on his rapier hilt, he turns his back on me and speaks to the wall. 'And you look too much like me. We are indistinguishable.' He whips round and instantly I see his rapier gleaming in front of my face, all the way back to his outstretched hand. My cheek stings – blooms into a great pain and sudden wetness. I bury my face in my hands and see them filling with blood! I look up at him in horror.

He crooks his arm, withdraws the rapier, and wipes it on the fur. The gash across my cheek burns and blood streams down into my collar. I fold my handkerchief and try to staunch the flow.

'Now people will be able to tell us apart. You won't creep back and become impostor king in my place.' He sits down on the throne, the rapier across his knees, and his hateful iridescent armour opals from metallic orange to bottle green. 'Goodbye, Raven.'

I bow to him and my blood drips on the floor. Oscen puts his hand on my shoulder and accompanies me out, past the awed ladies, to where mounted lancers are waiting, surrounding my black horse who neighs when he sees me.

Magnificent Rabicano, much the best horse in the world, the fastest courser and my only friend. Well groomed, hair like velvet, polished hooves and braided tail. It is just me and you now, Rabicano. I climb up into his saddle and sit with the blood pouring down my face.

Tarmigan is a better swordsman than I am. I swear I never saw his rapier move and then he sliced me like the lion. I bite my teeth together with hatred. I am resilient. It may take one year, it may take thirty, but I'll return with an army of my own.

'Have a swift journey, my lord prince,' says the damnably obsequious Oscen.

'Oscen?'

'Yes?'

'One day you'll call me king.'

A lancer with his visor down, like a masked executioner, takes Rabicano on a long rein and leads me from the camp, out of the woodland, and out of the manor I once called home.

Ha! I was in such a brown study there. I pushed my chair back and went to the fireplace, where whole logs were burning. I rested my elbow on the stone mantelpiece, put one foot up on the tiled surround and looked down past the carved strapwork designs and my blank escutcheon to the flames. Then I turned round and clasped my hands behind me, warmed my backside and the backs of my legs, while surveying the room with its rich tapestries and painted hangings and the red velvet seats either side of the window.

The first winter was the hardest. Some trappers in Skline village, a little lower down, took me in and gave lodgings to me and my supporters. We shivered and cursed in their miserable log shacks through the whole winter. Some of my followers, who had learnt where I was hiding, came to join me, bringing provisions that saved our lives. As the weather grew more clement their trickle swelled to a stream. Snipe was the first to arrive. Tarmigan had exiled him too, so he came to join me. He may have a multitude of failings but he is bone-loyal. So loyal, in fact, that he puts my interests ahead of his own. I was so relieved to see a steadfast ally that I made him my steward. He began life as a cottar and was only accustomed to farm labour, but he is proving very adept as my second-in-command.

When spring came the deep drifts began to melt. The torrent thawed and began gushing milky with rock dust from the glacier again. I started to build and Snipe descended to Rachiswater to call for settlers. He advertised in newspapers, pasted up posters, notified the town criers, and hundreds of people came to the meeting at his old farm outside town. Some were cottars with no better prospects in life, some were youths or ex-soldiers looking for adventure. Experienced hunters and miners offered their services and entrepreneurs appeared hoping to find riches in Darkling. So did any number of outlaws who realised I would give them reprieve if they worked for me. Every man prepared to work hard was a useful man, and they respected me too. The harsh conditions have made them dependent on me.

I designed the keep myself and sought masons experienced in construction from the battlefront, and we achieved the foundations before the first year's snows set in. Now, from my eyrie, I can literally look down on my brother, who probably gamed and chortled while I planned and pined. It is bizarre that we look so similar. Even when I rode out of the camp with blood flowing down my cheek, I looked the same as him, because on his face he still wore the blood of the lion.

I glanced up at a clattering in the staircase turret. Snipe swept aside the curtain and burst in. He ran into the middle of the room before he caught my disapproving expression, stopped and pointed energetically towards the stairs. 'My lord! There's something in the sky!'

'*What* in the sky?'

'The biggest bird in the world. An enormous eagle! The captain wants to shoot it! But I told him either it's something from the mountains – something we haven't seen before—'

'Or it's the Messenger.'

'My lord, I think it's Comet himself! Actually flying!'

My heart started hammering. I took a deep breath and nodded slowly, then stood and took the coat from the back of my chair. 'We thought the Emperor would send an Eszai to investigate. Do you remember what to do?'

'Yes, my lord.'

'Make sure the armouries are locked and the barracks are disguised as cabins. On no account must Comet be allowed to explore the keep without a guide.'

'I told the pikemen training to go inside, but ... but, if it is Comet, he's come so soon!'

'News travels quickly to the Castle. The Emperor can easily reach out here when the whole Fourlands is in his compass ... But even his power has limits, Snipe, don't you worry.'

'The eagle thing started spiralling round and round. What we thought was a forked tail could really be legs and ... I think he's spying on us!'

'I'll come up.' I smoothed my fur lapels and Snipe held the tapestry aside. I followed him into the draughty gloom of the spiral staircase, thinking rapidly. If the Emperor has heard I'm building the keep he will have guessed my plans. It doesn't take profound intuition to deduce I hate Tarmigan, and I have attempted a coup once already; the evidence is clear. But my plans are moving fast now. My troops are on their way. It's only a week until the main body of men will show up. I need to be rid of Comet before they arrive. That shouldn't be difficult. Only nine days to go until New Year's Eve; he will be raring to return to his parties. 'We must maintain a façade,' I said aloud. 'Be polite to Comet and give him what he wants. Then we can see the back of him as soon as possible.'

'What will he want?' asked Snipe.

'To dismantle the keep, I should think.'

'My lord!'

'Yes, and fine us into the bargain. I've built this without licence.'

Snipe looked back over his shoulder with a worried expression.

'We must manage him well,' I continued. 'We only need the keep for nine more days. We've already collected most of the weapons, most of the food. We have more than enough to barrack our soldiers. We can survive a siege if my brother launches a pre-emptive attack. But next week I'll be King of Awia, and forget Carniss! For all I care, the Emperor can grind this tower into dust ...'

I paused to catch my breath in the thin air, but Snipe gasped his way out onto the tower top. Rock salt crunched underfoot as I turned the last curve, running my hand along the frozen rope handrail, and emerged onto the tower top. I shaded my eyes to see five archers clustered around a brazier warming their hands, with their mitten fingertips fastened back from their fingerless gloves and their bows unstrung. The bright sunlight cast their shadows sharp across the flagstones.

I scanned the sky and immediately saw Comet – a black cross with his mighty wings spread, their feathers fingered at the ends to catch the current he was riding. I unpocketed my telescope and snapped it open but, looking through it, I just saw the same shape again, larger. It glinted, now and then, as the sun flashed on some metal he was wearing. He circled in front of the great arc of mountains confronting us, and every few minutes he passed directly overhead and his shadow flicked over us.

'That's him,' I said.

'An immortal ... Here.'

'They have to be somewhere.' I clicked the telescope shut. Every time I see one of the Eszai a shiver runs down my spine – and Comet is the strangest. Yes, the others are older than him – in some cases more than ten centuries older – but they resemble normal people, so I can occasionally forget their great age and talk to them as I am talking to you. But I can't even begin to fathom the way Jant thinks. I find it hard to read his Rhydanne eyes. I'm struck by their marked intelligence but have no idea what is going on in his mind. He looks too alien, too extreme. In the palace he appeared so incongruous that if he wasn't so bloody relaxed about everything he would have been a monster in our ballroom. Since I came here I've seen other Rhydanne and realised how greatly he takes after them.

And who can understand the mind of a man who can fly? Every

day he sees the world from angles I can hardly imagine. His mind is full of maps, wind speeds and air currents, like some seagull. He sails over rooftops and descries us standing below; where we see spires, he sees perches. Gargoyles for us are easy chairs for him. He could have landed by now, right in the bailey. Once I was engrossed in a novel in the palace library and jumped, startled to find him standing behind me, and the window ajar.

His shadow passed over us again. 'At least he's letting us see him approach,' I said. 'Trust the Emperor to have the most perfect spy.'

'What if he wants to destroy the keep immediately?'

I laughed. 'What, will the Castle mistreat a few innocent settlers? If you knew your history you'd recall that San didn't touch Eske Manor when Orraman Eske fortified it. And that was a rebellion against San himself.'

'He didn't send fyrd?'

'To assail his own people? No, he waited for Orraman to die of old age. Look, if San does move against us, Comet will take days to summon enough fyrd, by which time we'll be in control of Rachiswater. And if he moves sooner than I think, will he really want to besiege our little colony, which just happens to be on an unscalable cliff in the middle of winter?'

Snipe said nothing, but watched Comet approach. I tried to quell my rising anxiety: for god's sake, we're already outcasts. What have we to lose?

'My lord – a Rhydanne!' called the captain of the archers.

'Where?'

He came to the parapet and pointed down to the glacier on our left. It lay like a banded slug in the sheer-sided valley it had carved through Capercaillie. A tiny dot was moving at its wrinkled, folded margin. A native had crossed the glacier crown where the ice was whole, and now he was making turns left and right to avoid the yawning crevasses.

Jant sped over him, unusually low, his shadow swooping over the ice. He made a turn and stayed above the Rhydanne. 'He's checking out that native.'

'Could they be together?' asked Snipe.

I could hardly see them. The glare was giving me a headache, and every day the wrinkles around my eyes deepened from squinting into it. I said, 'At least they're not dazzled. Their eyes cut out the glare.'

'Could just have invented sunglasses,' Snipe muttered. I glanced at him. He was watching the Rhydanne with contempt – the expression of a mouse who had found a foolproof way of slaying cats.

The Rhydanne descended onto the mounds of snow beside the glacier and sat down to remove something from his feet, then climbed out of the gorge remarkably quickly. I kept losing sight of him against the brilliant white, but Comet stayed above him.

'They are together,' said Snipe. 'What's he doing with a savage?'

'Don't forget, he *is* half Rhydanne.'

'Not a very superior Rhydanne,' Snipe muttered.

'What?'

'A Shira.'

'Of course.' I turned and smiled at him – at his chin, anyway, because his peaked cap cast a shadow over his eyes. 'Thank you for reminding me.'

'Surprised it could slip your mind, my lord.'

A freezing gust whipped over the tower top. It rattled the wires of the flagpole bolted to the staircase turret and cracked spots of ice off the flag. It panpiped over the flagpole's hollow tube and sounded a rising, falling moan.

I stamped my feet. The water overlaying the paving stones had soaked my boots black and my toes had long since gone numb. Webs of ice clung to the parapet walls on all four sides and impacted snow stuck to their tops. This crystallised snow was turning into ice, just as firn patches in the hanging valleys give birth to glaciers. In fact, every crack in the wall was collecting its own tiny glacier.

Another gust of eighty kilometres an hour tore from the icecap behind the double peak, down the gorge and over the forest. Riding it came Jant. Larger every second, then he sped over us. We were cast into shade, suddenly colder. I could have reached up and touched the length of his body. Snipe and all the archers dropped to their knees. I looked up at the underside of his wings, strung with muscle, bent at the elbow, tiled with dark feathers. Then he was gone.

'Snipe, for crying out loud, get off the floor!'

Now above the end of the promontory, Jant lost more height and turned so sharply he stood on one wing. The archers left, so I was alone but for Snipe beside ... behind me. Jant glided straight over the bailey, wind hissing off his wings, swung into standing position and lifted one leg then the other as he passed over the parapet.

He stepped down out of the air. He ran a few strides, slowed and walked towards me folding in his gigantic wings.

'The Emperor sends greetings,' he said quietly.

'And I return them, I'm sure.'

He met my eyes, then looked down at my right cheek, distracted by the scar. 'Yes,' I said. 'My brother gave me a very visible autograph.'

'At least it healed well.'

'Ah, no. I look like a beaten duellist.'

A smile glinted on his face. 'A duel would be as illegal as this fortress, Governor Raven.'

'But this is no fortress. This is a colony of miners and lumberjacks. Come inside and have a glass of mulled wine.'

He studied me even more intently, then abruptly turned away and looked over the parapet to where the Rhydanne was approaching. The creature kept glancing up, his eyes flashing when the *tapetum lucidum* behind them caught the light. When Jant saw one of the flashes he waved and the Rhydanne below waved back. Very interesting, but more interesting still was the fact Jant was dressed in their clothes. *Used* savage clothes: I could see his mushroom-grey parka was made for a slighter man. It was also too bulky for his wings, which no longer crossed neatly. He'd shaved unevenly and cut himself in one place. He must have been travelling for days.

The wrists of his wings projected a couple of centimetres above his shoulders but the pointed tips of their primary feathers brushed his shins. The beautiful cross-hilt of a Wrought sword protruded from between them, its scabbard lacquered red and gold – the Castle's colours. Trust Jant to carry such a valuable sword so carelessly.

'San is interested in knowing why you have built fortifications.'

'These aren't fortifications!' I laughed.

'Don't talk bullshit. I see machicolations here ...' He waved a hand over the parapet, then turned to point at one of the ravines in the rock inside the bailey. '*That* is actually a drawbridge you've built over a fissure. But it isn't reinforced with iron so it can't be protection from Insects. You've enclosed the whole cliff top with a wall, with most of the cabins inside. The promontory is a natural salient. And I haven't seen the like of this gatehouse south of the Lowespass Front.'

'My masons are from Lowespass. They built according to their custom.'

'The walls are thicker than Slake Cross!'
'I heard it's the best protection against earthquakes.'
He faced me. 'There are *towers* in your wall.'
'Again, to strengthen it.'
'The tower tops have crossbow mounts!'
'No, platforms from which to view this astonishing landscape.'
'And the *parapets* have *arrow slits*!'
'Merely narrow windows to prevent the blizzards blowing in.'
He gestured up at the flag of Awia, field bleu du ciel with a white eagle displayed, armed and membered jaune, the head to the sinister. He said, 'You're flying the Spread Eagle. But this is Darkling and Rhydanne hunting ground.'
'Rhydanne may well hunt here, but Carniss is a manor of Awia.'
'The Rhydanne are defenceless. Raven, why have you built this? What do you plan to do to them?'
What? He thinks I've built against Rhydanne? I checked myself and mastered my expression. Excellent – if he's jumped to the conclusion that I care about savages, let him think that! Let him continue and I might discover why. But he was just as good at stalling and we fell into silence while he watched the lone Rhydanne approach and I lost the feeling in both feet.
He nodded at the savage, who was now passing the quarry. 'That's Shira Dellin. She asked the Emperor's aid because you're occupying her ground and trapping the animals she needs. The eternal Emperor San has decreed Rhydanne and Awians must live in harmony in Carniss. Show me your settlement, and we'll discuss how you'll achieve such fraternity. And I want that glass of wine.' He vaulted the parapet and fell out of view.
I leant over and saw him, wings spread, spiralling gracefully down like a sycamore seed. The Rhydanne girl had joined the track and was running between the cabins scattered outside the gate. She slowed to a effortless lope, then stopped by the arch and Jant landed beside her. She pushed back her hood and they both looked up at me, two pale triangular faces glowing with fitness. She was peculiarly small for a Rhydanne. They spoke together, then ran into the undercroft, their boots grinding on the strewn salt. 'Snipe!' I called.
He slipped off the stone seat built into the warm chimney breast and came over. 'Comet was travelling with that female Rhydanne,'

I said. 'If he was forced to go at her pace they could have been hiking for weeks! We'll win him round with a decent meal. God knows, if he's been camping like a savage we'll give him a feast and he'll sing our praises.'

Snipe smirked.

'So go and order an excellent spread. Make sure the fire's roaring and arrange a room for him, as comfortable as you can make it.'

'My lord.'

'If he speaks to you address him as Comet. And make sure the servants look neat and tidy, not like bloody filthy trappers.'

'They are trappers.'

'That's not the point. Then join us in the solar. I want you to listen in.'

Snipe sketched a bow and hurried cautiously over the wet flagstones into the staircase. As Comet and the savage walked through the undercroft passage four storeys below, I crossed to the opposite parapet and looked down on my settlers' chalets and barns in lines, their shallow roofs covered with clean snow. Deeply dug paths bordered with piles of shovelled snow ran in a grid between them.

At the far end thin clouds were blowing over the curtain wall, and beyond it the cliff fell away so sheer I couldn't see it, just the lowlands spread out like an undulating blanket far below. The snow had smoothed every feature, levelled everything to equality. It was a desert. Carniss snow is not the safe, cotton-wool snow I remember from my childhood, with our boot tracks and horseshoe prints, and the shallow indentations where we had rolled up the snow to make snowmen until we uncovered the tips of the grass. Carniss snow is snow universally, snow to a monotony, hanging fat on the branches till every tree is disfigured. This snow kills. It covers brutal ravines you can plunge into and perish. It threatens to avalanche into a wall of solid surf racing towards you down the mountainside. It will engulf you and bury you alive, metres deep.

The Pelt Road had vanished, woodland was hidden and, looking east, nothing but varying shades of white stretched as far as the eye could see. There is no point as high as this in the rest of the entire continent. Rachiswater town lies directly on this latitude, out of sight, and I wished I could see around the curvature of the globe to the columns of my brother's palace – *my* palace – in the distance.

Jant and his pet savage emerged into the bailey and stood looking around, taking everything in. I quelled the urge to drop a block of ice on their bloody heads, and went down to meet them.

'This is my solar, which has to double as my state room. But welcome! Welcome! Eszai, like musicians, are appreciated everywhere.' I led out of the staircase into my chamber, where a scent of cloves pervaded the air. Snipe was pouring mulled ale into three pint mugs on the table. 'I'm sorry we only have beer; wine is expensive to import.'

'Beer is fine.' Jant looked around the room, at the few hangings I had managed to retrieve from Rachiswater, including one where he himself was embroidered like a black and white stork flying over the heads of a horde of Insects. He surveyed the table covered in letters, ledgers and coins, my high-backed chair draped in wolf pelts, the whitewashed walls – clean and as yet unembellished with frescos – and the decorations my servants had already started draping from the rafters in preparation for New Year's Eve. They had wound holly and ivy garlands along the rails of the hangings and twined laurel and ribbons above the doors, green for the old year out, white for the new year in. They had hung red and gold glass baubles from the mantelpiece, each one reflecting the flames. Beside me on the table a wreath of mistletoe and variegated ivy, more green and white, surrounded scarlet candles that gave off a nostalgic scent of cinnamon.

'It's very meagre, but we do what we can,' I said.

Jant nodded, then glanced up to my chandelier. It hung from a reinforced beam in the centre, and its glistening droplets broke the sunlight into thousands of tiny spectra shining and swinging on the walls. His eyes widened. 'That's hardly meagre! You brought a *chandelier* from Rachiswater?'

'Yes, my one whim. It weighs so much we had to pack it into a brick wagon with a team of four carthorses. We hauled it across torrents and pushed it by hand up slopes too rocky for the wheels to grip. It cost me, but it was the one thing I wasn't prepared to leave behind. And my chest of books, of course.'

Jant clasped his hands around the mug, strode to the fireplace and stood on its surround, with his back towards it to warm his wings. 'And you're preparing for New Year's?'

'Yes.' I shrugged. 'But we celebrate in a very modest way. My people work so hard to survive, they deserve a festival but our indulgence is unsophisticated. They'll swig beer and dance in my hall. It isn't like Rachiswater. It isn't your kind of thing. And the mountain cuisine is terrible ... How much bland and rubbery cheese is a man expected to eat, I ask myself.'

'So, no Shattering?'

I paused. 'We *may* try a Shattering, but nothing like on the scale of the lowlands.'

He spread his wings and blotted out the whole four-centred arch and the crackling flames. He had wrapped shawls around his wings' biceps to protect their leading edges, and they had frozen plastered to his feathers. I appreciated how tough he had to be. He flexed their fingers so the massive primary feathers, twice as long as mine, fanned open and closed. Ice rime surrounded the edges of each one, like blades of grass after a heavy frost.

The Rhydanne woman was striding rapidly up and down the room, prying into everything with rat-like glances. The shiny baubles attracted her – she leant close and tapped a claw on them – so before she could break anything Jant pulled out a chair and instructed her to sit down. She folded herself onto the seat, with no intention of letting go of her spear. She was rangy – well, they all are – rawboned and loose-jointed with the scraggy look of a woman who exercises too much. Her hatchet face wore a determined expression, which I didn't like. She whipped her ragged ponytail from her collar and shuffled off her coat, which was adorned with savage accoutrements: snail shells, bones and even teeth, such as you see in illustrations of Rhydanne in picture books. Some of her trinkets were quite disgusting, but she also wore an astonishing amount of crude silver and I wondered if she knew of a mother lode. I sat down as close as possible to the heat and waved Snipe to take another chair, but Jant did not relinquish the fireplace.

'So the Emperor chose her as an advocate?' I asked.

'No, no. *She* sought an audience with him. Dellin says that the Rhydanne of this area are starving. Your trappers and hunters are taking their prey.'

'We have to ensure our own livelihood, Comet. In fact, the Rhydanne are stealing our livestock. They've driven off fifty sheep and goats, and slaughtered them.'

Dellin raked her filthy fingernails on the tabletop until Jant translated for her. She was as quick of limb as of eye, fierce of look, half-sullen and half-defiant. Her untamed attitude made me watch her even more than I kept an eye on the Messenger. She seemed always poised to pounce, ready in the pause before a crouch or a leap. She hates me, I thought, amused. I continued: 'As a governor, nay, as a prince, I am entitled to defend my land by force against bandits.'

'Rhydanne aren't bandits.'

'They act like bandits, so they are bandits, and I am allowed to shoot them, Comet. In Lowespass the governor can fortify farmsteads against marauders. On the ranches in Ghallain the governor can raise a hue and cry. Carniss is no different. I have even lost my favourite horse, Rabicano, the best courser in the kingdom. Did you know that?'

'No.' He paused, and I could tell he was lying.

'Two of them ran around inside the corral, laughing, killing – on a spree as savage as foxes in a coop. They pounced onto Rabicano's back and stabbed him like matadors! They were worse than wolves – so they deserve to be treated like wolves! My captain shot one who was devouring Rabicano alive, tearing my horse's guts out and eating them! The other one unfortunately escaped. Now, Comet. I know my rights. These are internal Awian affairs, not part of the Castle's primary interest. Does the Emperor allow a governor to defend his possessions or not?'

'Possessions!' Dellin exclaimed. I thought she was merely copying my words, and stared at her until she said in heavily accented Awian, 'Carnich my possession. Not yours.'

Jant rattled off something in Scree and she replied at ten to the dozen. Piqued, I asked, 'If you're going to confer at my table, perhaps you'd care to translate.'

'She said that Rhydanne are the original inhabitants of Carniss. Therefore, if people can possess mountains the same way as they possess objects – which is impossible as all men roam over all mountains – then Darkling is the possession of Rhydanne, not Awians.'

'But they have never drawn territorial borders.'

'They don't think that way.'

'Well, you can't assume Awians won't settle above a certain arbitrary altitude. My people are adventurous, Comet, and this was empty country. My brother recognised it was available to be claimed by anyone who wanted to develop it. Yes, it is wasteland, but if it wasn't, Awians would have farmed it centuries ago. It is in our nature to develop land. This is progress. We are bringing civilisation to Darkling. My frontiersmen and the villagers of Eyrie are pleased to call this Awia, under my jurisdiction and the sound traditions of my country. Before we came this was unused land; now it is being put to a purpose.'

'It *was* used. It's a Rhydanne hunting ground. How many have you shot?'

'How many Rhydanne? Four, I think ...'

'Four!'

'They killed fifty goats! Which were all my people have to live on! Comet, our stock must have attracted the Rhydanne, because when we arrived we saw no natives whatsoever. The villagers told me Carniss was completely empty and no savages frequented it. Rhydanne were never here before.' I looked at the woman pointedly, and she shook her arms, jangling her bangles belligerently until she rang like a round of bells. Then she rested her hands on her knees, letting me see her long talons and readiness to scratch; she was as brutish as a wildcat. I said, 'Perhaps they see what we've achieved, our animals and our cabins, and want them for themselves. Maybe that's why they've advanced their grounds. Perhaps she has fabricated this story in an attempt to make us relinquish the land we have managed to tame. At any rate, you can see her grumbling doesn't stand up in law.'

Jant poured another beer and gave it to the Rhydanne, although I would have thought cheap spirits would suffice for her. And sure enough she drank it without savouring it and brandished the glass for more. He said, 'No one will see a hunter if they aren't deliberately seeking them. And anyway, they're nomadic. Dellin hunts towards the top of the mountains in summer and moves down in winter.'

'So she doesn't actually *live* here? She could just return to other grounds? What's the fuss about?' I laughed, and motioned the butler to pour the last of the beer.

'She said she needs the whole area. You can't just shunt them together!'

'Why not? I thought they ignored each other?'

'She needs wide grounds and lots of game to survive. There are other hunters up-slope so Dellin needs this space. Rhydanne range widely but if food is hard to find and she competes with another hunter he'll attack her.'

'Like wolves?'

'Not like wolves,' Comet said levelly. 'Like Rhydanne.'

'I'm sorry,' I said. 'I wasn't aware you were on their side.'

'I am simply here to negotiate.'

'The Castle always excels at remaining neutral,' I said, and Snipe smirked.

The Messenger glared. 'Raven, you can deal with me, or you can deal with the Emperor ... if you really prefer.' I said nothing and he continued, 'Have you ever met the Emperor? Would you like to?'

'I'm sure it won't be necessary.'

The savage sprang up and paced hyperactively around the table. She ran up into the window seat and stood gazing at the view. Jant gave me another look, then went and joined her. 'Come up,' he said.

'I'd rather not. It's cold.'

We fell silent. I knew how obstinate immortals could be. They act as if they own any place they happen to visit. Now, to talk to him I would have to sit with the draught clinging to my legs, in sight of the fangs of Capercaillie. 'Come on, Snipe,' I said, and we joined them in the triple bow window. I could feel the chill radiating from the glass, so tangible I could almost push my hand against its smooth flow. Snow had caught in the corners of each pane, lying like hammocks on the leads, and frost crystals had formed here and there in minute stars or thin networks as if spun by a spider made of ice.

He tapped the glass. 'Quite a feat, bringing up so much.'

'Thank you. Assembling it was the hardest part.'

'You can see everything from here.'

'Yes, but have you noticed the window faces away from Awia?'

'Towards the mountains?'

'Towards the mountains. I have no option, Jant. Rhydanne may not want me in Carniss but I don't want to be here either. If I had a choice I'd still be in Rachiswater. But I must make the best out of misfortune and do my utmost with what little I have. Do you know, Rhydanne have caused damage other than killing our livestock. They cut into our water pipes last summer. We were pumping drinking water from the glacier torrent, and my scheme was working perfectly until a Rhydanne or maybe several chopped holes in the pipes – a deliberate act of sabotage!'

'They were probably drinking from them.'

'As if we were providing water for their benefit!'

'They're used to taking whatever they can from the land. They'll take what you leave lying about as if nature had provided it.'

'Our property isn't "lying about".'

Jant picked up the book I had left on the cushion, flicked through it carelessly and splayed it face down on his thigh, cracking its spine.

I bit my teeth hard together. 'So you agree they are causing the problem?' I asked. 'First, they raid our traps, eat the animals and sell the pelts. Second, they vandalise my water supply. My colonists work extremely hard but the natives cream off what they can.'

'I'll talk to them, don't you worry. I'll make sure any forays cease. But there can't be many Rhydanne in Carniss. I think it's strange that they could cause so much havoc. Nevertheless I will visit them and tell you what they say. Our talks might take longer than I thought ...' He paused. 'Why are you looking frustrated?'

'Oh, nothing. It doesn't matter. I was thinking that of course we'll provide a feast tonight, as lavish as we can manage, as befits the honour of your visit. Snipe will show you your room, upstairs.'

He shook his head. 'No. I should stay somewhere neutral.'

'But there isn't anywhere else! You can't sleep out in the drifts.'

'Maybe down in Eyrie village?'

'You'll hear many tales against the Rhydanne there, I'm sure.'

Snipe ventured, 'My lord, may I make a suggestion?'

'Of course. Comet – Snipe, my steward, one of the many who is finding his Carniss life more rewarding than drudgery in Rachiswater.'

Snipe hesitated, frowning, then said, 'There *is* a hostel that isn't partial to natives or pioneers, but it isn't the sort of place an Eszai would stay.'

'I'm not your usual Eszai.'

'Well ... it's a trading post, called the Frozen Hound Hotel.'

'The Frozen Hound! Yes!' Dellin burst out with a torrent of chatter so fast it's a wonder her pinched cheeks could encompass such rapid words.

Jant listened and laughed. 'She said she'll show me the way. She prefers it to my staying here.'

I thought she'd used stronger terms than that. 'If you insist. I have never been to the Hound, but my steward goes there – don't you, Snipe?'

'Yes, my lord. To trade with Ouzel. She only has a few rooms but she rents them to anybody.'

'Does she trade with Rhydanne?' Jant asked.

'Yes, Comet. She barters their silver and furs for hardware and the food they can't make themselves. Ouzel's a formidable woman. Very eccentric, but what do you expect? She's lived there for years!'

'Dellin said the Hound is half an hour away.'

Snipe looked doubtful and wiped a drop of beer from the corner of his mouth. 'I'd make it two or more ... Ha! Well, it'd take us two, but yes, half an hour for a Rhydanne and even less for you, Comet. It's a few kilometres west, on the cliffs this side of the glacier.'

'Thank you.' Jant nodded. He picked up *Myths and Legends of Ancient Awia,* which rested like a moth on his thigh, and glanced at the cover. 'By Lightning Saker Micawater.'

'Yes, one of many,' I said eagerly. 'Have you read it?'

'Huh. Life's too short.'

'Even for an immortal?'

'Especially for an immortal.'

'I read factual books too,' I said. 'The sort you prefer. But Snipe only salvaged five books out of the whole library before Tarmigan stopped him. See how dog-eared it is? I've read it so many times I've practically worn it out. I miss my library ...'

'That's between you and your brother,' he said abruptly, as if he had suddenly recalled the reason why I was exiled. I wanted to steer his thoughts away from Tarmigan, back to the Rhydanne, and not onto books either; any new publications Jant may enthuse about will only serve to rub salt in my wounds.

I stood up. 'Would you like to see the settlement?' Dellin, who had been fidgeting with her bangles as if she thought their jingling would intimidate me, bounded to her feet and down past the arras. 'Her too. There's half an hour before dinner. And Snipe, accompany us.'

My gloves and scarf were warming on the mantelpiece. I avoid going outside as much as possible; the grasping cold permeates every inch of my being. I wrapped myself in my overcoat, cloth-of-gold scarf, sable fur hat and fur-lined boots, which took some time, and while I did so Jant examined the huge panels of carved limewood forming the chimney breast. 'What's this?' he asked suspiciously, pointing to my coat of arms in the centre. It was a large shield with no features whatsoever, topped by my prince's coronet rather than a plain governor's circlet, and supported by two Rachiswater eagles with their wings closed and beaks agape. But instead of holding blue roses in their free claws, with thorn branches entwining to form the mantle – as in my brother's shield – they held wolf pelts draped into an ornate mantle around the crest.

'It's my coat of arms,' I said.

'But there's nothing on it.'

'I left the escutcheon above the gateway smooth as well.'

'I noticed. What does it mean?'

'I'm deciding what emblem to adopt,' I said, lightly in response to his grimness. 'Since my brother expelled me I no longer wish to use thc family's coat of arms, but I'm entitled to one. So I'll keep those shields blank until I think of a heraldic cognisance for Carniss I can pass down the generations. A pair of frozen feet, perhaps, on a field blue with cold.'

He laughed, relieved. 'I see, I see. Or a tankard of this excellent beer?' He poured himself the last of it and, as he turned back to me, the edge of his wing caught a stack of letters and sent them all cascading to the floor.

'Damn!' He stepped back and put his mug down, but Snipe quickly knelt and scooped them all up.

'I'm sorry,' he said.

'Never mind,' said Snipe, who reached up and deposited a handful haphazardly on the table.

'I really am sorry.'

'It's all right,' I said, polite but infuriated. I collected the rest and tapped them into some semblance of the original pile. The sooner I am free from him the better. I led on and he followed, bearing his cumbersome wings at a greater distance from the table but perilously close to the fireplace. We went to the hall and I swung the door wide so he could see the empty room with folded tables resting against the walls. Two servants were up on stepladders fixing holly garlands to the beams. Then we descended to the floor below, down the spiral stairs, and Jant swept his hand along the wall, trailing his fingertips over the cold, rough stone. The blocks were neatly squared black granite, which is difficult to cut, and I could tell he was impressed.

We stopped on the landing beside a barred gate. The savage sniffed the air for some reason, but I pretended not to notice and addressed Jant. 'This is my treasury. Like the rest of the settlement, it's open to your view.' I selected my largest key and unlocked the grille, then a chrome-covered key opened the inside door. I pocketed the bunch and lifted a heavy lantern from its niche.

Its light flickered on stacks and stacks of neatly folded pelts, receding into the darkness. Each pile was fastened with a cardboard tag, grading them according to species, colour and quality. Dellin cried out, 'What have you done?' She pushed past us and walked between the pelts, into the gloom, then turned to us and we saw tears running down her face. 'Such waste! Such terrible waste!'

Jant snatched the lantern and went to inspect the furs. I followed him in and sat down on my chest of silver and gems, surrounded by the warm smell of fur and suede, the white tang of camphor.

The nearest were pure white wolf pelts, then subtly patched ibex skins, stacked flat like playing cards. There was chamois tan and beige, blue-white vair from squirrels, dark-chocolate zibeline from martens, and luxuriant ermine: long milky strips with black-tipped tails. There was velvety snow leopard, clouded mountain cat, the glossy sheen of mink and the silvery fluff of fox. Horns tied together in pairs hung from hooks along the walls: the black prongs of chamois, ibex knobbly and bowed, surprisingly gigantic for the size of the beast. There were smooth red deer tines and palmate elk. There was also a mound of the natives' woven rugs, which some customers in Awia will buy, even though their retarded designs are no more than broad stripes and most have no designs at all.

The savage strode up to me and demanded, 'How can animals replenish their numbers if you kill them all at once?'

'Don't be surprised if our hunting is more efficient than yours.'

'Answer her question!' said Jant.

'Comet, what she said is meaningless. This is just a fraction of the tremendous plenty. There is so much game that our trapping could never make any impact, even if we hunted a thousand times more thoroughly than we do. The mountains teem with game of all kinds. We could never have any effect on their numbers, because obviously more animals will roam in from further afield to take the place of the few we harvest.'

'But all these skins!' she wailed. 'What do you do with the meat?'

'Feed it to the dogs.'

'Do you sell the skins to Tarmigan?' Jant asked.

'Yes. Every month I send a full wagon train down to Rachiswater, under Snipe's guard. My brother's steward and various other merchants pay Snipe, who purchases our provisions and returns.'

'I see.'

'So this is just one month's hunting?' she whined in amazement. 'It's a year's worth of food! The scale ... twelve times this? Why work so hard? Why waste so much? You could freeze the meat and live off it for the rest of the year!'

'We don't eat carrion.'

'Soon you'll be eating nothing, because there'll be nothing left!'

Snipe was standing in the doorway. 'If we keep trapping, there might be fewer wolf attacks,' he said.

'Ah yes, the white wolves have been a nuisance. We must protect our children and beasts from them ... and from other carnivores.'

Jant scowled. 'Clearing wolves is one thing, but overhunting and inadvertently starving out Rhydanne is quite another.'

'Comet, I am not overhunting, I assure you.'

'Show me the rest of your fortress.' He slammed the lantern back into its niche and we descended into the overpowering mountain sunlight. I led them through the bailey, between the chalets, as I had planned, using the track furthest from the armoury and our storehouses full to bursting – which would give the lie to my assurance that our livestock and trapping were all we had to live on. It was true, in a way – I needed every last sack of flour, because my troops will quadruple the population of Carniss.

We passed the dog compound and stable where the sleds were kept. The barking was deafening. 'Why do you have so many dogs?' Jant asked.

'They're sled dogs.'

'Yes, but hundreds!'

'Only one hundred. I'm making sure all my villagers know how to dog sled. Mushing is the most convenient way to get around.'

'What are those buildings over there?'

'The settlers' cabins. You can see how dedicated they are.'

'If we didn't work hard, we'd perish in days,' Snipe added. The log cabins in neat lines were indeed poor but meticulously kept as I had ordered. Every one had foundations of rough stone and covered stores of firewood in the space where their sloping roofs reached the ground. Their shutters were cheerfully open, and smoke poured from every chimney.

'And that,' said Jant, pointing to the empty barracks. 'What's that?'

'A new smokehouse, as yet unfinished.'

'I see.'

He doesn't believe me, I thought, and felt a rising sense of dread. He doesn't believe a word I'm saying. I fought the panic down, lest it show on my face, and breathed steadily in the thin air. I swung my arms casually, although my palms were sweating.

We ascended between snow-covered outcrops, every one of which we had used in our building, so the fronts of some cabins emerged from roofed-over cracks in the rock; a terrace of stables had been built against a crag providing their rear walls, and other houses were ingeniously constructed over shallow chasms, which gave them cellars for cool stores in the summer. We ascended a causeway between granite slabs stained red with iron ore and I noticed that neither Jant nor Dellin felt the need to use the hand-rail. Eventually we arrived at the end of the promontory, where on a clean swathe stood a tall pylon of flexible green pine. We walked up to its base and I patted its timbers.

'And what on earth's that? A bell tower?'

'Another of my innovations.' I said. 'For avalanches and earth-quakes. If the ground shakes, the bell tolls and gives us warning. What do you think, Comet?' I added proudly. 'Rather remarkable for two years' work?'

'It's extraordinary.'

Our Rhydanne guest had been gazing around with her arms tightly folded, paying no notice whatsoever. She was as petulant as a teenager on a school tour. It's typical of Rhydanne: as soon as you bring them to a serious topic their attention disappears, they become obstreperous and dash away to start drinking. Sure enough, she made some remark and set off back to the gatehouse, her moccasin boots squeaking the snow. We followed.

'She's hungry,' said Jant.

'They always seem to be hungry.'

'Fast metabolism. Otherwise they'd freeze.'

'So they must eat continually? Yes? And drink?'

'There's stuff in their blood that naturally stops them freezing solid.'

'Gin?'

'It's metabolised from alcohol. That's why they have to drink all the time. Would you be comfortable in a minus-forty blizzard?'

I winced. 'Considering she knows you're an Eszai, she doesn't pay you much respect.'

He smiled, as if he preferred it that way. 'You don't know the half of it! You should have seen me trying to put her in a coach.'

The awe-inspiring bulk of Capercaillie reared in front of us, dwarfing the gatehouse. Jingling goat bells echoed back from its rock walls, giving the impression that the mountains themselves were ringing. 'Capercaillie always takes my breath away,' I said, and laughed. 'Literally, at the beginning. Everyone had altitude sickness, and although we're acclimatised now it still sometimes affects us. But I believe my climbers will scale Capercaillie one day. We need to discover a means to breathe up there.'

'It's called Klannich,' said Jant.

'Pardon?'

'That mountain is called Klannich. Not Capercaillie.'

'Claniss?'

'Klann*ich*.'

'To you, perhaps, but not to us.'

'It means the Hitching Post of the Sun,' he insisted.

'How pretty. It had no name on our maps – none of them did – so I named them all.' I stopped and pointed to the long arête which joined the two summits. 'Raven's Ridge. And that one's Becard Spur after my father.'

Seeing me pointing, the Dellin woman demanded a translation. She heard it in dismay and clawed the air. 'No! It's always been called Klannich!'

'Then what do you call Raven's Ridge?'

'That's Klannich too!'

'And Becard Spur?'

'Chir Klannich too!'

'So all the mountains have the same name?'

'Becard Spur is part of Klannich. It's such a short run from the summit the Rhydanne see no point in giving it another name.' Jant continued warningly, 'You think you've travelled far, but by Rhydanne standards you're still sitting on your brother's doorstep.'

We began walking again. 'I had assumed Rhydanne didn't name places. I thought they lacked our impulse to categorise.'

'You have very strange ideas about them, Raven. Of course they name features. How else could they hunt if they couldn't refer to places?'

'Like pumas, I suppose – just taking down whatever game they come across. Many people say Rhydanne don't have exploratory minds. I thought they never classified the world around them. They certainly don't have any art.'

Comet switched to High Awian for effect: 'Raven, I have never heard such nonsense! It's a matter of degree.'

'Not of kind?'

'No! You exalt history and heroes in your place names; Rhydanne may remember where a great hunter killed a fearsome bear. They have little parables too, and let me tell you, their titles are more poetic than yours! Far behind Klannich, there's a mountain which no Awian has ever seen. It breathes sulphurous smoke and steam from holes on its bare slopes, and my grandmother called it the Mountain Where All Clouds Are Born. On the western rim of Scree Plateau is the residue of a lake; no water but just caustic soda – white crystals covering black grit as far as the eye can see. Eilean called it the Tarn of Stinging Salt. If you trek north to the furthest horn in the range, you'll see it ends in a mountain as large as Klannich. In the remote past an earthquake sheared it in half. The half that remains is a neat wedge. It looks out over the Paperlands with a two-thousand-metre rock face as smooth as an iron, and Eilean called it Bhachnadich: "God's Doorstop" . . .' He was becoming angry at himself for seeming to side with the Rhydanne. His speech dried up, like a stream into sand, and he sighed.

'Let it pass,' I said.

'Let it pass.' He reverted to the common tongue. 'You can call it Capercaillie if you want.'

I began to think it would be easier to deceive him than I had feared. His memories were his weakness. Beside the keep the northern wall wasn't yet finished, and some men on top were adding a course of stone. All were silhouetted against the sky, but a thinner black shape crouched nearby with his knees jutting out and arms folded across them, his long fingers hanging down like claws. Jant shaded his eyes and looked up. 'That one's a Rhydanne.'

'Yes. I employed him two years ago. He carried the first rope up the cliff, from which we ran thicker cables and mounted our pulleys. He's still useful if we need someone to scale rock faces to fix the first supports for our climbers. Or if the builders drop something, he shins down the cliff and fetches it.'

'So he doesn't do any building?'

'No.' I frowned. 'They're not capable of building.'

'They built Scree pueblo.'

'By an accumulation of small dens, as rabbits build warrens, so I'm told. There is something of a difference between Scree and Carniss.'

'Do you pay him?'

'Oh, yes. In meat and drink.'

Dellin was aghast. She raised her face and called to him. He ignored her, I was pleased to see, and when she continued her savage yells he shuffled around on the wall summit to face outwards, and presented her with the mute expanse of his back. She looked downcast and started spinning her spear as if to show she didn't care.

As we approached the staircase turret, hobnailed boots echoed in the undercroft beside it. A group of explorers walked out, blinking from the sunlight and laughing at some joke. Then they sighted the Messenger and turned as white as snow. My guard captain was leading them. He came to join us and bowed low, then put a finger on the bridge of his sunglasses and pushed them onto his forehead.

Three Rhydanne bearers loped out of the passage, covered in the climbers' equipment, with coils of rope across their bodies and karabiners jangling in bunches from their belts. They had adapted items of our clothing, and wore mismatched T-shirts and coloured scarves with their suede parkas. One had forsworn his native clothes completely and wore fyrd fatigues, which is understandable as our clothes are better quality. They all had necklaces made of pierced pound coins; they carried skis over their shoulders, and ice-axe handles projected from their rucksacks. When they saw that the explorers had gone inside they cheerfully dropped all the gear in the snow and dashed to the captain's house, where many Rhydanne footprints converged on a barrel on the veranda.

I said to Jant, 'I'm glad you have the chance to see we employ Rhydanne as porters – and guides too; they show us the best spots for prey, silver and gems. Don't they, Crake?'

'Yes,' said the captain, 'when they behave.'

'Don't they work well?' Jant asked.

'They tend to get bored. Then they dump our packs and shoot off into the corries. And they seem childlike. They don't understand money at all.'

'They're not stupid.'

'I'm not calling them stupid. They just don't see the point of exploration. And they have a really short attention span.'

'Perhaps that's a comment on the attractions of your conversation?'

I stepped in. 'Did you find anything?'

'Yes, my lord. Karbhainn found us a fissure with a vein of tin ore.'

'Tin? Not silver?'

'Not today, my lord. Cassiterite with tourmaline and topaz in the same vein. Possibly arsenic too.'

'I once read tin was easy to smelt,' I said. 'Can we do that here?'

'I'll look into it.'

'Excellent. Show the seam to the chief miner tomorrow.'

'Yes, my lord.'

'And give Karbhainn a double helping of gin.'

The Rhydanne began drumming on the lid of the barrel, chanting in Awian, 'Captain Crake, Captain Crake, Captain Crake, we've thirst to slake!'

'I'd better go pay them.' He smiled, cracking his chapped lips. He hurried to the barrel and the Rhydanne all stood back, jostling each other like crows. He brought a ladle and stack of tin cups from inside the house, levered the lid off, ladled out some gin and passed it to the nearest bearer – who downed it in one and reached for more.

The Dellin woman exclaimed, 'No! What is he doing?' She ran to the captain, dashed the ladle from his hand and pushed him hard. He slipped but regained his balance. He looked to me for help, as Dellin leant over the barrel. She sniffed it and grimaced in disgust. She put her weight against it, rocked it forward and over into the snow. Clear spirit poured out, melting straight through the snow then running in little gullies out of the soaked patch and sinking deep. The Rhydanne together gave a howl of dismay.

All three dropped to their knees and started scooping up the spirit. They knocked back handfuls, licked their palms, elbowing each other out of the way. A woman bedecked in beads snatched a cup and scraped slush into her water bottle. A youth lowered his face to gin pooled in the heel of a frozen footprint, and sucked it from the ground. Dellin set about them, yelling, kicking and slapping. She grabbed the youth and pulled him to his feet, but as soon as she let go he knelt down again, lapping the rivulets.

Karbhainn peered into the barrel and reached in with his cup. Dellin hauled at his ponytail. He batted her aside. She scratched his shoulders and kicked the barrel till it boomed.

All the Rhydanne bawled at her, and Jant shouted at them all until his cheeks flushed red.

'Just tell me what she's saying!' I said.

'Karbhainn!' Dellin was shrieking into the tall Rhydanne's face. 'You were a hunter once! What happened to you? What have you *become*?' The captain tried to grab her but she darted away and he flailed after her, as ungainly as a bear trying to snatch soap. 'Are you flatlanders, to work for pay? They're fobbing you off with worthless drink! With rotgut spirit! No Awian would work for that!'

The Rhydanne sat back on their haunches and regarded her with astonishment. They had scratched up all the gin-laden slush and now surrounded a large, ragged hole in the snow. 'Believe me!' she begged. 'I've seen the lowlands. Featherbacks have such riches that this is a joke. It's poison!' She booted the barrel so hard it cracked.

I said, 'Comet, call her off. She's upsetting my porters.'

'She has a point. That stuff stinks.'

'If you don't call her back, the guards will arrest her.'

'Listen to me!' Dellin pleaded. She whirled round and pointed at me. 'He's using you like goats – all of you! He is stealing your self-sufficiency. Turning you not even into herders but into herd animals! Karbhainn, aren't you ashamed? You used to be the best hunter in Chir Klannich!'

The tall Rhydanne did start to look embarrassed, so as Jant drew breath for his next translation I said, 'Call your wildcat off.'

'How much do you pay them?' he demanded. 'It hardly seems a fair wage.'

I turned to the gatehouse and prepared to call the archers.

'There's no need for that!' He glared at me. 'Dellin! Shira Dellin, violence won't win! You'll make the featherbacks hate you!'

'But they—'

'The porters made their own choices. Come here!'

She snarled and reluctantly returned to us. Jant took hold of her spear. 'Put your trust in me and the Castle.'

'Let go!'

'All right, but calm down.'

I said coldly, 'I can see who is the troublemaker.'

'She's under control.'

'She's completely unreasonable!'

'Raven, if you can't overlook this entirely, at least be noble enough to give her a chance.'

I turned my back and climbed the stairs, and did not speak until we were seated at the table in the relatively warm solar. The servants served goat's cheese soup, roast ibex and sauerkraut. Jant instructed Dellin not to drink from the gravy boat, then he turned to me and said, 'So you're using Rhydanne as cheap labour.'

'Cheap? No. Everybody has to work. You should see how little my people live on – I can't spare more for Rhydanne. But yes, we're working hand in hand with some Rhydanne, the enlightened ones. Isn't that what you want? We're bringing progress to Darkling. I keep telling you. Some have learnt a lot from us already. In fact, several hunters have been so keen to offer their services that they climbed into our compound.'

'Of course, they had no choice,' said Dellin. 'They're dying of hunger.'

'But we are supplying their material needs and improving their lot.' I said. 'Food and drink, so they no longer need to hunt. Comet, I am happy to cooperate, but you must stop their raids.'

Jant drew a deep breath, deeper and longer than anyone else in the world could, to fill big Rhydanne lungs, then the air sacs inside his long bones – femurs and humeri – and two deep in his back under the roots of his wings. It is a wonder he left any air in the room. Then he sighed long enough to empty them all at once. He seemed frustrated and downcast. For me, the worst thing about this place is the uneasy cold, obtrusive every hour of the day and night, but he will never be rid of the humiliating memories of his goatherd past. Good, I thought. An ego as strong as his can be brittle too and I can drive an apposite word into any crack in his self-esteem.

'Does Carniss remind you of your youth?' I asked.

'This is a holiday resort compared to Mhor Darkling.'

'Do you think the Rhydanne at the Frozen Hound will listen to you?'

'Yes,' he said. 'Yes, they will stop taking your domestic animals. Never fear. I should leave now, while there's still enough light.'

I glanced at the window and the sun was indeed grazing Capercaillie's nearer peak. Then it was coat, hat and boots again, and out into the attendant cold. Night comes on too fast in winter, and faster here than in Rachiswater, as Capercaillie rapaciously blots out the setting sun. The oblique winter light cast the long shadow of my gatehouse over the bailey – the snow had turned dark blue in its shade, and the colour dappled every hollow. We passed through the undercroft passage and Dellin curiously examined the carts parked on one side, with sacks of rock salt, bales of fodder and barrels of gin between them. At the gate, below my blank escutcheon, I said goodbye to Jant and watched them shoulder their packs. They took the gruelling ascent towards the glacier at a loping pace and gradually shrank into the distance, tiny at the heads of two long, regular chains of footprints – the only tracks over the snowfield made nacreous with all the colours of dusk.

JANT

We left the keep and began walking up to the trading post. Where the slope levelled out to a snowfield on the bank high above the glacier, I paused and glanced back down to the promontory.

Raven was still standing where we had left him, tiny at the entrance of his gatehouse. His black coat hung in cornet folds to his ankles, hiding his feet. His steward had left his side but he remained, looking up at us. I could just make out the blur of his face muffled up between fur collar and fur hat. God, his scar had shocked me. It was terrible – a crevasse from just below his right eye to the corner of his mouth. He might have lost that eye if Tarmigan hadn't been such an excellent swordsman. I know what Raven must have felt – I've felt the pain of a cut as deep as that. In fact, the Wheel scar carved into my shoulder by my gang leader in Hacilith is a good deal longer than Raven's blemish, but my Wheel was a sign of belonging, albeit to a gang. Raven's is a scar of exclusion. With all that's happened to him it's a miracle he could bear it so nobly; he was still every inch a prince.

The cloud was closing in and his figure faded as wisps blew past. In thinner patches his outline resumed its clarity: it firmed up, ebbed from view, then gradually became less and less visible until he greyed out completely and was gone.

Dellin continued to crunch across the snow. She realised I wasn't following and stopped to look back. I had grown used to her rhythmic footsteps, and when they ceased the silence was absolute. It thrummed, like a pressure on the ear. The still majesty of the mountains struck me, increasing until I was overwhelmed by the silence. Slowly I became aware of a constant, very distant sound like surf, the endless rush of wind in the high cirques kilometres away.

'Jant, we don't have much time!'

'I'm coming ...' I whispered, then cleared my throat and called, 'Coming, Dellin!' As I walked I felt inside my jacket and brought out the letter I'd stolen. If you know me, by now you'll have realised it was no accident that I knocked over the pile in Raven's room. The top letter had caught my interest – I was positive the handwriting belonged to Francolin Wrought – and tipping them all onto the floor was the only way I could think of pinching it.

I smoothed the envelope and studied the writing. I have often carried Francolin's letters and his crabbed script is unique. But he was involved in the rebellion and Tarmigan exiled him. Why should he be corresponding with Raven? The envelope had no seal – stranger and stranger – so I opened it and unfolded the letter. It was in code. Ah, Francolin, you hoary-headed son of a bitch, what are you up to? I scanned the lines of letters and knew immediately it wasn't a cipher I'd seen before. It wasn't any of those used by the Awian nobility, which are very prosaic and easy to crack – after all, they rarely hide much more than gossip. Neither was it one of the Eszai's codes, by far the most difficult to decipher – not least because I invented many of them myself. It shouldn't take me long to figure out. In fact the trickiest part will be interpreting Francolin's handwriting.

I read while I walked, treading in Dellin's footprints, and found Francolin's encryption was just a simple transposition. He had written in Plainslands, moved each letter four to the left in the alphabet and removed the gaps between the words. It was so laughably straightforward that I worked it out in my head.

November 29th

To Raven Rachiswater from Francolin Wrought, greetings.

As promised, I have dispatched my Select troops and you will receive them in approximately thirty days, depending on conditions at your end. It is considered good luck, is it not, to welcome a visitor to herald in the New Year? Well, you shall have five hundred.

Each man is loyal to myself – and to you, of course, my lord – and hand-picked for our purpose. You must ensure the sleds are in prime condition, for speed is of the essence.

I would be grateful for prompt payment. I have precious little here. I fear my steward left in charge of Wrought is lining his pockets, draining the coffers I have spent my life assiduously filling. The Castle keeps close control of Lowespass's finances. You would think a noose encircles this fortress with the rope extending straight to the Emperor's hand. If you send me funds I can scatter money around the court. Tarmigan plummets in popularity as the taxes levied for his indulgences soar, and our partisans grow in numbers.

My lord prince, keep your spirits high! I trust from the tone of your last letter that your mood has improved and I assure you again all is not lost. I understand the pain of enduring this bleak winter – Lowespass is a dismal valley. Constant sleet, Insects everywhere, my living quarters seem to predate the Pentadrica and the latrines don't work. You are isolated from the court but I am banished from the side of the daughter I love and, at the rate Wrought is falling into poverty, I fear for her future. This terrible state of affairs will not last. Two years is not too long to wait for the throne.

I risk you interpreting this as a bitter irony but, nevertheless, with all my heart I wish you a very happy New Year, and may our Wishes shatter and release the very future.

Yours faithfully, Francolin.

I see. This explains everything. I clenched my fist in rage and looked downhill – only the black parapet of Raven's gatehouse was visible now. He thought he could trick me. *Me*! He is pressing ahead with his ludicrous vendetta and all the time he *knows* this will bring the Castle into it. He's flouting Imperial authority. He's prepared to deny San as well as Tarmigan!

But I admit, I was furious mainly because he'd successfully pulled the wool over my eyes. Francolin said his men would be arriving around New Year's Eve – a week on Thursday. I should warn the king. No. I should inform the Emperor and he can decide how to tell Tarmigan.

'Raven Rachiswater!' I said aloud. 'How bloody stupid can you be?' I folded the note, slipped it into my jacket and ran to catch up with Dellin, thinking the while.

If Raven increased the archers on his towers and reinforced his gate, his 'compound' would be as strong as Lowespass, where Francolin already was. They both had fortresses. Francolin would have swarms of troops, so why had he only sent five hundred men? Five hundred couldn't possibly stand against the king, so Raven must be planning some ruse. A lightning attack? If he was fast he could storm the palace and seize the throne before Tarmigan knew what was happening. One division could overpower the palace guard if they had no time to call for reinforcements. Of course Raven knows every approach to Rachiswater, all the streets of the town, all the vulnerabilities of the palace, the habits of the sentries, every corridor and secret passage!

What's this about sleds? Dog sleds would be the swiftest way to transport five hundred men to the lowlands. Maybe they'd change to horseback once they reached Rachiswater, but up here dogs have every advantage – and Raven had so many. God ... Raven would want to catch the king unprepared ... On New Year's Day! Yes, I felt certain, either on New Year's Day itself or the following day. Awians celebrate so passionately that they have hangovers all the first week of January. When better to swipe the throne from under your brother's arse than on the biggest festival of the year?

I take it back: Raven isn't stupid at all. God knows what he wants to do to Tarmigan! But, for sure, if I let him attack Rachiswater he'll split the heart of Awia in two. We are looking at nothing less than civil war.

'You're being completely useless!' Dellin's exclamation rang on the air. 'What are you thinking about?'

'Listen! Raven is receiving soldiers to depose his brother!'

'Good.'

'But there'll be bloodshed in Awia!'

'Good!'

'I have to do something about it,' I explained, as if to a child.

'Stare at a scrap of paper, perhaps? Jant, we are walking through a *crevasse field* and you are taking *no notice* of your surroundings!'

'We're walking through a what?'

'A crevasse field! Here is a fissure. *There* is a fissure; who knows how deep? Some are covered by snow. I tried to lead you but you weren't even watching!'

I glanced about. Sure enough lenticular cracks were open all around us, in roughly parallel clusters. Looking back at our footprints I realised Dellin had zigzagged artfully between treacherous chasms rendered invisible by a thin crust of ice.

'I'm sorry.'

She threw a pair of crampons down at my feet. 'Put these on!'

As I buckled them on – metal ones, which I suspect had been Laochan's – she continued, 'I sincerely hope the featherbacks do start fighting each other! Are you going to help me, or join them?'

'I have to help you, as the silver man commanded.'

'But you didn't support me! You let Raven talk on and on! You saw the pelts from hundreds of kills?'

'Yes.'

'And the poison they were doling out to those hunters?'

'Yes—'

'Well, why didn't you *do* anything about it?' She flourished her spear. 'I could skin him myself! The way he looked at me, considering me less than a goat! Did you see that too?'

'Yes, actually.'

'But you didn't stop him! By the Huntress! This is the service the Castle gives Rhydanne!'

I sighed. Dellin had held her own against Raven with such magnificent determination I hadn't been able to keep from smirking. Now that she was turning that disdainful attitude on me, she was spicing my amusement with great admiration.

Her features set in anger. 'Stand still! I'm going to rope us together. See this loop? Thread it on your belt.'

I did so and she passed a rope through it, deftly twisted a knot and tied it around her waist. 'For want of a proper harness . . . If you fall down a crevasse your belt will cut into you like a lasso into bear fur and squish your guts but at least you won't plummet to your death. Now, it's nearly dark and a blizzard's coming.'

'How long will it take to reach the Hound?'

'The rest of our lives, if we don't look sharp!'

And so we ran. I followed her, her long legs scissoring ahead of me, elbows flashing at her sides, her tight bottom bobbing at the top of my vision. Her long hair flowed down her thin back. Our footsteps crunched lightly on the crust of ice covering the snow. It was transparent but pitted, having been warmed by the sun and refrozen every day. Toe down, the crampons bit; toe up, they flicked out tiny ice fragments, giving me the impression we were running across the surface of a gigantic crème brûlée.

On our right the cliffs soared up into a flaky arête. Fine powder snow hung in their folds and fanned out at the foot of each to merge with the snowfield. Glass-clear ice filled the cracks in the cliffs, in unbroken shafts for hundreds of metres as if it had been poured in to freeze there. Rock columns, their edges as sharp as knives, stood proud of the rock face. Shards shattered from them formed mounds at their base, smoothed by the deep drifts.

We crossed the long shadows of Klannich's aiguilles striping the snow, cast equally across the surface of the clouds building up below us. Our shadows angled over the ice as we ran on, out of Raven's manor and into an alien world.

On our right the crags closed towards us; on our left a steep pitch of fifty metres or so fell to the glacier. The snowfield was narrowing and becoming the Turbary Track, a trade route that ran unbroken alongside the glacier, up to its source and over the pass at the head of the valley. It ascended between torn peaks and snaked across cols for over a hundred kilometres, past the impossible cone of Stravaig, onto the high plateau to Scree pueblo.

The sun set behind the ridge at the head of the glacier and the temperature suddenly dropped. The snowfields greyed in the fading light. I took my sunglasses off and smeared grease on my lips from a little leather pot Dellin had given me. Grey-brown clouds were gathering over the head of the valley and yet more clouds were moving in placid herds around the contour of the cliffs and joining them. Thick nimbus was forming on the arc of Klannich's ridge, blowing off and building into one great mass – the cloud base was lowering until the summit of Klannich then the tops of the lower peaks disappeared from view.

We passed a cairn of rubble, to which Dellin gave a wide berth, so I called, 'What's that?'

'A crevasse marker!'

'Why is that one marked and none of the others?'

She huffed a laugh. 'It gave someone a nasty shock! Maybe their partner is still down there!'

The crevasses curved out on our left, like wrinkles on an old woman's face. Those closest to us were the shallowest, elongated ovals and almond-shaped holes. I could see recent snow at the bottom of the nearest one as if the old woman had packed make-up into her wrinkles. In the distance clouds were creeping down from the top of the valley and obscuring the source of the glacier. The glacier's surface was less dirty there, where the ice was new. Its broad tail curved up and branched into three, no longer striped but pure white, emerging from the snowfields of the cirques that fed it.

'I see the Hound!' Dellin cried.

'Where?'

She pointed to the cliff on our right, buttressed by a jumble of snow-sheeted boulders, but we were loping along so quickly I couldn't see where she was indicating. I stared at the boulders until my eyes stung – and a slow movement caught my attention. Above them a black shape was flapping like a huge bat.

'I see a flag!' I called to Dellin.

'Yes! So we can find the Hound against the snow!'

Where on earth was it, then? I scanned the cliffs and realised that the boulder pile below the crag *was* the Frozen Hound Hotel. Just as growths on tree bark resolve into a face, or clouds floating past morph into maps of the world, now I saw that the crevice in the centre was a doorway, and a zigzag cleft below it was a staircase carved into the rock. Diverse recesses at differing levels and of various sizes must be shuttered windows. I couldn't tell how far the Frozen Hound extended. It rambled away on both sides under the shelter of the cliff and merged indistinguishably into the rest of the talus froth and ice.

Dellin stopped and crouched down. I anticipated some disaster and braced myself with the rope but she beckoned me over. We had come upon a set of tracks proceeding in the same direction. 'A Rhydanne?' I asked.

'Yes, just one, about two hours ahead. A hunter, probably, and a poor one – he only has bone crampons.' She spread her hand like a bird's claw over one of the heel marks. 'It's good to have footprints to follow among these crevasses.' A snowflake landed on her nose. She brushed it away, grinned at me, then we were up and running again, with scarcely enough light to see by. All the time I was thinking, she's fantastic. I admired her skill, her knowledge of genuine things. And why did I never notice before how cute her bum is? Bobbing in repetitive motion, her bottom hypnotised me and I ran almost in a trance.

Further on, a double set of prints curved in and joined us. Dellin pointed out scuffed snow on the shelves of the cliff where two Rhydanne had climbed up, and we followed their footholds, sipping the freezing air with gritted teeth.

Another flake, white against the steel sky, then a gust of wind blew and the snow began falling heavily. I pulled my hood down to my brows, slitted my eyes and turned my cheek to it. In a few minutes I'll be in the warm with my hands wrapped around a glass of whisky, I thought. I couldn't wait.

We climbed through shrouds of snow slung between the rock pinnacles, kicking footholds clear in every crevice. The snow we dislodged fell and rolled down the slope, gathering more and ending up at the bottom as fair-sized snowballs. Flurries swirled across my vision, left to right from the head of the valley. The granite front of the trading post came and went through them. It was so deeply blanketed it rose in a smooth, white tump. Hummocks were extensions leading off on all sides, passages and rooms, their roofs all varying heights. Some had two storeys, others were tumbledown as if burrowing into the cliff face.

We reached some steps where yesterday's snowfall had been shovelled clear and piled on either side. The blizzard was now driving grey and the sky so black I could no longer distinguish between it and the outline of the cliff tops above us. Snow was sticking to our clothes and freezing there: I was covered in it like a suit of armour and Dellin was completely grey against the pitch black, with lines at her elbows, knees and around her neck where the snow had cracked away.

We passed a bothy where the heaped snow was dotted with trodden-in mule droppings, each one surrounded by a brown ring varying in size depending on how long it'd been there. Goat bleats swept on the wind; a low rattle of copper bells, then a louder jingle as one beast shook himself. We walked alongside the passage from the bothy to the front of the trading post. It was a door dark with creosote and two windows shuttered so tightly no light leaked from them. Smoke poured from a stout stone chimney and vanished immediately on the wind. So many extensions led off that the building looked like a grey mite: a rugged body surrounded by uneven, ugly legs.

I walked straight into a cane with a beer bottle on top and set it rattling. I stared until my eyes watered and could just make out a few more, planted in a line in the snow. Good signs to attract Rhydanne – and here was one for Awians: the creaking timbers of the flagpole. Its weather-tattered flag cracked and flapped in the blackness above us, showering us with ice grains and unfurling momentarily to reveal a device of a white dog rampant.

Dellin released the rope from her waist with a couple of deft moves, left it trailing and barged straight in. The door banged shut behind her. I sighed and coiled the rope around my arm. Alone now, I became aware of the colossal space around me, without being able to see it. Only gasping logic told me that the inhumanly vast valley pass still lay ahead, the glacier stretched from end to end of the landscape below me, and Klannich's array of spines skewered the deficient air a thousand metres above.

A multi-layered cornice as thick as a pie crust curled off the eaves over the door. I pressed my glove to the deeply weathered wood. Its grain projected like the bones on the back of the Emperor's hand. There'll be other Rhydanne inside, I thought, and felt apprehensive. Then a fine contempt rose within me. I can deal with any Rhydanne. I'm not a boy now, as I was when they hounded me from Scree Plateau. I worked a hand under my parka and tugged at my sword hilt but the damn thing had frozen fast into the scabbard.

Fuck it. My mouth was dry with dehydration, my tongue stuck to my palate and my face was so numb with cold I couldn't feel it. I pushed the door wide and went inside.

Many pairs of glowing pale gold eyes stared at me from a range of spiky silhouettes. The door slammed shut behind me on its springs. I stepped forwards, blinking at the brightness of the fireplace in the centre of the room. The silhouettes resolved into a handful of Rhydanne sitting at tables, backlit by its red light. Some further in lounged on cushions and rugs on the ground and against the walls. Others in niches recessed into the walls made the room look rather like a dovecote. I had never seen so many in one place before.

A few Awians, halfway through a game of cards, occupied the table nearest to the fire. I shrugged the rope from my shoulder, flung it on a table and eased the crossbow strap and scabbard from my back. Slabs of snow fell from the creases of my coat and thudded to the floor. I hung my crossbow bag on the back of a chair, unwound the scarf from my face, unhooked my frozen coat from my aching wings and dropped it on the table.

The Rhydanne uttered not a word and continued to stare like a pride of lions. The Awian trappers rustled their wings nervously and lowered their gaze but they hadn't continued with their game. They were listening.

The room smelt, I could sense it now my nose was defrosting, of a mixture of gloopy meat stew, the kind of thick, half-burnt gravy that sticks to the side of the pan; musty goat bedding; dog hair; creosote;

lanolin; the sandy smell of crushed rock and, above all, rugs soaked with slush and almost rotten. There was also sappy pine smoke and whisky. The scents I've come to associate with Rhydanne.

On all sides dark doorways led away. In the middle, on the stone chimney hood, hung an old dog lead, an iron spring trap and a shabby pair of snowshoes. Two huge, white avalanche dogs slept in front of the grate. Their ribcages rose and fell, their lips flopped back from drying canines. The breed was used by the Rhydanne for hunting, but their senses are so fine-tuned they can give advance warning of an avalanche. A couple of their canvas sled harnesses and the packs they can carry hung on the nearby wall.

I looked down the room for Dellin. She was already sitting on the floor at the far end, talking animatedly to a couple of hunters, but I couldn't hear what she was saying. The chunks of wood spat and crackled in the hearth and sparks whirled up the flue. A patter of feet and two Rhydanne children, one thigh-high, the other so small he ran under the table without touching it, dashed to me and stopped just short of crashing into my knees. They turned up their faces and stood regarding me solemnly with big cat eyes.

'Hello,' I said.

The smaller boy looked to the larger one. Their faces were very pinched, pointed noses and chins, framed by black hair tangled with neglect.

'If they bother you, just cuff their ears,' a voice resounded from behind the fireplace. It was a fleshy voice, and added in Awian, 'If you can catch them. I never can.'

I stepped to one side, peered round the fireplace and saw that it had been obscuring the bar. A woman stepped out from behind it, untying her apron strings. She thrust out her arm as brawny as a man's and offered me a hand like a side of ham. 'Ouzel,' she announced, in tones so loud she made the tankards rattle. 'Welcome to the Frozen Hound!'

I shook her hand, feeling rather put out. 'Call me Jant. You don't seem surprised.'

'Last March Dellin told me she was going to find the silver man, and when she came in just now – she's over there, see? – and said she had company, I thought: who else would the Emperor send? Though I never thought I'd see an immortal in the flesh. Ha ha. Excuse me, Jant. I'm sorry. Been up here a long time. Forgot my manners. Do you want some kutch?'

'*Anything* apart from kutch.'

She strode back behind the bar and vigorously slopped stew and dumplings into a wooden bowl. 'I only sell homebrew, kutch and spirit. Here you go.'

'Thanks. I'll have water and a whisky.'

She turned her back, unhooked one of the cups, opened the spigot on a cask, and filled it. Her voice was no less stentorian for her facing away. 'Only beer, kutch and spirit. You see, everything has to be carried up here. By mules and my good self, ha ha.'

'Where are you from?'

'Oh, where people are from has become important, has it? I thought that'd happen, though it never should, ha ha. Well, I'm from Rachiswater – but a very different Rachiswater from the one Raven knows.'

'Yes, Raven is the problem.'

'Well, it's very good of you to come and sort our problem out.'

The bar was a low wall of coarse stone topped by a great timber slab, its grain worn to smooth corrugations. Behind it, rows of small kegs on stands nestled like fat suckling piglets. Above it, hefty stoneware bottles, all carefully corked and labelled, lined the shelves from which all shapes and sizes of tankard hung on pottery or stitched leather handles. It was a bizarre mixture of crockery of various ages and farmhouse designs, but all was clean and neat. It gave an impression of belongings kept carefully for a long time and added to with the wisdom of extreme economy. The can-do effect was embodied – and what a sturdy body! – in Ouzel herself. 'Did you build all this?'

'I did.' She indicated a table, and the two Rhydanne sitting at it sloped away to lounge on some floor cushions. 'Eat your stew. Well, you won't do that without a fork, ha ha. Here's a fork.' She had a weird way of half-saying, half-laughing 'ha ha', but heartily, not suspiciously, with her head thrown back. 'I didn't build it all at once, of course. It took twenty summers. And not all by myself; with the help of my boys.'

'Your boys?'

She gave a piercing whistle. 'Snowblink! Spindrift!' The dogs by the fireplace pricked their ears, sprang to life, bounded over to her and collapsed like drifts onto her boots, which I saw were thick leather with reinforced toes. She tickled their tummies. 'My boys, ha ha. And my son – in the back room. And some Rhydanne, of course.'

'Raven said the Rhydanne aren't capable of building.'

'Raven knows nothing of Rhydanne! Nothing at all, ha ha.'

I cut into a suet dumpling and munched it thankfully. I knew I was hungry from the climb, and that would have affected my judgement, but Ouzel's cheese dumplings were one of the best things I have ever tasted, on a par with the pepper-glazed sirloin served at Rachiswater palace and Tre Cloud the Cook's signature chocolate torte. As I ate I watched Dellin, at the end of the room. She crouched and leant forwards to harangue another group of hunters bedecked in tooth necklaces and bangles.

I had never met a woman quite like Ouzel. She was enormous in every respect: her very physical presence, her capacity for talking and the fact she quite clearly didn't give a damn whether she was addressing the Emperor's Messenger or a muleteer. She had the practicality, but not the suspicious shrewdness, of the orphan girls I had known in gangland Hacilith. She was nothing like the drippy aristocratic women with whom I've mostly had to deal since I joined the Castle: the vain wives of governors, or the gold-diggers, crystalline with envy, who inhabit boudoirs and emerge fully fledged each night like basilisks into the ballrooms. She was nothing like the female Eszai, who were constantly intent on their work. She looked with matriarchal fondness on the people in the bar, Awians and Rhydanne alike. And to be honest, a room full of Rhydanne is rather like a room full of hyperactive six-year-olds. Ouzel's formidable vigour made all those other women look pale. Her rounded brown wings were too small for the rest of her. Her red check shirt was made of the same material as the curtains. She wore her sleeves rolled in a businesslike manner, and her trousers, swelled by her belly, were patched and darned to within an inch of their being. She was as rosy as a cask of very powerful cider and she gave the impression of seizing life and hugging it in her strong arms every day.

I became aware of a tugging on the back of my chair. The two Rhydanne babies had unlaced my crossbow bag, managed to pull out the crossbow and were investigating it. The older one poked his thumbnail into the cracks between the mother-of-pearl inlay. His smaller accomplice in crime, who couldn't have been more than a month old, was biting at the drawstring of the quiver full of bolts.

'Put that down!' said Ouzel, and leapt out of her chair.

The boys evaded her and nipped under the table. 'Tearaways!

Little terrors!' She reached under for the nearest and they both raced past her, almost quicker than the eye could follow. 'Told you I'll never catch them!' she said. 'Rubha, will you look after your children?'

The smaller child dropped the quiver and instantly his brother pounced and scooped it off the rug with one clawed hand. He rolled onto his hands and knees, tipped the bolts out onto his long palm and poked at them inquisitively. He had left the crossbow unguarded, and his brother hunted it down, dived onto it and tried to escape but was brought up short by the elder grabbing his hair. They began fighting over it. Ouzel waded in. They scattered. Then the taller one, who was probably only eight months older, rolled his brother over, cuffed him soundly and gained both crossbow and bolts.

I was about to intervene when a Rhydanne woman at the next table shot out an arm and grabbed him by his collar. He stopped at once and went limp. She lifted him up and put him on her back. He clung with his arms around her shoulders and his knees on her hips as if riding. I hastily retrieved my crossbow and reached for the quiver, but – too late – the other boy snatched it, zoomed under the tables, past legs and with a high-pitched giggle was soon hunting fleas and other peoples' belongings at the far end of the room.

I'd look ridiculous if I chased him. I looked to Ouzel, 'He took my bolts.'

'Don't worry.'

'But he might hurt himself.'

'Oh, they're quite used to sharp objects. We can get them later; he caches stuff behind the bar. Rubha, keep them under control – I've told you before!'

Rubha gleamed at me like an angry cat, and went to sit on a slanting ladder that led to a loft where, presumably, Rhydanne slept.

'Never mind,' I said. 'The lock just freezes anyway.'

Rubha passed a strip of dried meat to her baby, who chewed it eagerly. He pushed his mother's tangled tresses aside to ogle me over her shoulder. By the end of his second year he would be starting to hunt; he'd be a fully grown adult by the time he was ten.

Rubha's clothes were worn to shreds, her leggings stonewashed so many times they had faded from black to a brindled grey. She wore a threadbare Awian bodice, battered and with no eyeholes; she was so starved the edges of the material overlapped where it was laced. Bandages swathed her left foot, which looked horribly misshapen. Her ankle was purple and red threads of blood poisoning were climbing up it.

'She was caught in a trap,' said Ouzel.

'Her foot?'

'Yes. She was hunting in the forest and walked into one of the Awians' spring traps. The sort with jagged jaws that'll shatter a wolf's leg. It bit her to the bone. She was there for hours before she managed to prise it open with her spear. So I also had to treat her for frostbite.'

'That's terrible.'

'Yes. Last summer she was a proud hunter; now look at her. Pissed every day and with a Shira child. She was raped ...'

'By whom?'

Ouzel sighed. 'By some of the tame Rhydanne that Raven employs. She can't run fast enough to escape them any more. By the Huntress, she can't run at all!' She clapped her hands and the lame woman looked up. 'Rubha Dara, go and wash your foot again, the way I showed you. Rub some more silver ointment on it and use a clean dressing.'

Rubha nodded and climbed into the loft, her baby clinging to her naturally, the way he had known since the day of his birth.

'I keep telling her to find a husband to protect her. But of course no one wants to marry her because she can't run. The men think her worthless, even more so than if she was a Shira. So she's taken to drinking.'

'I see.'

Ouzel had surprised me by talking in Scree, the only non-Rhydanne apart from the Emperor I had ever heard speak the language. She had foiled the Awians trying to listen in on our conversation. 'I'm impressed by your fluency,' I said.

'Oh, I taught myself Scree. Twenty years trading with them, ha ha. I copied them, a little here and there.'

'I'm coming round to the idea I should be the first to write Scree down.'

'Shouldn't think it'd be a long task for an immortal. It's easy to learn – not that the settlers bother – but at first I couldn't make Rhydanne talk to me. A few sentences and they'd run off. I discovered booze was the best bribe. I said to myself, Ouzel, there's a mint of money to be made here if you go about it correctly, ha ha. So few Rhydanne haunt these valleys that I needed a trading post to bring them together. So I built the Hound close by the track which the Eyrie villagers used to get up to them, by the base of the cliffs where they hunt and shelter. The snowfield narrows here and gathers them together.'

'Very clever.'

'Thank you. All my own work. At first this bar was my bedroom. The trading room next. Then the outbuildings, ha ha. No Awian has climbed in Darkling as much as I have,' she said, and hoisted up one trouser leg to show a hairy calf harder than a block of wood and a shin bone as sharp as a knife blade. 'I owned nothing and had not one friend but poor Barguest. Sometimes when the wind howls I think he's scratching outside, asking to be let in. Passing Rhydanne helped me, in return for good meat and drink, ha ha. Not like the shit Raven's giving them.'

'I see.'

'They're a very interesting people. Forgive me, Comet. You obviously know! Oh, and by the way I'm sorry I swear. The words just slip out. I know who I'm talking to, but with all due respect, I'm rough.'

'That's all right. I'm pretty rough myself.'

'I know ...' She paused. Then she clapped her hands together and said, 'Do you want to see the back room? Where our actual commerce takes place?'

She pointed past the punters to a door with one of the Rhydanne kilims hanging over it. Dellin was leaning on the wall beside it, seemingly lecturing a hunter. I thought I might be able to overhear, so I agreed. Ouzel rose, light on her feet but bearing her paunch before her, and stepped between the Rhydanne sitting on the floor. They hastily snatched their criss-crossed legs out of our path. A smell of wet suede and meaty breath rose from them. Heads turned to us and beads rattled as they stared at me with awe or confusion and wondered what to make of a winged Rhydanne.

Gusts of wind swept around the walls. Wind boomed in the eaves, hustled ice-edged snow against the shutters and growled in the chimney. The burning stack of logs in the hearth collapsed with a crisp, metallic sound, shooting a twist of bright orange sparks up the chimney. But the shutters did not rattle, held by sturdy bolts, and the curtains drawn across them remained still, a testimony to Ouzel's constant improvements to the building she seemed to love so much. If the furniture had been crafted by her hand, her workmanship had improved, because the older chairs and stools had been knocked together but the newer-looking ones were very professionally joined. Away from the damp entrance, the floor was comfortable too, completely covered in kilims. The gigantic floor cushions were of the same bright weave: pashm and cashmere in hundreds of tones of earthy red and orange, indigo and woad-blue, comfrey-brown; dyed by plants of the mountain meadows. Very occasional diamond patterns attested to the staggering heights of Rhydanne art.

A greasy smell rose from the home-made candles on every table. Their holders had also clearly been made by Ouzel and were used so continually they were covered in tallow. Each was a fragment of crystal geode, sparkling clusters of quartz with a hole for the candle. She obviously had a professional eye for gewgaws. But the flames heading every candle were stunted, hazy balls a quarter of the size of a flame at sea level. There was just enough oxygen in the air to sustain them: they struggled and wobbled with every draught like beads on pins.

I passed Dellin. 'What are you chatting to these people about?'

She fell quiet and turned her back.

Ouzel held aside the curtain. 'Come in.'

I passed through, glanced over my shoulder and saw Dellin resume speaking with the hunter.

The trading room glittered, every surface reflected the light! A collection of crystals filled the shelves on every wall, lined their bases and the sills of two windows. A geode opposite me in the corner of the room was fully my height, chipped in half to reveal its cavern bristling with purple amethyst.

There were glossy black crystals, colourless transparent needles, pellucid cubes like mineral ice; all as lambent as Rhydanne eyes. Below the shelves, the contents of a line of hemp sacks glinted too: unsharpened knife blades, iron nails from tacks to nine-inch, brackets and alloy tent pegs. Brand new hammers hung from a rack. A shelf above them held packets of razors together with awls, files, chisels, saws, pliers, a crowbar and rolls of wire. Whetstones were stacked like child's blocks at the end of the shelf.

In another corner was a large chest with a pile of ledgers on top of it, and an enormous scale balance loaded with weights and a mound of ore. Two smaller chests, one full of native silver and the other of copper, looked as if their contents had melted and solidified again mid-flow. Beside them new, shining ladles were hooked all round the edge of an enormous cauldron packed full of cutlery.

Above coffer and cauldron, another rack of shelves positively groaned with an array of fyrd-surplus goods: brass pots and pans, canteens, mugs and plates, carving knives, metal matchboxes, strike-a-lights, combs, cases containing sewing sets, tins of boot dubbing, bales of cotton fabric. There were burlap sacks of oats and dried apples, a box of hazelnut flour with a scoop in it, and pyramids of tins and jars – the tins mostly of beans or vegetables and the jars mostly fruit, jam and boiled sweets. Five smoked and dried haunches of ham hung on thick strings from a row of hooks on the lowest shelf. And specifically for the Rhydanne there were boxes of silver beads, brown packets of salt – valuable this far up-slope – and a sheaf of spear shafts, even more valuable. In front of the chests a trapdoor led down into a dark basement, which seemed to be a pantry because I could just make out the top of another sack.

Beside the door a folded canvas filled the air with the smell of fyrd camps, as did coils of rope hanging on butcher's hooks and a pair of mended boots, reeking of goose grease and muddy laces. It was like a quartermaster's store, knocked through into a sweet shop on one side and a delicatessen on the other. If you had declared to me as a little boy that the shopkeeper was away and I could steal what I wished, I couldn't have been more thrilled. I took it in with delight. Then my gaze fell on the desk and I realised I had overlooked the most important item in the whole emporium.

'My son,' said Ouzel.

'Pleased to meet you,' I said.

'Macan, rouse yourself and shake Comet's hand.'

He did so, then sank back behind the desk and peered at me curiously. 'Macan' simply meant 'sonny' in Scree, and I feared he might be a half-breed like me, but on close inspection he had not a drop of Rhydanne in him. In fact, if Ouzel had bred with anything in order to produce him, it seemed to have been an owl.

'Can I use the desk for a while?' I asked. 'I need to write to the Emperor.'

'Certainly. Get out of the way, Macan,' Ouzel said. He relinquished his place at the desk, but neither of them seemed inclined to leave me in peace. She sat down on a sack of potatoes and shrewdly watched me write. 'This is about Raven's settlement, isn't it?'

'About Raven's plans.'

'Comet, that settlement is disturbing the Rhydanne. My customers, ha ha. It's starving them all and frightening them away. I don't know how they'll survive.' She opened the curtain and pointed to the bar. 'See him asleep in the corner? Lainnir?'

I looked up from my script and saw a hunter slumped against the wall. His face was rounded by fat and his belly was actually chubby. I had never seen a Rhydanne with any fat on him before. With his eyes closed he looked almost human.

'He's blind,' Ouzel said. 'He was one of Raven's porters but they paid him in alcohol so toxic it blinded him. He was no use to them then, so they sacked him. Now he just sits there and drinks.'

'We give him free stew,' Macan added.

'He's just waiting to die. It's so sad ... You'll see other cases about. Lesser cases but it's the same damn thing. Look for the whites of their eyes turned yellow.' She tapped a finger on her temple.

I said, 'Raven plans more than a settlement.'

'Doesn't surprise me. He's destroying the balance, ha ha. Fewer Rhydanne are bringing furs than ever before. If Raven's blundering turns them against Awians –' she spread her wings '– what will I do?'

'Are you afraid for your own safety?'

She glanced at her son. 'No, no. I'm afraid for the Hound. Raven's taking my trade ... I spent my life encouraging commerce and both Rhydanne and Awians benefited. But the Rhydanne sell to him now, instead of me, and he cheats them something awful.'

'Give him an example, Mum.'

'An example of the sort of crap Raven fobs them off with? Look here, Jant. Copper bracelets gilt with silver. And for a stack of wolf furs I give a Rhydanne a spear or two solid silver bangles. See what Raven gives them ...' She picked a spear head from the shelf. It was highly polished to catch the hunter's fancy, but three times the length of a normal spear point and much narrower.

'What is it?'

'Raven started exchanging one of these for a pile of furs as high as the spear point is tall. So he began making longer ones to get more furs for his money. The Rhydanne didn't complain because they thought bigger points must be better points. Fewer hunters come to me now, they want these. But these points don't last as long as mine do, and the Rhydanne are beginning to notice.'

'I see.'

'I'm worried that they'll conclude all Awians are giving them mean terms. Then they'll stop trading with me.'

'Oh, Mum,' said Macan, 'Carniss isn't all bad. She says it is, but it isn't. Their traders come here too and I charge them a lot.'

Ouzel nodded. 'And I'll be charging them more in future! That's the silver lining to this cloud, ha ha. As I always say: if life gives you marmots, make marmolade.'

'Carniss will open up Darkling and bring more business,' said Macan.

'Other traders?' I asked.

'To begin with. Then, following in their footsteps, scientists, naturalists, artists and then even holidaymakers. Can't you imagine it happening?'

I could, actually.

'Excise men! Trophy hunters! More of Tarmigan's convicts!' Ouzel said, and gruffly started rearranging boxes.

Macan grinned. 'She likes to get away from people. She's not amused by the fact other lowlanders are following her up here. Are you, Mum?'

'Huh. I wanted to see the savages my mother told me about when I was a girl. So as soon as I turned seventeen I left home and trekked to Eyrie. After a while I saw that Rhydanne aren't savages at all. I began to admire them. I even began to envy them. You hear that, ha ha? They're suited to the mountains and their ways are as good as the ways of city dwellers. Not that a city man will ever understand that.'

'I understand,' I said.

'Well, an immortal would be at ease in any place.'

'You'd be surprised how few are. But I'm a boundary crosser and so are you.'

'Ha ha. Thank you. Indebted for the compliment. You hear that, son? Most people never leave the surroundings they know. Most people are adapted to only one tiny region. City, mountain, they both have their faults and they should damn well leave each other alone. Any Rhydanne would be uncomfortable in Rachiswater.'

She's right, I thought, but Raven had been uncomfortable in Rachiswater too. He wants to destroy Tarmigan and raze every trace of his rule to remodel the kingdom around himself. Maybe only then would he find comfort.

'Boundary crosser as I am, I don't like the changes that are coming to Carniss. You've never left this valley, son; the changes will come to you. I don't welcome them as much as you do.'

I finished my letter, sealed it in an envelope and arranged with Ouzel for one of the Eyrie village traders to carry it post-haste to the Castle. I shook twenty, fifty, one hundred, two hundred pounds in fresh coins from my wallet and pressed them into her hand. 'The best horse they can find. No expenses spared.'

'I understand.'

Now I had to return to Dellin. What she was saying to the hunters had been preying on my mind all this time. I dropped Ouzel's pen in my pocket and looked out. Dellin was standing in the middle of the room, with the Rhydanne sitting around the walls listening intently. The Awian card players, with worried expressions, kept glancing through the gap between the hearth and its hood. Dellin was facing me, one graceful hand raised, and the orange flames seemed to cast a halo around her head, shining on her loosed hair, which flowed down almost to her waist. I could see the shadows of her long lashes on her upper cheeks. 'My heart feels like bursting,' she said. 'This is our land. Listen to me and I will guide you. The Awians have more food and belongings than they can carry. We will take what we need.'

A huntress interrupted her. 'I'm not starving. The featherbacks skinned forty wolves in the last few days and left the carcasses in the forest. I can show you where.'

'Are you scavenging, Miagail?' Dellin asked.

The beautiful huntress, kneeling on the rug with one leg tucked under her, blinked slowly like a self-satisfied leopard. 'Of course,' she said with liquid smoothness.

'Are Awians so wasteful they leave a feast of carrion?'

'Certainly. Feocullan and I have seen them.'

'So what will happen when they have killed every ibex, every wolf? At this rate none will be left to breed and Carnich will be empty. Then what will you do, Miagail Dara? The Awians hurl their kitchen scraps down the cliff. Will you scavenge those?'

Miagail, who was wearing several heavy necklaces of silver and fox teeth, snarled and settled back. Dellin spread her arms again and addressed the room. 'Listen, *daimh,* I love Carnich and its animals and will not part with them. I don't want to move to the high plateaux. I want my children to live in this abundant valley as I do.

We were born here, where there were no enclosures, where the wind blows free, and every huntress breathes freely and wanders where she will. Now the Awians have taken our country. They saw down the trees and slaughter the beasts. They think the very land belongs to them!' She paused, but there was silence and blank faces all round.

'The land?' said Miagail eventually.

'The Awians think they can take it as their property.'

'That's ridiculous. It can't belong to anyone.'

'Of course not. But we must think like Awians, tell them the land is ours and we want it back. This is why we feel degraded, without understanding the reason, although we were all happy before. They have been stealing from us without replacing the goods they take.'

At this a hubbub broke out, since every hunter knew the danger of pilfering from stores.

'We must protect ourselves,' she continued. 'How? By fighting. Fighting will save Carnich! Do not accept their trade goods!' The Rhydanne looked at each other. Some muttered and a few tried to shout her down, but Dellin raised her voice above them. 'When we accept their clothes and steel the Awians assume we agree their goods are superior to our own.'

'Some of their things *are* better,' said Miagail.

'No! They believe their goods are superior and so they conclude that they *themselves* are superior to us. So they think it natural we will cede Carnich to them. Just as we take the lives of animals, so they are justified in taking ours. Just as a swift hunter raids a slow herder, so they think us weak-willed. We should sew our own leather tents and knap our own points, because if we don't, in time we will forget how to. Our knowledge will be gone, and when we need it, we will be forced to rely on the Awians instead. Look at Lainnir!'

The hunters sitting on the floor looked round. Blind Lainnir had woken up and was leaning on the bar. His windburnt face was amazingly lined, his opaque eyes recessed in dark hollows. He was very old, as much as fifty years, a relic like those which melt out of the edges of glaciers.

'The Carnich drink destroyed his liver. You know their goods are shoddy and dangerous. They have no respect for us; they are laughing at us, thinking they can swindle us. We must not let them!'

Behind me Ouzel said, 'Attagirl!'

I glanced at her indignantly. 'Surely you don't want them to fight?'

'I've never seen this before, ha ha. I've never seen them standing up for themselves.'

'San sent me to do that. She'll wreck everything!'

'She's suffered, Jant. Let her blow off steam.'

Lainnir aimed his voice in Dellin's direction: 'The Awians brought us wealth. They made us what we are – better than the hunters in Stravaig.'

Dellin spat, 'You've picked up their dangerous ideas as well as their sluggishness! "Better"? Through owning many possessions? Whoever heard such a thing! How can you be better when they made you blind!'

'Age blinded me, Shira.'

'It was the gin and you know it! You Rhydanne—' she pointed at one or two who were wearing garish odds and ends of lowlands clothing '—who hang around their fortress are making fools of yourselves. Your ridiculous swaggering makes Awians laugh. You're wearing so many bangles you can hardly run! You traded them, not made them, so they mean nothing! You, why are you wearing a metal hat?'

'It's a helmet,' a young hunter said proudly, pulling it down until his hair stuck out in bristles.

'What did you pay for it?'

'The furs of one week's chase.'

'See! You look like a clown. How will a metal hat stop your ears getting cold? What's this chequered cloth? And a pendant made from a spoon! First, put your proper clothes back on and have some self-respect! Stop hanging around their fort! Second, stop hunting to excess, just to pay for jewellery. Have you forgotten we only kill animals we need? If we need a jacket, it's a simple matter to spear a snow leopard. But now you're hunting to give furs away! You're learning the Awians' greed! It's terrible to see ...

'The Awians are a sick people, because no matter how much they have it's never enough. They accumulate goods until it drives them mad. Eventually they collect mountains of polished rock and metal and live inside them. I have seen these hills of stone all crammed together – they made me feel trapped. The Awians also feel trapped; I can sense their sadness and frustration. They will trap you too, at last. They'll kill you, drive you away or send you as mad as they are. Greed saturates their lives; they overeat at every meal. They need so much grain they have to grow it. They proliferate, with more people in each family than everyone in this room. They never kill newborns. How can such a people live except by theft?'

Dellin gestured towards me and all the Rhydanne looked. She continued: 'Lowlanders have lost the skill of making their own clothes. If you also forget how to sew hides and find food you will have to rely on them – as Jant did – or you will die.'

Suddenly finding myself with an audience I strode forward to Dellin's side, introduced myself and said, 'Don't listen to her! You can trade with Ouzel, the way you always have. She isn't the same as the other featherbacks. The silver man says you should stay away from the keep altogether – until I tell you it's safe.'

There was general agreement at this, but Dellin clawed her hand. 'We've already spoken to Raven! He is treacherous; he considers us less than goats and our language no better than bleating. Do not make deals with the settlers. They are bound to cheat us. Do not learn the idea of money from them; money leads to greed. Every autumn the leaves turn a thousand shades of gold – that is all the gold we need. Every evening we see silver in the moon and in running water – that is all the silver we need. Be satisfied with your original life, a simple life, and you will be happy.'

She darted over to the card players. They had been staring at her throughout although they couldn't understand a word she said. One man was bristle-chinned, the other woolly-hatted, and their cards lay face down on the scored table. She batted the cards about until they flew all over the place, then leaned and yelled directly into bristle-chin's face, 'Greedy Awian!'

The Rhydanne fell about laughing – this was their sort of humour.

Into woolly-hat's astonished face she said, 'Slow Awian! You have taken our hunting ground and my heart revolts. I will never rest until I have driven you back to the lowlands where you belong!'

She flitted towards me and into the square of Rhydanne around the walls.

Instead of standing in full oratorical glory, she sat down in the middle, cross-legged, upright, and continued in a conspiratorial whisper, 'We meet here tomorrow night to defeat the Awians. I will show you how!'

I went to sit beside Dellin. I tried to make her recant but she wouldn't take back her words. She fell to conversing with Miagail, not the usual directions to find prey but about the location of prospectors' shacks. I couldn't stop her and I certainly couldn't use force after our journey through the snow. The trust between us when we were roped together had disappeared and she was independent again. I was so torn I gave up arguing, because the more I stayed near her, the more I enjoyed doing so. Her energy and enthusiasm shone from her, and even without touching her I could feel the latent power of her hard body. Her quicksilver potential for movement tingled over her even now. I sat for hours listening to her, the most talkative and the most eloquent Rhydanne I had ever met. Meanwhile in the background the Awians quietly resumed their game of whist and the Rhydanne baby chased a spider running across the floor, pounced on it and gleefully pulled all its legs off.

Dellin's powerful words rang in my ears. They multiplied like echoes and resounded through my mind. When Ouzel brought me a lantern, showed me my room, and I lay between the furs in a pallet bed on the floor, I was still wondering at her speech, and I thought of her all night.

RAVEN

In the window seat, I made good use of the light to go through the ledger and check my accounts. Our furs had earned an excellent profit, even more than I had estimated. I could have afforded more fighting men than the hundred I was mustering and the five hundred Francolin was sending. No matter, they would suffice.

Below me, Snipe occupied the table with his back to the fireplace, weighing silver nuggets on a scale and slipping them into cloth bags. Click, click, rustle. He placed the small weights on the plate, paused, then his pen scratched as he recorded the values. The clicking must have been going on some time, but once it registered on my consciousness it seemed interminable and annoyed me intensely.

I put the ledger down. Snipe, feeling my attention on him, scribbled a note on his blotting paper, peered up and smiled sheepishly. He was not a man blessed by nature with good looks. His forehead was high and his chin was long, but all his other features were squashed together in the middle of his face, leaving forehead and chin empty expanses. He looked like a human being reflected in a tap.

'My lord?'

'Have you seen Jant this morning?'

'No, my lord.'

'Hmm.' I was beginning to worry he may have sneaked in. It would be his style to question my staff without my knowledge – or worse, the Rhydanne porters. 'Has any servant seen him?'

'No. The bad weather could have stalled him, my lord. Or one look at Ouzel's spit-and-sawdust shack and he fled back to the Castle?'

'No, that's not like him. Trust me; I know.'

Snipe nodded, hunched his shoulders and fell silent. I scanned the snow-heavy sky.

Snipe came to life again. 'My lord, how old is Jant?'
'Ninety-five, or thereabouts.'
'Uck! He looks in his early twenties.'
'He is. He always will be. The Emperor freezes time for him.'
'Because he can fly? That's not fair.'
'Snipe, how in this life can you possibly have imagined that anything was going to be *fair*?'
'Sorry. He looks younger than you, my lord. Um, I mean younger than both of us.'
'Anyone treating him as if he's twenty-three comes to grief. He knew my great-grandfather; he comes from the era when the Tanagers were on the throne ... Yes, it makes me shudder too. As Phalarope once said, death defines humanity. If the Eszai aren't human I wonder what they've become ...'
'Who's Phalarope?'
I sighed. I wished this picayune picaroon had read something, *anything*; his ignorance cramped my style. 'Phalarope was a philosopher.'
He tapped one nugget on another. 'I never thought I'd see an Eszai in the flesh ... Once, when I was at school, my lord, a circus troupe drove by the yard. A train of wagons, one after another ... I remember it well. They were yellow and blue, and an Eszai was painted all gaudily on the side of each one: the Strongman, the Swordsman, the Messenger. They were in the circus. Not the real Eszai, of course. Performers dressed up.'
'The Castle *is* rather like a circus,' I said.
'Dame Goslin said if we behaved ourselves she'd take us to see them. So we were 'specially quiet all week and on Sunday she trooped us out to the big top – we got to sit high up, on the back row. But the "Eszai" weren't very good, looking back. They were a bit crap. The Messenger was a trapeze artist. And check this out: it was a girl.'
I laughed.
'A girl in jeans and a T-shirt. They got that right.'
'And was she a good likeness?'
'Perfect. Except her tits were much too big.' Snipe chuckled and returned to weighing silver. Behind the money bags, he looked like the hunchback Gog out of *The Miser King*. 'How much silver have we obtained this week?' I asked.
'Nearly seven kilos, my lord.'

'Excellent.'

He poured some more fetid juniper-berry coffee. 'I wish I could think of a way to make cat-eyes work faster. The sooner we leave this place the better.'

'Ha – it won't be long now! Send the profit from this batch to Francolin.'

'All of it?'

'Yes. It's the last he will receive from here. Next time it will be from the royal treasury.'

'But, my lord—'

'No buts.'

'It'd be all right if these snow-brained 'danne actually *brought* silver half the time,' he complained. 'They're too dumb to tell the difference between metal and any other shiny rock.' In one hand he picked up a chunk of steely crystals chipped from granite and in the other a heavy block of cubes, which all adjoined each other. 'She brought me magnetite instead of silver and iron pyrites instead of gold.'

'Fool's gold,' I said.

'Well, they *are* bloody fools. And she wanted bangles for it: "*Demre* bangles. Two. *Demre*." They have bangles on the brain.'

'Who brought it?'

'How do I know? They all look the same. This one is bauxite, of no use whatsoever, and this ...' He lifted a small slab dusted with peacock-blue powder. 'I asked for purple, meaning amethyst, but instead she brings me flowers of aragonite.'

'It's attractive.'

'It's worthless ... except as a paperweight.'

A sudden movement outside caught my attention. Five brown goats stampeded from behind a snow-laden cabin at the fringe of the forest. I sighed. 'Idiots, why don't they just teth—'

A darting movement. Stopped. I squinted against the brightness of the snow. Now the goats veered towards the trees, away from something in their path, a shape white on white. A wolf? I wished for my bow.

'Snipe—'

The shape moved, exploded into a sudden sprint after the goats. It was a savage, a Rhydanne all in white. Now I saw another flicker at the edge of my vision, a dash between huts.

I ran to the speaking tubes, flicked the cover off the connection to the roof and yelled to the sentries, 'Savages! Can you see them?'

Muffled shouting, then, 'I saw one!'

An arrow zipped past the window. I ran back to the niche and looked down to see an orange flight sticking out of a drift. Another savage was crouching in its lee, undoing the tethers of our llamas. Back to the tubes. 'Is Jant with you?' I yelled.

'No, my lord.'

'Is he flying over?'

'No!'

'Then bloody shoot them. All of them!' Then the tube to the guardroom: 'Everyone on the roof! With bows! Now!'

I jumped down, swirled on my coat and pulled my gloves from the pocket. Snipe swept the tapestry back and we ran up the stairs.

I emerged onto the top, light-headed. The freezing wind nearly tore my coat from my body. The two sentinels leant over the parapet, scanning the snow, seemingly at a loss. I took hold of it to brace myself and looked down. All was silent below, nothing to be seen but the swathe of snow between our curtain wall and the margin of the forest, along which settlers' cabins were scattered. A clamour from the stairs and then Captain Crake was beside me, his archers stumbling up behind. 'My lord—'

A crack of splintering wood blew on the wind. Two settlers pelted out of one of the more distant cabins and ran towards us, heading for the gate. A second later a savage appeared in their doorway and set off, long legs sweeping. He sent quick glances around as he dashed, so fast the settlers, running at full speed, looked sluggish.

'There!' I pointed. 'There!'

A couple of archers drew but loosed wide. I made the mistake of letting my gaze follow the arrows – with my attention deflected for a second the white figure disappeared against the snow. I clenched my teeth in exasperation.

At the same time the captain cried, 'I see one!' Six bows flung heavy arrows hissing in the opposite direction. I whipped round, stared along their line of fire and saw sheep scattering, just the bottom of their feet kicking up against the whiteout. A savage drove them, hood raised and spear in hand. A slick of blood darkened the cabin door where he'd speared a sheep – no, two – and left them dying messily.

The wind skewed our arrows, thrust them into the ground, and the archers could hardly see to shoot. The next gust bunched up an eerie whistle, whisked it away. Another whistle answered from among the cabins and we saw a glint of silver in a snow-filled alley between them. 'My god,' said Snipe. 'How many are there?'

'It could be the same few.'

A second flight of arrows snicked into the snow well short of the thieving wretch and the archers drew again. The savage just dropped to the ground, lay still. Beside me Crake, looking down the length of his arrow, muttered, 'Where is he?'

'I can't see him,' said another, and lowered his bow.

The wind crashed around the tower and I turned away from ice grains flying off the parapet. When I looked back I couldn't see him either. Spindrift snow chafed over the patch where he'd lain flat, filling in his footprints and those of the sheep he had spirited away. There was nothing save the smell of our lunch cooking ripping past on the wind.

Snipe broke the silence. 'I see one! There, between the trees ... He's gone.' The captain glared at him.

'It was nothing,' I snapped. 'Keep searching.'

Two figures came racing out of the forest. One flitted into the shadow of a cabin and I heard him break the door with a well-aimed kick. He vanished inside and the settler's whole family poured out, three little boys and a mother in a red skirt. The mother scooped up her smallest son and they fled to the next cabin. They hammered on the door, shouted till it opened, admitted them and slammed again.

Goats and sheep spilled out of the opened cabin onto the snow, some of them bleeding, all bleating, and the Rhydanne flashed after them. Long hair straggled from the sides of his hood and red-stained necklaces slapped the front of his parka. His barbaric regalia struck fear, then hatred, into my archers. He whacked the beasts with his spear butt and turned them towards the forest but a settler followed him out of the cabin, axe in hand, and set his foot on the trailing tether of the last goat. The savage turned to face him and the man brandished his axe. I felt proud.

The savage raised his spear, levelled it at the settler, then as I thought the brave man's last minute had come, one of those barbarous whistles cleaved the air. The savage sidestepped faster than we could follow, shepherded the goats at a sprint towards the forest. The burly woodsman looked after him, bewildered, still with his foot on the rope and the goat bleating beside his leg.

The savage reached the trees, swung round to face us, ran a few paces and hurled his spear at the settler. It transfixed with chilling accuracy the goat, which fell dead. Snipe swore beside me.

Another raider dashed in from nowhere, pulled the spear out and used its point to slit the rope. They hunt in packs. No, in pairs. He flung the goat onto his shoulder and set off after the other, overtook him in the cover of the trees, and tossed the spear back to him. They both disappeared into the forest and again the gale swept up ice grains and hurled them straight at us, forcing tears from our eyes. The sky lowered minute by minute, darker with snow.

Out of sight around the corner of the parapet a dog was barking furiously. I crossed over and looked down to see the door of the largest barn swinging wide. Every time it banged shut I could see behind it. A savage was there, driving the last of the sheep into the forest. He evaded the dog as it snapped at his legs. It bounded higher and with an irritated motion he spun round and thrust his spear into its neck.

The dog collapsed and the plunderer ran on. He had strung settlers' cups on a belt across his body. Cutlery in the cups rattled as he ran, and under one arm he bore off a haunch of smoked ham. He had stolen too much to carry, and dropped a trail of objects. His accomplice appeared and, crossing and re-crossing his trail, stooped to pick them up.

A young woman stood by the banging door of her ransacked cabin, looking in their direction, blonde hair streaming in the wind. Shivering visibly, she clasped a blanket around her and clutched a broom as if it were a mace.

Snipe joined me, his features screwed even more tightly together with fury. 'Send someone out. The savages will rape her!'

Maybe. Who knows what they'll do? Their instinct to chase is strong. I nodded, then looked beyond his shoulder to the captain. 'Crake, split the men into five squads. Send one out to that lady; give two to me. One man in each squad to act as a spotter for the others. Pick targets; shoot in concert. Stop gaping and move as fast as they do!'

Two sets of five archers joined me at the parapet and searched the ground now etched with footprints. Another raider dashed from the trees, crouched in the cover of a drift. The spotter yelled, the archers drew, and waited. The settler had retreated inside her house and the black sheepdog was limping in a circle, emitting a ghastly whine and dropping blood on the snow. Like a dart the Rhydanne broke cover and dashed towards it. Ten arrowheads tracked him with confidence and the arrows whirred away. He threw up his arms and fell face down in the snow. The archers reloaded, satisfied, but the savage raised himself on one elbow and one knee and began crawling towards the forest, with three flights pinned in his shoulders.

My archers drew and loosed again, and again. They had the range now, and poured flight after flight into the savage as he writhed and twisted. He crawled on, shuddering as they hit and eventually lay still, with one arm extended and fingers clawed into the snow. Hardy breed, I thought. Takes a lot to kill them.

We waited, and the wind blew between my groups and those of the captain, who had shot briefly before falling silent. At length I called to him, 'Do you see any more?'

'We saw a pair, but we missed them.'

'We got one. Only one.'

'Congratulations, my lord.'

The two settlers who had been running towards the gatehouse, were inside the bailey. I crossed to the far parapet and looked down to see them puffing clouds of breath as they stared about. My reeve emerged from his house with some rugs, which he wrapped around the poor couple and ushered them inside.

The captain joined me. 'I think it's over—'

'Keep watching!' I snapped. I didn't appreciate his surly, independent expression; it was defiant, almost a sneer.

'It's your responsibility to keep us safe ... my lord,' he said quietly.

'Of course I will. But only if you follow orders!'

'Because the villagers don't feel safe, and after this I reckon they'll mutter to me even more.'

Was he daring to threaten me? With a feeling of sinking hopelessness I realised this raid would be the settlers' major concern. I gritted my teeth. I don't *want* any more setbacks. I don't *want* any more wasted time. I swore I would be seated on the throne this time next week – but the Rhydanne flit in like hail on the wind and disturb the people toiling to build my force.

The captain waited. 'What are my orders?'

'Shoot every one of those degenerate creatures that sets a foot outside the forest! I want watchers up here all day and night. I want you to move every villager into the bailey – there should be cabins enough for them there, but if not they can sleep in the hall until they build more. There's no need for them to be outside the walls in winter. Send archers to accompany every hunting party to leave the gates and guard the prospectors in the woods ...'

'My lord?' he said with curiosity because my voice had trailed off. A black dot crossing in front of Capercaillie's rock face had turned and was careening towards us at extraordinary speed. Jant's here. All my foreboding crystallised at once: where the bloody hell has he been?

'Snipe? Snipe!'

'My lord?'

'Our unwanted guest.' I nodded at the dot, which was rapidly increasing in size. 'Ready yourself.'

Jant suddenly folded his wings in and dropped like a stone out of sight behind the parapet. I rushed to it, looked over and saw him fall below the level of the treetops. He opened his wings at the last minute, jolted with the drag, swished out in a forward arc and sped low over the ground. He flared his great wings like fans, landed neatly next to the Rhydanne's corpse and knelt beside it. The arrows in its back projected like spines. I was surprised to see him carefully turn the body onto its side.

'What's he doing?' asked Snipe.

'I don't know. Come on.' Together we descended the staircase, went through the undercroft, out of the gate and strode through the shin-deep snow, the wind flapping our coats behind us. We passed the dead dog, its head twisted at a revolting angle, and as we approached, Jant looked up.

I had never been subject to such a baleful glare in all my life. The wind blew his hair in tangled fronds across his face and his eyes were red-rimmed. He was paler even than usual and his real age lay like vicious ice below the surface. He looked distraught, then realised we had observed it and his expression tightened into fury. Snipe slowed to a dawdle behind me. We were close enough now to tell the body was that of a female.

He had snapped the arrows from the woman's shoulders and laid her on her back with her arms by her sides. He had closed her eyes and pushed her wet, bright scarf and necklaces away from her mouth and pointed chin. The splintered ends of the arrow shafts projected from her shoulders, sunk over half their length in her body. Orange flights also surrounded us, growing at the same steep angle from the snow like crocus buds.

Jant spoke haltingly, 'This is Miagail. At first, I thought it was *her* – I mean, it could have been Dellin.'

'She was one of the raiders.'

'I saw that. I saw everything!'

He had arranged her as if for burial, which piqued me. Uncivilised Rhydanne don't bury their dead. They don't even respect the bodies of loved ones but simply heave them over the nearest precipice.

'You murdered her . . .' he said with a dry tongue, swallowed and began again: 'You tried to shoot the others.'

'They were robbing us! See what we've lost?' I pointed to the goat tracks, the dead dog and belongings in the snow. 'My people demand safety.'

'They weren't in danger! Yes, the hunters took food, but no lives. They could have chased down those silly trappers a hundred times over.'

'Up here those animals are our lives! Are we to grow crops in ice? Trade with the roads buried under snow? They will starve us!'

'You had no right to kill Miagail!'

'Miagail?' I looked at the body but felt nothing other than disinterest.

'She was called Miagail! A solitary huntress! She had a name, you know!' He stroked back the locks blowing across her face.

'I'm surprised the death of one savage affects you so much, Comet. Haven't you witnessed the deaths of thousands of mortals? Did you know her?'

'No.'

'And another thing I find odd. You went to the Hound to tell the Rhydanne not to attack us, but this is the worst yet! We've never been assaulted by more than a pair before.'

'They're driven by hunger.'

'So you keep saying. You could have stopped it. I expected you at breakfast.'

'I lost Dellin,' he said, with a most uncharacteristic flutter in his voice. 'She was gone when I woke up.'

'Well, she's probably joined them.'

He hesitated. 'She isn't in her cave. I told her not to come here.'

Yes, it is to be expected, I thought; they don't have the staying power. She will have melted away like the others, and we'll next see her appear on one of these random raids.

Jant glanced at the furthest cabin, where some guards were standing on the threshold, giving the surprised occupant notice to move. An excellent chance, I thought, to get him and the Castle off my back. If I take Rachiswater swiftly and neatly – and I must, to have a chance of winning against my brother – the Castle will fall in behind me to preserve the peace and I will be incontestably king. In the meantime I must free myself to proceed with my plans.

'All right,' I conceded. 'I'll try to restrain my people and allow the Rhydanne to roam unharmed. You see I'm moving the villagers and livestock within the walls and I'll also put out meat.'

'They'll take that as an insult. Rhydanne want to hunt.'

'It's a start. But only if they cease these raids.'

He nodded and stood up swiftly. 'I'll return to the Hound and inform them. But first I'm going to visit your archers and order them, from the Emperor, not to shoot at Rhydanne again.' With a whisk, he took off, and landed a few seconds later by the patrol.

'Much good may it do you,' I said loudly. I began the uncomfortable trudge back to the gatehouse. A bristle-backed avalanche hound had set upon the dead sheepdog and was noisily tearing flesh from the wound on its neck. As Snipe and I walked past I kicked the hound away, grasped the dead dog's raised hind paw and its stiff pads crunched together in my palm. I began to drag it after us.

'My lord, why did you say you'd "restrain" us?' Snipe demanded.

'To put Jant off the scent.'

'And those terms! After the 'danne did this, are you really going to feed them?'

I waved my arm so the dog's carcass inscribed an S-shaped track. 'Scraps, Snipe. Scraps.'

JANT

That night I sat in the Hound, infuriated by a day of reasoning with Raven. I couldn't tell him I had stolen the letter. Not yet, anyway. I picked at a bowl of Ouzel's stew and hardly touched a mug of beer. I was trying to overhear Dellin in the back room. A group of ten or twelve Rhydanne had gathered around her and more were dropping in every minute. The last, a willowy huntress who couldn't have been more than ten years old, had brought the news of the death of Miagail. Dellin's shocked response convinced me she had nothing to do with the raid. She stood with her spear pointing downwards, twisting its point and boring a neat hole in the rug as she urged them to listen.

She was impatient and, thinking my negotiations overly slow, had grown disdainful. When I tried to join them she took the other Rhydanne into their cubby holes or out into the snow, leaving me standing alone. When I retired to my table, their huddle reformed. I hesitated to interrupt again, in case I drove them away to continue their powwow in the deepest part of the forest. Dellin had asked the Castle's help but now she was bloody well intent on proceeding without me.

I rested my head in my hands and stared down at my congealing plate without seeing it. I was listening hard, trying to catch a few stray words. Nothing in all my years as an Eszai had prepared me for a situation where my title and all the authority of the Castle was simply irrelevant. The Rhydanne gave nothing to the Empire and took nothing from it. I had no hold on them. I peered at Dellin through my fingers. Truly she made all other women look lumpen and clumsy. She runs on instinct, trusts her senses, but her mind and will were as strong as a governor's. Her voice waxed and waned as she paced up and down. Her bangles jangled and her tooth necklaces clacked together. She hopped her bottom up onto one of the ledges, jumped down, constantly moving. She stirred her spear eloquently with one long hand, as if it was part of her. Her eyes flashed when she turned to talk to Feocullan. I became alert. Feocullan was an accomplished hunter and I couldn't tell if she liked him or not. He raised his hand to signify agreement and leaned back into the shadows. I began watching her again.

'...can't even find rats,' one of them said.

'Yes, we are hungry,' said Dellin, 'But if we all attack separately we fail. Look what happened to Miagail. We must all attack together, as if the featherbacks are a herd of deer.'

As far as I could tell, the Rhydanne were listening more seriously than last night. Miagail's death had brought the danger home to them. How was I to stop them getting killed? Dellin had no idea of the Awians' power, pride and hunger for profits even after today.

Ouzel approached with her hand wound in a tea towel, holding the lug of a heavy pan. 'You haven't touched your stew at all.'

'I'm not hungry.'

Nevertheless she heaped more dumplings on top of the already-cold remains, set the pan down, drew out the chair next to me, threw herself onto it and crossed one leg over the other. Her trousers rode up, showing her mountaineering shins. 'The guards are coming,' she said.

'What ...?' I was watching Dellin's hair. She has such long hair, but when hunting she binds her ponytail with an ochre-dyed scarf and pins the sides back with combs. The combs are carved from bone—

'Jant,' said Ouzel. 'You haven't heard a word I've said.'

'Sorry.'

'The guards are coming. Can't you hear them?'

A distant noise I had, in fact, heard in the background without really registering it was growing in volume and resolved into male voices reciting in marching rhythm. It struck a familiar chord in this unfamiliar place; it was one of the 'one, two, sound-off' rhymes fyrdsmen invent when on the march. They often describe Eszai or captains in altogether uncomplimentary terms, but these men's voices, louder now, had a triumphant ring. Their footsteps crunched an accompaniment as they climbed the icy steps:

The foot folk
put the 'danne to the poke

by way
never heard I say
of readier boys
to get the joke
and make some noise
damn the 'danne all
may they rot where they fall
hey, boys!

This is the last thing I need, I thought. Ouzel looked at me questioningly but at that moment the door barged open and six archers, heavily bundled up in hats, greatcoats and gaiters, spilled into the room. They stood by the door, laughing and chaffing each other, unslinging their bow bags, unbuttoning their coats, unwinding their scarves, stamping their feet and leaving little geometrical blocks of impacted snow from their boot treads on the damp rug. The first unwound the tail of his indigo liripipe hat from his head till it turned from a turban to a woolly tube, lifted it off, leaving his blond hair standing up in sweaty spikes, and I saw it was Snipe. He beckoned to the others, 'Come in, come in.' They flocked in with a clatter of scabbards and a flap of coat skirts and occupied the table next to mine, where they peeled off their mittens and regarded me speculatively.

'Sh!' I said, trying to listen to Dellin, but Snipe clapped his hands exultantly. 'Beers all round! And some of your never-ending stew, my lovely.'

Ouzel brandished her wooden spoon and disappeared behind the bar. 'The face that lunched a thousand chips!' Snipe added as soon as her back was turned. The men laughed – though rather cautiously since she was as big as they were. She brought jugs of beer, holding four together at a time, and supplied them all with mugs and food. She returned to sit beside me and approvingly watched them tuck in. After a few nervous glances at me they realised my attention was elsewhere and relaxed into their business, trying to put themselves on the outside of as much food and drink as they could. When they fell relatively quiet I could hear Dellin again.

'If we raid them over and over they will eventually tire and give up,' she declared. 'Not raids like the one you stupidly carried out today, but proper hunts. Featherbacks flounder in the snow. On a night like tonight they would freeze solid! They have already withdrawn inside their great pueblo, so Feocullan tells me, and every Awian who ventures out is armed to the teeth. See those who just came in over there? Raven sends them to check on us. He fears us, and well he might, for in the forests and on the cliffs his people are more helpless than fawns and we are pumas. We can drive them like deer and beat every last one out of cover. We will push them out of our land, into their fortress and down the slope. Then I will say to them, "You are free to return to your own country."'

Ouzel looked at me questioningly. 'Did you hear that?'

'Every word.'

'She doesn't understand that Carniss Manor is here permanently.'

'None of them do,' I said. 'Dellin has as much chance of driving the settlers from Carniss as she has of hitting the moon with an arrow.'

'The moon with an arrow!' A voice guffawed from the next table. 'That's good, Comet. Good and true. We're rooted here now and no bloody talon-hands are going to shift us. Did you hear that, lads? Comet said the cat-eyes have as much chance of disturbing us as they have of hitting the moon with an arrow. Which, seeing as they can't shoot, is no chance at all. We're not shaken by a single raid, are we?'

In a chorus of uproarious denial, they banged their beer mugs on the table and roundly damned every Rhydanne.

I said, 'If you respected them it would be a start.'

'Respect them? Why?' Snipe asked innocently, then began laughing again. 'Do we respect the tabby cats our wives keep as pets? Because you know, Comet, they can't organise themselves any more than cats do. Today was proof. Eh, lads? Today was a fine score: Carniss one, Rhydanne nil.'

They all laughed. 'And open a tally for our beer, Ouzel, darling,' he leered, though at a look from Ouzel he had to glance at his mates for support. 'It's expensive. Three times the price of Rachis beer, by god.'

'This house brew is the only beer for thirty kilometres,' she said. 'If you want cheaper, ski down to Eyrie.'

Snipe pulled an aghast expression. 'With planks on my feet like a Rhydanne? Do you want me to burrow in the snow like them as well?' He turned to the other five, who were enjoying the warmth of the fire on their wind-ruddy faces, occasionally still blowing into their fists to ease their defrosting fingers. Melting snow dripped from the hems and sleeves of the greatcoats hung over the backs of their chairs. I was surprised to note their bows were first-class quality. They looked very much like a fyrd squad – they would all have done service – and although Tarmigan would never allow Raven to have actual Select Fyrd, Raven had found the means to kit out some of his ragtag collection of cottars, criminals and entrepreneurs almost to the same standard.

'Oh, I forgot your due, Glede,' Snipe added. 'Have some beer for that excellent shot today. As much as you can drink, on our lord. Yours is the shot that felled her, I'm sure. Other arrows hit her, but yours was the first to bring her down. Hey, Ouzel! Fetch some more!'

Ouzel removed one of their empty jugs, refilled it, and slashed a fifth mark across a tally of four she had chalked on her blackboard. The woodsman who had shot Miagail eagerly drained his mug. Snipe, satisfied, dug his hands into his damp hair again and pulled them up, raising his hair into a single curious tuft. He looked like an onion on top of a potato. He grinned, showing yellow teeth against wind-tanned skin. His skin had an oily sheen, probably from all that cheese, and a pimple stood proud on the muscles of his brawny neck.

I caught a snatch of Dellin's conversation: 'Feocullan, you will man the snowbank with your partner.'

Feocullan has a partner, I thought, and for some reason I felt more relaxed.

'Prepare the branches tonight,' she continued. 'And the means to light them. Do you have any dummies?'

'Yes, Dellin.'

'Then you are in charge of them. Airgead, I want—'

Snipe's voice drowned her out. He had followed my gaze and was watching Dellin with extreme distaste. 'Feline rank smell in here, isn't there?'

'Oh, shut up,' I said.

Ouzel said to him, 'This is their pub too. In their opinion you're the stranger and you smell like prey.'

He ducked his head, giving himself a double chin. 'I don't know what they think, *if* they think, and I don't care. They're imbeciles. If they mess with us, the only land we'll give them in Carniss is two metres each, like the one we buried today.'

'Hear, hear,' said Glede, holding up his mug in a toast.

'If we hadn't roused them, they'd stay in their backward state for ever. Playing like children, always shirking hard graft.'

'Please be quiet,' I said. 'All of you.'

Snipe took a long drink and I hoped for a second he was going to shut up, but he continued in a lower voice, 'I grant you they may be able to run, but they can't outrun arrows. I grant you, they land on their feet mostly, but not always. That one today landed on her belly.'

'That's the attitude that causes the raids,' Ouzel upbraided him.

'Huh. I think we should leave some offal outside as bait, go up on the parapet and have fine sport. There are fewer 'danne than we have arrows; we'll keep score until they're all dead or fled to their holes.'

'Stop looking for a quarrel!' I snapped.

'Huh – if they seek a quarrel they can have one,' he mumbled. 'A crossbow quarrel!'

I glanced at Dellin, glad that she couldn't follow the Awian but at the same time wishing she knew, so she could defend herself. My glance grew to a gaze: she was crouching and arranging two lines of small stones on the rug, and the other hunters watched intently. They looked for all the world like Eszai poring over a map table in the Sun Pavilion, drawing up their plans of war. I gradually became aware that Ouzel was watching me nervously.

Snipe was staring into his beer. 'It's strange, really,' he murmured. 'That one we shot today – when crows pecked her eyes out she looked quite human.'

'Do you have a problem with my eyes?'

He looked up, then broke away from my stare. 'Ah, Comet. I was thinking of someone ... My poor wife ... No, of course I didn't mean ... It's obvious that you –' he gestured at my wings '– that you aren't one of them ...'

The other archers, oblivious to our exchange, guffawed at some half-witted joke. I looked away from them in disgust, trying to eavesdrop on Dellin again. Snipe gulped beer. Out of the corner of my eye I saw Glede, red-faced with drink, nudge him in the ribs. 'Hey, Snipe. Ever thought what it'd be like to fuck one of them? One of those skinny little 'danne women?'

'Huh! Man, woman: they all look the same to me.'

Another voice: 'Glede, you probably had a go at that one today before we threw her in the hole, you dirty bastard! Dropped one in her hole before we dropped her in the hole!'

I turned, slammed the table with my hand. 'Enough!'

'Why?' said Snipe. He nodded and grinned at Dellin. 'Are you looking to have one or something?'

'Right!' I jumped up, darted to him and grabbed his throat. His bristly skin was clammy. Head tilted back, he looked down the length of his nose. I released him, sideswiped with my other hand and whacked him across the jaw. His head whipped sideways. I drove my fist into his solar plexus and he doubled up.

I clenched both hands into his sweater and dragged him away from the table. Out of the corner of my eye I caught a glimpse of Ouzel's aghast expression and the archers stumbling to their feet. Snipe straightened up. His hand went to the knife in his belt and a centimetre of blade gleamed. He swung out the knife but I dodged it – in leisurely style but I doubt he saw me move.

Revelling in my speed, I gave him no chance. I punched again, felt it connect with his eye socket, punched the other hand into his nose, felt it crack and give, then an uppercut under his chin and his head flicked back.

'Stop it!' yelled Ouzel. She strode in and tried to grab my arm, but I was too fast. Snipe, half-blinded, lashed out with the hand not clutching his knife. I pivoted forward and whacked him in the mouth with my full weight. He staggered back, over the chair and onto the table. He turned onto his side, supporting himself with both hands on the table, and spat out a tooth. His mouth open, saliva mixed with blood drooled out. Behind him, Glede was fumbling to string his bow. He caught my look and stopped.

Fury shone in Snipe's eyes and his split lips tightened. He pushed himself off the table and dashed at me, knife outstretched. Great, I thought; give me an excuse. I slipped aside, let the blade pass, seized his wrist and twisted his arm up behind his back. His fingers uncurled and the knife tumbled to the floor.

'Leave him!' Ouzel shouted.

The mist was clearing and a vision crossed my mind of the Emperor, furious, rising from the sunburst throne. My grip relaxed. Snipe tore himself away, flung himself on the ground and got up, knife in hand.

He came at me again. I looked around and saw their ice axes and ropes piled by the door. I ran to them, snatched up the nearest axe and whacked him full strength across the stomach with its long shaft. He dropped to hands and knees. I booted him at the top of the leg – the pressure point dimple where it joined his backside. He yelled and collapsed onto his side, breathing feebly. Now you know how it feels to be kicked by a Rhydanne, I thought, altering my grip on the shaft. It's like being kicked by a racehorse.

Even now he was reaching out for his knife. I raised the axe above his neck.

'No!' Ouzel grabbed the shaft. 'Leave him!'

I lowered it and gently touched my boot toe to the nape of his neck and the base of his spine. 'If you pick up that knife it'll be the end of you.'

He curled up limply, dribbling blood from his spongy nose and mouth. His friends surrounded him and Ouzel knelt down in their midst. She took the tea towel from the table and folded it under his head. 'Why did you do that, Jant? Why?'

'Why did he have to make out I fancied Dellin?'

'He was only joking! Oh, I see ... Bloody hell.'

My white-hot fury had subsided but she sparked a throbbing anger. 'I'm sick of this prejudice! I'm immortal, not Rhydanne, not Awian! But I can't make them listen to each other!'

'For an immortal, you're a dirty fighter,' she said.

'There's no such thing as a fair fight where I come from.'

'Hacilith?'

'Darkling.'

She lifted Snipe onto a chair with his friends' help and his head drooped like a beaten boxer's. She dabbed his bleeding mouth and I paced up and down, tapping the axe against my palm. I was still angry but I felt the tiniest butterfly stir its wing in my stomach. What have I done? Shit ... if the Emperor hears of this, he'll ...

A scream behind me brought me to my senses. Ouzel had just set Snipe's nose straight. The Rhydanne beyond the fireplace pealed with laughter.

He shouldered Ouzel aside and stood up roughly, holding a wad of lint against his damaged mouth and nose. His friends clustered around him and helped him put on his hat and coat. They gathered their gear and hurried out, with Snipe leaning on the shoulder of the most sober.

I closed my hand over cold metal and realised what I was holding. They hadn't asked for the axe back. I rotated the shaft and examined its sharp pick opposing a narrow, serrated chisel, with a spike at the foot of the shaft. Metal loops at both ends held a long canvas strap. What a useful weapon, I thought. I'll have this. I slung the strap over my shoulder and looked round.

Dellin was gazing at me ... straight at me, with pleasure and appreciation glittering in her eyes. The Rhydanne around her seemed admiring, too. She smiled and skipped towards me. She pressed a beaker of vodka into my hands and gently guided me over to sit beside her in a corner, on some bear furs rucked and folded over a soft pile of cushions. 'Well done!' she said warmly. 'That was worthy of a hunter!'

'I *am* a hunter.'

'And so swift! Snipe didn't even land a blow!'

'You're the swiftest I've seen,' said Feocullan, and I felt incredibly grateful to him for a second. I said, 'Listen, Dellin, when I was young I rounded up red deer hinds on the mountainside, thinking they were escaped goats which had somehow lost their horns. That's how fleet of foot I am.'

She smiled at me. Now maybe I would learn their plans, I thought, but they wanted to hear from me instead. They treated me like a hero. They brought me cup after cup of spirit while I sat beside Dellin, acutely aware of her movements and turning her words over and over until they embossed my mind. I didn't want to miss anything she said and I began to unsettle myself, wondering if any of her remarks were about me.

She was flawless, strong and wild. I hadn't noticed her beauty before, and I suppose that was because I was used to elegant women, superficially elegant women. Dellin was so much harsher than they, but her poise was a type of elegance all her own. She's like a sculpture come to life, I thought, light-headedly. I wanted to hunt the Rhydanne way with her. I wanted her to teach me. The wind on my face, setting my own strength and skill against the power and grace of the deer. Her skin smelt of pebbles; her hair of woodsmoke and gales. No doubt from sleeplessness and the vodka I began to feel light, as if I was floating. But a great energy surged through me. The little annoyances – the uncomfortable draughts and terrible vodka paled into insignificance. I had tapped an immense, calm, golden energy and I could go on for ever. I wish I had this energy while flying. Why now? Whether it was adrenalin from the punch-up, or because the Rhydanne had really, at long last, welcomed me as one of their own, I didn't know, but I was certain of one thing: I didn't want the night to end.

Next morning I woke long before the servant entered to light the fire. I rose promptly, for there is no point in lying abed with the same unpleasant thoughts about my brother circling in my mind time and again. As I dressed I planned how I would consolidate my grasp on the kingdom. I would love to set my brother's corpse on the throne, dressed in his most regal finery, and taunt him: 'You weren't the only one born to the throne. Why did you presume to hold it without sharing it with flesh of your flesh, blood of your blood?' Then, when I have satisfied my humour, I will cut off the hand that caused my scar and throw his body in the Rachis River.

I opened the curtains, unbolted the shutters and pushed them wide, breaking the film of ice that had formed over them. The drab blue sky around Capercaillie, by now a familiar backdrop, was just beginning to leak dawn, but the air seemed more still and silent than usual. I rubbed the sleep from my eyes and looked up at the pine skirts of the mountain. Darker strands seemed to reach from the sky to the ground – a phenomenon of the clouds, perhaps? No ... palls of smoke rising into the air. They rose calmly and sedately from several places in the forest, as if they were the last smoulderings of much larger fires, and each column reached to a third of the height of Capercaillie before its smoke levelled out into gauzy cloud.

Seven, eight, nine columns. One ascending from a hollow where the pines were still night-black, several by the trail where it crooked to meet the stream gorge, and one further away over the tree-covered shoulder of the mountain. One at every site where my prospectors had thrown up cabins or commenced quarrying. But why light such fierce blazes in the middle of the night? While I wondered, a lone horse walked out from the trees onto the snow, its saddle empty and its bridle dangling. Then I realised, and a horror like the cold stole into me as I watched the smoke from my people's razed homes climb and disperse. The Rhydanne had retaliated.

OUZEL

After an uneasy night, the drama between Jant and Snipe had so worried me, I went into the bar to coax the candles alight. It was completely empty. Usually at least a few sleeping Rhydanne litter the floor, but this morning there were no bodies to step over – everyone had gone. No, not everyone; Jant was sitting on the cushions, half-lit in a shadowy corner, in exactly the same place as last night. He had wound a striped kilim around his shoulders, but although the temperature outside last night must have dropped to minus forty, the chill in the bar didn't seem to bother him.

I circled the room, then stubbed out my taper, bent down and stirred the fire into life. Jant didn't greet me. In fact, he hadn't moved, head in hands and his wings half-open, resting on the floor.

'Good morning!' I enthused.

He removed one hand from his face and regarded me blearily. Dark shadows ringed his eyes, and they were bloodshot too, as if Snipe had given him a shiner rather than the other way round. In the gloom he was spectral white, and his hair all black tangles. Slumped in this manner, it struck me he looked much like my son in one of his welters of thinking too much. Nonsense, I told myself; letting superficial appearances fool you. He's far too old to succumb to angst. But he did seem to be suffering some type of anguish. Maybe he felt guilty at having overstepped his authority. Perhaps he was regretting having beaten Snipe – if he had spent all week calculating how to alienate Raven and the whole bloody colony he couldn't have done any better.

'I've porridge for breakfast,' I said. 'If you're in a rush, toast and sausage will be quicker.'

He shook his head. 'I don't want to eat.'

'But you must eat! I'll make you some porridge.'

He sighed rather dramatically, but an Eszai is an Eszai so I left him to his Empire-scale contemplation and went to pack faggots in the oven. I warmed a bowl of goat's milk, stirred in oats and set it before him. He didn't register it for a time, but I pressed a spoon into his hand and he idly began to pick flakes of ash out of the porridge with it. He sat head bowed and high-shouldered, like a vulture with no appetite, which alarmed me. You need good food to fortify you against the cold. I've never seen a Rhydanne anything less than voracious, and quite rightly so. Their lives are so demanding, they must keep their energy up.

'Dellin and the others have gone,' he said.

They certainly had. They had plotted and supped late into the night and Dellin had fallen asleep with Jant beside her. However, I think she had only been pretending because when he was deep in slumber she got up and roused the rest. They lit torches in the fireplace to light their way and dashed out. They left a tense atmosphere behind. I'm finally troubled about what might happen to Macan and myself. That girl hates Awians. She hates too powerfully for a Rhydanne, all in all.

'They might return tonight, ha ha.'

He pressed his lips together: he didn't seem so sure. 'I thought I'd won her over, but she'd gone when I woke up. I expected to run with her today but, damn it, she's going ahead with her plans and I'm not even part of them.'

'Rhydanne are thoughtless,' I said. 'They come and go their own way.'

He traced a double S-shape in the air. 'She let me lie close behind her, right here on the floor. Our bodies fit together well ... I even put my arm round her, and she didn't mind. We might have been hunting partners, but today she's gone! Does she have more caprice than the worst tart in Galt or was she just using me for warmth?'

'She probably didn't intend to hurt you.'

He sprang to his feet and strode to the fireplace, whirled round to face me. 'I'm not hurt! Don't be ridiculous!'

'Sorry.'

'*Her*, hurt *me*? An Eszai? I've hardly any time for this. I must go and see Raven.'

'My mistake,' I said. 'I'm glad you're here to do business with Raven, because – ha ha – if by any chance you were harbouring feelings for Dellin, she would hurt you every single day. She can't help it.'

He returned to the porridge and thankfully began eating with a healthier appetite. As he leant forward a pendant on a surprisingly sheer gold chain swung from his unfastened collar. It was a garnet double-sided seal on a finely wrought swivel, and I caught a glimpse of the Castle's sun engraved on one side. I wouldn't hazard to set a price on it.

'Where do you think she's gone?' he asked, too nonchalantly.

'I haven't the faintest idea. I never know where they go. But, Jant, will you be staying here for long?'

'Until I've prevented Raven carrying out his schemes.'

'Good, because I feel safer with an immortal under my roof.'

'Have the Rhydanne threatened you?'

'Not directly, but the atmosphere couldn't be worse. I haven't traded so much as a snowflake since Dellin made her speech. And after last night I don't think Snipe's men will come here again.'

He paused, possibly reflecting on his part in our dwindling business. Good, I thought. Eszai have no right to beat up mortals, especially in my hotel. He was supposed to act as an adviser, not like a bloody gangster! I wanted him to get rid of Raven, not wreck my livelihood.

'I wish I felt better myself,' he admitted. 'I'm just tired, though ... Last night she was encouraging, then she left me. No wonder I'm perplexed.'

'She has to hunt,' I said soothingly.

'Bollocks. I'll buy her the best dinner you can offer. She can have the best Tre Cloud can cook. There's no need to hunt.'

'She prefers her way of life.'

'And won't let me join it.' His wing nearest me flexed open a little and closed, and I noticed he had clasped bangles around its broad wrist. 'I wanted to stay up all night, talking to her about anything and everything. In all her speeches I thought she might be hiding some sort of message for me ... What she wanted me to do ... Hmm ... Maybe I said the wrong thing and put her off. Have you got any whisky?'

I fetched a bottle, poured two slugs into cups and he knocked his back. It gave him confidence, or at least a moment of clarity, because he leant forward conspiratorially. 'I've never had this feeling before. Nothing as strong as this ... I actually feel sick. Don't tell anybody, will you?'

'Who on earth is there to tell?'

'Good.' He nodded, one hand on the bottle. He knew his eyes were striking, and he was so vain he kept eye contact longer than normal, in a very mischievous manner. 'Raven's men – Snipe, Crake, all of them – say that although Awians and humans are people, Rhydanne are more like animals.'

Life is too arduous to waste time and energy by being angry. I felt my anger rising sure enough, but I laughed it down because no good ever comes of it, as he'd proved yesterday. 'No, Jant. Don't lose perspective by talking to the colonists, ha ha. Don't let their stupidity sway you, when you were right in the first place. Rhydanne are the rightful occupants of Carnich.'

'The Castle's Doctor told me they were indigenous. She was interested in Rhydanne, so when I joined the Castle she studied me thoroughly.' He spread his wing across his lap, plucked a broken feather and crumpled it, deep in thought. 'She said Rhydanne could have been humans who came to the mountains long ago ... maybe even hundreds or thousands of years ago ... and the harsh climate changed them. The mountains altered them, a little every generation, until they were suited to live here. Whenever I drank too much, she tried to keep me on the straight and narrow by saying, "The mountains were your ancestors' gymnasium. You'd never have won into the Circle without being so fit."'

'Ha ha! So Rhydanne are more than human!'

'No. Neither more nor less, just different. Rayne said, "Everyone knows things gradually improve. The Castle shows us that. The Castle keeps the best of every skill, which always improves as better practitioners come to light. Similarly the best of every species survives, and people and animals grow to be the best match for their surroundings." But Dellin ... well, somewhere along the line Rhydanne lost the need to rely on each other.'

'Oh, I think every human secretly wishes for that.' I poured another whisky and he sloshed it down. To be honest, I wondered how he ever got anything done. He seemed too impractical to be the Emperor's Messenger. He was as impulsive as a schoolboy. I squeezed the bicep of his wing, quietly comforting. His feathers were hard and sharp, the muscle taut and powerful – a *working* wing. There was little I could say to comfort him, because I've never been in love myself. As far as I see it, our emotions, noble or despicable, are nothing more than those of animals raised to a higher power. All our fine philosophies and epic tales are nothing more than the refined grunts of beasts. Our high art is degraded instinct, and we shouldn't flatter ourselves on being more than animals, because we form a continuity with them. Yes, we're all animals: Rhydanne, Plainslanders, Morenzians and Awians too – and if that's a blow to your pride, let me tell you: pride is an animal emotion. I said quietly, 'Every emotion I've seen in people, I've also recognised in my hounds.'

'What about love?'

'What do you think?' I whistled, and Snowblink bounded up from the fireplace to loll at my feet. 'You talk to me about love, Jant, but the only thing I ever loved I killed.'

'A man?'

'No. A dog. A faithful dog, Snowblink's grandsire. I was even more hound-surrounded then than I am now, ha ha.' My eloquence is hardly up to Jant's standard, since I live alone, but telling the story might take his mind off Dellin. 'Well,' I said, 'I came to Carnich twenty years past and I brought an avalanche dog called Barguest from Eyrie village.'

'Barguest? Like the great wolf that Rhydanne tell stories about?'

'That's right. I named him after the great wolf. And he was great: he dragged his own weight of supplies up here on a sledge. He was a fine companion and saved my life on a few occasions. I once toppled into a crevasse and he pulled me out. When I lost my bearings in a snowstorm his nose sniffed us home.

'I loved that great white hound more than anything. Don't believe those people who extol the virtues of dogs or cats to the skies: dogs follow their vanities just as much as men do. Dogs are similarly prone to envy or greed, ha ha. They'll squabble and try to be top dog in the same way as a man will. But in some ways they're better than men. With a dog you have a partnership, and if you honour it and keep your side of the bargain he'll be constant and faithful to the end.'

'And cats?'

'Are just the same. Human ego is pretence, Jant. Even the most lauded Eszai are crawling on all fours through life. I boggle at why we look for the human in our animals when we're utterly blind to the beast in ourselves. We love to see dogs act in human ways, don't we? Those are just the animal ways we share with them. When I started to build the trading post Barguest helped by hauling sledloads of logs. He carried water. He lugged rocks around, and we finished the roof before the first winter. We practically broke our limbs with working every hour of daylight and I wriggled into my sleeping bag exhausted every night. The icicles on the lintel grew so long they caged us in. Every morning I broke them and shovelled the snow. Otherwise it would've buried the whole cabin. We swept slush from the terrace every spring and received the Rhydanne goatherds travelling up to the meadows. We liked them because they trade rugs and kilims. The hunters never bother to weave.

'Anyway, Barguest would sit on the step and guard the house. He'd bark a welcome when he saw them. Then came Macan's father, an Awian trader, proof that men are more fickle and disloyal than dogs, ha ha. If you offer them a partnership they're sure to take advantage.'

'Like my father,' said Jant.

'What?'

'He might have been a trader too.'

I felt embarrassed because his father might have been anybody. As you know, Rhydanne arrange marriages for their children, to ensure there are two parents committed to bringing up any offspring. His mother was single and never had an arranged marriage, so being a Shira he was lucky to survive.

'It was many years ago,' I continued. 'But that winter was more than usually severe. Rhydanne sensibly time their births to fall in summer, but I hadn't calculated for Macan and I dealt with the birth right here, on my own. One day the blizzard was driving so powerfully that I didn't want to take the baby outside, but I had to check my traps. I laid Macan in his woven cradle beside the hearth and left Barguest to keep him company.

'I did the rounds of my snares, struggling through the drifts and stopping to disentangle a hare from each noose. The afternoon became evening; it grew dark and I trudged home. The gales battered me, the flung snow stuck to me and I bent double under my sack. I could just make out the cabin. The doorway was a black rectangle, the door open, crashing loose in the wind. Something was wrong.

'Barguest bounded out and frolicked over the snow to greet me. His tail was wagging – but his muzzle, jaws and chest were wet through and through with blood. I froze. He saw my expression, backed away, though still barking happily. He ran rings around me as I hastened inside. Snow covered the whole floor. It had blown in and lay in drifts all over the furniture. Macan's cradle was knocked off its stand and lay upside down. The blankets had spilled out and they were soaked with pools of blood. My baby was nowhere to be seen. I screamed, "You've killed him!"

'Barguest cowered and fawned. He tried to lick my boot and I saw blood on his fangs! "Evil hound! Murdering hound! Did you *eat* him, as well?" I grabbed my axe and swung. Barguest darted away – the blade chopped off the tip of his tail and buried itself in the floorboards. He yelped, dashed out of the door trailing blood drops and fled into the blizzard.

'But at his cry a baby started wailing. I moved the fallen cradle and there was my son. He had been hidden underneath it and fast asleep. I scooped him to my breast, and gathered up the blankets. Snow powdered from them, a drift collapsed and revealed the monstrous body of a wolf with its throat torn out.

'I hurried to the door. Barguest had gone; the snow had already covered his pawprints. I called, "Barguest! Barguest!" I called for hours and walked round and round the cabin with my baby inside my coat, but the gales blew my words back into my mouth and Barguest did not return.

'I was haunted by his look of betrayal, the confusion in his eyes as he fawned at my feet. He'd slain the wolf that tried to devour Macan, so why had I turned on him? The brave lad couldn't understand it. Now, Jant, if you jump to conclusions as quickly as I did, if you're fast to anger rather than taking time to comprehend, you will only destroy the one you love.

'Next morning I unfastened the latch and something dragged heavily when I pulled the door open. It was Barguest, frozen solid, and the fur on his back had stuck to the door. Late during the night, my dog had returned to sit on the step as he always did in the daytime, and he was covered in a layer of ice which held him sitting up straight, guarding our house even in death.' I nodded at the door. 'I buried him out on the terrace and raised the flagpole on his grave. Barguest the Frozen Hound. Poor boy ... See his lead hanging on the chimney breast? I had a terrible struggle with the wolves after he died. They knew my other dogs lacked his courage.

'So, Jant, I think misunderstanding someone is worse than hating them, because at least with hatred they have the luxury of hating you in return. Misunderstanding destroys any relationship, and even if they love you they will be helpless to respond ... So you had better understand Dellin, and more vitally make sure *she* understands *you*.'

He swallowed hard and nodded. 'I'd better go find her ... I still feel terrible.'

'No offence, ha ha, but you look terrible.'

'Console me!' He put his head on one side, swept a curve of hair away from his face and whined mournfully, like a dog.

'Cut it out.'

'Cut it out? Yeah, I should. Sorry, Ouzel. I just feel miserable ... I feel hope, remorse, longing—'

'All at the same time?'

'All mixed up. There's a hole in the middle of my chest, as heavy as lead, but empty. Last night she was encouraging, but ...'

'You're smitten.'

He nodded so abjectly that I placed my hand on his shoulder. It was strange to be comforting an immortal, but he seemed distraught out of all proportion. He shook his head and muttered, 'Comet, you've gone soft.'

'Last night gives the lie to that.'

'Hm? Oh ...'

'Yes, *that*!' I said. 'If you meet Snipe, would you consider apologising to him? Please?'

He folded his wings and buttoned his parka, lost in thought. Then he pulled a little leather pot of lip balm from his pocket, and seeing it seemed to cheer him up. 'I'd enjoy defending Dellin against anyone who insults her.'

'Not in my bar!'

'Even in Raven's solar. Bye!'

'Goodbye, Jant.'

The door banged closed on its spring and I heard his footsteps outside crisping faster and faster. Then they stopped abruptly – he had taken flight. I turned back to the table and discovered that the bottle of whisky had gone. I laughed. He was so ridiculously charismatic, his smile so quirky, that for hours afterwards I had a clear impression of him, as if he was still here before me.

SNIPE

It were still snowing, had been since cock crow. It fell thickly in front of us, on the track, and straight down on our shoulders. It were building thicker on the branches of the trees on both sides. Every now and then a branch dropped its snow with a thump. I was listening to the chat and the hoof falls of the squad I were leading to Lanner's place. We were heading to the lead mine.

Glede rode alongside and asked, 'Can you still hear Crake's squad?'

'Too bloody right. With all their crashing about the 'danne will hear 'em a mile off.'

He shrugged and grinned savagely. 'All the more for us then!'

Clumsy in leather gauntlets over my usual gloves, I pulled the rein of my horse left, to keep her on the track. I rested my other hand, holding a bow, on the saddle. My four men were scanning the trees to either side. Trees and more bloody trees. More trunks in the spaces between 'em. Between *them* more trees, and between them nothing but blackness. Darkling pine, Skline spruce and the odd silver fir. I don't like 'em. Anybody could hide behind 'em. We watched the lower boughs too: wildcats lie in wait on them and drop onto you. As do Rhydanne.

Raven had sent out five squads to discover what had happened to the prospectors. None of those poor sods had returned to the keep and everyone thought the cat-eyes had done for 'em. Raven had told us to beat through the woods, dislodge all the 'danne hiding there and kill them. We were to check the prospectors' cabins first, then fan out and drive the forest clean back to the keep. He knows his hunting techniques, does Raven. But he's edgy, more highly strung than normal. Recent events are getting to him. I told him: carry on preparations for Francolin's troops; don't forget to let me know what's happening and you can leave the savages to me.

The men were eagle-eyed, hungry for revenge. On Raven's behalf I'd promised a hundred pounds for each 'danne head. Spirits were high. The horses were in good nick and Raven had opened the armoury for us. He'd issued some of the gear we'd collected for Francolin's force. The squad wore gorgets to counter bolases, and our cuirasses, greaves and chain were proof against any of the cat-eyes' flint spearheads or the crappy metal ones we'd sold them. All this steel didn't half get cold though. Its chill sank straight through my clothes. And I had little hope of good news when we reached the cabins. The poor buggers there must have been sleeping when the 'danne struck.

My mare tended to the side again and I drew her back. Her shoes were wider than usual and spiked to grip the snow. I searched every space among the trees, and now and then I looked to the sky to see if that shit Comet was sailing round and round up there. I had slapped a beefsteak on my eye to stop the swelling but it did no good. I could hardly see. It were a garish purple and the freezing air made it sting, even though I'd pulled my hat down over it. My split lip was even worse: I hadn't eaten anything but soup since. The gash in my hooter had wrecked my looks – I was no longer the man my wife knew and loved. But at least it was going to heal straight. My broken tooth was the worst of all. I was always going to have a nasty gap to remember the bastard by.

The pain and humble pie weren't as bad as the feeling of helplessness. But all these were practically worth it when I told Raven what had happened. He descended from the window seat where he likes to sit so high and mighty, and gazed at my fizzog. Then he laughed and said, 'We're both disfigured now! Snipe, we have both been badly treated by those in charge, but now Jant has played into our hands!'

'Why?' I asked. I like to play dumb sometimes, though Raven's so convinced everyone else is an idiot it doesn't take much effort.

'He's given us an ace to play against him. Strange that he should lose self-control to this extent ... I thought he was the one who invented blackmail.'

'He was unreasonable,' I said.

'I can see that. Stay out of his way and be the card I play when the time's right. Try not to heal too quickly.'

I just nodded, which is safest when I can't be sure of the tone of my voice. Raven may think me sullen, let him think it. He doubled my wage before sending me away. The beating had some other advantages too: the men are in awe of me – that I've been thumped by Comet himself – and I let them know I gave as good as I got. I told the silly sods that if any of them had been up against Jant, he'd've killed 'em.

'I saw something!' Glede called from the rear, and we all drew up.

'What? Where?'

He stuck out a gloved finger. 'There, between the trees!'

The others looked where he was pointing but I glanced to the trees on the other side. 'You dumb oaf! Don't yell, just shoot.'

'It's gone now, anyway ...'

I clapped my hands so they looked at me. 'It could have been a 'danne. They move like smoke. Don't shout, just shoot – it's the only way. I want 'danne hands on my saddle bow, as they have bear paws. We're going to get those bastards. OK?'

'Yeah!'

'Did you hear something?' Sparrow, the youngest archer, said.

'What?'

'A twig cracking?'

'Sh!'

'Come on.' I tapped my mare and we trudged onwards.

Now *I* thought I heard the snow crackle, and a giggle, instantly hushed. I stared in that direction – but couldn't see anything – and my horse carried me past. I was sure something was keeping pace with us. I was sure we were being watched but, staring, all I could see was the damn bark, the snow lying in hollows. I hadn't been out this way since the snows began in earnest and the whiteness was disorientating. It masked all the familiar landmarks.

Glede behind me yelled and loosed an arrow.

I pulled up so suddenly his horse ran into mine. 'Nothing there.' I said.

'Sorry, steward. Nothing there.'

This is no good, I thought. We're getting spooked. 'Look, if Rhydanne were around, our horses would smell 'em. They're relaxed, so the bastards are bloody miles away.'

'All those trees,' grumbled Glede.

'So it's taken you two years to notice we live in a forest! Now come on, it's not far now.' Sure enough, the pall of smoke from the mine works was rising in front of us, just down the track, but we couldn't yet see the cabins. We rode on, into the shadow of a rock outcrop, one of the buttocks of Capercaillie. A definite crunch sounded behind us. We all heard it this time.

'That isn't snow falling,' said Glede.

'Where'd it come from?'

'There ... No, there.'

'From *behind* us.'

'I can't see anything,' said Sparrow. 'I know something's there, but I can't see it.' He flexed his arms, half-drawing then relaxing the bow on his knees. 'They're fucking with us.'

We waited, but heard no other sounds apart from the whisper of the flakes.

'Must've been a branch breaking.'

'They're fucking with us, they're fucking with us ...'

'Stop that! Men, we kicked their arse yesterday. And we're going to kick them again today. Let's have that song again: The foot folk/ Put the 'danne to the poke.'

'By way.'

'Never heard I say,' muttered Glede.

All together: 'Of readier boys to get the joke.'

I glanced up to the profile of the outcrop against the sky, and on its very edge a thin figure leaned out in silhouette. It held on with one hand, the other arm extended and the fingers clawed. Its profile was jagged, the outward knee bent. It let itself be seen, then it drew back into the cliff, seemed to merge with the rock and was gone ... as if a gargoyle could suck itself back into a castle roof.

I drew, loosed, and my arrow cracked off the rock. The men stopped singing abruptly. I scanned the cliff face for movement. Something fell towards us. A stone, about the size of my fist, lodged in the snow to my left. More began to shower down from above – one bounced off my cantle. God, they have good aim. 'Come on!' I yelled, and spurred down the track, but the falling rocks kept pace with us. God knows how many were up there, running along the ledges, clinging to niches. I scanned the cliffs desperately, squinting against the sun. 'Can you see them?'

'No!'

Abruptly a 'danne stepped into the path about thirty metres ahead, waving something. A slingshot banged off my shoulder guard. Before I could draw, he darted back behind a tree. 'There's one! Give it feathers!'

I spurred to a gallop. I could see the 'danne running in the fringe of the trees, parallel to the path ahead, its parka white against the trunks. An arrow cut past from behind me – too wide – and the thump of hooves told me the others were following. I had no chance of shooting it while galloping but if I could keep the thing in sight we could work together and corner it. I blew two blasts on my horn: when the other squads heard they'd circle up ahead and the 'danne would be trapped between us.

Suddenly it changed direction, vanished under the boughs and I feared we'd lost it. Sorrel, my mare, carried me to the spot in a second, and I could see it had turned down a small deer track running off the path. Now it didn't have to dodge trunks so much, it was beginning to accelerate away. I followed without pause. At the very least the path took us away from the cliffs and the rocks raining down.

I held my bow low to stop it snagging, ducked under the branches flailing my face, and sped on. Trunks flashed by; the path twisted and narrowed. We emerged into a clearing, a gash torn in the forest by a fallen spruce that lay half-buried. I couldn't see the 'danne anywhere now. The others piled up behind me, horses and men panting steam into the air.

'Where?' gasped Glede.

'Don't say we're lost,' wailed Sparrow.

'I don't get lost riding from the keep to the mines. Not unless someone has turned the forest around. Now shut up and listen.'

We had lost sight of the 'danne but he had to be around here somewhere. My breathing seemed too loud and the icy air tore at my throat. Up ahead I heard approaching hoofbeats.

'Crake's men are coming – hear? We'll catch that cat-eyes between us.'

A whoosh. I felt the passage of air behind me, and Glede was carried off his saddle. He hit the track, something tall waving above him. A spear. He screamed a wide-jawed scream, and my other three men loosed their arrows indiscriminately into the trees. They fumbled for more, drew again. Their shafts needled between the trunks, struck bark, ricocheted off. 'Stop! Stop!' I bellowed. 'Mark your targets!'

Glede flexed and kicked on the ground, screaming. The spear had gone through his cheek, through his mouth and out his other cheek. He was holding the shaft upright, his head on the snow.

He couldn't close his mouth, couldn't pull the spear out. From the dumbness of his screams it had severed his tongue. From the clacking it had knocked his teeth out as well.

Now a bolas came whirling from between the trees on the other side, whacked Sparrow on the shoulder, tangled around his bow and whipped it out of his hands. In its wake the forest edge erupted with Rhydanne. They dashed into the clearing and towards us like a flight of arrows. Three, four, five, that's all. Howling and shaking antler rattles they bore down on us. Sorrel bucked so deeply I were almost over her head, and she swung round so all I could see were a line of trees. I opened my wings to steady myself, felt the cold stab at them, and forced her to turn back. With a kick in the ribs and dragging her rein I won the battle of wills and saw the 'danne split up.

Two ran round me on each side and passed by a whisker, melted into the forest still shrieking and rattling. The last alighted beside Glede, who tried to kick away. Its hood bent to Glede's screaming face; it grabbed the shaft and with a swift twist and thrust shut Glede up permanently.

It turned and ran for the forest. I drew, loosed. It dropped its spear and fell flat on its face, my arrow projecting from its back. Take that, murdering cat-eyed scum! At once the howling and rattling started again. Two of the things bounded from behind a fallen trunk; two dashed from the trees on our right, forming a circle around us. Spears pointed at us – in their other hands they shook rattles or flaming branches, and their yowling was unearthly.

Sorrel reared so high I thought they'd dash in and spear her belly, turned and came down hard. My mates were squashed round me as their horses pitched and panicked, trying to turn but jammed too close. We tangled in a mesh of horses' hindquarters and our knees pressing together. The 'danne looped round behind us and closed in.

Sorrel pawed the ground, combing up the snow, lurched this way and that, then bolted. I tightened her rein but she kept bloody going, out of the clearing, away from the path. Trees loomed either side of me, then I was between them. She carried me, dashing between the trunks. Cries told me the others were following. Yowls further back as the 'danne chased us. My mare stretched out her neck and went hell for leather.

Terrified by the savages' hooting, terrified by their stink, and maddened beyond terror by slingshots, Glede's riderless horse plunged on behind me. Their aim was deadly – slingstones smacked off my helmet with such force they shoved my head forward. Sorrel wouldn't respond – I couldn't rein her up – at that speed if I tried to guide her she'd smash into a tree.

Damn 'danne could come from anywhere. A spear through the branches at any time! They were everywhere and I couldn't fucking see them! I was helpless. I was fucking helpless! They could snuff my life any time now, so why were they chasing us? Why were they chasing us? Why didn't they just kill us?

Sorrel crashed on. Snow flew up from her hooves. My quiver rattled on the saddle bow – I unclipped it and let it fall. I folded my coat back and checked the hilt of my snickersnee – I'm braced to take one of the fuckers with me.

I heard more cries to my right – human voices yelling, bawling, keeping pace with us. A second later I saw them through the trees – fleeting, pine trunks in the way like an illusionist's trick. A bay horse, the rider clinging to her mane, not the reins, his blue scarf streaming out behind. Another horse with blood streaks down her withers and froth all over her muzzle. They were the patrol – what was left of them – on our right, who'd been riding to Lanner's place. The savages were chasing them too.

I turned in the saddle and glanced back at Sparrow. His face was a mask of fear and his wings clamped tight. The other team was coming closer and closer. Rhydanne were driving them, and they'd have joined with us but our horses were starting to veer to the left. Cries were now coming from their other side – I glimpsed more horses among the trunks. Another squad. I recognised Crake's bellowing, his voice raised high in fear. They were out of control as well, and stampeding nearer and nearer. Were the scum hounding them too?

Now a snow pile loomed on my left, a long ridge between the trees. A savage appeared from behind it, leapt onto its summit, waving firebrands in both hands and yelling. Sorrel plunged away; all the other horses did too, carrying us closer than before to the team in the middle – now only three or four trees away. God, if we'd only brought dog teams instead of horses!

The ridge continued – it must have been shaped by hand. It rose half the height of a man and the 'danne had stuck branches in the top, sticks with rags and rattles on them. Our horses hurtled straight along it and I tried even harder to rein Sorrel back, but she was running for her life and cared for nothing. Had the 'danne built this bulwark? I thought they lived in potholes and tents. They're not capable of building! Tiny dwarf-creatures bounded up on top of it, howling and shrieking, waving flaming torches. I raced past. What were they? What the fuck were they? They were the same leggy shape as 'danne – dressed the same way. They had damp patches on their knees where they'd been kneeling, hiding. Then I realised – they were Rhydanne *children*.

I'd never seen one before. They were acting like adults. Shit, they were creepy. They were hunting us. Hunting *us*! I set my jaw. Can't get through my armour, can they? Then I'll damn well outride them.

The team on our right merged with us, thundered beside me at arm's length. Now something else on top of the ridge. Angular scarecrows of black and white with fluttering twig fingers, all along the crest. Can I break through? I gathered Sorrel's reins and tried to force her left against the mound. She swerved closer, closer still and then I saw ropes strung between the trees, at the level of her withers. The 'danne had netted the trees! The ropes looked as thin as threads, but for me to see them at all, they must be sturdy. The sort the savages climb with. The sort they make from their own hair.

I eased the rein and she bent to the right again. We were among Crake's squad now – ten riders left alive and two, three riderless horses including ours – and another squad was close ahead.

I hadn't known, none of us had known, there were so many 'danne. The forest had been silent, but now they were everywhere! How many? Twelve? Fifteen? No more than that. We should be able to kill them, easily, but Sorrel won't stop!

More jumped out from behind the barricade. They let us pass then sprinted after us. Those previously screeching on our tail lost pace and climbed up the barricade. They were exchanging places with the new relay. It's like a racetrack, I thought wildly, and then they're funnelling us together. They're funnelling us together! *Where are we*?!

We descended an incline. The ground became rougher, the snow more powdery. Sorrel and everyone around me plunged down without breaking pace. One brown horse lost her footing and went down in a whirl of snow – the rider catapulted over her head, smashed against a tree and lay still.

Screams sounded from the squad ahead. It's a cliff! A fucking edge! I pulled the reins with all my strength but Sorrel stretched her neck and the bit ring snapped. They went loose in my hand.

The horses in front of me went over – heads and forelegs into space, their butts shining, rear hooves raised. The riders screamed and looked down in front of them. They threw out their arms. One grabbed his horse's neck; another prepared to jump – too late! There was clear air between the saddles and their arses. All were in free-fall. Then they were gone.

I struggled to kick my foot out of the stirrup – the tab on my boot wedged and all the time the cliff edge was getting closer. I wrenched my foot out, kicked the other free, swung my leg over the saddle and dived.

I hit the ground, my arms around my head. I rolled over and over till I crunched into fresh snow. The hooves of the following horses charged past, beating the snow. They pounded across my vision, kicking up clods. Thunder and crunching all around me, the riders yelling, trying to rein in their horses. The horses jamming to a halt with all four legs and sliding. Some tumbled. Others stretched out galloping without pause straight over the precipice. They fell, slamming into each other. The heads and upflung arms of the riders were last to vanish.

The last group hurtled towards me and with them Crake, his face set in horror. I yelled, 'Jump!' He slipped back on the saddle, then threw his leg over and crumped to the ground – didn't roll – and all the horses following went over him, throwing his body this way and that. They stormed over the precipice and shrieks rang out ... faded ... horses and men falling a great distance through the air. Distant thumps as they smashed against the rock ... fainter ... fainter ... and a remote series of thuds and crashes.

Crake lay still, extended and rigid. His back was broken. His hands shook. Between us hoof prints and gouges scored the snow to the precipice about five metres away. Shit. They were all dead. Thirty good men, all killed.

I was about to run to Crake when a light crunching signalled the arrival of the 'danne who'd been chasing us. Two ran past me to the cliff edge and looked over. Teetering there, spears in hand, they started laughing. I boiled with fury and hatred. I lay still. Their fur-bordered hood openings turned to each other; the smaller one nodded and pointed downward. The other actually dug his talons into the snow and lowered himself over the edge! He turned, facing me. I caught a glimpse of his weedy, beardless face, then he climbed down the cliff and disappeared.

Another couple stopped beside Crake and stood with spears raised, wondering where to thrust between his armour. It'd be folly for me to move. I wanted to be up and running but they're like dogs – if you run they register you as prey and chase you. I figured I had bugger all chance of living through this and I had best lie still and not give them the pleasure of hunting me.

The small 'danne left the cliff edge and joined the others around Crake. One of them tapped his spear on the plates of armour – his head on one side. He raised his spear and tried to thrust it into the gap between Crake's gorget and breastplate. Ching! The flint point broke. He threw his spear aside in disgust, hunkered down and drew a knife. He began sawing into the gaps between the joints of Crake's armour – armpits, throat, the backs of his knees – wherever he could find a slit, until blood spurted onto the snow. Crake was alive all through this and they cackled louder than ever.

Eventually the short savage figured out how to unbuckle the gorget. He took it off, gave it to his accomplice, then cut Crake's throat with one neat slash. The tall one, having got the idea, eagerly started stripping Crake's armour. The little one left him to it and ran towards me. Halfway over I recognised her as the small woman who'd come to the keep with Comet. The one who'd chattered to our porters and spilt the barrel. She had more bear claws on her belt than the other savages and they rattled.

Recognition flickered across her face as well. She crouched an arm's length away, her spear at the ready. My fingers curled numbly round the hilt of my blade but I knew I could never draw it before she'd finish me. This is it. I braced myself for the thrust.

Her eyebrows drew together. She spoke and was halfway through the sentence before I realised I understood her. She was speaking *Awian*! I could hardly hear it through her accent. 'You are Steward Snipe, yes? Raven's man? The bruise eye man?' She reached out her spear and the point came at my face, circling round and round.

I nodded, scraping my cheek in the snow.

'Steward Snipe. Jant hit you.' She laughed and her cold eyes glittered. 'Jant hit you hard and good. Now I beat you too. What you think of this?' She flourished her spear at the precipice then trained it on me again immediately. 'Go, tell Raven this. Tell Raven to leave Carnich or I hunt him. I hunt you *all*!'

I scrambled to my feet, slipped and stumbled. I forced myself up again and ran, sure she would pounce. The male 'danne looked up from claiming Crake's armour but she barked a command at him – a *command*! – and he shrugged.

I passed other 'danne squatting by my dead friends or sitting on their snow bulwark. They all eyed me keenly and their babies trotted alongside me but not for very far. They were obeying the words of the huntress.

I staggered back into the forest and began to follow our footprints. I was shivering and gazing wildly round, thinking more Rhydanne would appear like ghosts. The light were fast ebbing and even the fucking trees seemed alive. The 'danne behind me fell quiet and when I looked back they'd gone. Crake's body lay alone, surrounded by wide bloodstains, sprayed out onto the snow from every joint.

I found the track as dusk were falling. I walked all the way back to the keep and emerged from the forest long after dark. The tower rose before me. I were shivering so violently it hurt; my face was numb and stinging, my lips cracked and bleeding, and I couldn't feel my arms or legs, let alone my bloody hands or feet. I stumbled like a dying thing out of the wilderness, and all the way I hummed to myself to take my mind off the pain. I clambered over the snow piled beside the path and the guard at the gate drew his bow. I called to him and he looked horrified at the state of me. No one in front of me, no one behind. I was the only survivor.

JANT

I flew for hours trying to find Dellin – I mean, trying to find any Rhydanne, or the troops Raven had sent after them. But the forest thickly cloaked the slopes, rising over its buttresses, descending into its gullies, and I couldn't see down between the pines. Pines grew solidly on every centimetre of land that wasn't vertical and bristled on the tops of the cliffs. They covered the cliff's slopes and ledges on all sides, surrounding rock faces which showed as black granite scars. Where the forest petered out, a fresh snowfall enlarged every hummock, disguised the crevasses, and smoothed away every sign of Awian or Rhydanne footprint or ski trail.

Where was she? I flew so low that my wingtips touched the treetops, but I couldn't hear her howls. I landed several times to rest my wings and listen, but it was nearly impossible to find clearings and just as difficult to take off again. Flying was no use, but if I borrowed skis from Ouzel it would be just as frustrating and even more disorientating criss-crossing among the shadowy trunks.

Snowflakes drifted down with endless patience – a patience I did not share in any way. I tore the sky in two looking for Dellin. I no longer cared whether I lived or died.

Then in the distance I heard a whistle. A Rhydanne whistle. I strained to catch it, but the swoosh and batter of my wings kept interrupting it. Up-slope slightly; in that direction nothing but blackness, the trees merged into the bulk of Klannich. I glided, straining to hear over the roaring airflow. Then ... voices ... and drumming!

The forest suddenly plunged away under me. I had flown over a cliff concealed by the trees. I gasped, checked I was still flying straight, and looked down into the black depths that had opened up below me. Way down below was a blossom of yellow light no larger than a mountain flower. I leant and turned – the forest soared up around me, then above me – and I spiralled down in front of the rock face.

The yellow light was a campfire in a large clearing at the foot of the cliff. It cast a halo on the snow and flickered on the dappled brown surfaces of some rectangles around it. I now heard Rhydanne voices and laughter, loud raillery, the occasional whistle, and the drumming.

I landed with a crunch and walked towards it, tentatively feeling each step in the half-light. The snow squeaked under my soles and the Rhydanne around the fire fell silent. Now I could hear another sound as well, like pebbles being struck together. 'Chack! Chack! Chink!'

The glow of the bonfire illuminated the ring of tents around it, casting their tapering shadows long over the snow. The ends of the tents facing me merged blackly with the night, but the flames reached high above their ridges, dancing so the orange glow lapped back and forth, sending sparks in a stream to the sky. The smell of smoke and a wonderful aroma of roast meat enticed me. Dellin must be here. I stepped over a windbreak and made my way between the buff-coloured tents. About twenty Rhydanne lounged around the fire, warming their soles or sitting with their legs covered with pelts. Their eyes reflected the fire as they stared at me, but the 'Chack! Chack!' continued for a second. On the other side of the fire – Dellin. She had a doe-skin kerchief over her nose and mouth. She glanced up, saw me, and pulled it down to reveal a broad grin. She removed a piece of hide from her lap, bounded around the fire and took my hand.

'He's on our side,' she said to the group. 'He's our friend!'

As one they whooped and whistled. I belonged here! I felt a remarkable rightness that I hadn't felt since first entering the Castle. I felt I was home.

Dellin tugged my wing, inviting me to sit down beside her on a chamois skin. Its small, pointed hooves reflected the bonfire light; its hair was like soft, beige moss. She pressed a cup of whisky into my hand and arranged a fur over my legs. 'Have a drink and warm up. Did you hear our drums?'

'Yes, I did.'

'We've been calling Rhydanne in since sundown. We've had a successful hunt!'

Indeed, a huge haunch of meat was spitted over the fire, dripping fat into a tray lying among the flames. Every so often a huntress would lean forward, baste it, and give the spit a turn. Dellin forked a slab of meat from a pile of carved chunks on a hearthstone, plopped it into a piece of leg armour which made quite a good plate, and passed it to me. I drew my knife and cut the wobbly, pale fat from its edge.

She was so beautiful, and I was sitting beside her! She had rubbed red ochre powder in her hair and it hung in hard, red twists. Her parka was unbuttoned down as far as her breasts. Its toggles were tubes of eagle's bone and she had threaded porcupine-spine beads on its lacings. All my anxieties of the last hours melted away. Now I was here the journey seemed inconsequential.

The firelight fell vividly on the stretched leather of the tents around us and the beautiful, rolling grey folds of the fur I wrapped round me like a shawl. Dellin picked up her apron, raised the kerchief over her nose and resumed her flint knapping. She raised a pebble, dinted at the end from previous use, struck the core she held in her other hand, 'Chack!' and peeled off a blade. It was as long and straight as my knife. She placed it gently on a neat stack, turned the core, deciding where to hit next, and struck off another identical blade. She laid it down carefully.

I picked it up and examined it reverently, as if the clear stone could melt into black water and slide between my fingers.

'Careful,' said Dellin. 'Flint is fragile.'

The kerchief muffled her voice, and as I looked up I cut myself. A line of blood appeared on my fingertip but the blade was so sharp it didn't even hurt.

Dellin laughed. 'Did you just draw blood?'

'Mm.'

'It's sharper than steel. But don't worry, it's cleaner too. A cut from black flint will heal a week earlier than a cut from steel.' She struck off another blade, her hands moving with deceptive lightness.

'Are you making knives?'

'These are to be spear points. But I start by making a knife, then I shape it. We've stopped using Awian metal but flint points do break easily.'

'Have you all stopped trading with Awians?'

'Yes! Everyone in Carnich has agreed that we'll stop being cheated. We're in control of our lives again – we're returning to our own ways. But not just the hunters of Carnich, look, there are many more. Raven's people drove their porters out of the keep and they've joined us. Now they're living like Rhydanne again! I called in hunters from Chir Klannich for the chase, and even a pair from Stravaig came to see what was happening. They hunted with us, so they can eat with us. We have food for everyone!'

Her originality impressed me again – no other Rhydanne would conceive such a plan and no other would have the force of character needed to put it into operation. She actually had them working together!

'They're following you even though you're a Shira!'

She waved the taboo aside. 'That doesn't matter any more.'

'They've made you their leader.'

'Leader? No ...' Her face clouded. 'That's an Awian word. These are all top hunters, Jant, my equals. They see the wisdom in my suggestions and accord with them, that's all.'

I turned the blade over, wondering at her craftsmanship.

Waste flakes were gathering around her legs; she tipped some off her apron and used it to brush them into a pile. She said, 'I learnt to knap when I was an over-winterer. When I was younger and looking for a partner, I stayed on the summit of Klannich all year round. That's how I met Laochan. There's no steel traded on Chir Klannich, of course, so Laochan showed me how to make our own knives. He was a great craftsman with flint and red chert; he used to say that because it breaks predictably, it is more reliable than people. Now I understand what he means ...'

I hoped she wasn't referring to me. 'You'll always find me reliable.'

'Will I?' She lowered the corrugated core and looked at me strangely, and I felt embarrassed at being found out ingratiating myself. She struck off a few more blades, though each was successively smaller, and dropped the exhausted core. She rummaged in her rucksack for another flake the size of my hand and began to trim it into a new core.

I pretended to take her skill for granted, because astonishment would just mark me as a foreigner. She had picked flint from Klannich summit and carried it in flakes. Just as the mountain and forest gives her free food, flint is also free. It's her knowledge of what to do with it that's valuable.

I watched as I munched the excellent boar. It was as salty and fatty as pork but much firmer, with the texture and grain almost of beef. Dellin refilled my cup, took one of her blades and shaved more meat off the roast, the flesh parting as easily as mine had.

The fire had been built on a platform of pine boles, and green branches were the main fuel, so tarry they crackled and spat. The Rhydanne were supplementing them with fresh bones piled like logs. The bones burned with a yellow flame; grease melted out of each one and spread along it, a translucent, oily liquid as if they were candles.

I looked around at the company, who were chatting merrily, telling hunting stories and exchanging directions. All the Rhydanne from the Frozen Hound were here, even Rubha. Her two babies peered over the low windbreak, licking meat grease from their fingers. There was blind Lainnir, holding the end of a chunk of boar in his teeth and sawing his knife across it. He seemed to know I was watching, because he nodded slowly as he sucked the cut meat into his mouth and chewed it. His front teeth were worn from chewing leather to soften it; most of the older Rhydanne made clothes that way and they all used their mouths to hold tools temporarily, each like a seamstress with pins between her lips.

Behind Lainnir, his tent was covered in black charcoal hand-prints, an impromptu pattern by someone with dirty hands and a sense of humour. All the tents were taut, pegged straight into the snow without need of guy lines and weighted around their edges with ice blocks. Each had been rolled out from a hunter's knapsack, with spears as tent poles and their shafts projecting. Each flint spear point high above faintly reflected the fire. This group could certainly teach lowland soldiers a thing or two about camp craft, I thought, chewing the tasty crackling.

The children ran about, brandishing their toy spears and giggling. Rubha had given them cups of beech-leaf liqueur. They hid in a tent and ambushed two young hunters, who came into the circle of firelight carrying another haunch on a spit between them. Dellin retouched a blade along its length to prevent flakes breaking off it and showed me how to use it as a knife.

All the Rhydanne – there were twenty, all told – worked as they talked. They knew it was vital to keep their gear in good condition, so they were all engaged in different activities. Many were sewing their jackets or boots. Some were repairing their spears, fitting new points to the original shaft and binding it round with the same string. They affixed long, curved blades along the shaft itself, the better to make the spear spin in flight and cut through hide.

The huntress sitting on my other side was piercing and threading teeth. Another Rhydanne was carving a beautiful spear thrower from a length of bone. He put down his flint gouge and rubbed the notch where the spear would rest with a rawhide strip coated in grit to polish the bone smooth. Usually when in camp they would be making bangles – the quantity signifying how efficient a hunter is to enjoy so much leisure time. But Dellin's followers had given up wearing them, an innovation as unprecedented as the Castle abandoning its sun-in-splendour. Dellin was incredible – the control she had over her followers! 'There's not a glimmer of silver to be seen,' I said.

'Hah! Silver's meaningless now it's tainted by trade with Raven. He sold so many bangles that even the humblest goatherd has a whole armful. You know what silver bangles mean now? Fraternity with the Awians. We want none of it!'

'You'll be giving up drinking next.'

She looked at me, surprised. 'What are you talking about? Drinking is Rhydanne! We've always made our own! Here, try this vodka. I distilled it myself, in my cave. It's better than Raven's. We're all returning to making alcohol, not buying it. See here, we are making our own bindings and our own belts and packs.' They had planted their axes upright as anchors for weaving the bright straps they used to bind trousers and sleeves.

Dellin tested the new haunch and proclaimed, 'It's cooked!' Everyone raised a shout and she carved off the first chunks. She passed them round without wasting the tiniest morsel and the ravenous Rhydanne ate their fill with gusto. I feasted just as heartily; flying gives me an appetite. 'Usually the Daras take the best cuts of meat,' I said.

'I've changed that too.' She laughed. 'Every hunter must accept we're all equal, or they can't join our feast. No more Daras hogging the hearth and gobbling the fat; no more Shiras pushed to the cold outskirts. Here Daras and Shiras can lie together without squabbling. Here, Jant, have some of this sweet stew. It's made from black lichen and maple syrup. Eat well in a time of plenty ...'

Hunting pairs lay peacefully draped over each others' bodies. The children now dozed, one in Rubha's big amaut hood, the other tucked under the hem of her parka. Above us the stars spun slowly round, some frost-white, some pinkish and some ice-blue; their paths crossed the sky.

When Dellin had finished she addressed the huntress beside her: 'Do you have the green amanita?'

'Yes. I brought it from the beech woods.' She opened a pouch of dried fungi. Dellin nodded, took it and secreted it under the folds of her blanket. I was once apprenticed for six years in a chemist's shop, I know well that green amanita are the most lethal fungi in the world. 'What are you doing with that?'

'I'm going to poison the featherbacks. I found a way into the keep last night. I climbed a wall, went through a window and into a long room with a stone floor, where women were roasting game.'

'The kitchen.'

She shrugged. 'They had pots of every kind of food, including dried mushrooms. I will replace them with these and our problems will be over.'

'No! You'll only make things worse! You'd kill some innocent cook. Raven would blame you immediately and persecute you even more.'

She continued regardless, 'They melt the blocks of ice we've seen them cutting from the glacier and pour the water into a gigantic stone box.'

'A cistern.'

'Yes, if you say so. I can easily drop an old carcass into it.'

'No!' I reached under the pelt and grabbed the bag of fungi. 'Don't poison Raven's men! Trust me; I'll bring him round to seeing sense. I'll throw these away.' I stood up and my feet crunched her flint chips.

She took hold of my leg and I felt her nails through the leather. 'Don't go out there. Stay here with me ...' There was a silky seductiveness in her voice I had never heard before. She smiled sincerely and ran her fingers over my thigh as I sat down. 'Stay with me,' she repeated. 'I want you to. You're one of us.'

'Yes ... I am. I know.' Was it strange that I thought so or strange that it had taken me so long to realise?

'Tell me about Scree plateau. The highest pueblo in Darkling.'

'Our capital.'

She considered this. Rhydanne don't think of Scree in the same way as the flatlanders do; it isn't a centre but a place to stay. She asked, 'Did you go to the pueblo itself?'

'Oh yes, all the time. Passing hunters always visited. It has a trading post, a storeroom and the biggest distillery in Darkling. If you run west from there you can find a place where hot water bubbles out of the rock.'

'I'd like to see it.'

'Well, I'll show you. We can run up the Turbary Track together. The whole altiplano can be ours; we can hunt the guanaco every day. The lowlanders wouldn't disturb us; no featherback ever climbed six kilometres into the sky!'

Dellin pondered. 'If I visit Scree, then by the time I return the featherbacks would have destroyed Carnich. I must get rid of them first.'

'You're much stronger than they are,' I told her dreamily, 'so you'll win. When I joined the Circle the Castle's Doctor was so surprised at seeing one of us that she carried out all kinds of tests on me. She said that we have bigger lungs to breathe this air. We have more blood than lowlanders do, and blood of a brighter red colour, and to pump it we have bigger hearts. We can chew gristle and cartilage, and digest it, but Awians would simply waste it. We can climb with our nails; we can see in the snow glare. Have you seen Awians using ice screws to climb and wearing snow goggles? We can see faster than them as well. To them the legs of a running hare are just a blur, but we see them crossing and stretching. We see individual drops flying from a waterfall, but lowlanders would see nothing but mist. And they can't survive outside on a night like this.'

She listened with a hesitant smile but her eyes betrayed confusion. She seemed to get the gist but Rayne's Morenzian terminology meant nothing to her, and I struggled to repeat it in Scree.

I wanted Dellin to tell me everything about herself. I wanted to become familiar with all her acquaintances, all the places she knew. But she was reluctant to talk about herself, which was actually refreshing since lowlanders never do anything else. For example, she had raised two daughters, but all she would say about them was, 'Children grow up and run away.'

She turned to the twenty satiated Rhydanne. 'Tomorrow we will attack the keep itself.' They blinked drunkenly at her. 'I have been watching the gatehouse and I noticed that when the guard reaches the end of the wall he turns his back. I can climb in and open the gate. Feocullan, you—'

Feocullan said, 'Dellin, you are a very angry woman.'

'We must not give Raven time to catch his breath.'

'Why bother, now we have enough food?'

'Yes,' said a lazing huntress. 'I'm going back to Sgriodan.'

'We're returning to Stravaig,' said another, 'taking our meat with us.'

Others raised their voices dozy with drink. 'I'll return to Chir!'

'I have enough food to reach Caigeann.'

'And me. Enough to cache till the melt, then I'll find more of the same.'

'Why go near the keep?' said Feocullan. 'I don't want to risk their arrows. We can go places the featherbacks can't. We can stay out of their range.'

'But Raven will hunt you!' Dellin retorted.

'Out here *we* hunt *them*. If we enter the keep he'll have us penned and shoot us easily.'

'Yes,' said another. 'I don't want to die like Miagail.'

'Or Laochan.'

'I've never even seen a featherback before,' purred the huntress from Sgriodan. 'What do I care about Raven?'

Dellin was trying furiously to come up with a reason for them to attack the keep. 'Eventually he will reach your hunting grounds too,' she said, but the Rhydanne only chuckled.

'When?' said Feocullan. 'Next melt?'

'Some time in the future.'

'Ha ha ha.'

'All right,' she said. 'I only need one or two of the stealthiest to help me find Raven inside the keep. It's an exploit you can tell your children.'

'Being shot means no children!'

The lounging huntress said, 'We've stopped them coming out of the keep. We frightened them into their refuge and they're staying there. Isn't that what you wanted?'

Dellin said, 'Cutting Raven's throat is the quickest way to rid ourselves of all Awians. They'll go home!'

'Dellin, you've been in the flatlands so long you think like them. Who cares?'

She looked down in frustration. If she hadn't been so drunk she might have thought of another argument. 'Tomorrow I'll talk to you again,' she said. 'By then you'll have realised the sense of my words. If you want to save yourselves, you'll stay with me.'

Tomorrow they're all going to be very hungover, I thought. Then, if they still have meat and drink they'll convey it to their caches. Dellin would find it difficult to rally them, although I thought she might be able to and I'd have to warn Raven. I grinned inwardly. Without the others, Dellin's vendetta would collapse, I could get Raven to give ground and then I'd have her full attention.

The fire was allowed to burn down to powdery sheaves of ash and calcined fragments of bone. The cauldron was scraped empty and Rubha was snoring. Everyone began stripping off their parkas and retiring inside their tents. Above us the moon hung like a coin. Tatters of cloud blowing across it gave the impression it was sailing with great rapidity towards the peak of Klannich. I was so tempted to track its flight across the sky that the fact it was stationary puzzled my eye. And, at this altitude, it was so pin-sharp that the man in the moon's face lost its distinction. I realised what Dellin must have known all her life: that high cordilleras and tranquil plateaux just the same as Darkling ran over the surface of the moon.

She plucked at my wing. 'Come inside.'

'With you?'

She laughed. 'Of course, with me. Do you prefer to sleep outside? Some men do.'

'No, no. I'll come in.'

On the spear pole of her tent behind us hung a magnificent elk skull with a two-metre spread of antlers. They cast a shadow over the neighbouring tents like a pair of gigantic hands.

Dellin undressed to nothing but black pants, bare breasts and supple skin. She stretched and crawled into her tent. Even the way she disappeared inside, little feet last, stirred love in me. I was tired from constantly being in the grip of emotion, but it was giving me a lot of energy to be tired with. I took my clothes off and carried them in before the intense cold gripped me. Inside was completely dark and wonderfully warm. Three or four layers of fur covered the groundsheet and Dellin wriggled underneath like a fox cub. Outside the temperature was plummeting and stark frost petrifying the forest, and we were snuggled together. I was so aware of her presence and my heart beating that I doubted I'd ever sleep. I might be awake all night watching over her.

I spoke quietly, so my voice coming out of the blackness wouldn't startle her: 'What are you thinking?'

'I will kill Raven. I will kill more Awians and eventually Raven himself. Somehow.' She yawned and shut her mouth with a click. I was too disappointed to answer and she soon fell asleep.

I woke with Dellin's head resting against my chest and my arm under her. Immediately I was wide awake, intensely aware of her. Her company, her body; I scarcely dared breathe for fear of breaking the moment. She had snuggled against me in the night and now lay with her top half naked and the cosy fur around her waist. With every exhalation the deep pelt rolled over her belly button. Wild huntress, not yet tamed but, for the moment, not moving. She lay with her arm on the pelts, and wisps of hair covered her forearm like the faintest growth of lichen on a silver birch branch. The few ochre dreadlocks in her hair splayed over the pillow and smelt of rock. Her body was hard with no fat under the skin whatsoever; in fact I could see the grain of muscle fibres in her shoulder where her skin pulled tightly over them. It was a strange effect because she was still completely feminine. For all her hardness, I knew I was lying next to a woman; in fact her posture, her scent, her pointed little nose and her delicate face intoxicated me. She was so determined but so vulnerable ... The slope of her shoulder descended to the pale plateau of her chest; on the subtle rises of her breasts, her nipples were like buds.

I wanted to wrap my arms around her but that would wake her. I wanted to nuzzle my face over her midriff. I was terrified of disturbing her, because when she wakes, she'll leave, and I would lose her again.

I lay on my back, feeling the nap of the furs under me and her antler rattle pressing into my shoulder. Condensation droplets had formed all along the ridgepole and shadows speckling the outside of the tent showed there had been a fall of snow. Dawn light filtered through the hide walls, a lovely orange-pink blush. Dellin looked as if she was glowing the colour of embers. I looked longingly over her ... so precious ... her trophy necklace seemed crude and misplaced against her delicate shoulders. I followed it down to her breasts; the bear's canine lay in the hollow between them. On her left breast lay a horse's incisor, wolf fangs, then some freshly pierced teeth with bloodstained roots and gold fillings. *Gold fillings*? Oh, oh oh!

I ran from the tent. I stumbled around the camp pulling on my trousers, tripping over the hearth stones, yanking on boots and parka.

She had killed an Awian and taken his teeth! The tents were all silent, their flaps laced, sprinkled with snow. The cliff loomed over me, fringed with pines – and there were great spills of blood on its snow slope! Big red patches and little flesh-coloured figures dotted the ground below the rock! I dashed from the camp and climbed to the closest of them. He lay splayed, his head downhill. He was stripped naked and all his limbs had been flayed to the bone. By god! By god! Flanges of muscle remained, cut ragged close to his joints. His hands and feet looked hideously big, attached to arms and legs that were just bone sticks. Handfuls of feathers stuck to the snow around him: his wings had been sawn away. His ring finger was missing and – horror of horrors – the crown of his head had been axed open. I bent down to look. His brainpan was an empty, gory cup with flakes of snow blowing into it.

What had I eaten last night? *Who* had I eaten?

I scrambled up to the next body. A man lay bent unnaturally sharply in half, his spine snapped in his fall from the cliff top. His broken back had caused an erection which had frozen fast to the inside of his leg. His face was caved in where he'd hit the ground. The Rhydanne had filleted him too – limbs, back, shoulders and chest. He was little more than a bloodied skeleton and his guts adhered to the ice slope around him. And there was something that looked like cloth. Oh god! It was his skin, piled in folds! Through the snow dusting over it I saw hairs and an old blue tattoo. The name of his girlfriend.

Dellin had driven these men over the cliff. They had all been butchered efficiently, spread-eagled next to their horses' broken carcasses. Their clothes, armour and saddles were missing. I stepped back and looked up to the cliff edge roughly two hundred metres above. Wind howled off its edge. Its snow was trampled away, its cornice broken – thick chunks of it scattered the ground around me. One man had fallen onto a pinnacle and lay draped over it.

I had eaten so much meat! I had eaten my fill! And it was ... was ... And the burning bones! I gulped, gazed around, needing to understand but not wanting to look. Here one man lay like a limp doll, but thoroughly frozen, his hair and pubic hair black dots against the slope.

All the shreds of flesh caught between my teeth! I found myself on my hands and knees, scrubbing my mouth out with snow. I spat, dug snow with my fingernails, packed my mouth with it, rubbed my finger against my gums and spat again. At length I looked up. The horror was still all around but the tingling in my gums grounded me. I counted the butchered men: twenty bodies in all and thirty horses. Tracks wound down the slope, drag marks spattered with blood – they led to a row of bodies placed neatly shoulder to shoulder at the base of the slope.

I slithered down to them: nine more men lay stiff and mottled blue-white. Their necks and limbs were twisted at odd angles, some pushed into their bodies, and enormous bruises where they'd hit the ground. They were whole apart from where Rhydanne had severed fingers to remove rings, and each man's detached fingers had been placed on his chest. Ice rimed their hair, every strand frozen like white netting. Some strands stuck to their faces, others to the ground. A film of ice sealed their eyeballs like opaque marbles. The nearest one was only a boy. I touched my boot toe to his hip; he was as hard as rock. Dellin was caching them for her followers.

I pressed my hands into the pit of my stomach. Although I felt hollow and empty, a heavy dread filled my chest. Rhydanne didn't consider Awians people at all, but simply animals permissible to eat. Dellin could feed her starving followers, and now they had the taste for Awian flesh they would hunt down more men, and yet more. No one could stop them.

Her camp had turned into an ominous lair. Its low windbreak pulsated in the breeze a stone's throw away. The spear points jutted from their tents like spines on the backs of beasts. I could see Dellin's elk antlers. She would fix some poor Awian's head there next.

She was dangerous. Not my lover, dangerous. Not vulnerable, dangerous. I looked down at the frozen men. You poor buggers, was my first coherent thought. You poor buggers, coming up here to meet your deaths. You had no idea. But, light-headed with shock, I was surprised I didn't feel sick. No one must ever know I ate ... And if nobody knows, nobody ever knows, it will be all right. I didn't kill them, wouldn't have killed them. And anyway they didn't taste at all bad.

Even now, I was loath to leave Dellin. Perhaps I could talk this through with her? Her eager stance and rascally smile flashed across my mind's eye. I had the potential to forgive even this. But no ...

she wasn't the woman I thought she was. She was a brute, a killer, and she can never change. I turned my back on her cannibal camp and took off for the keep.

The wind tore down the slope of Klannich. It howled through the glacier's gorge, scattered the clouds before it, seized me, and I rode it like a wave.

I raced to the keep and curtain wall standing proud on their promontory. Cloud poured off the edge of Raven's cliff, streaked out by the wind. Around and far below, a clear view to the snow-covered plains. I shed height with my wings half-closed and dropped into the bailey.

I landed in front of the settlers' cabins. All their shutters and doors were closed. The keep itself had shutters fastened over every window as if its eyes were squeezed tight in revulsion. Every embrasure in the encircling wall was bolted. Bowmen stood alert on its summit and some soldiers in the furthest corner of the parapet, busy with rope, block and tackle, seemed to be fixing sharp staves along the top, facing outwards.

I ran to the staircase portal, but the guards standing outside it crossed their spears. 'Let me through. I want to see Raven.'

They glanced at each other. So they were under orders not to admit me? I had no time for that. I barged between them and they snatched their spears out of the way. Then I was in gloom, running up the steps to Raven's chamber.

His door at the top opened and Snipe popped out. He peered down in trepidation, slammed the door behind him and its bolt snicked closed. I came to a halt a few steps below him and looked up. His face was a mess. The black eye I had given him was swollen and puffy, but now for some reason he also sported chapped lips and a waxy, yellowish sheen of frostbite on ears and nose. He must have had exposure, because extreme cold had dappled his big forehead red raw. The multicoloured effect reminded me of the corpses I'd just seen. He carried a loaded crossbow.

'Let me through. I want to see Raven.'

He rubbed a hand across his mouth and I saw his fingers were blackened at the tips. 'Comet, Raven isn't here. He's gone hunting.'

'I know he's in there, hiding in the solar. I want to talk to him.'

His sunken eyes glared. 'My lord rode out a few hours ago. To kill some fucking 'danne.'

'In reprisal for last night?'

'What do you know about it?'

I shook my head. 'Raven's in there. Is he afraid? Let me through, in the Emperor's name, for the will of god and the protection of the Circle.'

He shook his head.

I leant on the clammy wall. Nobody had simply refused me before. Refused *me*! Raven's door looked extremely solid and Snipe, in its archway, rested his necrosed fingers on the crossbow's hair trigger.

Abruptly I turned and descended the spiral stairs, out to the bailey and passed the guards. As I did so, I remarked over my shoulder, 'If those spikes on the parapet are to stop Rhydanne climbing in, you'll simply be giving them new handholds.'

The guards said nothing but crossed their spears again. Their closed faces and hooded eyes revealed prejudice like granite. They think I'm a Rhydanne. They think I'm in with Dellin and they're terrified.

I followed the track between the nearest cabins and the few shutters still ajar slammed as I passed through. Eyes watched me from behind fretwork holes and metal glinted. Fear hung over the settlement like greasy smoke. Their distrust was so palpable I could hardly breathe. News of the cliff-fall deaths must have reached them and they knew the Rhydanne were winning. They probably hadn't yet discovered that Dellin's hunters had devoured their fathers, brothers and sons, but the atmosphere of dread had taken on a life of its own. I doubted any Awian wanted to set foot outside the keep; their fear trapped them inside. They had always whispered rumours but now they believed every one. They jumped to conclusions. They had always alleged Rhydanne were man-eaters, now some scout would report the grisly remains and justify all their fears, all their belligerence. They were bent double under the weight of terror and they stayed in their houses. They knew what people like me did to Awians.

I considered as I walked to the end of the promontory. I am the most junior Eszai and I have very little clout with Raven. My very heritage, and the reason I'm Eszai, now made him mistrust me. I wished Tornado were here. No one would have dared lock a door against him – a pointless gesture to the Strongman in any case – and now I regretted not letting him join me.

As soon as Raven's troops arrive he will invade Rachiswater and seize the throne. He knows that the Emperor does not intervene in any country's affairs. How the Awians choose their king, or whom they choose, is up to them.

Even though I'm sure the Emperor wouldn't like Raven as much as Tarmigan, the Emperor would let Raven's uprising go ahead – and use me as spy to inform him of every detail. San would want to save lives and prevent Awia from losing strength against the Insects. So if Raven presents the Emperor with a fait accompli, once he is crowned the Castle would probably support him.

I wondered whether to inform Tarmigan. The Emperor wouldn't approve, but I was confident I could fix things so I wouldn't be the obvious source of the warning. But then what? Tarmigan would collect his Royal Select and set out to meet his brother. One way or the other I would push Awian troops into battle against each other, which as far as I know has never happened before. Of course, if Tarmigan won he would be grateful, and a king's gratitude is not to be sneered at, but how could I hide it from San? And what would happen to the Rhydanne if a royal army besieged Carniss?

I thought about Lightning and Mist. They were Eszai too and they own manors of Awia. Maybe I could ask them ... Of the two, Lightning was better; he was more steadfast. He's one hundred per cent noble as well as being the Castle's Archer, so everyone would be keen to know his opinion. He usually maintained a judicious neutrality in internal Awian affairs, but he'd have to get involved if soldiers crashed through his vineyards. Lightning has fifteen hundred years' experience of being a governor and the best archer in the world. Raven certainly couldn't ignore him as rudely as he'd just ignored me.

I stopped at the foot of the avalanche warning tower and heaved a sigh. I didn't want to ask Lightning's help because ... because it's admitting defeat. The world will know that my talks with Raven broke down so I called for the aid of an older Eszai. Well ... I'm doing it for Dellin, really. And Lightning might offer me some advice there too ... Oh god, now I sound as wet as he does.

He certainly mustn't find out about Dellin's taste for Awian flesh or he'd support Raven against her. A mere battalion of Micawater archers could wipe out every Rhydanne in Carnich. She isn't stupid, though. She'll hide the evidence of her feast and – I shuddered – she'll store the frozen bodies where even the wolves won't find them.

I spread my wings. Where would Lightning be at this end of the year? Feasting in Micawater? No, he said he wanted to spend a quiet New Year's in Foin Hall. In that case he's probably brooding again, and I should wake him up: a little excitement will do him good.

I took off, beating hard, flew up and over the curtain wall. The cliff dropped away below me and I was airborne, already three hundred metres above the fir-clad slopes. The view was so clear I could see Eyrie village tiny as a model in the distance. I turned south towards Micawater.

LIGHTNING

I was taking morning coffee in my study when a crisp impact outside surprised me and I looked to the window. Comet was at the end of the lawn, crouching where he had landed in a patch of grazed snow. He folded his wings and, without wasting a moment, sprinted towards the house. I crossed to the bay window and watched him approach, so fast over the snow-blanketed grass he seemed scarcely to touch it. At first I couldn't identify his clothes. Then I realised it was a Rhydanne outfit such as Dellin had used for a bedspread. He must have bought it in Carniss; perhaps the mountain climate had given him a change of heart.

A second later I could only see him through the sidelight, then he passed into the porch and the bell sounded. My reeve, who keeps few servants, answered the door himself. A hasty sotto voce conversation ensued then the reeve's footsteps pattered along the corridor followed by Jant's rapid tread. My door swung wide and the reeve's head appeared in the gap. 'My lord,' he announced. 'Comet—'

Jant pushed past him, muttering, 'He knows, he knows.' His shoulders hunched and hood up, he was unshaven and glistening head to foot with ice crystals. His coarse jacket and trousers glittered like sandpaper made of diamonds, an effect which lasted but a second; they melted to damp suede and I noticed the front of his coat was spattered with grease. He looked much stronger, built up by the arduous mountains and their denizens' meat-rich diet. He scanned the breakfast table with a look of relief, picked up the cafetière and poured coffee into my glass, drank it as if it was vital and poured himself another. Then he dragged out a chair and sat down gratefully.

'Have you gone native?' I asked.

'What?'

'Those clothes. That ice axe on your belt instead of a sword.'

'Oh ... yeah. For the conditions ... the conditions up there.' He pointed at the ceiling.

'Have you brought me any letters?'

'No ...'

I folded my arms. 'Then what *have* you brought? The flu? You went to Carniss. Have you finished talking to Raven?'

'I've just come from Carniss. Dellin's still there. I don't know what Raven could be doing to her – hunting her with dogs this very minute. She ... It's all ... Everything's gone wrong.' He tucked one slush-wet boot under him on the chair cushion, unbuttoned his parka showing nothing but a T-shirt underneath and fanned out his wings to shake drops from them. He looked like a black peacock. He looked like an old crow. 'Saker Micawater,' he whined. 'What the shining fuck do I *do*?'

'Why? Have you caused some kind of disaster?'

'*I* haven't caused anything!'

'Then to what do I owe this visit?'

He began counting on his fingers. 'Raven built a fortress as defensible as Lowespass. Covering a sheer crag – it's not a manor house at all! Fyrd are on their way to him from Francolin Wrought in Lowespass. As soon as they arrive in Carniss Raven is going to attack Rachiswater. The palace itself! He hates his brother.'

'I know he does.'

'He's going to seize the throne! And Dellin—' He counted her off too, but I interrupted him.

'I should have known Raven would make another bid for the throne. Have you told Tarmigan?'

'No. I thought I'd tell you first.'

'And the Emperor?'

'No! Not until everything's fixed!'

'Do Raven or Francolin know you've discovered their plot?'

'They have no idea,' he said and leant forward, head in hands.

'Good. Good.' I retrieved my newspaper from the table because ice was dripping from his hair and soaking into it. 'Is Raven's attack imminent?'

'New Year's Day, to catch Tarmigan unprepared.'

Yes, he needs the element of surprise and, knowing the king's banquets, everyone in Rachis would be stuffed too full to move. 'But aren't the roads impassable? The snow is bad enough here; I thought Carniss would be cut off?'

'He's banking on Tarmigan thinking that. Yes, the Pelt Road looks blocked – from the air it's a sheet of white – but it's not impassable to anyone with knowledge of how to travel in snow. Raven can get through: he learnt about dog sleds and snowshoes last year ... from the Rhydanne.'

'I see.'

'He's halted all contact with the lowlands to give the impression he's stranded. He isn't cut off; he's preparing. The keep is full of stockpiled weapons, so I think Francolin's soldiers are travelling light and Raven intends to equip them in Carniss. They might lose some lives to the Rhydanne, though.'

'Rhydanne? Why?'

Jant emerged from behind his clasped hands with a sombre expression. 'Raven is persecuting the Rhydanne. He wants to cleanse Carniss of every last one.'

'Why?'

'Because Dellin ... Dellin's defending her forest and prey. The Rhydanne are starving, Lightning, they have to find food. She—'

'How much damage have they caused?'

Jant placed a worried hand on his forehead and pushed his hair back. 'They killed at least thirty settlers. Raven's retaliating. I'm worried he'll pen Dellin into a small area and trap her. She moves so stealthily I hope she can sneak out, but you know how single-minded Raven is.'

'To the point of insanity. But his hands are full on two fronts.' I pushed a platter of bacon towards Jant. 'Would you like some breakfast?'

He shrank from it and stared at me with wild incomprehension. 'We don't have *time*! How can we, when Raven's forcing her to hide in the forest, subsisting on ... on whatever she can find?'

'I thought they always lived that way. Look, spend a minute on breakfast and hunger won't hinder you in a couple of hours' time.'

'You sound like Ouzel,' he grumbled, but he selected a couple of pieces of toast and began buttering them neatly.

Unfortunately I could envisage no way to be rid of him. I had been avoiding any exchange with the outside world and I didn't appreciate Jant barging into my peaceful, snowbound retreat, where I had planned to stay sequestered until after the festivities and long into eighteen ninety-one. I only rarely managed an escape from the parties of the self-conscious nobility or those Shatterings I feel I have to hold myself. Out here in Foin I have an excuse to decline the conviviality and the sleigh rides. The last thing I wanted was to be wedged in a sleigh with some governor's wife shrieking with laughter, first-footing to Bitterdale and beyond, as if I needed to visit everybody's halls again. So I had quite deliberately ensconced myself in the smallest and furthest-flung muster of my manor. The reeve knew to leave me to my comfortable melancholy; he respected my wish to be alone. The dim light and quiet woods soothed my memory of Savory. I had been spending my time at archery practice and in the weight room; long evenings standing with my violin by the fireside playing sonatinas; watching the reeve's children build winged snowmen; watching the figures in dark coats trudging through the snow-bound woods. These were the dregs and dog-ends of the year, when the people's weariness rubs off onto the land itself.

Now Jant appeared looking like a savage and with the apparent intent of dragging me into the machinations of the Rachiswater twins. If it wasn't the Tanagers or Shearwater idiot Mist it was the fractious bloody Rachiswaters. I sighed and sat down. 'Support for Raven is more widespread than you might think. You wouldn't know, having been in the wilds, but Tarmigan is losing popularity and Raven is gaining.'

'Is Tarmigan unpopular?'

'He is becoming so.'

'Why?'

'He keeps levying taxes to reward his favourites and extend his palace. People mutter against it; they don't like having to dip into their pockets time and again, especially with only five days until the festival. But Tarmigan will collect the taxes and Rachiswater Palace grows ever more ornate. And tasteless, incidentally.'

I looked out to the lawn, the outbuildings of the hall on either side, down to the gable end of the tithe barn just visible by the river. Ice so thick it looked like snow coated the trees uniformly white, their branches meshed like lace. The sky was pregnant with yet more snow and the morning silent. The tessellated panes of glass in the leaded window had, over the years, settled at slightly different angles, so even in this overcast light they glittered like the scales of a fish.

'My steward told me that two days ago someone climbed

Tarmigan's statue in Rachiswater Grand Place and carved a scar on its face.' I drew a line across my cheek.

'A scar?'

'Yes. Turning King Tarmigan into King Raven with one stroke of the chisel! Right in the centre of the square, bang in the middle of the capital.'

'Do they know who did it?'

'No, it was under cover of darkness. The night watch covered the statue straight away but enough revellers saw it for the gossip to spread. Many people are turning against Tarmigan; my steward tells me their whispering grows bolder every minute. If Raven pushes now, he may well topple him.'

Jant's eyes widened. 'Who would you declare for?'

'Comet, Comet. I support the throne, no matter whose backside is on it, Tarmigan's or Raven's. And if no one's is, then I support the idea that someone's should be. I support the idea of the throne itself.'

'Would you send archers to protect the king?'

'The last thing I want to do is arm my manor or his.'

'And about Dellin?'

'What *about* Dellin?' I paused and turned to him. His preoccupation, his appearance so unusually neglected, his adoption of their dress, the distant look in his eyes reminded me of how I felt with Savory. I studied him and grew more certain. Certain? It was obvious! 'Tell me of Dellin?' I offered, just to be sure, and he bowed his head. 'You love her, don't you?'

'If you'd seen her slay a bear single-handed, you'd be in ... you-know-what too.'

'In love?'

'Oh god, don't make me say it!'

Well, well. Could it be that all this time Jant simply needed to find one of his own kind? I had never thought it possible. I had thought him utterly devoid of the ability to love, not least because generosity is a prerequisite of love and Jant was so thoroughly self-centred that he had little passion to spare. In fact, I sometimes wondered whether he even realised other people had independent existences and thoughts – other than those about himself.

He kept himself as hard as his orphan days. If he had been born with the ability to love he had mislaid it in the backstreets of Hacilith or had it frozen out of him on the altiplano. Segregation had suppressed it; poverty had parched him of it; and adversity made him hate more easily than he could find it in himself to love. He could ask 'Where's the brothel?' in ten languages, but he has never said 'I love you' in even one. He just drifts through life casually side-stepping any sort of anguish. It was completely uncharacteristic of him to submit to the most exquisite torment of all.

'That's why I came,' he admitted. 'I thought I'd ask the expert.'

'I'm hardly an expert.'

He raised a grimy hand theatrically. 'You said, "My love for Savory was the greatest the world has ever known. Love flowed from me like waves, the colour of waves of heat. A love as strong as this could not exist for long because its intensity threatened to drive me to madness. I struggled day and night to recover, but in vain."'

Yes, those were my words. I can tell you what book he cribbed them from if you like. He had started sarcastically but ended miserably and added, 'That's how I feel.'

'It's pointless asking you to forget about her?'

'Yes.'

'So what do you want from me?'

'Some advice.'

'Some advice? Let me see ... Remember what happened to Savory? Well, Dellin is at risk of dying too, and so soon – being Rhydanne she will race through life and be old before she's forty. She'll leave you lonely and bereft, Jant. There's hardly enough time to befriend and court these mortal women before they die ... Time is short. She will change so much in a year that you'd be shocked and disgusted with yourself for falling in love with her in the first place. I have known women fascinating for one night and repellent a mere six months later. For love to persist you must change at the same rate they do and, believe me, it isn't easy. So be with her as much as possible. Isn't it unbearable to be away even this long?'

'Yes. But we have to stop Raven.'

'For god's sake, Jant. If you're Eszai you can do both!'

I walked to the stone fireplace and stood watching the brassy flames with my back to him. I suddenly felt tired of the mortals' constant striving for supremacy, whether a village blood feud such as ended Savory's life, or the never-ending stream of Challengers for my position in the Circle, or the Rachiswater twins wrestling for the crown of the most powerful country in the world. No two mortals, like no two snowflakes, are identical, but their aspirations are all the bloody same.

'The twins are stubborn,' I said. 'This won't pass without bloodshed. Such a terrible waste of life ... Aren't the Insects enough to contend with?'

Jant shook himself. 'All right! I'll forget Dellin! The Empire's business comes first!'

I doubted he would be able to give her up. Willpower is something Jant sadly lacks. I had never known him so agitated. I've seen him exhausted by flying and drunk seven eighths to oblivion. I've seen him with his shoulder broken – by myself – in a joust, but each time his natural energy buoys him up. Now it seemed to be driving him to distraction.

I glanced around the room at the oak-panelled walls, the low ceiling, the bulbous turned legs of the furniture, my violin on its stand wreathed in sheet music, my kitbox for fletching arrows, and lastly down at the now-cold coffee, plates of bacon and toast on the table. So much for my quiet New Year. So much for archery practice and long evenings stoking the memory of Savory ... I sighed and reconciled myself to trailing north to Darkling. 'I will come with you.'

Jant's face lit up. Then he bit his lip. 'But it's three days' ride in the snow.'

'How long did it take you to fly here?'

'Um ... Just under two hours.'

I laughed, impressed, but he leapt to his feet.

'Why should I be in love? Am I only flattering myself? Why should I go through this? What does it matter!'

Let him disown love. He twists on the hook because the emotion is new to him.

'I shouldn't concern myself with anything that isn't Messenger's duty,' he ranted. 'I nearly let the rot set in! Already! If I give way I'll be prone to all sorts of luxuries ... Love? I'm being soft! Lackadaisical. Unfit! If I go on like this a Challenger will beat me. I'll lose my place in the Circle. It mustn't happen!'

'You can tear your heart out and concentrate on nothing but your work, but you'll end up as hollow as the Architect. You should welcome feeling different for once in your life; you should make a virtue of it.'

'A *virtue* of it? It's horrible!'

I returned to the table and pressed his wing reassuringly. 'Fly ahead and prepare the way – at each stage a meal and quarters for the night. I don't need a change of horses; Balzan is better than any of theirs. Tell Raven to expect a guest for the Shattering. Send him into a scuffle for the best roast ox and hot negus, and clay for the Wishes. Don't tell him either of us knows about the coup.'

'What will you do?'

'I haven't the faintest idea. I'll only know when I see his face. But somehow we'll check his reins. Watch for my arrival and give me the latest news.'

'And Dellin ... I hope she hid— I mean, moved camp.'

'Certainly you must find her,' I said, and this time I couldn't keep the envy from my voice. He has a chance to be happy and I have left all my chances behind in the deep past.

He offered me his hand. 'I'll land at Irksdale hunting lodge, Toft coach inn, Plow reeve's hall. I'll tell them you're riding, warn them to be ready: every stage, all the way through! From Plow take the Pelt Road to Eyrie village and up for six kilometres through the forest to the keep. The track's marked by posts and notches on the trees. And ...'

'And what?'

'Beware of Rhydanne. In the forest you wouldn't even see Dellin before she lands on your neck.'

I nodded. 'Then three days. Goodbye, Jant.'

'Goodbye, Lightning.' He gave me a grateful half-smile, then was out of the door. He let himself out of the porch and I watched him open his vast wings, sprint down the lawn and jump, flap up over the ridge of the barn and into the sky – smaller and fainter into the low cloud until he disappeared from view.

I quelled the surge of envy I always feel on seeing him fly. Seventy years since he joined the Circle and it's still a novelty. My wings twitched and I spread them – if I stretch, I can just brush the mantelpiece with my feather tips, and the wall on the other side. Oh, well, maybe I will learn to fly on the day he learns to shoot straight. I reached over and pulled the bell rope.

The reeve appeared instantaneously – almost, I surmised, as if he had been listening outside the door. 'Ready Balzan,' I told him. 'His winter caparison, ice shoes – everything for Darkling. I must go north for some days, perhaps weeks.'

'But the festival, my lord?' He was crestfallen. Months of planning, baking, preserving, ordering everything from the traditional ox to spiced apple sauce, vanished in an instant.

'Believe me, Foin, I would stay if I could.'

'I understand: the Castle's duty.' He nodded sorrowfully. 'Does the Messenger *ever* bring good news?'

Soon afterward, muffled in scarf and greatcoat, my lidded quiver of arrows and two longbows in cases on the saddle, I rode out of Foin and up over the fell. The pristine snow covered the long hills seamed with drystone walls and the bristling trees in the woodland below.

The fresh air revived me and I smiled. The hog's back hills and the sweeping vista revitalised me, with the eerie light of the lowering sky swollen with snow. Something to do at last – to pit my wits against Raven! I urged Balzan to a gallop and ice flung from his hooves. A white horse almost invisible against the white hills of Rachis Moor. Riding hard I leant forward on his neck, my mind singing with excitement. Jant in love and Raven poised to snatch the throne: the world is changing again and I will put out my hand and turn it the way I wish.

Three days later Balzan climbed laboriously through the snow in short, sliding steps. It had set in snowing at daybreak and it now snowed hard. I had left Eyrie village some hours ago and entered the forest. Here, under the trees, I was sheltered from the worst of the flurries and the snow on the ground was shallower too. But the woods were so dark I could hardly see: the weight of snow topping every sagging branch sealed the thickly meshed canopy above me and barely any light penetrated. There was no sound either, no birdsong, only the faint hiss of powder snow trickling down between the boughs. Occasionally, deeper in the gloom, a branch of a tree shed its load and rebounded, sending snow cascading off the branches around it.

I rode with my bow on my knee and an arrow at string – aware of the trees on either side, wondering if Rhydanne could really see better than me in this murkiness. Flickers of movement here and there were only tricks of the light. The trees were ranged like waiting sentinels, bulges of snow eerily resembled shrouded bodies, and I passed no tracks of animal or human. In fact, as I rode, the snow filled Balzan's own trail and left no trace of our passage.

I had a terrible thirst. My water bottle, tucked in my coat lest it freeze, was already running low. Balzan was suffering too: he huffed and blew like a blast furnace and shook the snow from his mane as he walked.

My thoughts turned to Jant and I began to doubt whether he could be in love. He had never been able to shake off his street urchin days. It would be more his style to crave Dellin as a woman beyond the grasp of his lust. He was in many ways still a teenager – with the power of the Castle to back his vanities. Perhaps this was simply another way of seeking attention.

Then again, his very immaturity may be the cause of his passion. He is used to having so many women that Dellin's inaccessibility must have unsettled him. That could tip him into love. He's accustomed to women throwing themselves at him. He sleeps with them all and flies away the following morning. None has a chance of marrying him and gaining immortality – he is having far too much fun as a bachelor. And, by Murrelet, he attracts hundreds: gold-diggers and honest admirers alike. I suppose he treats them well. He adores their conversation and wine flows like the Gilt River. He prefers their company to that of men and flits from one to another, whereas I suspect he considers men more of a threat.

Once he had grown tired of the novelty of sleeping with aristocratic ladies he discovered the warrior girls of the front, then back he winged to Hacilith, to chat with the maids at the apple carts and chestnut stalls. At no time is love ever mentioned. Whatever happened to him in his gangland days has given him skin thicker than an Insect's carapace and taught him to raise defences like shield walls. However, he might be vulnerable inside, through lack of practice.

So, does he love Dellin? Love is both the antithesis of friendship and friendship gone mad. Love strikes without reason and cannot be controlled; you can never resist it intentionally and remain unharmed yourself. Seven decades ago I wanted to be together with Savory, but I have to admit I hardly knew her. How much less does Jant know Dellin!

In fact, this forest was much like Savory's, although they never have snows this deep nor slopes this steep in Cathee. As I rode, the silence and pines crowding the track brought back my memory of my wedding night. The murderers escaped into the forest; I ran after them but lost them among the trees. The other villagers fled to their houses and barred their doors against me. They wished me gone and indeed, having buried my wife, I did leave, and I swear on the Sunburst Throne I will never see Cathee again.

Jant thought I was stupid. Six months later he landed on my windowsill with withering contempt and a letter from the Emperor. He explained that as Savory's husband I could have continued the blood feud. No wonder the Cathee had been terrified of me! A word to the Governor of Hacilith, another to call up my archers, and I could have burned their village to the ground. But why cause more bloodshed and waste of life, heap agony upon agony? I was not vengeful, I was devastated. I wanted the blood feud to end with me, if that meant it would be over for good. I stayed in my palace, half a year whirled by, and the only thing that brought me out of my shell was that pointed letter in the Emperor's own hand.

The track wound higher and higher in relentless hairpin bends, and now large outcrops covered with ice rime and undersized pines showed where rock was forcing through the snow. The forest gradually lightened: there was more open ground between the trees and snow flurried down as thickly as before, settling on my shoulders and coat skirts. Tendrils and wisps drifted between the trees and across my path, greying-out the pines, thinning again so they regained their colour, then thickening into solid cloud. I had no choice but to ride into it, and I could no longer see anything but a shifting grey wall a metre or so in front of Balzan's muzzle.

The forest seemed to end, and we climbed a completely white slope. The only sign of a path was a trench worn in the snow and about every fifty metres Balzan's hooves crunched by the top of a black post, the last few centimetres of wood projecting from a drift shaped like a sand dune. I was riding on the inside of a grey sphere, the cloud puffing and bulging towards me, drawing back leaving gossamer fragments, blistering out and sucking into itself, throwing up twisted fingers of mist to the sallow disc of the sun which was backlighting everything bright grey. It smelt of a myriad droplets of numbingly cold water; it caught in my raw throat as if I was riding through a room full of freezing steam. All the time the snow still fell.

Balzan and I cast a vestige of a shadow, which moved along on the snow on our right like a miserable little cloud. My breath and Balzan's crisp tread were the sole noises in the intense silence. I could be the only man alive in all creation, riding the only horse.

This is the highest altitude to which I've ever climbed. Every step is a first – which shows that no matter how long you live, a hundred years or fifteen hundred, you'll always find yourself doing something new. As the penetrating cold grew yet more biting I hugged my coat tightly around myself and wished fervently I was back in Foin Hall. Yes, I may have spent hundreds of New Years in my manor, but there are always sufficient variations and new combinations to make it never boring. The immortals who, tired of life, go searching for ever more outré thrills, exploring Darkling, for example, generally do end up dead.

I could tell the cloud was thickening further as less sunlight filtered through, disorientating me with the illusion that twilight was drawing close. The shadows deepened, giving me the impression they were deadening sound, as my mind tried to rationalise the silence. No sound from outside, only my breathing; I am alone. But I'm not alone, am I? Someone is walking beside me, a little behind me, just out of sight. It must be Jant, coming to meet me. I called to him and listened ... Nothing but silence returned. I hesitated, and there he was again, walking just outside the scope of my vision, behind my right shoulder, a familiar presence in the palls of mist. I grew convinced he was dogging me and finding it privately very amusing. No, I assured myself, it's a delusion, but I couldn't shake the clear impression he was there, walking as steadily as Balzan, at the same pace and with no emotion. 'It's not funny!' I said aloud, and glanced behind me. Nothing. Nothing but thick bands of mist blowing across the track like the ghosts of a thousand wolves.

What do Rhydanne *do* in this all day? What a horrible life, by god; I would trade it for that of a dumb beast. I rode on, every fear that crossed my mind projected on the colossal canvas of the clouds – the thirst, the silence, and my companion just out of eyeshot who walked and walked, forever at my side. I could not dispel the illusion, and eventually I simply had to put up with it. By god, I felt sympathy for Raven – he was cut off from everything, even sanity! No wonder he had built a little manorship on his crag, for what else was there to keep a man from madness? If I was in his position I would do the same.

Balzan raised his head and whinnied as if greeting another horse. I stared ahead – the weirdly dulled sunlight still had the strength to sting my eyes – and perceived a movement too rhythmic to be the swirling of cloud. It gradually darkened into a blurred form, swaying towards me. It approached, closer and darker still, and resolved into the figures of two men on horseback, riding with their heads bowed. All was colourless, shades of grey and white, and cloud strands blew in front of them, curling across the track.

I called, 'Good morning!'

The men made no answer; their hooded heads made no motion and their mounts kept the same slow trudge.

I reined in Balzan and hailed them again: 'Is this the way to the manor?'

The first man turned to his comrade and raised his arm, beckoning as if to say, 'Pay no notice to this fellow.' The shape of his muffled body, a pack on his saddlebow and the slow-stepping horse passed some distance away and gave no answer. Another illusion. I shuddered, then suddenly infuriated I flexed my bow and shot an arrow into the top of his pack.

He halted immediately. Good, so they are men and not hallucinations. I flicked the lid of my quiver open, drew out another arrow and nocked it.

He turned his horse and walked it towards me, followed by his second. He was a curious man, with a scarf pulled up over his mouth and hat down over his brows. His face in the slit so produced was pale, but a huge, plum-coloured bruise covered one eye and half his cheek. He carried a bow with an arrow at string, a Lakeland type with a draw weight of about fifty kilos. So, granted, he was strong, but his bow was shabby and the wax worn off around the grip, the string frayed at the tips and he carried no spare. It looked as if he did not take a great deal of care of himself.

'Is this the road to the manor house?' I asked again.

'Yes.'

'Maybe you will show me the way?'

'We're on the lord's business.' He gruffly slipped my arrow out of his pack and threw it on the ground as if to say, 'Lucky shot, but if we weren't in a hurry it would be the worse for you.' His friend was gazing at me. Awe crept into his face and he removed his arrow from string. He had guessed my identity. He dismounted and knelt. I inclined my head to acknowledge his obeisance but Blackeye just scowled at me.

'What business is that?' I asked.

The awed man faltered, 'Carrying a message from Raven.'

Blackeye spat, 'Get up! Why kneel to a highwayman? What's wrong with you?'

I made Balzan step forward, to give him a view of the Castle's sun in tooled leather on the saddlebags, the strength of my long-bow, Balzan's matching livery in burgundy cordovan, the gilded stirrups shaped like bows, and my immaculate white thoroughbred himself, worth more than the compounded wealth of both their lives. I lowered my hood and asked, 'Who is this message for?'

Blackeye stared angrily, and who I was slowly dawned on him too. He rocked back in his saddle and gave a great exasperated sigh. I was angry, starting to shiver and my head ached from the terrible cold. I was in no mood to be messed around by mortals. 'Yes,' I said. 'Lightning the Archer. In Carniss. Visiting Raven. Now, you with the patch like a sheepdog, tell me where you're going.'

'A communiqué. Can't say. Raven's orders ... my lord.'

'And you are?'

'Snipe. His steward.'

'Then show me to your master's keep and I will ask him my-self.'

'We must deliver it!' He kicked his horse and it leaped away, vanishing with him into swirls of mist. His friend remounted but sat as if frozen, watching me with a petrified expression. We waited a short while and the snow obliterated our horses' prints until, again, we could be the only two men in the entire world.

'Tell me,' I prompted.

'My lord Eszai, the Rhydanne are killers! Raven sent us to ... meet ... some people. To warn them of the danger and bid them hurry.'

'Some people?' I mused. 'What sort of travellers would be climb-ing on a day like this, on the eve of New Year's Eve?'

He was saved from answering by the return of Snipe, who had not trotted far downhill before he realised he was alone. He looked daggers at his friend: you had better not have told him *anything*.

'Take me to the keep,' I ordered.

'But, my lord ... Oh, very well. Follow us ... and stay close. We're due for an avalanche and anyway the weather can turn in an instant.'

'I thought this *was* bad weather.'

He laughed bitterly, pulled his scarf up over his nose and, still laughing, rode into the cloud and disappeared.

*

The cup of hot coffee warmed my hands. I relaxed on the maroon velvet cushions of Raven's window seat and looked out at the truly incredible view. How beautiful it was! How wild and remote! The fog had completely cleared, the sky was brilliant blue and the enormous double peak of Klannich filled the window. It reared from its forested skirts, which seemed to have been creased and torn with the strength of the mountain eager to reach the heavens. The bare rock of its nearer summit faced to the four points of the compass and its smooth walls met in a point crowned with ice.

If I pressed my face to the cold glass and looked left, I could see the second summit some distance behind it, a tower of rock ending in a tilted summit like a thorn, hooded with white. Plumes of spindrift curled off it, blowing round into a complete spiral. Indeed, the whole peak looked as if it was bowed under a raging wind. Between the two peaks a narrow chasm hung like a vertical sword cut in the solid rock, crusted with ice and filled with a nameless glacier.

It was breathtaking. I exulted: this was my reward for yesterday's ordeal! The view was worth the climb. The more effort one makes, the more one is repaid by seeing such treasures. I was still aching, but now, surrounded by halls of air stretching to the roof of the world, I felt as if I could lean out and take flight over the forest. The occasional snowflake feathered against the window, but they somehow fell from a completely cloudless sky. I filled my eyes with the view: I feasted on it. Then I wondered why there was no trace of Raven's activities. After two years had he made no impact on the forest? The pine trees carpeting the lower third of Klannich seemed untouched, pocketed with curls of rising mist. Their branches, fattened with snow, seemed black in contrast, and peculiarly sharply focused in the frosty air. My eyesight is excellent but, ranging over the forest far below as if I was gliding, I imagined my vision perfected to the acuity of an eagle's.

I began to notice, here and there, scars of sawn wood and broken branches standing out among the snow-rounded mass. The forest was so immense that the efforts of Raven's settlers had had little impact on its overall appearance. This landscape resists efforts to tame it – no Awian terms can ever be forced upon it – it will always remain wild and unbowed. Raven would never own gardens like those his brother enjoys, no, not even if he lived to be immortal.

A man could find peace here, bounded by the knife-sharp

horizon, with the shadow of Klannich passing over him as if it were a sundial, and quilted with silence deeper than the drifts. I would not change one pine needle of it, if I could have that peace. But peace is the last thing Raven wants.

I sighed and descended to the table. I poured myself another cup of coffee, black because the only option was goat's milk. Raven had not been expecting me. Jant hadn't warned him of my arrival – in fact, he apparently hadn't returned to the keep at all since I saw him – and my entrance sent them into a panic. Raven was out hunting Rhydanne, so Snipe took charge. He gave me his own room, in his log cabin in the bailey. A glass of mulled wine, a hot bath and a change of clothes cured me of my shivering. I conversed a little with him and found him to be an intelligent and capable man, if uneducated: a fine choice for a steward. In an unflustered manner he related the latest news I'd hoped to hear from Jant. Raven and his men did not return until well after dark, and I didn't see him. I slept well and I felt acclimatised this morning, ready to meet him.

Jant still showed not a feather. He must be off searching for Dellin. It was natural and right for him to search for his love. Given how he feels he can act no other way. I hoped he'd found her and could convince her to feel the same – no man can win a woman without a great deal of talking – and the thought of their love warmed my heart.

Noises drifted up from the hall below: a guitar being tuned, hammering as a blacksmith installed the kiln. I love New Year's Eve. This is the winter solstice; tonight is the longest night of the year. As calculated by the Starglass, after tonight we leave December behind for January. The days will slowly grow longer and we will again be heading into spring. This night is always special. No matter how long I live the excitement will always steal up on me. Servants bustled hither and thither, preparing tonight's feast, putting the final touches to the arrangements they must have been planning for months. Across the country, preparations were taking place on a massive scale, and here too, although it was December above the snowline, the whole keep was in a sweat.

I loved the atmosphere of waiting, of delighted anticipation and secrecy. The presents were wrapped and rafters decked with holly. The Shattering was always my favourite time of year.

I took my coffee to the fireside and relaxed into a high-backed chair with arms of sensuously silky, warm pine. They curved into scrolls like the heads of violins, an oddly familiar shape. I stood up and examined them, then I lifted away the wolf skins hanging on the chair's back and seat. Elegant art nouveau tendrils spanned the back, which spread, with room for wings, and tapered into stylised blue roses with clinging briers. The slender legs, beautifully bowed, segued down to eagle's claws clutching rosebuds. It was a replica of the Silver Throne! Oh, Raven, you silly fool! You would do better to hide your ambition than to sit every day in a wooden copy of the throne of Awia! Laughing, I threw the skins back over it, arranging them as before, and as I did so I noticed how, in his anxiety, he had scored tiny scratches at the end of one of the arms with his ring.

I tried the throne for size again and stretched my legs towards the fireplace. You can tell a great deal about someone by examining their room, and infinitely more so if they have designed it themselves. The damn chandelier was the first thing I saw when Snipe showed me in. No one could fail to notice it. It dominated the room like a gigantic jellyfish, suspended from the ceiling with its candles all askew. It was not to blame. I hated what Raven meant by it. Strings of crystals, clutters of baroque pendants and its chain heavier than an Insect leash, it had been an heirloom of the previous dynasty. Around eighty years ago Raven's grandfather had seized it from the bankrupt Tanagers when he had taken Tanager Hall and the crown of the country. The Rachiswaters had kept it for two generations with their other prizes, the spoil of their success. God knows how Raven had dragged it up here, but maybe he wanted it to prove he was still heir presumptive – or, even worse, as a superstitious trinket to ensure the nation would be his one day. He had never liked the chandelier when it hung in his brother's palace – he cannot like it now. So, you see the heart of a possessed man: clear and flawless ice, always frozen, never melting.

He was like a musical instrument pitched to one note but producing two sounds: one melancholy, the other fearsome. When he was melancholy, I found it incredible that he would ever be cheerful again. When he was absorbed in some project he became cheery, and I could not believe he would ever be dejected again. I turned my back on the chandelier and dwelt instead on the coat of arms carved over the fireplace, which interested me most of all. As I studied it Raven entered. 'Happy New Year's Eve!'

'Happy New Year's Eve, Lightning,' he said. 'Good to see you!'

We shook hands and I relinquished the faux throne to him.

By god, he looked older – he looked haggard. His short dark hair stood up like iron filings with a nearby magnet, and his eyes were a peculiar pale grey, without any flecks in the iris – like silver coins – which is a feature of the Rachiswater family. The alarming wound in his face had knitted but the scar tissue was still pink and shiny. He had cured it well, but not so the wound in his heart, which he kept fresh and bleeding every day in his lust for revenge.

'To what do I owe this visit?'

'Good wishes from Micawater. I haven't seen you for two years. I thought I'd ride up and see this manor house you have built for yourself. And I am overwhelmed by your feat. Designing and constructing this in such a short time! You're a polymath.'

Raven was all smiles. He gave a convincing performance of being beside himself with joy. 'You should have sent word you were coming. I haven't even a New Year's present to give you. A pity the Messenger is too busy with the Rhydanne.'

'As a matter of fact I did send him ahead, but he seems to have been waylaid. A case of the hare and the tortoise.'

Raven switched to the High language, the royal tongue, so I did too; it must have been years since he had used it.

I presented him with a package containing two books which I'd selected from the shelf in Foin and the reeve's son had wrapped in marbled paper. Raven accepted it eagerly. Although, of course, he was supposed to wait until tomorrow, he took a knife from the table, sliced the string and unwrapped the books so reverently I felt embarrassed. They were a leather-bound volume of Conure's poetry from the twelfth century and a new libretto of *The Miser King*.

'Thank you,' he said, overcome with gratitude. 'Thank you very much.'

'You're welcome.'

'I have almost no books, only the few I brought here. Did you know my brother was starving me of them?'

'No.'

'You know I've a thirst for books, Lightning. But since I arrived Tarmigan has only let me have five and, believe me, I know them word for word.' He moved aside an untidy pile of letters and rummaged about until he unearthed a very worn copy of *Myths and Legends of Ancient Awia*. He pushed it triumphantly in my direction. 'One of them was your own! Don't you think my brother was cruel not to let me buy more?'

'Yes.'

'Truly we're living through the age of unenlightenment!'

I said, 'I wish I had known. When I return home I will send you some crates full.'

'Really?'

'Yes. You can rebuild your library. Just list the titles you want, or you could always leave it to my taste ...'

'Both, I think! A little of both. Thank you very much.' He picked up *Myths and Legends* and handled it with respect. 'I have read everything you've written. I started with all your works on archery, which I know word for word.'

'So do all my Challengers.' I laughed.

'Then I went on to read all your fiction. *Insects at Murrelet Manor. The Bride of Summerday.*' He opened the book at its mark and tapped the story headed, 'Lynette and Telamon, or, the Rose of Ressond'. 'I especially love the bit where Telamon shoots all the Insects.'

'That never happened, you know.'

'Oh, I realise. But the description is so detailed, such rich coloratura. Your imagination is superb ... I especially love Conure. Thank you, thank you ... Tonight I'll find you a present in return.'

'There's no need.'

'It's traditional. Why break tradition? You of all people know its value.' He poured himself some coffee and added some of the dismayingly musty goats' milk.

'I was admiring your fireplace. Is that your new coat of arms?'

'Yes. New is the word. I only chose it last week, and the herald's office in Rachiswater hasn't yet confirmed it.'

'They will.'

'I'm sure they will. My brother has no say in the matter.'

He mentioned his brother more easily than I had imagined, and appeared so relaxed you would have thought him innocent. Not the slightest vestige of doubt, hatred, or the struggle and horror of the battle to come clouded his silver eyes. The emblem was carved with an unsettling vehemence: a crescent moon transfixed by a vertical arrow. 'What does it signify?'

'Something the Messenger said. He was in a trading post, high up on the bank of the glacier. My steward occasionally conducts business there, and he found Jant carousing with the Rhydanne. Their ringleader, Shira Dellin—'

'I know her.'

'Was inciting a pack of them to attack us. She was rousing them, preparing them to eat us.'

'*Eat* you?'

'Yes. Didn't you know they have been murdering and devouring Awians? Our countrymen, Lightning, roasted and eaten! My steward said that Jant told those animals they had as little chance of hounding us from Carniss as they did of hitting the moon with an arrow. He was right! So I made it my symbol. Shoot at the moon, Rhydanne, if you can!'

'Do they truly eat people?' I asked, shaken.

Raven was nettled. 'Yes. Snipe told me. Ah ... this is something Jant didn't tell you, am I right? I've lost fifty men! Lightning, you're the best archer of all time. Can you shoot the moon? No? If you can't, no one can. Those beasts are too primitive to know the use of the bow. They have no chance whatsoever of shooting the moon, and we will never leave Carniss.'

'Are you safe here?' I asked. 'Do the walls keep them out?'

Raven shuddered. 'I think they can climb any wall they are inclined to, but my bowmen deter them. When I built Carniss I thought they could never act in concert, but Dellin has deviously taught them to ambush my patrols in the backwoods.'

'Your difficulties with the Rhydanne interest me.'

'So we discover the reason for your visit!'

'Jant told me he's been unable to stop you persecuting them.'

'Wouldn't you persecute beasts that devour your people! They tear us apart with their teeth!'

The statement chilled me, and I wondered if Jant knew all of Dellin's deeds. My own experience with Savory proved how sightless love can be, and he was so besotted, Dellin could easily have deceived him. Surely she couldn't be so terrible as to eat people? I felt heavy and cold inside. 'If this is happening to our countrymen you must do everything to stop it,' I said. 'But are you sure? Do you have evidence?'

'Lightning, you *are* here in an official capacity.'

'The Emperor wants this war to reach a peaceful solution.'

'Oh, so now it's a war, and the Castle feels justified in stepping in! Dellin raided my settlers' homes two days ago. Twelve families – thirty men, women and children – vanished! Dellin burnt the houses but we found no bodies inside, so she must have carried them away. She took all their goods too. I sent armed patrols to look for them and of those men only Snipe crawled back, suffering severe hypothermia. The others met their deaths, driven over a cliff by Dellin's horde.'

'Is that how Snipe gained his black eye?'

Raven paused. 'No. We'll come to that in good time. And we no longer ride; the horses take fright too easily. The Rhydanne tore Rabicano apart with their talons; how would you feel if they killed Balzan?'

'There will always be another Balzan.'

Raven stood up. 'Why are you Eszai supporting the natives? Are you so opposed to progress? This colony is a glorious thing for our country to achieve. Lightning, I wish you could see the innermost heart of Carniss as I do; much of your sympathy would subside. The Rhydanne savages are on a level with the brute, not even to be compared with the noble character of the dog. They are in a crude state. They have no gratitude, pity, love, nor self-denial, no idea of duty, not even knowledge of the Castle, but covetousness, ingratitude, selfishness and cruelty. All are thieves, idle, envious and ready to plunder. Please feel free to speak to my terrified settlers. Imagine how you would feel if the citizens of Micawater were too afraid to leave their homes? I have a duty to protect my people, the same as you do. The settlers look to me for help. You know what it's like. No one wants to leave the keep. I had to order soldiers to collect firewood or there'd be no roast ox tonight.'

'If you stop trawling the woods for Rhydanne, Jant can persuade Dellin to cease.'

'You know as well as I do that Jant has no influence over her.'

Privately, I agreed with him. I guessed that Dellin had all the influence and Jant was a paper boat on her river. 'She talked at length with the Emperor,' I said. 'He supports her. He said, "In the Throne Room the column representing Darkling stands beside the column for Awia. The Rhydanne are part of the Empire."'

'Does their silver column carry as much of the Empire as our blue column? I think not.'

I returned to my question: 'Have you any evidence to prove Rhydanne have ... consumed Awians?'

He frowned but said nothing.

'No eyewitnesses?'

He paused. 'No.'

'So you heard it from Snipe, who heard it from a soldier, who heard it from a schoolboy, who overheard an old woman muttering? It is hearsay, Raven, nothing more!'

He heard the relief in my voice. 'Very strong hearsay, since everyone believes it! Even if you prefer to side with the killers!'

'I agree they're killers, but not man-eaters.'

'It is misleading that they have a roughly human shape, for they are wolves. If you had only seen them sprinting out from the trees. At first, nothing. Then – everybody's dead! Silence again, and you're standing surrounded by the bodies of your friends!' He paced across the room, from the fireplace to a tapestry and back, casting nervous glances at the window but never approaching it. 'At least you can hear Insects coming!'

'They're not as bad as Insects.'

'They're much worse – as you'll witness for yourself, because the festival won't diminish their attacks. I will kill them, Lightning, *all* of them.'

I leant back in my chair and rested my elbows on the arms, and he responded to this relaxed posture by calming visibly. He paused by the arras and added, 'My decision is correct. It is the fate of princes to be ill-spoken of for doing well.'

'Even princes cannot break the law with impunity.'

'The law of the Empire or the law of nature?'

'Immortality apart, the two are much the same.'

'Immortality is a thorn in your side, not mine.' He sat down again in the timber throne.

'The Emperor wishes for peace. Your manor has less than a tenth as many Rhydanne than settlers. The Rhydanne have nothing to eat, so if you cease to provoke them, they will disperse naturally.'

'*We* are a source of food. You and I, Lightning. Dellin is attracting more killers from the wilderness to prey on us. They have a taste for our blood! They lurk in the forest, waiting for someone to step outside so they can carve the flesh from his bones. They gnaw the bones! The soldiers say they even suck out the marrow!'

'I'm surprised you can be so gullible,' I said coolly. 'I'm surprised that the author of *A Mirror for Princes* can fall for the same superstition as a cottar.'

Raven paused and thought awhile. At length he muttered, 'I am still a son of Rachiswater. Your complacent life in the lowlands has led you to favour Rhydanne over your own countrymen.'

'Not at all, if Rhydanne are murderers.'

'Jant is the same. I have seen the way he looks at Dellin.'

'He looks at all women like that.'

'He beat up my steward. You've noticed Snipe's black eye? Jant gave it to him.'

I was shocked. Raven saw this and continued, 'In the Frozen Hound trading post. Jant stood up for Dellin and beat Snipe so badly he has more than a black eye: a broken nose and a gap in his teeth. Jant was prepared to go further – he raised a hatchet to kill Snipe – but the owner of the bar prevented him.' He paused. 'I do have witnesses.'

Knowing Jant, I believed him. This changed everything. Immortals must not assault mortals. Unless fighting Insects we have no authority, only influence. We're not even supposed to take sides in their quarrels, let alone get involved. Jant had undermined me, the whole Castle even. I had no position from which to mediate and my anger rose against him.

Raven saw he had won and continued with mock regret, 'A brief letter will inform the Emperor. Assault is a crime, and in my manor Jant is subject to Awian law. I must try him and if he's found guilty jail him.'

'San need not know of it yet.'

'On the contrary, I think it's vital he knows.'

'Do I have the honour of being invited to your feast tonight?'

'Yes, of course.'

'Well, let us talk further then.' I was about to continue but a noise outside interrupted me and I turned to the window. A dog sled raced out from between the trees, heading towards us. Eight enormous dogs, pale grey with darker masks like wolves, leapt and strained. Tethered in pairs, they hauled the sled smoothly towards us. On the driver's seat a very stout figure, hooded in a brown parka, held the reins in fatly mittened hands.

The shining metal runners curled up at the front, beaming lanterns lashed to them. The rest of the sled was wood laths between which I could see the snow, and towards the back a passenger in a white parka sat hunched behind a pack. It reminded me of a kayak, as it snicked over the ice with rapid grace, leaving a wake of two ruts over paw-packed snow.

'Who's that?' I asked Raven, who looked apprehensive as he joined me at the window.

He saw the sled, relaxed and smiled. 'Ouzel. Ouzel with no surname. The proprietress of the trading post and one of the witnesses I mentioned. She saw Jant thrashing Snipe, and if it hadn't been for her, Jant would have killed him.'

'If the Rhydanne eat people, why haven't they eaten her? She's more than one good meal.'

The sled sped closer, until I could only see it by looking directly down through the lowest panes of the window. Ouzel pulled the reins and her team slewed to a halt. She disembarked in an ungainly fashion owing to the thickness of her breeches and walked down the line of dogs, releasing the reins from the harness on the back of each one. They were barking energetically, leaping up and woo-wooing. She threw something to each in turn, which sent them sniffing in the snow then lying down to chew.

The passenger opened majestic wings for balance as it disembarked. It was Jant. He looked up at the window and waved. I snorted: *wait till I talk to him.*

He blew out the lanterns, hefted the pack, and helped Ouzel pull a tarpaulin over the sled and peg it down. The dogs milled around them, and when he and Ouzel started towards the arched gate, directly below me, all eight dogs bounded forward as one, seeming to bear them into the gatehouse on an exuberant tidal wave of grey fur.

'I invited her to the feast,' said Raven. 'She supplied most of our beer.' He stepped down and returned to his throne. I made small talk, complimenting the fine petit point tapestries and the New Year's decorations, and soon footsteps were heard on the stair. In burst a vigorous woman with curly hair, her parka flapping open over a knitted jumper and hide breeches tightly circumscribed around the waist. I liked her immediately – it's easy to like someone who radiates an aura of loving everything. She rolled a rotund and rubicund bow to Raven and cried, 'Merry New Year's Eve, my lord!'

Raven laughed. 'Ouzel, compliments of the season. Let me introduce you to Lightning Micawater.'

I rose in the window seat. She looked up and opened mouth and eyes wide in astonishment. 'By god. Never thought I'd— Pull yourself together, girl.' She rallied, inclined a bow and said, 'My lord, I have something of yours. I'd like to return it.'

'What is it?'

She pointed a thumb back over her shoulder. 'Your Messenger.'

Jant came into the room, carrying a pack clinking with bottles.

He dumped it on the rug and collapsed into a chair. He looked even more wan and drawn than before. 'Isn't it good luck for a handsome man to bring in the New Year?'

'*After* midnight,' Ouzel corrected him. 'Before then he's just another pain in the backside ... My lord Raven, may I call in my lead pair?'

'Very well, but only if they behave.'

'Hist! Snowblink! Spindrift!' she yelled, and two of the sled dogs bounded in. They ran leaping across the room like an avalanche, bustled into the recess and pressed against my legs. I stroked the first, who had black ears and a dark widow's peak, making his face a pure white mask. He had saddle markings and a proud tail curled over his back. He jumped up, sturdy on enormous feet like furry snowshoes, and blotted my trousers with melting snow. The second was just as powerful. My fingers slipped over his sleek, grey guard hairs and sank deep into the incredibly soft rolls of white fluff beneath. Their brown eyes were full of laughter as they licked my hands stickily, with rough tongues that smelt of old meat. Dogs this strong could be of use in the Insect war, I thought, and wondered how to introduce them to the lowlands.

'Good boys. Which of you is Spindrift and which is Snowblink?'

'Avalanche dogs, ha ha.' Ouzel bellowed, in a way I began to realise was her norm. 'Bred by the Rhydanne.'

'They are remarkable. Dogs of this sort may be useful at the Lowespass front.'

'Oh no, my lord. Some things are not for your war. Some things are not for sale.'

OUZEL

Raven, Lightning and Jant's conversation was extremely strained. Raven couldn't stand Jant and didn't want to speak to him. Lightning tried hard to smooth their ruffled feathers. He was very polite and debonair but he was obviously furious with Jant as well and couldn't resist resorting to sarcasm. Nobody I've ever met could turn on the sarcasm quite like Lightning Micawater.

After a while I left them to it. I visited a few of the Carniss folk I've come to know and helped out in the kitchens, where I felt more at home. At seven p.m., when the governor and Eszai retired to dress for the feast, I went to feed my dogs.

Something odd was happening. Men were coming through the gate, at first in dribs and drabs. Then, on my way back from the kennels I saw the trickle had become a flood. Soldiers were arriving in ragged double file, all muffled up in greatcoats. As soon as they were inside they lidded their lanterns and looked around leerily. I know fyrdsmen when I see them. And I could see no end to them. They were crossing to the captain's house and looking in. Some stood on his veranda; others wandered off in twos and groups to the chalets and sneaked inside. A very grim wassail indeed.

The owners of the chalets were up in the hall and I wondered if they knew. In fact, everyone was in the hall, starting the feast, and the servants were still busy in the kitchens. I crunched across the snow into the tower and up the spiral stairs. Shoddy workmanship, this building. They mixed the cement with too much grit and too little concrete and it's crumbling already. I could do a lot better myself. And half the rafters were unseasoned pine, so of course they've split. It isn't difficult to dry pine, but Raven was too hasty. I should give him some advice.

My heavy skirts swung, brushing the steps. I was glad I had changed but unfortunately I had tacked together this old frock years ago. It was my best and only dress but it could hardly be described as a ball gown ... especially now its hem was soaking with slush and the dogs had slavered down it.

Coloured glass lanterns in the niches cast a jolly glow of green and red. A crimson carpet had been rolled out over the stairs and fat garlands of holly and mistletoe draped low from the ceiling. Their bright berries, glossy leaves and shining white ribbons criss-crossed the receding spiral of the steps above. A wonderful smell of baked bread and mulled ale drifted down to meet me. I was so hungry my stomach churned. I hurried up. I couldn't wait to fill my belly with roast ox, and plum pudding with brandy butter.

'So, is it true?' Lightning's voice came from around the next turn of the spiral. I stopped and listened – I didn't want to barge in on one of the Eszai. His shadow – and Jant's – were cast on the curved wall in front of me. They stood on the little first-floor landing outside the treasury door. I wondered what to do and decided that rather than push past them I had better hold on till they returned to the hall. I rested my hand on the clammy rope rail and waited.

Jant said something in an undertone.

Lightning huffed. 'You say there's no truth in it, but how did the rumour arise?'

'Like any other rumour,' Jant replied plaintively. 'Out of the villagers' imagination. They've seen Rhydanne and they've seen wolves snatching their children. It doesn't take a great playwright to meld the two together.'

Lightning's shadow nodded. 'All right, I thought that must be the case. And the next point – how *could* you beat up Snipe?'

'Oh ... Did Raven tell you?'

'How could you think I wouldn't find out? Snipe looks as if he's been hit by a mail coach! Brawling in a bar, Jant! Are you mad? Have you any idea what the Emperor will think?'

Jant must have had an idea, because his shadow on the wall looked at its feet. He muttered, 'Snipe was insulting Rhydanne.'

'That will be a poor defence in court! Yes, in court! Raven can try you, and he intends to!'

'I only blacked Snipe's eye!'

'And broke his smile. You'll have to pay a fine or take a prison sentence. I hope it's the former – you won't be a useful Messenger in prison! Do you think San will keep your position open? Do you think he'll wait out your sentence? I don't think so!'

'What would he do?'

'Open a competition for a new Messenger!'

Jant leant on the wall and covered his face with his hand. Further angered by the gesture, Lightning poked him in the chest. 'Are you sorry?' he demanded.

I shrank back involuntarily. In the silence that followed I could hear the night wind piping in the upper reaches of the tower.

'Are you sorry?'

'No, I'm not,' Jant said eventually.

'Well, you had better pretend to be! When we return to the table, apologise to Snipe. Make it sound genuine and make sure Raven hears it.'

'No! I told you. I punched him because he kept insulting the Rhydanne.'

'And would you let a Rhydanne get away with derogatory remarks about Awians?' Another pause in which Jant hung his head. 'Look at you in that costume,' Lightning continued. 'The King of the Rhydanne! I know how you feel for Dellin but love has turned you into the worst diplomat of all time. You've crumbled the ground from under us. Now I've no position from which to negotiate, and if we fail, the kingdom is lost!'

'Then Dellin can have Carnich back. The Emperor will be pleased.'

Lightning let out an exasperated yell and shoved Jant all around the landing. I heard him clang off the grille of the treasury. 'All right!' he bridled. 'I'll apologise to Snipe!'

'Very good,' said Lightning breathlessly.

At this point I suppose I could have stomped up a few steps, feigned surprise at seeing them, called a cheery greeting and escaped into the hall. God knows the smell of spiced beer was tempting enough and the freezing draught blowing down the steps was making my knees knock. But this was the best entertainment I'd ever had. I figured that between them Jant, Raven and Dellin had wrecked my business, so the very least they owed me was the chance to listen in on their New Year's cabaret. And now Lightning had joined them: the Archer himself, over a thousand years old! I'd never thought I'd hear the Archer tearing a strip off the Messenger. And Jant certainly deserved it. I shrank against the wall and continued to listen.

'About Raven,' said Lightning. '*Will* you concentrate?'

'I guess ...'

'This is what we do: we wait until tomorrow, until the very moment he arms his troops for the march, then we swoop.'

'Will he assemble his men with us here?'

'He doesn't know what to think. I tried to confirm his assumption that our mission is concerned with Dellin, and I believe I was successful. Whatever you do, don't destroy that impression in the next few hours.'

'Of course not.'

'I have no doubt Raven has sent word to Rachiswater and his supporters are preparing as we speak. Have you seen all the soldiers down there?'

'I saw lights in the stable block.'

Lightning folded his arms to wrap his coat about him, rested his foot behind him with the boot sole on the wall and leant back on it. 'Those are just the vanguard,' he said seriously. 'If you listen you can hear more ...'

They listened, and I held my breath. Sure enough the rhythmic thud of booted feet was echoing through the undercroft.

'The barracks are already full,' Lightning continued. 'Snipe's house is next to them, so I had a good view of them just now. I estimate about two hundred men so far, which means the remainder of the division are still climbing. Raven is billeting them with the villagers and in the stables. Even the horses are making room for warriors.'

'He's hiding them.'

'Exactly. We must be quick now, because he will worry that we are snooping about and come looking for us.'

Lightning was right: even the kenneller's house had been packed with strangers. They had looked rough and practically frozen. They were warming themselves around the fireplace until their long coats ran wet with melting ice. They had kept their boots on and piled their accoutrements – waxcloth knapsacks and snowshoes – up against the wall.

'They'll be pissed off at missing the Shattering,' said Jant.

'Forget the Shattering; they will be glad of a hot meal. Listen, Jant, we must not let Raven leave. He must stay in Carniss. Do you understand?'

Jant's sapling shadow on the grey wall nodded. He sat down on a step. 'And Dellin ...?'

'All in good time,' said Lightning, and a trace of sympathy transfused his voice. He reached out and rattled the grille. 'We cannot let this fortress stand. Not only is it the base for his offensive but it's grossly in breach of Imperial law. Tomorrow when we arrest Raven I will take command of his soldiers and we will dismantle the keep ... in front of his very eyes.'

'May your Wishes come true, Raven Carniss ...' Jant muttered.

'The soldiers must be aware we're here.'

'Yes, they're very quiet.'

Unseasonably quiet, I thought. Nasty, in fact. I'd called 'Happy New Year!' to them but received only suspicious stares in return. I had hoped they had money to spend and hearty appetites. The Hound needs new customers untainted by Dellin and Raven's battles, but this bunch wanted more than a bowl of stew to warm them.

'Then stay in the hall,' said Lightning. 'If they see you, they'll think we have informed Tarmigan of the coup.'

A coup!

'They'd assume right,' Jant agreed. 'I can reach the king in a couple of hours.'

'They will know that if they've lost the element of surprise they'll be heading to their deaths. If Tarmigan is prepared, he'll massacre them. So now they will fear his retribution and be loath to follow Raven. I will gather them in the bailey and tell them we won't deliver them to Tarmigan if they cooperate.'

'Will Raven stand by and watch?' Jant asked, dubiously.

'What else can he do? Our authority over the fyrd is greater than his.'

'He could tell them to hack us to shreds?' Jant's dual shadow, cast by the two coloured lanterns, separated and thinned. He had turned to ascend to the hall.

Lightning delivered one last barb. 'Don't ever, *ever* beat a mortal again.'

'Sure,' Jant said flippantly. 'Never again.'

'Oh, very well,' Lightning snapped. 'Go on, we're missing the Shattering.' His shadow merged into Jant's and faded as they climbed.

I breathed out. How could I enjoy the feast now I knew Raven was secretly plotting a revolt and the Eszai were trying to foil him? Well, the answer's straightforward: with baked potatoes and tipsy cake, of course! What difference does a war in Awia make to me or the Hound? I waited awhile, then hitched up my skirts and sauntered after them into the hall.

The feast was in full swing. The hall was packed with people – I had never thought I'd see so many in my life again. Carniss was a town, a walled town, and Raven had invited all his people. I joined Jant and Lightning, who were sitting next to Raven and Snipe – in that order – along the same side of the table so as to have a good view of the hall. A number of bottles of wine were clustered in front of Raven and the Archer, but waiting for me was a jug of beer and a tankard, and Spindrift was lying under the table, chewing Snipe's bootlaces.

There was no main course yet, just snacks of pinwheel rolls filled with raisins and currants, or with cow's cheese – a rare treat. The tables were arranged in a square and in the centre, on a stand of red and white glazed bricks, stood the kiln. I have seen Shattering kilns of all shapes and sizes, but this was by far the most ornate. It was shaped like a lantern of openwork wrought-iron curlicues. Raven's initials embellished it and the gold Rachiswater eagle perched on its apex like a standard. It was two metres tall and open at the top so the flames rose around the eagle. I thought it was truly the possession of a prince; it burned so fiercely that the two fires in the hearths had been kept to a minimum. Only a few lamps were lit and cosy shadows crowded the corners.

To watch the kiln, the woodsmen, prospectors and their families sat around the outside edge of the square. And in the space left for safety between the fire and the tables, servants walked to and fro with laden plates and jugs of beer. Here, a little girl stuffed her face with bread; there, a boy fed Snowblink under the table.

'I thought I was late,' I said. 'But I see there's no clay yet.'

'It will be brought in shortly,' said Raven. 'In the meantime, please help yourself.'

'Thank you, my lord.'

Imagine me rubbing shoulders with two Eszai and the king's brother! Rachiswater and Micawater, a Lakeland full house – if I cared for distinguished company I might find myself flustered. But I'd much rather meet Tornado. Out of all the Eszai I loved hearing tales of his exploits best. He could be handy around the Frozen Hound; he appreciates a pie and mash, and; tell me true, what woman would turn down the opportunity of exploring a mountain of solid muscle?

Lightning's bearing showed he was used to being the centre of attention and I made up my mind there and then not to be impressed. But I couldn't stop looking at his broad shoulders and the girth of his biceps, which, with the rest of his big frame, were very graceful. His eyes were somewhat baggy and the beginnings of blond stubble was rather a shame as it hid his jaw. He wore his hair below shoulder level and tied in a ponytail, odd for an Awian, as long hair is a sign of mourning. Unlike Jant I wouldn't find him lying drunk on my floor ... I think.

A procession of servants emerged from the staircase and everyone gave a shout. The first ten waiters bore huge bowls of water. All our excited conversations grew louder as they walked among the tables, leaving a hand basin on each. A lad placed one in front of me, and I looked down to see dried blue petals floating on delightfully rose-scented water.

Now they brought the clay! It was very black and clean, in smooth domes like gigantic puddings, each on a silver salver. A servant placed one before Raven. It had been embossed in a mould with holly and ivy leaves. Sprigs of mistletoe decorated the top and it had been embossedbrushed with water to make it shine. 'Carniss clay!' proclaimed Raven. 'As good as any in the lowlands, I promise you.'

'It looks edible,' I said and everyone laughed.

Raven picked up a palette knife. 'For months I've been sending out patrols searching for the right type. Eventually they found this in the glacier outwash. It's perfect.'

Lightning teased, 'I bet you tested it thoroughly.'

'Of course,' said Raven seriously. 'A fifty-fifty chance. I'm certain it will work.' He sliced into the dome with the mock ceremony of a groom cutting a wedding cake. Grit scratched on the knife; he cut the dome into five segments and motioned that I should take the first. I held out my plate and received a slice.

'As usual, every dome of clay contains one gold acorn. Who has it? Who's the lucky one?'

I pressed my clay flat. 'Not me.'

The servants brought a stand of five bowls, each containing coloured powder. Raven spun the stand and the bowls revolved like a spice tray. 'We have blue, red, green, pink and purple. I will be blue. Ouzel, what colour do you want?'

'Pink, my lord.'

'Green!' said Jant.

'Lightning?' Raven asked.

'I will be red.'

'That leaves Snipe with purple. To match his bruise, eh, Jant?'

We each took a dish and kneaded the coloured powder into our clay. The clay was smooth but contained the tiny quartzite grains that weather out of Darkling granite. It was not as silky as Rachiswater clay but still malleable and delightfully cold to the touch. I dug my fingers in and started rolling it into a sausage. What animal will I make to carry my wish into the new year? A rat, perhaps? No, an otter – sleek and playful. I tore off a piece and rolled it into a tail, then started sculpting an otter's frisky body as best I could.

'I've got the acorn!' said Snipe.

'Finders keepers,' said Raven. How could he seem so cheerful when he was hiding so much?

Jant separated his clay into several chunks and moulded them into complicated shapes, but on his other side Lightning was very adeptly fashioning a deer. He pulled the clay into legs with elegantly minimal curves, and nipped one end of the body into a stylised head with an arched neck.

'That's beautiful,' I said.

Jant grinned and shrugged. 'He makes the same thing every year.'

With a few deft impressions of the edge of his fork, Lightning gave it eyes and criss-cross shading on its flank. He plucked two holly leaves from the wreath left on the platter and poked them into the deer's head to form elk horns. Then he placed it on his plate and it stood with sophistication. 'A wish deer,' he said. He cupped his hands around it and whispered into them as if telling the deer a vital secret.

'What are you wishing for?' asked Jant.

Lightning leant back. 'You should know by now that if you tell anyone, it doesn't work.'

'Rubbish. I bet you can all guess who *I'm* wishing for.'

Lightning glanced at him and he fell quiet. Raven seemed to be making an eagle, and on his other side Snipe was elongating his clay into an S, but I couldn't tell what animal he was making. I concentrated on my otter, which was not proceeding to plan. The clay was too soft for it to stand and it kept sagging. I decided it would have to be an otter couchant, lying in the way my dogs sleep, with its tail wrapped around its nose. Jant peered at it. 'What's that? A dormouse? Or a toad? A wish toad?'

'It's an otter,' I said, laughing.

'An otter that's been run over?'

'It's not finished!'

'This is not a competition,' said Lightning.

'Ha ha, I am pretty crap at it,' I conceded, then vaguely wondered if that was the correct way to address an Eszai.

'Well, it looks very much like an otter to me,' said Raven. 'At home in the River Rachis.'

'Thank you, my lord.' I picked up my knife and scored hairs in its tail.

Around us the shouts, as people found their acorns, had all finished and conversations were a low murmur as everyone concentrated on fashioning their Wishes. Occasional bouts of laughter broke out as they appraised each other's efforts or gave up making difficult animals and plumped for snakes or owls. When I had finished my otter I held it in cupped hands and whispered, 'Hello, otter. This year I have a new wish. I wish that Raven's selfish Awians and Dellin's militant Rhydanne would *fuck off* out of Carniss so that peaceful Rhydanne and Awians can continue trading more profitably than ever before.'

'What did you wish for?' asked Jant.

'The same as always. That next year my trade will be better than ever and that Macan will continue to grow strong and healthy.'

He wrinkled his nose as if he considered this boring.

'It *is* supposed to be a secret,' I added. 'If you find other people's secrets commonplace, you have only yourself to blame for asking.'

Raven used his signet ring to impress his shoot-at-the-moon emblem on his eagle, and set it on his plate. It stood clasping a clay mountaintop with crooked claws and its beak had a very disdainful expression. Snipe had finished his model too, a lizard with holly berry eyes, but Jant was still sculpting intently.

'It doesn't have to be perfect,' Lightning told him. 'It is only a game.'

'Perfection is in the eye of the beholder!' Jant dipped his fingers in our hand-washing water, gave his sculpture a shine, and placed it on his plate. He had made a model of himself! A tiny Jant, unmistakable with roguish face, sitting cross-legged with a platter on his knees as if it was making a smaller model.

'You're supposed to make an animal,' I said, laughing.

'Raven insists that the Rhydanne *are* animals.'

'Jant!' said Lightning. 'Not now!'

'Who better to carry my wishes into eighteen ninety-one than myself?'

I placed my admittedly rather squashed-looking otter with the rest of our Wishes onto the platter and a servant carried them down to the kiln. Throughout the hall, servants were collecting wish animals from all the tables: salvers full of black clay hedgehogs, rabbits and piglets, robins, tiny dormice and fat marmots. All were decorated with berries and leaves that the revellers had found to hand, but only ours were coloured. It's the perk of the High Table to be first to know whether our Wishes will come true. Everyone else had to wait till morning, when they could pick over the cooled trays of ceramic figurines on display on the trestles and discover whether their animal had shattered or not.

The servants carefully took the animals – a huge, inventive variety so every maker could identify his Wish tomorrow – and placed them on great iron trays. They slid each tray into the kiln on runners. Ours was first to go in and, for an instant, I saw the silhouettes of our figurines black against the flames. Then the flames roared high; blue, green and red leapt from the top of the kiln and the audience watching cooed, 'Ooh!'

Meanwhile, more serving boys were bringing in the feast. Two lads carried between them a whole roast ox on a tray more like a stretcher. They placed it in front of us then moored gravy boats and ramekins of hot horseradish sauce around it.

'Amazing!' I said. 'It's as big as a man!'

Jant choked on his beer and it frothed up over the rim of his glass onto the table.

'What's the matter?'

He glared and wiped his mouth. 'As big as a man? Help yourself to him.'

I dealt some slices of beef onto my plate and poured on strong Bitterdale blue cheese sauce with mushrooms. Then came baskets of roast potatoes, tureens of crisp swede and parsnips glazed with honey, sauerkraut, carrots and peas shining with vinegar from the pickling jar, baked batter puddings, fried rice balls stuffed with figs and sultanas, and sausages wrapped in bacon. Platters clustered around the ox till there was no room left on the table.

Raven must be pining for a traditional Awian New Year. If the sweet course was just as customary I might almost be prepared to forgive him for wrecking my trade. I loved plum pudding in a moat of double cream and packed with cherries, almonds, all kinds of candied fruit, cinnamon, ginger and cloves. Not to mention a festive splash of brandy.

Every table bore the same. The serving boys were queuing up on the staircase outside and bringing in ox after ox, roasted as dark as mahogany and lying with their legs tied on their trays. Domestics in Raven's new livery entered to carve them and slices of rich meat accrued on the platters.

'There's nothing Darkling here at all,' said Jant.

'Nothing Rhydanne, you mean,' I said.

He nodded. 'We should ask Raven to give us some kutch.'

'I think that would be a very bad idea.'

'What is kutch?' asked Lightning, leaning forward to look at me over Jant's heaped plate.

'A drink the Rhydanne brew,' he said. 'Any kind of meat stewed with any kind of alcohol.'

'Often with water, blood or milk,' I added. 'It makes a sort of broth.'

Lightning considered this. 'By god,' he said, at length. 'The horror.'

I ate happily, looking at the gorgeous decorations. All the beams were bedecked with satin ribbons and gloriously fat scarlet and pearl-white baubles. Each one reflected the flames of the two fireplaces and the flickering kiln. Wreaths draped the fireplaces, too; boughs of berried ivy looped up to bunches of mistletoe, with gold pine cones and purple baubles in their centres. Between the fireplaces was an enormous portrait of Raven looking haughty astride a black horse, but its grandiose frame was hidden by tinsel made of foil and silk, which fluttered in the rising heat. Decorations of gold bees and acorns – symbols of hard work and the subsequent rewards – hid among the tinsel. Beside the painting hung an ornate brass pendulum clock, at which everyone kept glancing. It now showed half past nine.

Whether it was accurate to Starglass time or not we didn't care.

It was Carniss time, our own time in this bizarre bubble Raven had made, and we were waiting excitedly for its twelve chimes to bring in midnight and eighteen ninety-one. A quartet of musicians, two violins, one viola and one cello, arranged themselves on chairs at the foot of the dais and began playing. Raven brightened considerably on hearing the first bars and nodded to Lightning. 'They're far from their best in this damn climate, but listen how they play *The Comic Turn.*'

'One of your favourite pieces.'

'Yes. They were part of my household in Rachiswater but only four were loyal enough to join me in exile.'

'You could make Carniss a place of inspiration for musicians and artists,' Lightning suggested.

'Ah, it pleases you to laugh at me,' said Raven.

'I'm not laughing.'

'You must agree no artist or poet will ever climb this dreary crag. You must agree our feast is modest compared with what you're used to. Or compared with my brother's masquerades ... his orchestras on the bridge ... Remember his sleighs pulled by horses with gilded manes. Or his kilns floating on gondolas on the river?'

'Yes, I do,' said Lightning. 'But this is far more memorable.'

Raven snatched at this: 'Will you remember?'

'Yes.'

'Do you promise?'

'Yes,' said Lightning, startled by his vehemence.

I wanted to tell Raven that he should put all that stuff about his brother behind him. There's enough to do in Carnich without bothering yourself with the misery of the past. But he began to muse. 'If you remember this for ever, in a small way I shall never die. You might live for another thousand years, Lightning. Maybe two thousand ... or even more.'

Lightning said nothing, so Raven continued, 'And among all your memories, sometimes at a Shattering you'll recall Raven Rachiswater, now lost in the depth of time. You'll think, his very bones must be dust by now. I will live on in your recollection. All the more reason to give you a present; it will act as an aide memoire.'

'There is really no need,' Lightning said.

'Yes, there is. Here.' Raven dug into the pocket of his beaver-fur-collared coat, which hung on one post of his chair. He brought out a silver hip flask and placed it on the table. It was engraved with his old, royal coat of arms. 'This is at hand. For want of something better, take it as a memento.'

Lightning took the hipflask, realised it had liquid inside, unscrewed the lid and sniffed it.

'Brandy,' Raven said. 'Will you remember me by it? Whether it's a Rhydanne spear that ends me, or whether I'm crushed by an avalanche?'

'Yes, I promise,' said Lightning.

Raven's whimsy was making me uneasy. If he was setting out to fight the King, of course death would be preying on his mind. But it's no wonder he's obsessed, I thought, bearing the reminder of such a deep wound on his face. His own twin did that – the king! Of course it would twist his thoughts and make him rashly crave revenge; the lords of Awia are more vicious than any starving vassal in his plough ruts or any Rhydanne hanging by her fingernails from the crag.

A snap resounded from the kiln – the animals had started to burst and the show was about to begin. Clicks and cracks resounded, and then one exploded – bang! It turned the flames purple. Fragments of hot pottery erupted out of the top of the kiln and showered down into the space between it and the tables.

'That was one of ours!' I said.

'Purple!' said Snipe. 'My lizard.'

'Your wish will come true in the new year. Good for you!'

Then a second and third blew up together, throwing out debris and colouring the flames bright red and pink. 'Pink!' I said. 'That was my otter, ha ha. I knew it was a winner!'

'Oohs' and 'aahs' combined with mock screams and shouts of hilarity as pieces pattered down on the tables. Someone stood abruptly, brushing her head, and ran for the corner of the room, leaving her friends in uproarious laughter. The next tray of wishes began exploding all at once. The bright flashes and bangs unsettled my dogs and a small howl emanated from by my feet. I ducked under the table and reassured them.

'What about mine?' said Jant in dismay.

'Give it a chance,' I said. 'It's still warming up.'

'I want my wish to come true!'

Lightning said, 'If it cooks without breaking, then at least you will have another ceramic figure for your mantelpiece.'

'But I want it to release my wish! How can my wish come true if it won't let it free!' Jant picked up his beer glass, swirled it and shrugged. 'Anyway, it's all nonsense ...'

'It's just a game,' I said. 'You can't always win if it's random.'

The bursting Wishes kept on, some all at once, then pauses, sporadic bangs that seemed the loudest, and series of pops as exploding animals set off adjacent ones. Raven laid his knife and fork down and said, 'I should go among my people and wish them Happy New Year.'

'Of course,' Lightning said.

Raven motioned Snipe to join him and descended to the trestle tables. We watched him moving among the colonists, shaking woodsmen's hands, clapping the backs of the miners and joking with them.

'He's rallying them!' said Jant. 'Some of those will join his troops, I'm sure.'

'I have no doubt they will, and he's probably telling them not to fear us.'

'He's making sure they're stoked up with beer.'

Lightning watched Raven as if he could lip-read. 'Yes. But we wait until they make a move.'

All this time the Wishes continued exploding, showering fragments with exhilarating pops and bangs.

'I haven't seen a flash of blue either,' Jant said. 'Raven's eagle hasn't blown up yet.'

'A blue Rachiswater eagle,' Lightning assented. 'Poor Raven, no amount of melancholy and no degree of single-mindedness will make his wish come true.'

'I wouldn't call him poor.'

'He would make just as good a sovereign as his brother, with the same appearance but a different style. Being reduced to a merchant gave him something definite to do. Tarmigan couldn't have rolled his sleeves up and achieved all this. But Tarmigan is as good with people as Raven is with abstract concepts. I couldn't say which would be the better king.'

Jant was about to retort but bit it back, and the two fell silent. If only they would talk as freely in front of me as they had on the stairs!

SNIPE

Raven was shaking Whimbrel's hand. He took my upper arm, gripped it tightly and turned me away from the Eszai. 'You should have done it before,' he hissed.

'Locked them in the room?'

'Yes! Before the troops started arriving. Never mind. I will do it after the feast.'

I stayed mum.

'Tell Comet and Lightning I will meet them in the room by the solar. When they are inside I'll come out and turn the key. No windows. Jant won't be able to fly out. Then we will assemble the men.'

I still said nothing. Locking up Eszai has got to bring some retribution. Raven had said he'd release them when he was on the throne. By then, they wouldn't be able to stop him.

He shook the hand of Grebe. 'Happy New Year!'

'Happy New Year, my lord.' Grebe had a glint in his eyes – he were mindful of our business and ready to join us at first light. Raven smiled at him, as cool as can be. But I could feel the immortals' eyes boring into the back of my neck. Wouldn't surprise me if, along with eternal life, the Emperor had given them the ability to hear us whispering. Or read our minds. I couldn't believe Raven was sticking to his plan under their very noses.

'Have you spoken to the Lowespass captain?' he asked.

'Yes. Nearly half are in already. All five hundred will be safely inside in a couple of hours.'

'Give them plenty of food and make sure they rest. Tell them to form up by the kennel compound at daybreak. While I talk to them, you gather the settlers.'

'They know the Eszai are here.'

Raven shook another man's hand and spoke to me at the same

time. 'They only know rumours. They'll never see the immortals. They know not to come into the hall, and in an hour or so Lightning and Comet will be out of sight. Snipe? Snipe?'

'Yes, my lord?'

'Pay attention. Go outside and wish the kenneller a happy New Year. He'll be preparing the dog sleds. It's not just the longest night of the year, it's the longest night of our lives.'

OUZEL

The fact that Jant was dressed in Rhydanne gear couldn't have escaped Raven's attention. I thought Jant looked magnificent. He had managed to clean the white parka and tasselled trousers, and lynx fur tippets hung from the lacings at his hips.

Lightning refilled his glass and asked innocently, 'Did you find Dellin?'

'Yes,' Jant said. 'I know where she's hiding.'

'Does she still want to drive Raven out?'

'Yes. She swears it.' Jant shuffled his wings and let them droop slightly open. 'Awians swear oaths on their blood, but Dellin's smarter than they are – she swears it on *Raven's* blood.'

Lightning nodded. 'Can you possibly stop her terrorising the villagers?'

'No. She's determined.'

'I remember her determination from the Throne Room. Do you know where she is now?'

'Oh yes! She's outside, among the rocks.'

'Outside the keep?'

'Yes.'

'Without shelter?'

'She's watching the gate.' Jant chuckled.

A frown creased Lightning's forehead and he turned to whisper impatiently, 'Pull yourself together! When we insist Raven stays in Carniss, he will wreak his fury on the Rhydanne instead. He'll immediately cut their forest back as much as he can. We can commandeer his warriors but he'll use the colonists and ask for more. He'll denude the slopes until there are no trees near the keep for Dellin to hide in. This morning he told me he won't stop until he has wiped her out.'

'God! I have to tell her!'

I stayed quiet; I wanted to hear as much as possible. Lightning didn't want to mention the coup but he had no problems discussing Rhydanne in front of me. He seemed to have cottoned on to the fact that Dellin and Raven between them had ruined my business completely. The Frozen Hound was absolutely empty; we hadn't seen a customer for days.

He raised a hand. 'If Dellin stops her raids, I have a small chance of bringing Raven to terms with the Rhydanne. He won't negotiate, so he declares, but he doesn't have my patience. Go outside now, and tell her to stop.'

'But ... but ... No. I can't.'

'Tell her the silver man says so, ha ha, ' I suggested. The two immortals looked at me. Lightning kept me in his clear and searching gaze, wondering whether I was trustworthy, useful, or both.

Jant shook his head, 'She's past that now; she wouldn't listen. The silver man is five hundred kilometres away and she has the courage of her own convictions.'

'Tell her she must stop.'

'No. There must be another way ...'

It was terrible to see Jant struggle. We all knew that if he tried to stop Dellin, she would never speak to him again.

Lightning bided his time and watched. I was surprised to see a look of grim satisfaction cross his face. He twiddled the stem of his wine glass. His hands were remarkably powerful, fingers broad and flattened at the tips, accustomed to holding an arrow at nock. His short nails were meticulously filed and, on his wedding finger – as if he was married to his manor and no one else – he wore a signet ring of silver. No, platinum, with a sapphire bearing the Micawater lozenge. It must have been a copy of a very old ring because it was an oddly antiquated design.

Jant gave up and buried his head in his hands. 'I can't think of any alternative. But, Lightning, I need to be on her side. I've already prevented her poisoning everyone in Carniss. If I tell her to stop, she'll think I've ceased to support her. She'll continue her raids and I'll have achieved nothing apart from losing her. I can't ...'

Lightning smiled faintly. 'Why don't you marry her?'

'*Marry* her!'

'Sh! Tell me honestly, had you never thought of proposing?'

'No ...' Jant stared. 'I never ...' Then everything clicked in his mind. The puzzle was solved. A mad gleam came into his eyes. 'Yes! I can, can't I?'

'We all have that ability,' said Lightning, swirling his glass.

'But ... it'll make me lazy. Self-contented. I'll grow too fat to fly!'

'If you marry a Rhydanne?' I said. 'Nonsense!'

'Well, yeah ...' He paused again then smiled.

'Maybe you need it,' said Lightning. 'Maybe in your life the time has come – by god, I never thought it would – when you are ready. You look more exhausted than if you'd been at the battlefront all this time. Imagine feeling so tired for the rest of eternity? Would you suffer, if you had to live without her?'

'I think so.'

'Then offer her your hand in marriage. Tell her you will bring her to the Castle. You will marry her before the Emperor. He will link her to the Circle, through you, and make her immortal.'

'I don't know ... Rhydanne accept the fact they die. She might not understand immortality.'

'Immortality is a quality every woman understands.'

'We'd be together for ever.'

'Yes. Preserve her beauty. Doesn't the Castle need a touch of wildness?'

'She'd be dependent on me for life ...' Jant looked inside himself again, still trying to come to terms with using his power seriously, rather than as a fail-proof chat-up line.

'If you want to give her love, what better way than to give her life?'

'That's right! That's what I want!' He jumped up and snatched a platter of meat. 'I want to make her happy, because that will make *me* happy! I'll bring her food – that's how Rhydanne propose!'

'It seems rather less enduring than a ring,' Lightning murmured.

'I'll give her my ring as well!' Jant cried, and hurried out. The last I saw of him was the fur trim on his parka hem disappearing down the staircase.

'A good night's work!' Lightning smiled. 'And an excellent way to round off the year. Ouzel, may I? To eighteen ninety-one!' We clinked our glasses.

JANT

I hurtled down the stairs, out onto the snow and dashed into the gatehouse arch. So many soldiers marching through it, one after another. Their coats were white with hoar frost; they carried only light packs and each man's pallid face was like a lantern floating above the amber lamp that swung in his hand. Each was lined with exhaustion, and lit with sudden surprise as I ran past.

Time would tear Dellin from my side. I keenly felt its inexorable flow separating us even now. I felt as if she had been walking beside me, then suddenly lost her footing and chuted down the icy slope, out of control, hurtling faster and faster into the distance. Time would rip her away – she would crash into all its events and it would kill her. Rhydanne live too quickly. How cruel reality was! How cruel time was, as we walk like parasites on its rushing body. Time: as the twelve strokes of midnight drew nearer, I felt it tangible in the air, a sense of expectation, anticipation. It was so cloying, I couldn't stand it!

If I don't save Dellin, she will die. There suddenly seemed to be very little time left – if I don't save her in a matter of minutes she will die imminently! Why had I been fooling about for weeks when I had no time to spare?

I ran out of the gateway, to the track with shovel-loads of snow piled high beside it, along which the soldiers were still coming. Their lanterns cast long shadows over the snow mounds, turning every lump into a mountain. Every hollow became a crevasse. I scrambled off the path onto the untouched snow. A gaggle of lights in the distance glimmered as they ascended between the trees. More soldiers.

The storm lamps on the parapet cast an orange glow down the curtain wall. Their arcs of light pooled around its base, shining on the enormous blocks lustrous with verglas. Beyond was nothing but blackness. I ran alongside the wall, on snow coloured orange by the lamp light. My forked shadow licked beside me on the drifts. The ground sloped away in tiers, then vanished abruptly in a sheer drop. Far below, I could hear the wind moaning against the rock face.

The curtain wall rooted straight onto the cliff. I searched its puckered and exfoliated rocks but Dellin wasn't here; I was quite alone. I reached a little crag, lambent with ice and veiled with snow. The wall stepped down it before disappearing into the darkness. I held the plate to my chest and climbed down the crag, with the drop sheer to the lowlands beneath me.

A cornice crusted over the top of the crag like icing on a cake, and lower down the rocks showed through. I was at the very edge of the light emanating from the keep, and I came to a halt on a ledge surrounded by the void. The cliffs were dim and I could no longer hear soldiers' voices or any sound from the hall: everything was still.

'Dellin?' I called quietly. 'Dellin, are you here?'

She stood before me. One second I was alone. The next she simply detached herself from a shadow in a fissure and ran forward a few steps.

She looked meaningfully at the tray of meat so I gave it to her. She crouched and bolted every piece, then dropped the tray and wiped her fingers on the snow.

'Thank you,' she said, and I smiled. I had tamed her that much.

As she stood up she met my eyes. I took her hands and she did not pull away. 'Dellin,' I said. 'Will you be my wife?'

Her glance flicked down to the tray. Yes, I could procure food like the best of hunters. She thought for a while, her hand over her mouth and her pale face turned away from me.

So, she will not dismiss me out of hand, but I couldn't stand to wait. I reached out and touched her collar, wanting, but not daring, to tilt her face to mine. 'Come with me to the Castle. We'll be married in front of the silver man. He'll make you immortal. You'll be part of the Circle, Dellin. You will never die. Never! We can see the world a thousand years from now.

'Everyone will come to our wedding. The whole Circle will be our audience in the Throne Room, then we'll have a feast. I don't mean you should act like a flatlander! I don't want you to dress their way; I want you the way you are. Everyone in the Castle will accept you

... They aren't prejudiced against us. You don't even have to leave the mountains, if you prefer not to. We can be married here. You can stay in Carniss for ever.'

She looked up. 'Yes! I will be your hunting partner.'

The delicate curve of her beautiful eyebrows over her almond, green eyes. Her skin, as clear as the silk inside a chestnut shell ... Her black hair in contrast, pinned by a bone comb ... I wanted to kiss her but instead she leant forward – she smelt so rich and heady – embraced me powerfully and licked my throat. Her teeth closed on my skin and nipped me. She let go and breathed out at the same time, her eyes closing in pleasure. Intoxicated, I held her. She whispered in my ear, 'Chase me!' then she leapt away and scaled the little crag confidently, pulled herself over the top and was gone.

What on earth? What was she doing? Why had she left me? A sense of rejection rose and I teetered on the edge of anguish then – yes. It means yes! She wants me to *chase* her!

Without time to think, I climbed the crag after her. I clutched my fingers into the snow and hoisted myself over the cornice. Dellin was running for the forest edge, already small at the edge of the light, her faint shadow racing ahead of her. I stretched my legs and ran my fastest, and began to close the distance as the wood loomed closer. I could just make out her sylph-like legs. She jumped a rock, slipped between the trees and disappeared. I cleared the rock in a stride and followed her into the forest.

It was pitch black. I couldn't differentiate anything. I halted, panting. I put out my arm, strode forward, and gradually my vision improved until I could just distinguish her footprints, darker grey on the grey snow. The tree boles were black shafts, streaks of empty space, and Dellin had zigzagged between them, climbing all the time. I ran on, over her prints, trying to glimpse movement, but she had already vanished and she ran so nimbly I couldn't hear her steps.

The forest was silent and the snow striped steel-grey and impervious black, crusted over like old sugar so I broke its topping with every footfall. I was so fleet of foot, running was effortless. A light feeling in my chest seemed to raise me up and filled me with warmth. She loves me in return! This was going to be so good! I'll take her to the Castle and show her the whole world. I'll introduce her to everyone as my wife. What would she think of Hacilith? She's so inquisitive she'll love it!

I had an image of her smiling face surrounded by the long wispy trim of her hood. I wasn't sure what to do. I had seen Rhydanne run but what happened at the other end was a mystery. Will she give herself to me, or does she expect me to bring her down in the snow? Something wonderful will happen, but I didn't know exactly what. I'll have to do what seems right. One thing I knew for certain: she was leading me to a special place where we will be alone together.

I'll be tender. I'll teach her how to kiss. She'll learn my love and I'll learn hers. Hope filled me. When she's mine, we'll do this again and again in innumerable ways. We'll fight the Castle's battles side by side and fill up the Northwest Tower with Dara children. How we will shock the ambassadors! Dellin, sitting beside me at the feast, in shorts and vest, and her party trick climbing all the way over and under the table without touching the floor!

A light breeze stirred the branches. The trees were thinner here and I glimpsed the sky. A rocky mound rose some distance in front and my lover's tracks led straight towards it. This is it! She must want to give herself to me on the summit. I realised I preferred the hard and glassy snow to any eiderdown. Better than any boudoir, above us we would have the biting air and limitless stars. The peaks of Klannich will witness us making love.

I reached the knoll and began climbing. I thought I saw snow brushed from the handholds she had used less than a minute before, but I still couldn't hear her. I reached over outcropping boulders, found a crack among them and followed it. I reached one arm over the final projection, to the summit, slithered my belly over the rimy rock and pulled myself onto the top.

Knees bent, poised to spring, I looked around. Dellin was not there. The domed summit was empty – she must have descended the other side. I ran across and examined the edge for footprints, but the crust was untouched.

Where *was* she? I smiled and it froze on my face. Never mind. Perhaps she was tempting me. I had to admire her talent. She had thrown me off her trail, but if she loved me she'd retrace her steps and let me glimpse her. We would run on and I would want her the more when I caught her.

This was a magnificent viewpoint. The forest spread out in all directions, rising to the silhouette of Klannich against the dark purple snow clouds. The forest dipped smoothly down, folding into gullies, and at the foot of the incline gave onto blank snow and the keep. On the keep's parapet, orange haloes surrounded the storm lamps. Semicircles of light scalloped the walls below them and fringed the snow.

The lancet windows of the hall, halfway up the tower, were lit yellow and flickered from within. The Shattering was continuing down there. With midnight and the new year fast approaching, it was a magical place to be.

But where was Dellin? I must be misunderstanding something; had I done something wrong? I cast about but found no trace of her and was about to slip back into the forest and retrace my steps when the light from the keep bloomed twice as intensely. I crouched and watched it. The kiln must be raging.

The light pulsed again and shone on clouds rising behind the keep. Not clouds – smoke! Second by second the brightness increased, and now a glow began to flicker in Raven's window seat above the hall. It was on fire!

The Shattering must have gone wrong. Sometimes a spark from a kiln can cause a blaze. I'd heard of it happening. I didn't want to call to Dellin because she'd think I was admitting defeat, but my friends were down there! I hesitated, torn between them and Dellin. Would she give me another chance to show how much I loved her? I might never see her again!

'Dellin!' I shouted. 'Dellin, if you can hear me, the keep is burning!'

No answer but the hiss of the breeze. I stood, paralysed by indecision, and all the time the blaze increased. Raven's window filled with dancing flames. I spread my wings, took one last frantic look around, then launched myself off and glided down towards it.

The cool air sped past me, the treetops of the forest below. The tower came up swiftly, a starkly solid black shape in the diffuse orange glow. I drew nearer. It looked squat and foreshortened; now I could smell the smoke. I passed over its square top and felt a burst of rising heat.

I looked down into the bailey. Figures were spilling out of the tower stairs and clustering on the snow. Some in groups, others alone, they looked up at the keep and cast fans of shadows by its guttering light. I pulled my wings half-closed and dropped. I flared my wings, dangled my legs and skimmed along the surface of the snow till I slid to a halt.

Villagers and soldiers were swarming out of the narrow staircase and gasping for breath in the sudden freezing air. One after another – there must be a crush inside – they ran towards me and spread out, searching for their loved ones in the crowd. I saw a man running to the open arms of his wife, a lady in thick skirts gathering up a young boy. Soldiers were joining their comrades, shouting and pointing at the windows.

The glass in the hall windows was still sound but the curtains were aflame. I could see a fraction of the ceiling: the garlands were burning fiercely. One detached and swung out of sight, in a shower of sparks.

Over in the darkness Ouzel was yelling at some women to bring buckets and scoop up the snow. Lightning was standing by the doorway, keeping the flow of escapees as fast as possible, patting the back of each one passing, keeping them running over the snow till they were well clear.

I skirted round them and ran to join him, skidding with every stride, but as I reached him the flow of people stopped. Lightning stared up the staircase.

'Was it the kiln?' I cried.

He looked to me with eyes wide, but turned back at a commotion on the stair. Raven plunged down the steps. His expression was thunderous and he was dragging someone behind him. He burst out onto the snow, pulling Dellin by the wrist. *Dellin?*

Struggling, her hair flying, she looked more beautiful than ever. She dug her heels in, flexed her arm and bit Raven's hand. He tugged her so hard he pulled her over and strode on, towing her behind him. She regained her footing and hauled back.

Snipe, with sword drawn, then a couple of spearmen, followed him out of the turret. Snipe ran to his master's side and the guards closed behind Dellin.

'Let her go!' I said.

Raven stormed on, black with fury. His hand was running with blood. As he hauled Dellin past she glanced at me in mute appeal. Then she resumed yanking, scratching, and riving his feathers out, as he towed her in the direction of the stables. He cut through the crowd, which parted in front, then drew in behind him so more and more staring people followed in his wake. I kept pace with Dellin. She was fighting with all her strength but Raven had an iron grip.

Lightning joined me. 'Not the kiln. *Her.*'

'Dellin?'

'She set fire to the treasury *and* his room.'

'How? Has everybody got out?'

'Yes. Smoke was pouring into the hall. It was streaming along the ceiling. Then a guard ran in yelling, "Fire!"'

'Any casualties?'

'None. Raven kept a clear head. We stopped the panic and got everyone out, but the treasury's destroyed. Raven and Snipe ran up to his chamber ...' Lightning coughed. 'They caught her there. It's still burning.'

The treasury below the hall had been full of furs. No wonder the fire caught so quickly and so much smoke was billowing out. But Dellin shouldn't be here. She was supposed to be in the forest. We were supposed to be making love. Only half an hour after we were engaged to be married, she was digging her feet into the snow, as Raven dragged her away so powerfully I thought he'd wrench her arm off. I felt there must be two Dellins, one here and the other still out in the woods, waiting mournfully for me.

Nonsense. She must have doubled back early in our chase. Could it have been when I first lost sight of her? Could I have been following a false trail all that time? A cold feeling clutched me: could she have *planned* this?

A tremendous explosion sounded behind us. I swung round in time to see flame bursting from the undercroft. Another explosion followed and another, throwing shards of wood out of the glare.

'What was that?' Lightning gasped.

'Barrels of cheap gin. The Rhydanne porters' wages.'

Now the faint chimes of the hall clock drifted out, striking twelve. Several people hesitated and turned to listen. Snipe glared round at them, whooped and flung his arms in the air. 'Happy New Year! Happy bloody New Year, all! Open your presents. Hoosh! Go home. Go to your sodding homes! Do you want to catch your deaths?'

Raven cast no glance behind him. He stormed straight past the stables to the kennels and climbed the steps onto the portico. It was covered in a thin layer of impacted snow, as slippery as satin. Dellin grabbed the rail with her free hand and pulled Raven to a halt. He turned and kicked her hand brutally – she screamed and let go. The dogs in their open run were making an ear-splitting din. They jumped up at the wire mesh, clung with their forepaws, barking furiously as Raven pounded past. He stomped along the portico and into a room at the end. Snipe followed him, then Lightning and myself. The plank room was dark, its fireplace empty and shutters closed. The livid light of the burning keep was shining through fretwork holes in both shutters and pulsing orange hearts and stars on the floor.

A bear cage, about two metres square, stood in the corner. Raven ripped its door open and flung Dellin inside with such force she buckled against its far side. He slammed the door, locked it and dropped the key into his pocket.

Dellin crouched and tucked her broken hand into her armpit. She glared at Raven with utter hatred. Then she threw herself against the cage door with her full strength. 'Let me out! Out!' She picked herself up and cast herself against the bars again and again until they rang.

Her struggles had no effect on Raven, who was calmly winding a handkerchief around his bitten hand.

She lunged from one side of the cage to the other, jumped and thrust her palms against the roof, dashed herself to her knees and tore at the bars of the floor. Finding no weak points, she turned her whirlwind energy to rattling the door.

I knelt by the cage. 'Dellin!' I said. 'Listen. *Listen to me*! Calm down and wait. You won't be in there long.' I looked up to Raven. 'This will kill her. You have to release her.'

'From the cage? I have no other room that will hold her.'

'She can't stand being enclosed. For god's sake, have a heart!'

He tucked in the end of his bandage and said nothing.

I turned to Lightning. 'Remember she couldn't stand being in the coach? She doesn't even like houses, let alone a cage!'

'The girl is used to open spaces,' Lightning told Raven. 'She can't abide to be trapped.'

'You'll drive her mad!' I said.

'Better than she should drive me mad. All my money, all my books, gone!'

'You can keep her in custody, but not like this. It's inhuman.'

'She isn't human.' Raven's lips twisted in triumph. Behind him, Snipe opened the door and we saw the settlers and soldiers had formed bucket chains into the keep. Their shadows jumped and flickered across the trampled snow. They seemed to be gaining control of the blaze, but the hall windows had lost their glass and smoke like dark grey fur was pouring out of them.

'For god's sake,' I said. 'She's a thinking woman, not an animal!'

'Then she should have thought harder before committing arson. The cage stays locked. Comet, Lightning, if you release her I will charge you with jail breaking. Tomorrow we will, as civilised people, try her. Then there will be a hanging. Snipe, come, let us see the damage.' He put his injured hand in his pocket and walked out.

Dellin was ferociously poking her fingernail into the keyhole. I tried to touch her hand through the bars but she jerked it back. I said, 'I can pick locks. I learnt in the city. Trust me.'

I drew my knife, slipped it between the mortise and the frame, and tried to push the catch back. When it became clear that this was a high-quality lock, I slid the knife into the keyhole and began trying to turn the tumblers.

Dellin stopped watching me and slumped in the far corner, her expression vacant. Lightning paced back and forth, clutching his coat tight and making no move to stop me, but after I had been at the lock for ten minutes he asked, 'Is it too difficult?'

'I can't do it. Damn it, all my tools are at the Castle.' I threw the knife down. 'I'll stay with her. Send someone for blankets and food and drink.'

'Of course. But please come away. Leave her alone.'

'I can't.'

He nodded, sadly, and left, passing on the way out a pikeman arriving under orders to guard the cage. The man began setting logs in the hearth and I sat beside Dellin, on the other side of the iron grille, but she did not acknowledge me at all nor seem to draw solace from my presence.

I had a pain in my chest, in the depth of my heart. My years in the city had taught me that violent emotion brings on real and physical pain. Now I felt my heart cracked and bleeding. Whatever the Castle's Doctor says, the heart is truly the place where love originates and Dellin had broken mine for good. My only other sensation was one of disbelief. How could she do this to me? The thought was too excruciating, so I gently pried at how she could have found it in herself to lead me into the forest, then double back and climb into the keep. She had let me chase her and duped me. We were supposed to be hunting partners – not an hour later she was Raven's captive and I was numbed by her duplicity. How could it all have gone so badly wrong?

Dellin stirred and, from staring at nothing, her pine-green eyes rolled to focus on me. 'Help,' she whispered desperately.

'I will, Dellin.'

'Free me, to run in the forest again.'

'Yes,' I said, though I was sick to the core.

'If you don't free me, I will tell Raven ...'

'What? What will you tell him?'

'That you ate a man like him ... You ate the meat of an Awian.'

'God!' I recoiled. Anger swept through me, numbing my aching heart and hollow stomach. 'Everything's a barter for you, isn't it? I'll free you because I love you – don't you believe that? Or loved you – I don't know any more! Why do you think you have to bargain? Don't I mean anything to you?'

I felt she was certainly capable of telling Raven. I would never be able to trust her again. Raven knew she was a man-eater and he'd think she had no reason to lie. He would believe her and I would be firmly in his power.

If a Rhydanne eats an Awian she isn't, strictly speaking, a cannibal, but I had consumed the flesh of my own kind. I had been the only true cannibal that night! If Dellin opened her mouth the news would snowball through the Fourlands and everyone would hear it, no matter how much I protested. All the Eszai, all the governors, the Emperor himself!

She held the bars and leant her cheek against the cold metal. I drew away and rested by the wall. I had thought I'd found a woman wild and untainted, but her love was a lie and she was mercenary scum like all the others. Emotions swirled within me, as if I'd heard news of the death of my closest friend. Thoroughly lost, thoroughly shaken, I abandoned myself to sitting in that grey room, on the hard floorboards, with the freezing draught stealing in. I would never feel the same for her again, that much was clear, but I couldn't know, could not determine, which way my cards would fall.

LIGHTNING

At dawn the trodden snow was frozen solid, with all the dirt of last night pressed into it. Fragments of ash, shards of charred wood, pieces of foil tinsel would stand witness to the blaze until the spring. Under the ugly, blackened archway the snow had partially melted and re-frozen with the iron hoops from the gin barrels embedded in it. I trod over the medley of footprints to the kennels.

Jant was sitting against the wall, huddled under his folded wing. His head rested on the wrist of his wing and he watched Dellin. She was kneeling behind the door of her cage, grasping one of its bars. She was rocking a little, and every time she rocked back she tugged the door, jarring it with her weight. She stared vacantly and her thick hair hung unkempt. Her lips were cracked and sore at the corners, and her eyes deep-shadowed, sunk in their sockets.

The guard saluted me and resumed warming his feet at the grate. I touched Jant's wing and more keenly felt his anguish, as if it coursed into me. 'I suppose you haven't slept?'

'No.'

'Then go to bed. Go on, I'll look after her.'

He nodded once, gathered himself and staggered out. I sat on a crude chair and watched Dellin. She wasn't staring into thin air; she was watching the window. Its shutters were bolted and she could see no more than two hearts and stars of agate sky, but she attended to them deliriously. Her whole body was so tense she shook, prepared to spring from the cage and out of the window in a single bound.

Tears streaked her dirty face. She pressed her lips together and moaned quietly in time with her rocking. The blankets and leg of beef I had brought lay untouched in the corner of the cage and, against the wall, a pool of urine spread on the floorboards. I hoped the guard had averted his gaze.

I leant forward. She snapped out of watching the sky and turned dulled eyes on me. She tapped her nail on the lock. 'Make. Me. Out.'

'Dellin, I can't.'

'Make me out.'

'I'm sorry, Dellin. Look ...'

'"I'm sorry, Dellin. Look."' She hooked her fingers over one of the bars and I saw she had worn her nails ragged. The metal showed polished around a crack in the frame – she must have been trying to prise it apart. She had set her hopes on a minuscule gap that didn't even go all the way through.

'Oh, Miss Wildcat,' I said, 'why did you do it? You could have been immortal this time next month.'

She slipped her hand between the bars and reached out to me. It may have been the shadows, but her bones seemed more prominent than before and her wrist thinner than I would have thought possible. Jant had said that she has to eat all the time. If she refused to eat I thought she would die very soon.

'I'm cold,' she whispered. 'I want ... I want ...'

'Yes?'

'I want a drink.'

I dug Raven's hip flask from my pocket. 'Here, some brandy. Altergate XO. Have as much as you want.'

She stroked my hand – her skin was cold to the touch. She took the hip flask gently and turned it sideways to pass it between the bars. She sniffed it and sipped, sucking in her pinched cheeks. I raised my hand to say she should keep it and drink at her own pace.

'Make me out, Lightning, please.' She said 'please' so hollowly I wondered if she knew its meaning. Was it only a sound she was shaping, no more than a key to obtain what she wanted? I understood her need to be free and I even admired her determination in pursuing her hostilities. But setting fire to the keep while we partied? Wasn't that the act of a savage?

'No,' I said aloud. 'You're not so different from us, it's just that your desires are different. You want to get rid of Raven. I've heard a lot worse. Your wants are at odds with ours, your understanding of the world is different. But I'm afraid for your people, Dellin.'

She leant close to the bars, tilted her head with her too-fast movement. She listened.

I said, 'The Castle wants me to bring Rhydanne and Awians together. But Rhydanne don't want to live with Awians. Your people have pride just as Awians do; they don't want to rub shoulders with us slow herders. You are both good, proud peoples, but if I force you together you'll just fight the more. It will make things worse. You both have rights but I'm not sure how you can share Carniss ... This is beyond me.'

'Make me out.'

'I've done all I can to win Raven round.'

She rattled the bars.

'Dellin, you're the blank card. We don't know what you'll do if he releases you. Not even Jant knows what you're thinking ... Especially not Jant.'

'Outside ...'

'Yes.'

'Out to the forest,' she moaned in desperation. She hugged her knees, so tense she must be aching with cold. 'Lightning, *Dealan* Lightning, *is fheudar dhuit teasaiginn mi.*'

Even if we could understand each other's speech, I could tell her nothing. She would find all the wisdom of my long life completely meaningless. Was she capable of loving? Rhydanne or not, I've known many women who aren't. I wondered whether she simply didn't love Jant or whether she was devoid of the ability to love at all. What emotions were involved in being a hunting partner? Could they possibly be as insidious and addictive as love?

'Please let me out.'

'Jant says your language has no word for "please". Do you have any idea what he's going through? What you've done to him? I told him he should try to sleep, but I doubt he will. You should try to sleep too.'

She resumed rocking, murmuring, 'Make me out, make me out, make me out,' tugging the bars every time she said 'out'. She seemed thinner every minute, inside her bulky clothes. She stared at the holes in the shutters, which were now brightening though the room stayed dim. A dash of light reflected on the hip flask and on the tears in her red-rimmed eyes. The nails in the floorboards, polished by the passage of so many boots, shone like a sultry set of stars.

Footsteps crunched the salt on the portico and Snipe swung into the room. He saw me and stopped, startled. He was carrying a full bottle of whisky.

'Ah ...' he said.

'It's all right.' I stood up. 'I'm going to talk to Raven now, anyway. Thank you for bringing her drink, and for god's sake get her to eat something.'

'Um ... yes. Yes, my lord.'

'And San protect us all.' I nodded to him and left for the keep.

JANT

I tossed and turned, thinking again and again how Dellin had made such a fool of me. I turned from her image in anger. Nobody treats me that way. I'd have killed any man who showed me that much disrespect. I had done before. They knew it in Hacilith – nobody ever burned me on a drug deal. They knew it in the Castle too; I'd grown used to the deference that comes with my position, which was no more than I deserved. But Raven had stamped all over my self-respect and now Dellin had put an end to it permanently.

The inner street kid laughed and sneered. I should be ashamed. I'd been acting like a naive stripling not an immortal. I had let a girl tie me in knots and bluff me into chasing her without pausing to consider her real aims. I must have grown very soft indeed to end up the willing lapdog of a savage.

So why, if I recoil from her image, does it keep recurring in my mind's eye? I lay on the couch in the guard room with my parka spread over my chest and thought: it isn't right that I should think of her smiling when in reality she's shaking the bars of a cage, snarling and spitting in emerald-eyed loathing.

Love seemed more than ever to be like a disease. I had caught a virulent infection and it had spread through my body until I had been completely overcome. Unrequited, it had caused a fever and now thankfully my natural defences of independence and injured pride were kicking in. I was at a transition stage, sometimes coherent, sometimes lapsing to love, and I hoped that if the fever broke I could return to my old self.

In the meantime I had better see Dellin. I jumped off the couch and searched in my rucksack for my original clothes, my Castle clothes, and put them on deliberately. I left the bare room. Lightning and Raven's voices emanated from Raven's chamber opposite, talking in a low, earnest tone. I didn't go in. If I saw Raven at this moment I'd bury my ice axe in his head.

I hurried down the stairs. The staircase stank of smoke. Remains of decorations hung from the ceiling, shrivelled to spider's webs. Strands of blistered tinsel with baubles attached lay sadly on the steps. I kicked them aside.

I ran past the kennels – the dogs were unusually subdued – opened the door and slipped inside. The cage was empty. Dellin was gone.

The cube-shaped cage shone dully in the dim light. I ran to it and found it locked – nothing inside apart from a congealed joint of meat and some blankets still creased where Lightning had threaded them between the bars. In front of its door lay a hip flask. I kicked it across the floorboards and sat down, head in hands. What had Raven done to her? He could have let me talk to her one last time before dragging her to her execution! A hundred terrible eventualities flooded my mind. There was no blood on the floor, only piss. Had he strangled her? I could see no clues – the guard had gone and the hearth was ash. Had he laid hands on her and dragged her out to a firing squad? I imagined her pincushioned with arrows, imagined her swinging from a branch, imagined her crushed down onto the snow under his strong arm, as he drew his sword to slit her throat.

I paced back and forth, making no effort to collect my thoughts. Dellin was gone. Raven had put an end to her without allowing me a final farewell. I was desolate, empty, and fitful gusts tore through me.

Her scent lingered in the cage, enough to bring tears to my eyes, but the tears became those of anger as I gradually gathered my senses – they rushed together and erupted in a great spout of wrath. I'll kill him! I'm going to bloody kill him! So what, if I spend a mortal's lifetime in jail? That was nothing compared to life without Dellin.

No. Wait. I might be in time to save her! I leapt up and ran out, so fast I never felt the ice ridges under my boots. I whisked into the staircase tower and sped up the steps. Lightning and hateful Raven's voices droned on up ahead, in the same conversation. Were they talking about her? I spun left on the landing and into the room.

Jant appeared in the doorway, his face a mask of fury. His eyes venomous and mouth open in the middle of saying something, he belted across the room and dived on Raven, grabbed his collar in both hands and shook him thoroughly. Tried to shake him; it was like a rawhide weasel trying to shake a tree. Raven fended him off and smoothed his coat. Without losing any dignity he left his throne and walked to the fireplace, to put some distance between him and Jant, who stood still, panting.

'Jant!' I said. 'What are you doing?'

He yelled, 'Where is she?'

Raven paled. 'Who? Dellin?'

'Of course, Dellin! What have you done to her, you bastard? At least ... at least let me see her body.'

Raven reeled, placed his hand on the table. 'Another disaster. I can't ... Is she not in the cage?'

'Don't feign ignorance! You know where she is! Have I time to save her?'

'Jant,' I said calmly. 'Did you just check on the cage?'

'Yes! She's gone!'

Raven breathed out. Suddenly like an old man, he buckled, managed to grasp his chair and sank onto it. He leaned forward until his forehead rested on his hand on the table edge. I have seen mortals die this way – the skin of his face was ashen and jowly. Jant suddenly looked very worried. I believe he thought he had killed the man.

Raven straightened up slowly, but the light had gone from his eyes. 'She's gone?' he asked. 'She's escaped. Damn it, is this a trick of yours?'

'Not me,' said Jant. 'The cage was locked and empty.'

'Snipe!' He looked to his steward. 'Go and check the room.'

'Yes, my lord.'

He felt in his coat pocket, brought out the key and stared at it. 'But how? There's only one key and it's been in my pocket all the time. I don't understand. Did you break the lock?'

'No. It's sound,' Jant said, astonished.

'With no Rhydanne inside. Can they walk through iron bars? Do they vanish on one side and appear on the other?'

'Of course not,' I snapped.

'Then who released her? Was it you, Lightning?'

'She—'

'She'll hound me again! She'll mastermind more schemes of terror ... I caught her right there! There, see, in the window seat! I should have thrown her through the pane! I caught her with the *torch in her hand* and now she'll do the same again!'

His gaze wandered desolately around his ruined chamber. The venerable chandelier had crashed onto the table, and its weight had broken one of the table's legs. It now lay half-on, half-off the sloping top. Its dusty chain dangled, still attached to a metal rose with screws embedded in a lump of charred wood. Its strings of jewels no longer hung free but tangled the bronze candleholders. Smoke had dulled the crystals and most were either cracked or shattered. A few, free of their wires, scattered the table and floor. Under its ornate arms Raven's letters were no more than fragments of carbon strewn everywhere. Dellin had been thorough.

The table itself and the throne were singed. The carpet crisped underfoot. On the far wall the sumptuous tapestry was reduced to a miserable strip hanging from the hooks on the rails. Gold threads projected from its scorched fringe like tiny, twisted wires. The plaster behind it was blackened by smoke in a thick band up to and halfway across the ceiling. The New Year's wreaths had shrivelled to practically nothing. Holly leaves were parched and curled, the laurel blistered brown. Dust from burnt silk and shards of broken baubles covered the floor.

Raven had stripped the charred wolf skins from his chair and thrown them in the fireplace. On the mantelpiece his five books had fused into one mass, crinkled and so brittle their edges were flaking, but the middle of the cover of my book had survived – I could just make out 'gends of Ancient' and half my name.

The cushions in the window seat were leprous with black-edged holes. Their down stuffing had puffed out and dropped on the steps like snow. Dellin must have only just set the torch to them when Raven caught her, because, judging by the rest of the room, she would have destroyed them completely if she had had chance.

Raven regarded all this dismally and without words, his expression so blank and vanquished it was terrible to behold. He was like a man who had escaped a deadly storm and arrived at a mountain refuge which, while he was thankfully recovering, had been blown down around his ears and left him outside once more in the gales and blizzards. He had been buffeted too much and his strength to withstand fortune's blasts had declined with each blow, until this latest disappointment had cut him to the quick. He moved his head side to side, sapped of strength.

At length he became aware of us. He wiped his palms on his handkerchief and said quietly, 'Well then, I must ride out and catch her again, and this time I will behead her.'

Jant walked around the table until he was opposite Raven and had his full attention. 'No. However Dellin escaped, this marks an end to your struggle. Let her go and the Emperor will be pleased. You must not pursue her. You also must not invade Rachiswater to wrest the throne from your brother.'

'*What*?!'

'We know you plan to launch a coup. The real reason why you've summoned so many warriors. Francolin Wrought sent them.'

'How ... Oh god, how?'

Jant wound his fingers in one of the chandelier's crystal strings, which clinked as he spoke. 'Fortification is the prerogative of the Castle, you know that well. We have a use for your soldiers. We'll command them to demolish this tower and the curtain walls, immediately ... From the ashes you can build a new manor house where you can live in peace.'

'A single-storeyed hall, as befits a governor,' I added.

Raven looked at me. 'Lightning, so you're here to defend my brother? Did he ask you personally? And, Jant, as a Rhydanne, you take sides with Dellin.'

'Don't call me Rhydanne,' Jant said sturdily. 'I'm saying this as the Messenger.'

'And as the Archer, I support him,' I said. 'Not on behalf of Tarmigan, but to maintain peace in the Empire.'

Raven let his hands fall to his lap. He looked aimlessly around his chamber and after a while he murmured, 'Everything's gone. My books, my chandelier. I can't replace anything ... He won't let me. So must I stay here with no books, no money, and surrounded by killers?'

'I said I would send you some books.' I reminded him.

'After this do you think I can bear to receive gifts from *you*?' He swayed to his feet ponderously, yet still with regal dignity. He turned his back on us and ascended to his window seat, rested himself on the burnt cushions, which puffed out more feathers. He drew his coat around him against the wind blowing in, and stared out of the broken glass, down to the tracks in the snow and the edge of the timeless forest.

Some of the mist has stolen in from outside, where a thick bank of cloud covers Carniss. It lies low and hides the houses; only the ridges of the roofs and the chimneys poke through, as if the smoke from last night had fallen once more. For the last two hours lights came and went within it, now all is dark with only an occasional cluster of lanterns travelling through as the patrol makes its rounds.

I have been watching all this time. First in my mirador, then I crossed to the smaller windows on the other side of the hall to watch Lightning and the Messenger drawing up the troops in the bailey. The soldiers have begun to raze my house. My greatest achievement is being dismantled, torn down around my ears.

A sergeant led a group of men into my chamber and climbed the steps to the roof. I heard them raking out cement and hammering the great stones of the parapet. They replaced the pulley, slotting its timbers into the holes I had designed, but this time they began to lower the same blocks that I had raised a year ago. They started to re-erect scaffolding around the outside wall, and I watched it climb towards my window as if time was running backwards and this was my scaffolding I was seeing rise again, stage by stage. You see, the Archer and the Messenger, being of the Castle, act without wasting time. Being of the Castle, they are not interested in the finer things in life, the achievements of mortals in architecture or husbandry, but are only interested in destruction. And, being of the Castle, immortal and stagnant, they detest progress, our latest additions and improvements to the world. They know in their hearts that determined mortals like myself could do without them, so they refuse to give us free rein. Or free reign. They know we don't really need the Castle: we can protect ourselves. We don't need them to interfere in our lives. They know that and will not let us be independent, for then they would be redundant, so they clip our wings with severe rules ... and demolish Carniss Keep.

Let them. They have already breached the wall alongside my tower; cloud drifts through it into the village. My people are afraid and angry. They know the Rhydanne will run in and prey on them. Snipe told me that they oppose the destruction, but the soldiers obey Jant and the settlers have no choice.

Since the fire I have not eaten, washed nor shaved. I scratch my stubble and my fingertips slip into the scar. I clutch my fingers in its rift as if I could hook them deep and tear my cheek. I will *never* beat my brother now! He's won – again! I will never have another chance to repay this welter of pain and humiliation. Instead, I am shamed again; losing my keep is the worst mortification of all. All my exertions have brought me nothing. I am condemned to live in exile in this wasteland, reduced to the same penury as when I arrived.

I could salvage something. I could build myself a manor house, as beautiful as possible, drink my life away and recite poetry to the peaks. But I'd face raids every day and I'd have to live surrounded by the settlers. My god, I thought, clenching my teeth, I hate them. I despise their ignorance. What kind of life would I lead, protecting and served by people who have never read a word, who know neither Conure's poetry nor the choreography of the *Pennate Ballet*? The women are sottish and raucous, the men's conversation turns only on goats and cuts of wood. Snipe is just as boorish. I cringe at the thought of seeing his ugliness before me every mealtime, as if the fool were one of my family.

How can I live with the image of my brother in the mirror, reminding me of my failure and taunting me? I have not looked in a mirror since Dellin escaped, but now the cracked glass itself has become a mirror backed by darkness and I see his face there once again. Ah, Tarmigan, now you have a real reason to jeer. The Eszai will tell you my plans and laugh with you at my expense. I will know you are laughing long and loud while you feast on the fruits of the kingdom, but I will never have the proof of seeing it with my own eyes. Did you have a good New Year? Will the tale of an aborted coup make it even more memorable? And every December the thirty-first you'll repeat it to your sycophants. Or perhaps you will forget me, as you're swirled from day to day in the tattling eddies of court gossip. You will enjoy filling your time with idly shooting the cloud-hidden crane and the mottled hind, with never a thought for your twin, when I must truly hunt to survive. And in return Dellin hunts me.

Dellin. In all my drifting thoughts today, as I sat alone and the brandy decreased in the bottle, I could not understand how she escaped. The key was in my pocket – in fact I have it now. After Jant left to assemble the troops I inspected the cage myself. Jant is hot-headed and volatile: he would have hacked it open with an axe to free his love. Lightning is obstructive, unjust and calculating: he would have called my blacksmith to prise a bar loose and weld it again after she'd slipped away, but I saw no signs of tampering and the smith seemed too hungover to wield a hammer ... Unless the fellow was putting on an act.

Ouzel. It must have been Ouzel: she's friend to the savages and she accuses me of disrupting her rough and ready haggling with them. No wonder she returned so quickly to her hideaway this morning. I have little inclination to chase her there, and anyway she's in cahoots with the Eszai and loved by my settlers too. I cannot trust any frontiersman – none are decent people. Even the guard I sent to watch Dellin is nowhere to be found.

I wondered for an instant if I myself was mad. Did I let Dellin out without knowing? Am I chasing round in circles, subconsciously undoing the deeds I've worked so hard to achieve? No, I have no evidence for madness. I am as sane as the cold crag. Others, not myself, cause my downfall time and again. The savage was not able to free herself from the cage, therefore somebody let her out. The immortals must have freed her. They are rats gnawing the edifice I made, and between them they have had over one thousand years to practise deception.

Now the niveous bitch is lurking in the forest or hiding inside Carniss itself. Maybe she's concealed in the kitchens now, with Jant feeding her my best meat. She will lie in wait for me. She will stalk into my bedroom when I'm asleep and unaware, and plunge her knife into my throat.

She's outside somewhere. Where? I imagined myself plunging through the snow, blinded by the blizzard, struggling to catch her while she skulks in the drifts and cackles at me. The wilderness is her playground: free in the too-vast forest she'll howl to summon more beasts to join her. She will lead her pack, skeeting swift and light over the snow like blown ice crystals. And my people will curse me for leaving them prey to her glistening fangs. I do not want to live this way.

I do not want to live here for the rest of my life. I can call no pictures to mind to imagine how I would spend it. Time would pass slowly and I would watch myself age, knowing that my brother in the palace was not gathering such deep lines of care and weather-tanned skin. He would look ten years my junior and, no longer identical, it would seem as if I should be crowned as the older. The years would pass quickly for him, slowly for me. I would spend them watching the glaciers shrink back every summer over their expanses of smooth rock, and every winter I would see more splinters slough from the cliffs and the glaciers would extend their fingers over the bare mountainside again, until I grow old and lethargic and seven-eighths iced-over, when I will waste and die from boredom and be buried in the screes.

While I have stood thinking, the cloud has peeled away under the influence of the night wind blowing down from Capercaillie. The night is quite clear. I see my village cloaked in snow. A thick covering sits on the roofs and the lids over each chimney pot. The paths cleared and snow heaped beside them now have a sparkling topping of ice. Most of the houses are dark, with yellow light shining through chinks in their shutters and around the doors; a few have lamps lit on their sills. The natural rock crags out between them, black voids shining with ice. This is the village I have built, and when the walls fall it will be open to the Rhydanne pack. This is Carniss, where the thought of living circumscribed and caged fills me with disgust. This is Carniss, of which I am heartily sick.

The drifting moon intercepts my line of sight. Dellin's face in the moon, pinched cheeks and narrow nose. That thin face, as I had seen her crazed with defiance, but now laughter crinkles the skin around her cat eyes. If only the clouds would cover it, if it were not always poised in endless view.

It gradually slips away to crouch behind the architrave. She casts a shadow over my life. She mocks me. She was under my hand, she screamed for mercy, and now she is free to raise fires again. I no longer want to live with it. I no longer need to live.

I realised I was gazing at nothing and turned away abruptly. As I moved, the window reflected the side of my face without the scar and I glimpsed my brother. I picked up my scarf – now every action seemed weighty and significant – wound it on calmly and opened the door. I descended the steps with my boot soles patting every one – there are thirty and I know the shape of each by heart. I alighted onto the landing, opened the door beside the treasury and went out onto the wall walk.

SNIPE

My lord just walked past. Knowing his moods, I hadn't expected him to leave his room so soon. He didn't look in to check on me and he had such a serene expression I was pretty surprised. I got up, ran over the burnt banknotes and peered out of the doorway.

He was standing with his back to me, unlocking the arched door that leads to the parapet walk. He opened it and a draught of icy air blew in. He walked out onto the parapet, leaving the door open and the key in the lock, with all the other keys of the keep dangling from the ring. Why was he going out there this time of night, bareheaded and with no gloves? Oh god, I thought. He must be following his plan to lock Lightning up. But since Lightning's in my house, he must mean to keep him there. He could still arrest Jant. Then he'll try to gather his men and start for Rachiswater. But they've been working all day! They'll be knackered before he begins! He must be bloody crazy.

The thought of Lightning being locked in *my* house made me quake. I didn't think anyone could trick him. Only a madman would try, especially since he's got his bow at hand. This was too much. I couldn't go along with Raven but how could I stop him? He was a man possessed.

I looked down at the silver ingots I'd been salvaging from a burnt casket and thought *fuck this*. I closed the treasury grille quietly and followed him.

RAVEN

The night air is pleasantly cool and caresses the warm cocoon I have made around myself. Wrapped in my coat I am comfortable up here for perhaps the first time. My boots crunch the gritted walkway and at its edges the ice crust encroaches on the rock salt like a hem of lace. Individual salt nuggets have worn holes deep into it.

At either side the untouched, frost-sealed snow glitters. More stars cover the path than there are in the sky – they twinkle at every step, a sheen of tiny diamonds as if someone has crushed the jewels of my chandelier and strewn the dust in my path. It is apt and fitting that my last walk is on a carpet of stars.

The rough parapet wall to my right is encased in verglas and ice rime. Over its surface fragile crystals like glass straws had formed, raised fluting all running parallel in the direction of the prevailing wind. On top of the wall, between the blocks, the sun's light during the day has melted small puddles, which at dusk have frozen in stages so now the very thin panes of ice covering each hollow have white rings like tree rings.

My mind is untroubled and unsullied by worldly worries. I see everything with more-than-usual intensity, a clear percipience. As if I am observing the world for the first time, every object seems vibrant and peacefully itself. Would that I could have lived my whole life with such an uncluttered mind.

Beyond the wall there is nothing but blackness, a sense of the mountains' lonely space and empty air, but I can see nothing apart from the abnormally bright constellations above.

SNIPE

What *was* he doing? He walked with measured tread, hands clasped behind him, but there's nothing out here. Jant put all the guards to demolition duty, and they're asleep after a hard day's work. No one's set foot up here since the lamplighter. Halfway along, though, a flight of stairs led down to the bailey. He must be going to my house, all right. He must be going the long way round to escape Jant's notice. But the steps were covered in ice and dicey. I strained my eyes to see if soldiers were converging on the house next to mine. A glow in my cabin window showed the Archer was inside, but I couldn't see any movement.

Raven always walked with his head lowered, like he was tugging his whole body along by his forehead. He was pondering more deeply than ever, as if he was sleepwalking. I kept him in sight – a darker patch on the dark path. I hugged the wall and dashed across the light cast by one of the lamps, into the shadow between them.

Had he heard my footsteps? I paused, but he paced on. He passed another lamp and his shadow jumped like a clock hand, from lying behind him to angled in front. It glided on, as if keen not to be trodden on.

Perhaps he is sleepwalking and I should wake him. I prepared to run up and rest my hand on his shoulder, but curiosity stopped me. I really did need to know if he was going to barricade Lightning in my house. I followed, with my skin crawling, 'cause I thought any moment he'd swing round and shout, 'Gotcha!'

RAVEN

This is certainly the perfect night for it. The ice shimmers more strongly around the storm lamps' flames, as if practically alive. This is what eighteen ninety-one looks like. Quiet and peaceful, barren and void, and damnably the same as eighteen ninety. I have seen too many men overcome with fear when the end draws nigh and I would never be so craven. I am pleased to find myself just as I imagined I would be: composed and without qualms.

Jant's destruction of Carniss, and my loss, is inevitable in a way. No matter how determined I am, the ignorance of others will always win because it is effortless. Stupidity and laziness are without cost of exertion so they will always outlast and prevail over any effortful work. Similarly, natural decay will always overwhelm our buildings and, at length, our own bodies. A multitude will always overpower an individual. The Castle will always prevail over a mortal ... and the manor I have spent years building will be overturned in days by the reversion of the ignorant to their usual habits. No matter how much effort I have put in, the mountains are more powerful than I am because they are mindless. I have struggled to the last of my strength but in the end they have won.

SNIPE

Nearly slipped! Careful! I had to stay in the centre of the walkway or I'd crunch the ice, but I leant close to the wall. On the other side, the railing was plastered in icicles, hanging over the drop to the bailey.

Raven would have told the guards to gather in the captain's house – that's next to mine – and they would creep to my cabin and turn the key in the lock. The cabin's sturdy enough, but they'd have to bar the window to stop Lightning getting out. Yeah, but even if Raven succeeded without Lightning shooting him, Jant would take to the air and vanish. How's he supposed to arrest a man who can fly? He's going to call down the wrath of the Castle as well as the king!

Raven reached the top of the steps and walked straight past. He didn't even look down to the bailey but kept going and climbed another couple of stairs where the rock crags up. I followed him along an exposed section, our shadows slipping ahead of us. He's walking all the way to the end.

I couldn't understand what he was doing at all. I wondered if I should just shout to him, but then I'd have to explain why the hell I was following.

RAVEN

The promontory is narrowing. I am nearly there, but I walk no slower, nor any more hurriedly. I will take things at my own pace. Ironically, the immortals never have the leisure to feel as sedate as I do now. They are always rushed, fending off Challengers, fighting every crisis. Only a mortal can feel as if he has all the time in the world.

The cliff cuts in here and the wall grafted exactly on top of it sweeps in a long embayment. Below, I can see nothing. The three-hundred-metre drop is invisible; it is like looking down into a lake of ink. Thin, fine clouds drift below me. I have the impression the wall is afloat like a ship and the clouds are reflections in immeasurably deep water. I pass the last of the dimly lit houses in the bailey. Nothing else remains. Capercaillie peak with its serrated forest outline is just a black space blotting out the overcrowded stars. Carniss is all that exists, floating in the void, darkness lapping against it like water against a harbour wall. I shudder. By god, may I leave Carniss to those who deserve it.

It is colder out here, towards the tip of the cliff, and a breeze is blowing. The promontory is coming to its point. I can just make out the bell tower and, very indistinctly, the curtain wall on the other side. Sky and wall merge in the darkness so the storm lanterns on the opposite wall top hang like a line of stars.

I know what I am doing. I have never been more sane. Has any other King of Awia faced it with as much noble calm as I do? I arrive at the point of the promontory and walk past a small turret where sentries may shelter. The cold wind plays on my face and stirs a little melancholy in my soul. What man about to leave the world would not feel melancholy?

But my world is no longer Rachiswater but Carniss: I hate and abjure it. I feel no fear. I look down as I unbutton my coat. I can see nothing below. The drop may be three hundred metres or three thousand. All the same, it will be short. I shall feel the wind rush through my feathers as if I am flying. Thankfully, I will see nothing. It will be a brief rush of air, a shock and then oblivion. I welcome it.

I remove my coat and fold it neatly on the parapet. Then I put my boot toe into a crack, climb up carefully onto the top of the parapet and stand with my wings spread.

SNIPE

Shit – he's climbing up! He's going to jump! I shouted and ran towards him. He was looking straight ahead. He raised a foot and—

RAVEN

I step out.

SNIPE

He's gone! I ran to the parapet and looked over. Nothing below. Nothing but the pitch darkness and a few shreds of mist. He'd fallen out of sight. Three hundred metres, he was probably still falling!

My legs buckled and I sat down, leant against the wall, clutched my fingers into the ice. For fuck's sake don't let me fall! Everything was spinning – the walkway could vanish and drop me into space!

He had stepped out and, as his foot met empty air, tilted forward till he was falling horizontally, with his wings spread like hooked canopies. He was looking past this world and his flight feathers were bending, already fluttering, as the air began to race.

My ears strained but I heard no noise. No cry, no ... collision. God, it was the cliff fall all over again! After a few seconds the freezing water soaking into my backside brought me to my senses and I stood up. I felt my way along the parapet and gathered his coat. It was still warm.

I looked down into the abyss and realised I was shivering violently. No point shouting; he's dead. He's dead ... down there ... smashed on the rocks ... and already freezing. Besides, if I shouted, who knows what might answer?

I pressed the coat to my chest and hurried back along the walkway towards the lights of the keep. It seemed that I had crept the opposite way hours earlier, though it had only been minutes. The sensation was so powerful I could almost see myself tiptoeing in the shadows, following my lord, who walked with sure tread some distance in front, and still walked there, just out of the corner of my eye. Something told me that Raven – his back broad, his head bowed – will always be walking along the top of this bloody wall. Every night, when the oil in the lamps is running low, the flames guttering out and ice is forming on the stone, he'll walk here. By god, the sooner we demolish the keep the better!

But even if we level Carniss, I know I'll always see him, up at the height of the wall with no parapet to support him, or pacing the ground below, or any-bloody-where – even if I'm walking through the market in the middle of Rachis town – because he's branded on my mind's eye.

I shuddered. Pull yourself together, I told myself. The dumb fantasies of nobles and immortals must have rubbed off on me. I've been mixing with 'em too long. So I made an effort to think carefully. I'm the only one who knows Raven is dead. Who knows Raven has … has committed suicide. If I find the Eszai and tell them straight away, I'll be more likely to escape any blame. I know Lightning's in my house, and last time I saw Jant, he was moping at the top of the tower. I took a deep breath. Brace yourself, man, I thought. This time, when I find them I'll tell them the truth.

Some time after midnight I was sitting by the fire, putting the finishing touches to a letter to Tarmigan, in which I detailed how we had prevented the planned putsch. The night was silent apart from the crackling of the logs in the grate and the scratch of my fountain pen across the page.

I folded the letter and turned the end of a stick of sealing wax in the candle flame, watching it become glossy and rounded, which is always very satisfying. There was a knock on the door. 'Come in!' I called, but the knocking continued with brisk desperation.

You're not in Foin now, I thought, irritated, and pushed my chair back. 'All right, all right, I'm coming.'

I opened the door to Snipe, with Jant behind him, who had changed back into Awian clothes and wore an even more tortured expression than before. Between them they blurted out the news. The shock swept over me, dulling my hearing. I stood, not thinking of anything, and it took me a while to come to myself and realise I was looking down at the rag rug and Snipe's boot toes. Both Snipe and Jant were waiting like anxious schoolboys for my reaction.

'This is *your* house,' I said to Snipe, and turned aside for him to enter. They sat down either side of the square table in front of the fire. I whisked the letter into my pocket and drew up a third chair.

'It was suicide,' Snipe repeated. 'Suicide. I saw him just step off. Lightning, he spread his wings as if ... as if he was going to fly ... and strode off the wall. Off the cliff.' He raised his hand and tipped it from vertical to horizontal, then closed his fingers. 'Gone.'

Jant flinched and his wings twitched. I doubted that he had come across suicide before. Snipe certainly hadn't; he was even more stunned. His shoulders were bowed – not with the servility he faked when in Raven's presence, but in genuine shock. His pallor was so sickly it cast his black eye into lurid contrast. He was no longer the man I had met on the cloud-bound path, when he had mistaken me for a soldier of fortune. He was shaken to the core.

He went on, 'Honestly, if I'd known I would have stopped him. I would have, before he reached the end. I wouldn't have even let him leave the keep.'

I hastened to reassure him. 'Of course.'

'Raven was strong. Stronger than me, yes – and a swordsman too. I was a long way behind him – ten metres behind him, all the way.'

'Don't worry,' said Jant. 'Nobody is accusing you of having a hand in his death.'

Snipe swallowed and nodded. 'Good, good. I swear I only saw it.' He heaved a great sigh and stood up. He went to the dresser and opened a door, brought out a bottle of whisky and stoneware cups. He plonked them down in front of us, uncorked the whisky and filled his cup. He knocked it back, sank onto his chair and filled it again.

We sat in silence, wondering how desperate Raven had to be to kill himself. Suicides are very rare, and even then it's almost always the elderly, the insane or those with excruciating diseases without hope of a cure. You only have one life, and if you choose to leave it for oblivion, you should at least heft a sword and use the opportunity to bring down as many Insects as possible. Everyone wants to win immortality, to live for ever; who would take the losers' way out? I thought it an act of cowardice. Raven had felt trapped, as much as Dellin had been trapped in her cage. He was not prepared to compromise, so chose to die rather than adapt himself to life here. I looked into the top layers of his desperation and I recoiled. Give me solid ground and certainty, I thought. From the way Jant was staring into space I could tell he was thinking much the same.

'Lightning, Comet,' Snipe said softly. 'I must tell you, or I'll have this on my conscience for the rest of my life ... along with everything else. I swear, if I'd known Raven would react like that I'd never have done it. I thought it would anger him, frustrate him, certainly. I never thought he'd throw himself off the cliff. I shouldn't have done it. I'm sorry. Honestly sorry.' He shot us a quick glance from under his brows and I saw how frightened and guilty he was.

'What did you do?' I asked.

'I let Dellin out of the cage.'

'You?' Jant sat up. 'But you hated her!'

'I didn't know that freeing her would make my lord kill himself,' Snipe moaned.

'No,' I stepped in. 'Nobody could. Snipe, we are not blaming you, so do not blame yourself. But tell us, why did you release her?'

Snipe rubbed his mouth and thought awhile before answering. He had lost the end joints of his little finger and ring finger from both hands, rendering them stubby, blunt and oddly blind where I expected nails to be. His other fingers were blackened at the ends, and the skin of his hands and face was patched red and numb frost-bite yellow. I doubted whether he would ever regain his original complexion. He would bear the marks of having been Dellin's prey until his dying day.

'I had good reason to loathe her,' he said slowly, 'and fear her too, but when I saw her in the cage it all began to melt away. She was lying against the bars ... not looking at anything. I tried to speak to her, but she wouldn't turn to me. She was dying, Jant.'

'I know.'

'I couldn't let it happen. I've seen trapped wolves lie down that way, when they give up struggling and just wait to die.'

'You pitied her?'

'Oh, you're surprised. Don't think me capable of pity, do you, Messenger? Let me tell you something. I was married – once. In Rachiswater, when I was a servant at the palace. How do you think a mere ploughboy came to be Raven's retainer, anyway? My wife, Gerygone, was seamstress to the queen.

'A year before Raven and Francolin started plotting, Gerygone became pregnant. Now I need to tell you how beautiful my Gerygone was. She was lovely. She surpassed all the maids of honour. Her name meant "echo" and she was so ethereal – I mean slight, so to speak ... She had such grace that you'd have thought her an echo far too delicate for this world. She died in childbirth ... while giving birth to our daughter. Two days and nights she struggled in agony, pain so bad I never thought a human frame could bear it. She were very brave ...' He looked at his rainbow hands. 'But the baby wouldn't come. In the end it sapped her strength. The Queen's own doctor tried to cut her, but she had no stamina left to endure the operation. He should have tried it on the first day. She just lay there, not looking at anything. Then she gathered her energy and focused on me. She smiled at me, a faint little smile, and she died.'

'I'm sorry,' I said. Jant said nothing, and perhaps rightly so, because the 'correct' words often sound false.

Snipe sniffed and rubbed his nose. 'Our daughter had died hours before. I buried them together. Gerygone and little Owlett, who never saw the light of day.'

As if strapping on armour he pulled himself together, hiding his grief beneath a pioneer's tough pelt. 'Now you know, immortals. Now you know why I wanted to come to Carniss. There was nothing but bad memories left in Rachiswater. Nightmares every night. Mistaking other women for her in the street. At least out on the frontier, with the fresh air and my hands full of work, a whole half-hour might pass without me seeing her.'

'I know what you mean,' Jant said quietly.

'When I saw Dellin lying in the cage, she looked exactly as my wife did – so frail she couldn't possibly live. The more fragile they seem, the more precious. I don't know why that should be, but it's true. I couldn't let it happen again. I couldn't let her breathe her last. God knows I did all I could for Gerygone, but it was beyond my power. So I saved Dellin.'

He looked at his cup of whisky. 'I gave her her freedom and I didn't expect her to thank me. She couldn't understand ... It's like, if you let a caged bird free she doesn't thank you, but it is good to see her fly away. Would that I could have saved Gerygone so easily.'

'By mercy we show we are civilised,' I said.

'Yeah. Dellin caused us terror, but we still shouldn't lock her in a cage. She stood against Raven's might. I kind of appreciated her pluck.'

'Raven captured her,' said Jant. 'He stopped her running around, but he could never tame her. Nothing can change her. She'll die defiant. She'll die a creature of the mountains whether we trap her or no.'

'I don't know about that,' said Snipe. 'All I know is, when she hunted me in the forest she beat me fairly. I had no chance in her world. She could have eaten me, but she spared me and let me go. How low would I be if I didn't return the favour?'

I expected Jant to answer, but he was looking into the mid-distance and dreamily fingering his earlobe as if testing costly silk. So I prompted Snipe gently: 'How did you open the cage when Raven held the key?'

Snipe shrugged. 'He left his coat on the hook while he cleared those burnt pelts off his chair. When his back was turned I picked his pocket. Simple. I took a bottle of liquor down to the kennels and got the guard drunk. He'd been on duty since the fire and he's fond of a drop. I told him I'd relieve him if he wanted to sleep, and he went to bed with gratitude. For all I know, he's sleeping still. As a steward, I find it helps to know people. Raven never did – he thought we were all one mass.'

'You unlocked the cage,' Jant breathed.

'Yes. With sword in hand! I wasn't going to let her claw me to shreds. I needn't have worried, though. As soon as the key turned she burst out. She streaked out the door. I've never seen *anything* move so fast. Not even you.'

'So, she's safe?'

'I don't know. I haven't a clue where she is. She sprinted out the gate, as straight as a rule, and into the forest.'

Jant looked preoccupied and morose, more serious than I had ever seen him. Snipe sipped his drink nervously, but when he spoke his mouth was dry. 'What do we do? Lightning, Comet, we're the only ones who know about Raven. The watch changes in about fifteen minutes. In three hours everyone will start to wake.'

'Come daylight we will retrieve Raven's body,' I said.

'Yes,' said Jant. 'And I'll tell Tarmigan everything.' Snipe sucked in a breath. Jant added, 'He won't lay the blame at your door.'

'It's not that. It's just ... I don't know whether to tell you.'

'Tell us what?' I asked.

'Nothing. Nothing. It's just ... Lightning, losing Dellin added to Raven's woes, I get that, but whatever burden any man's under, he shouldn't jump off a cliff.'

Jant said, 'Snipe, you've never considered killing yourself, I suppose.'

'No!'

'Not even when you lost Gerygone?'

'No ...' he said suspiciously. 'Why should I?'

'And you would never miss living in Rachiswater?'

'I told you. I don't belong there any more. I'm a Carniss man now.'

'Then, Steward Snipe, will you be the next governor of Carniss?'

Snipe blinked. He ducked his head so his chin almost rested on his chest. He became the very definition of humility. Then he sat up straight. 'Yes. Yes, Messenger, I certainly would.'

'When a governor dies without leaving an heir,' I put in, 'his steward is usually appointed the new governor. There are many recent examples.'

'Yes, yes.' Jant waved me away. 'But that isn't the point. The point is, he's ideal for the job.'

'And I accept,' said Snipe. A new light of hope was beginning to break over his face. As his face was so large and rugged, it was taking quite a long time.

Jant said, 'Lightning and I will recommend to King Tarmigan that you be the next governor *if* you accept two conditions.'

'What conditions?'

'First, you must not harm any Rhydanne whatsoever. Leave them alone and let Shira Dellin be.'

'What if she eats us?'

Jant leant back and folded his arms. 'After this day dawning, I doubt you will ever see her again.'

I recognised Jant was having difficulty controlling his emotions. Snipe also seemed to appreciate how much the loss of Dellin was affecting him. He knew from experience Jant was dangerous and feared his tinder temper. He said uneasily but now with the voice of a governor, 'If Dellin doesn't prey on us, or lead marauders, then we will never ride against the Rhydanne.'

'Nor molest them in any way?'

'No.'

'Swear it on the Emperor's name,' commanded Jant.

'I swear it by the Emperor San,' he said simply. 'By the Castle's Circle and the Sunburst Throne. What's the second point?'

'You must set boundaries. Already there aren't enough animals left to support all your settlers. You need meat and furs to sell, but you'll have scant pickings because you've worn out the land. Luckily for you the Rhydanne are drifting away. They've gathered enough food ... um ... yes, food, to make the journey to new hunting grounds. You must care for Carniss until it has grown rich again. You must not expand further into Darkling.'

'I agree,' Snipe said.

'You know the eastern border adjoins Rachiswater. Now listen. Your south border is the south bank of Carniss glacier. Your north border is the first spur of Caigeann, forty kilometres on. As for your western limit, the furthest you can go into the mountains is a line drawn across the glacier and Klannich just below the altitude of the Frozen Hound Hotel. Ouzel's bar is the marker; it will be outside your manor and she'll thank you for trading with the Rhydanne there.'

'So I have the forest, two promontories, the glacier and its stream?'

'No more than that. Leave the head of the glacier, Klannich's summits and all of Darkling beyond to the Rhydanne.'

Snipe shrugged. 'All right. We can't breathe up there, anyway.'

'Then I will draw up a covenant to sign. Lightning, how does one do that?'

I said, 'Fly to the Castle and ask Gayle the Lawyer to help you. Show the agreement to the Emperor, then take it to Rachiswater and present it to the king. If Tarmigan consents he will set the Royal Seal upon it. Then Snipe will be the second governor of Carniss. Snipe Carniss.'

'Snipe Carniss ...' Snipe repeated, as if tasting the words.

'Yes,' I said. 'The King will invest you governor and you may choose your own insignia.'

'I think I'll keep the shoot-at-the-moon. After all, Jant was right that we'll never leave.'

Jant looked rather pained. He said, 'I'll also get the Cartographer to chart Carniss so there may be no disagreements in future.'

Snipe thoughtfully rubbed his split nose. All of a sudden he leant forward and rested his forearms on the table with the cup between them. 'Archer, Messenger, when you mention my name to King Tarmigan you'll find he already knows it. I were the one who shopped Raven to him in the first place.'

'*You* were the informer?' asked Jant.

'Yes. I was the grass.'

'Excuse me?' I said.

'Two years ago. He told Tarmigan about Francolin's coup.'

'Yes. I wanted to tell you earlier. But I can't keep it secret any more.' Snipe stood and crossed the room in three steps, to the box bed. The closed partition hid it from view and, apart from the runners, you would not know there was a cubbyhole behind, with a pallet filled with clean straw and a shelf for a candle. He slid open the panel and sat down on the bed. The coverlet and pillowcase were covered in embroidery – crewel work, the folk art of northern

Awia – tiny flowers of saffron-yellow, blue, red and violet. Their stems and foliage intertwined innocently, symmetrical and somehow very wholesome.

The flowers were so delicate they could have adorned the dress of royalty. I realised they were the work of Gerygone's hand, Snipe's memento of his wife, and food for thought for another reason: the flowers of Rachiswater meadows will never bloom in Carniss. I hoped Snipe would never crave tapestries of damask silk and gold thread, miniver fur or velvet cushions, festoons or chandeliers. As long as he stays with cotton and folk art, he will be the governor Carniss needs.

It was proper of him to have relinquished the bed to me, but I couldn't sleep on Snipe's memories. I made up my mind I'd stay in the keep.

He said, 'When I was swept along in Francolin's plotting, it scared the shit out of me. Raven and Francolin seemed unaware how much the palace staff gossiped and how often they listened at doors. At any moment a valet or chambermaid might overhear and spill their plans to Tarmigan. There'd be a noose for every neck! I was terrified but I thought on it and decided to take matters into my own hands. I sought an audience and told him myself.'

'Your loyalty is to be commended,' I said.

'Loyalty?' His voice tilted into ridicule. 'Nothing to do with it! I was trying to save my skin. And I thought His Royal Highness would give me a stonking great reward. Well, Tarmigan gave me nothing, as it turned out, but he did let me walk free. The following day he swooped on Raven and the others. Raven thought Tarmigan had sent me to join him in exile. Ha! How likely is that? If Tarmigan had arrested me, he'd've chucked me in jail and built a scaffold in the square. The tumbril would've come for me just as soon as there was a big enough crowd.'

Snipe went to the window and for the first time I noticed he walked with a limp. If frost had bitten off the ends of four fingers and blackened the rest, I preferred not to imagine what had happened to his toes. He poked the oilcloth pinned over the shutter's vents, which were shaped like gingerbread men, then leant against the sill.

'Anyway, I had to go along with Raven's assumption or he'd have suspected me. I ask you, if I hadn't been the informer, what was the chance of me being pardoned? I've been living on my nerves since then, thinking at any minute Raven would come to the obvious conclusion. Fortunately, he never thought deeply about his liegemen. He would've been surprised to find we had lives and histories of our own. I know every settler in Carniss and that's why I'll be a better governor than him.'

'I am sure you will,' I said.

Snipe glanced again at the oilcloth, then unlatched one shutter and pushed it wide. The chill mountain air drifted in, but with it the grey light of dawn. From the direction of the kitchen, knocks and bangs and muted conversation told us people were already awake. He asked, 'What time is it?'

I flicked my watch open. 'Six.'

'The patrols are changing. Bunting will be setting the hearths in Raven's apartment. I had better make an announcement ... Lightning, will you help?'

'Certainly.'

We rose and joined Snipe by the window. Outside, the snow trampled by footprints had turned to solid ice, grey-white and translucent like banded agate. The curtain wall cast a thick strip of shadow. Of the keep itself we could only see the undercroft passage, its gates left purposely open, and the snow around it dotted with trodden-in fragments of burnt wood and cinders. Smoke had streaked the wall above the opening of the staircase tower and the arch of the passage. The ice on every lintel had re-frozen into undulating fringes. A deckle-edged mass of ice draped in the apex of the arch, from which hung enormous icicles as clear as blown glass.

I could just make out the cobbles under the arch, hoary with frost, then a band of snow and the first trunks of the forest. The chiaroscuro of black, white and pine green reminded me of Dellin: her black hair, white skin and eyes as green as chrysoprase. I wondered where she was now, and Jant looked so wistful I could tell he was thinking the same.

Snipe picked up his crampons from the fireplace and went out. I followed him. Jant closed the shutter and tagged on behind. We passed into the other room of his log cabin, out of the front door and into the bailey, as the second day of January, eighteen ninety-one dawned crisp and clear.

In the shadow of the low-pitched roof Snipe paused to slip his feet into the crampons then strode out towards the keep. Jant ran a couple of steps in front of us. He whipped round, hair straggling on his shoulders. He threw his arms wide. 'I have to go. Give me four hours.'

I said, 'If you need more time, feel free.'

Jant shook his head, smiled wildly, then turned and sprinted away. His footfalls echoed under the arch, then he ran out of view behind the curtain wall. A second later he lifted into the air and flew up, away towards Klannich.

JANT

Once outside the keep I took off and spiralled up. I rode the constant wind blowing down from Klannich, turning and turning again into it so with each twirl into the current I rose a bit higher. The margin of the forest fell quickly below, till I could see the whole keep on its promontory. Condors and crows had gathered at the furthest tip, screaming and cawing and circling down to feed on something at the foot of the cliffs.

Higher still, and the promontory diminished until the keep looked natural, no more than a pile of stones. All human activity shrank to nothing and disappeared into the landscape. The whole of Carniss now fitted into my field of vision, and more – glaciers on either side – the promontory just one of a range of headlands jutting out over the lowlands. All around me the vast mountains and the plain of Lakeland Awia were opening out. Raven and Dellin had been fighting for such a small piece of land!

I flew still higher, now at a level with the double cusp of Klannich, now above it, and I could see greater mountains, dimmed by distance, rising towards the plateau. They linked together and paled into the distance until they merged in the haze. They looked almost like the sea, transformed into waves of granite, standing high above the land.

In the opposite direction, Rachiswater was one blue-white unending plain, stretching out of sight. Plow Hill was a minuscule molehill rounded by snow. The sun cleared the horizon and stood upon it, as if on the edge of a plate. It cast gold rays across the whole of Awia.

Up here I could see no trace made by any living creature. The works of Awian, Rhydanne and human faded to nothing. I was alone in the calm, remote sky, and the fringe of mountains turned slowly beneath me, on the taller prong of Klannich, as if it was the hub. I was suspended between Awia and Darkling, as I always had been. My future lies in the flatlands, not the peaks, but perhaps now I will be able to balance them better.

I breathed deeply the thin air and became immeasurably relaxed. Raven's death, my losing Dellin and the forestalled coup faded and my mind became quite blank. Nothing existed. Up here I was beyond names – no Darkling, no Awia – the landscape was a continuum and I became part of it. An inanimate part, as if I will always exist here, pinned on the sky.

I sailed on in the wonderful air, making small adjustments with wings and feet to steer in a circle, otherwise in seconds I would be kilometres south, heading towards the Plainslands. Completely out of view to anybody on the ground, the land itself an inconsequential mass, I played with the currents of air and started to prepare myself for what I had to say.

Higher still, the subzero air began to gnaw and a dizziness overtook me. I sensed a cold stream of air flowing eastward. It wasn't the usual katabatic wind, but something immense, too powerful. I'd only felt it once before. It was the global air stream that cast me from Scree pueblo all the way to Hacilith city when I was just fifteen years old. That river of air has been blowing all this time and is still blowing now. It will never stop. It caught me like a dandelion seed and bore me east, so I ducked down out of it and spiralled past the summit's prongs, past the cirques biting semicircles from the smooth rock of its horn, to the level where features recovered their names. I flew over Carniss Glacier and the forest on its far bank, to the cliffs called the Stone Flames. Closer, a black ribbon seemed to cut the cliffs in two. A thin rift cave, Uaimh Dellin: Dellin's Den.

I landed on the terrace. A line of small footprints led into the cave, and the snow around its entrance was scuffed and crushed. Gauzy woodsmoke was issuing out of the top of the rift and dispersing. I could smell kutch cooking.

I approached quietly, but at the sound of my footfalls there was a quick movement in the cave mouth and Dellin ran out, her spear at the ready. She looked larger than she had in the cage; her brilliant eyes flashed in the oblique sunlight. When she saw it was me she lowered her spear and relaxed. 'How did you know I was here?'

'I just knew.'

She examined me, taking in my Awian clothes with a grim comprehension. Then she perched on the same ice-covered rock where she had fought the bear. She tilted her face away from the sun in her eyes, or maybe she was flinching – I hoped having been imprisoned wouldn't affect her for life.

I sat on the rock beside her and said, 'Dellin, you must go. Leave Carniss. Raven is dead. I just wanted you to know that. I also wanted to tell you that I ... to tell you that I made Snipe governor and the settlers will remain.'

'Did you kill Raven?' she asked quietly.

'Leave Carnich, go far up-slope, to the plateau. You said you always wanted to see Scree pueblo, didn't you? Now's your chance. Hunt on the plateau, beyond Klannich, beyond the head of the glacier. You must never return.'

She said nothing and I waited too. Then we both began at once: 'Did—?'

'Why don't—?'

We stopped. 'Go on,' I said.

'Why don't you come with me?' She looked directly at me. 'Run with me, Jant. Or I'll come to the Castle. I'll marry you. Yes!'

'Please tell me, I have to know. Did you lead me into the forest so I wouldn't stop you setting fire to the keep? Or was it because you loved me and didn't want me to burn?'

She paused. 'I do want to marry you. I'll be your hunting partner for ever.'

My spirits fell. I felt loose with disappointment. Was she just mouthing these words? She had turned me down once and now she tempted me with my own proposal. But I was wiser now: I knew her better. With calm self-control I said, 'No, Dellin.' And my heart grew so heavy I felt as if I was sinking into the rock.

'I want to hunt with you. Let's run to Scree together.'

I heard the loneliness in her voice. She must be the last Rhydanne left in Carniss. I still wanted her so desperately I ached, but I knew she would hurt me again, some time in the future. She would follow her instinct and consider rules as nothing. She would cause me pain for the rest of eternity. I knew that, now. I couldn't bind myself to her.

'No, Dellin,' I said. 'It's too late. There'll be other hunters at the pueblo. Join them in the new grounds.'

Her eyes glistened with tears. She turned her head away and composed herself. When she looked at me again her lips and eyes had assumed the hard expression of a woman baulked in her intentions but who will no longer plead. She rose swiftly, spear in hand, and slipped into the cave.

I breathed the cool air and regarded the shadows of the clouds chasing over the glacier. Dellin reappeared, wearing her rucksack and with ash on her boots from smothering the hearth. She held her spear over her shoulder and looked out at the incredible vista. Then, without saying a word, she turned to the cliff.

She stepped up onto a ledge, as if calling a path into existence by her footsteps. She ran up, along a straight stretch, and then zigzagged higher on the ledges. Now she was lost to sight behind massive columns of rock, now she emerged between them. I strained to watch her, because I knew I'd never see her again, for the rest of my life and hers. The cage door is open and her path diverges from mine. In a hundred years' time I will look back on this. In a thousand years' time I will remember her, wonder what happened to her, and try to imagine how she met her end.

The cliff ledge debouched onto a scree chute. Dellin climbed the large boulders at its edge, up into a hanging valley filled with snow. She was a tiny figure crossing the white patch, leaving an infinitesimal trail of prints. Sometimes she merged with the great wall of rock, sometimes I could just distinguish her. She reached the head of the valley and passed through a notch in the skyline, onto the top of the cliff and was gone.

I turned away, back to the keep. Back towards Awia.

Thank you to Garrett Coakley, web designer extraordinaire, for
www.stephswainston.co.uk

Love and thanks as always to Brian.